W9-AVC-187

Praise for
Mean Streets

"Readers will be delighted with this collection of original novellas tied to popular crime/fantasy series.... All solid and suspenseful, these stories are sure to please."
—*Publishers Weekly*

"Entertaining excitement ... Four great stories you won't want to miss, as they seem to fill in some of the gaps between novels and give you a peek into the characters' lives you like to read about."
—*SFRevu*

"These four new novellas by top urban noir authors will entertain while showing the seedier, darker side of town and human nature.... Imaginative yet humanizing story lines with familiar characters make this collection a treat and a great introduction for readers new to the genre."
—Monsters and Critics

"Each tale is well written, feeling complete even in the novella format, and [they] complement one another as the writers rose to the occasion of expectations from their fan base. An obvious must for readers of any of the four paranormal sagas, [and] newcomers will appreciate the introductions to these literary legends as they investigate the otherworldly *Mean Streets*."
—Alternative Worlds

"Four stories that are sure to keep readers engaged. They're equally well told and intriguing, to the point where I found it impossible to say that any one stands out above the rest. This is a keeper that will easily rise to the top of the list of favorite anthologies for fans of the genre."
—Darque Reviews

"This is a good collection for urban fantasy and noir lovers, combining mystery and magic in thrilling story lines."
—*News and Sentinel* (Parkersburg, WV)

"Four of today's most talented urban fantasy authors combine their magic to deliver an outstanding collection. Walking in these characters' shoes is enlightening, frightening, and not for the faint of heart!"
—*Romantic Times*

MEAN STREETS

JIM BUTCHER
SIMON R. GREEN

KAT RICHARDSON
THOMAS E. SNIEGOSKI

A ROC BOOK

ROC
Published by New American Library, a division of
Penguin Group (USA) Inc., 375 Hudson Street,
New York, New York 10014, USA
Penguin Group (Canada), 90 Eglinton Avenue East, Suite 700, Toronto,
Ontario M4P 2Y3, Canada (a division of Pearson Penguin Canada Inc.)
Penguin Books Ltd., 80 Strand, London WC2R 0RL, England
Penguin Ireland, 25 St. Stephen's Green, Dublin 2,
Ireland (a division of Penguin Books Ltd.)
Penguin Group (Australia), 250 Camberwell Road, Camberwell, Victoria 3124,
Australia (a division of Pearson Australia Group Pty. Ltd.)
Penguin Books India Pvt. Ltd., 11 Community Centre, Panchsheel Park,
New Delhi - 110 017, India
Penguin Group (NZ), 67 Apollo Drive, Rosedale, North Shore 0632,
New Zealand (a division of Pearson New Zealand Ltd.)
Penguin Books (South Africa) (Pty.) Ltd., 24 Sturdee Avenue,
Rosebank, Johannesburg 2196, South Africa

Penguin Books Ltd., Registered Offices:
80 Strand, London WC2R 0RL, England

Published by Roc, an imprint of New American Library, a division of Penguin
Group (USA) Inc. Previously published in a Roc trade paperback edition.

First Roc Mass Market Printing, January 2010
10 9 8 7 6 5 4 3 2 1

CONTENTS

THE WARRIOR

JIM BUTCHER

sat down next to Michael and said, "I think you're in danger."

Michael Carpenter was a large, brawny man, though he was leaner now than in all the time I'd known him. Months in bed and more months in therapy had left him a shadow of himself, and he had never added all the muscle back on. Even so, he looked larger and more fit than most, his salt-and-pepper hair and short beard going heavier on the salt these days.

He smiled at me. That hadn't changed. If anything, the smile had gotten deeper and more steady.

"Danger?" he said. "Heavens."

I leaned back on the old wooden bleachers at the park and scowled at him. "I'm serious."

Michael paused to shout a word of encouragement at the second baseman (or was that baseperson?) on his daughter Alicia's softball team. He settled back onto the bleachers. They were covered in old, peeling green paint, and it clashed with his powder-blue-and-white shirt, which matched the uniform T-shirts of the girls below. It said "COACH" in big blue letters.

"I brought your sword. It's in the car."

"Harry," he said, unruffled, "I'm retired. You know that."

"Sure," I said, reaching into my coat. "I know that.

But the bad guys apparently don't." I drew out an envelope and passed it to him.

Michael opened it and studied its contents. Then he replaced them, put the envelope back on the bench beside me, and rose. He started down onto the field, leaning heavily on the wooden cane that went everywhere with him now. Nerve damage had left one of his legs pretty near perfectly rigid, and his hip had been damaged as well. It gave him a rolling gait. I knew he couldn't see out of one of his clear, honest eyes very well anymore, either.

He took charge of the practice in the quiet, confident way he did everything, drawing smiles and laughter from his daughter and her teammates. They were obviously having fun.

It looked good on him.

I looked down at the envelope and wished I couldn't imagine the photos contained inside it quite so clearly. They were all professional, clear—Michael, walking up the handicap access ramp to his church. Michael, opening a door for his wife, Charity. Michael, loading a big bucket of softballs into the back of the Carpenter family van. Michael at work, wearing a yellow hard hat, pointing up at a half-finished building as he spoke to a man beside him.

The pictures had come in the mail to my office, with no note, and no explanation. But their implications were ugly and clear.

My friend, the former Knight of the Cross, was in danger.

It took half an hour for the softball practice to end, and then Michael rolled back over to me. He stood staring up at me for a moment before he said, "The sword has passed out of my hands. I can't take it up again— especially not for the wrong reason. I won't live in fear, Harry."

"Could you maybe settle for living in caution?" I

asked. "At least until I know more about what's going on?"

"I don't think His plan is for me to die now," he replied calmly. It was never hard to tell when Michael was talking about the Almighty. He could insert capital letters into spoken words. I'm not sure how.

"What happened to 'No man knows the day or the hour'?" I asked.

He gave me a wry smile. "You're taking that out of context."

I shrugged. "Michael. I'd like to believe in a loving, just God who looks out for everyone. But I see a lot of people get hurt who don't seem to deserve it. I don't want you to become one of them."

"I'm not afraid, Harry."

I grimaced. I'd figured he might react like this, and I'd come prepared to play dirty. "What about your kids, man? What about Charity? If someone comes for you, they aren't going to be particular about what happens to the people around you."

I'd seen him display less expression while being shot. His face turned pale and he looked away from me.

"What do you have in mind?" he asked after a moment.

"I'm going to lurk and hover," I told him. "Maybe catch our photographer before things go any further."

"Whether or not I want you to do it," he said.

"Well. Yes."

He shook his head at me and gave me a tight smile. "Thank you, Harry. But no thank you. I'll manage."

Michael's home was an anomaly so close to the city proper—a fairly large old colonial house, complete with a white picket fence and a yard with trees in it. It had a quiet, solid sort of beauty. It was surrounded by other homes, but they never seemed quite as pleasant, homey, or clean as Michael's house. I knew he did a lot of work to keep it looking nice. Maybe it was that simple. Maybe it was a side effect of being visited by archangels and the like.

Or maybe it was all in the eye of the beholder.

I'm pretty sure there won't ever be a place like that for me.

Michael had given a couple of the girls—young women, I suppose—a ride home in his white pickup, so it had taken us a while to get there, and twilight was heavy on the city. I wasn't making any particular secret about tailing them, but I wasn't riding his back bumper, either, and I don't think either of them had noticed my beat-up old VW.

Michael and Alicia got out of the car and went into the house, while I drove a slow lap around their block, keeping my eyes peeled. When I didn't spot any imminent maniacs or anticipatory fiends about to pounce, I parked a bit down the street and walked toward Michael's place.

It happened pretty fast. A soccer ball went bouncing by me, a small person came pelting after it, and just as it happened I heard the crunchy hiss of tires on the street somewhere behind me and very near. I have long arms, and it was a good thing. I grabbed the kid, who must have been seven or eight, about half a second before the oncoming car hit the soccer ball and sent it sailing. Her feet went flying out ahead of her as I swung her up off the ground, and her toes missed hitting the car's fender by maybe six inches.

The car, one of those fancy new hybrids that run on batteries part of the time, went by in silence, without the sound of the motor to give any warning. The driver, a young man in a suit, was jabbering into a cell phone that he held to his ear with one hand. He never noticed. As he reached the end of the block, he turned on his headlights.

I turned to find the child, a girl with inky black hair

and pink skin, staring at me with wide, dark eyes, her mouth open and uncertain. She had a bruise on her cheek a couple of days old.

"Hi," I said, trying to be as unthreatening as I could. I had limited success. Tall, severe-looking men in long black coats who need a shave are challenged that way. "Are you all right?"

She nodded her head slowly. "Am I in trouble?"

I put her down. "Not from me. But I heard that moms can get kind of worked up about—"

"Courtney!" gasped a woman's voice, and a woman I presumed to be the child's mother came hurrying from the nearest house. Like the child, she had black hair and very fair skin. She had the same wary eyes, too. She extended her hand to the little girl, and then pulled her until Courtney stood behind her mother. She peeked around at me.

"What do you think you're doing?" she demanded— or tried to. It came out as a nervous question. "Who are you?"

"Just trying to keep your little girl from becoming a victim of the Green movement," I said.

She didn't get it. Her expression changed, as she probably wondered something along the lines of, *Is this person a lunatic?*

I get that a lot.

"There was a car, ma'am," I clarified. "She didn't see it coming."

"Oh," the woman said. "Oh. Th-thank you."

"Sure." I frowned at the girl. "You okay, sweetheart? I didn't give you that bruise, did I?"

"No," she said. "I fell off my bike."

"Without hurting your hands," I noted.

She stared at me for a second before her eyes widened and she hid behind her mother a little more.

Mom blinked at me, and then at the child. Then she nodded to me, took the daughter by the shoulders, and frog-marched her toward the house without another word. I watched them go, and then started back toward Michael's place. I kicked Courtney's soccer ball back into her yard on the way.

Charity answered the door when I knocked. She was of an age with Michael, though her golden hair hid any strands of silver that might have shown fairly well. She was tall and broad-shouldered, for a woman, and I'd seen her crush more than one inhuman skull when one of her children was in danger. She looked tired—a year of seeing your husband undergoing intensely difficult physical therapy can do that, I guess. But she also looked happy. Our personal cold war had entered a state of détente, of late, and she smiled to see me.

"Hello, Harry. Surprise lesson? I think Molly went to bed early."

"Not exactly," I said, smiling. "Thought I'd just stop by to visit."

Charity's smile didn't exactly vanish, but it got cautious. "Really."

"Harry!" screamed a little voice, and Michael's youngest son, of the same name, flung himself into the air, trusting me to catch him. Little Harry was around Courtney's age, and generally regarded me as something interesting to climb on. I caught him and gave him a noisy kiss on the head, which elicited a giggle and a protest of, "Yuck!"

Charity shook her head wryly. "Well, come in. Let me get you something to drink. Harry, he's not a jungle gym. Get down."

Little Harry developed spontaneous deafness and scrambled up onto my shoulders as we walked into the living room. Michael and his dark-haired, quietly serious daughter Alicia were just coming in from the garage, after putting away softball gear.

"Papa!" little Harry shouted, and promptly plunged forward, off my shoulders, arms outstretched to Michael.

He leaned forward and caught him, though I saw him

wince and exhale tightly as he did it. My stomach rolled uncomfortably in sympathy.

"Alicia," Charity said.

Her daughter nodded, hung her ball cap on a wooden peg by the door, and took little Harry from Michael, tossing him up into the air and catching him, much to the child's protesting laughter. "Come on, squirt. Time for a bath."

"Leech!" Harry shouted, and immediately started climbing on his sister's shoulders, babbling about something to do with robots.

Michael watched them exit with a smile. "I asked Harry to dinner tonight," he told Charity, kissing her on the cheek.

"Did you?" she said, in the exact same tone she'd used on me at the door.

Michael looked at her and sighed. Then he said, "My office."

We went into the study Michael used as his office—more cluttered than it had been before, now that he was actually using it all the time—and closed the door behind us. I took out the photos I'd received without a word and showed them to Charity.

Michael's wife was no dummy. She looked at them one at a time, in rapid succession, her eyes blazing brighter with every new image. When she spoke, her voice was cold. "Who took these?"

"I don't know yet," I told her. "Though Nicodemus's name does sort of leap to mind."

"No," Michael said quietly. "He can't harm me or my family anymore. We're protected."

"By what?" I asked.

"Faith," he said, simply.

That would be a maddening answer under most circumstances—but I'd seen the power of faith in action around my friend, and it was every bit as real as the forces I could manage. Former presidents get a detail of Secret Service to protect them. Maybe former Knights of the Cross had a similar retirement package, only with more seraphim. "Oh."

"You're going to get to the bottom of this?" Charity asked.

"That's the idea," I said. "It might mean I intrude on you all a little."

"Harry," Michael said, "there's no need for that."

"Don't be ridiculous," Charity replied, turning to Michael. She took his hand, very gently, though her tone of voice stayed firm. "And don't be proud."

He smiled at her. "It isn't a question of pride."

"I'm not so sure," she said quietly. "Father Forthill said we were only protected against supernatural dangers. If there's something else afoot . . . You've made so many enemies. We have to know what's happening."

"I often don't know what's happening," Michael said. "If I spent all my time trying to find out, there wouldn't be enough left to live in. This is more than likely being done for the sole purpose of making us worried and miserable."

"Michael," I said quietly. "One of the best ways I know to counter fear is with knowledge."

He tilted his head, frowning gently at me.

"You say you won't live in fear. Fine. Let me poke around and shine a light on things, so we know what's going on. If it turns out to be nothing, no harm done."

"And if it isn't?" Charity asked.

I kept a surge of quiet anger out of my voice and expression as I looked at her levelly. "No harm gets done to you and yours."

Her eyes flashed and she nodded her chin once.

"Honey," Michael sighed.

Charity stared at him.

Michael might have slain a dragon, but he knew his limits. He lifted a hand in acceptance and said, "Why don't you make up the guest bedroom."

*   *   *

By a little after nine, the Carpenter household was almost entirely silent. I had been shown into the little guest room kept at the end of an upstairs hallway. It was really Charity's sewing room, and was all but filled with colorful stacks of folded fabric, some of them in clear plastic containers, some of them loose. There was room around a little table with a sewing machine on it, and just barely enough space to get to the bed. I'd recuperated from injuries there before.

One thing was new—there was a very fine layer of dust on the sewing machine.

Huh.

I sat down on the bed and looked around. It was a quiet, warm, cheerful little room—almost manically so, now that I thought about it. Everything was soft and pleasant and ordered, and it took me maybe six or seven whole seconds to realize that this room had been Charity's haven. How many days and nights must she have been worried about Michael, off doing literally God only knew what, against foes so terrible that no one but him could have been trusted to deal with them? How many times had she wondered if it would be a solemn Father Forthill who came to the door, instead of the man she loved? How many hours had she spent in this well-lit room, working on making warm, soft things for her family, while her husband carried *Amoracchius*'s cold, bright steel into the darkness?

And now there was dust on the sewing machine.

Michael had nearly been killed, out there on that island. He had been crippled, forced by his injuries to lay aside the holy sword, along with the nearly invisible, deadly war that went with it. And he was happier than I'd ever seen him.

Maybe the Almighty worked in mysterious ways, after all.

Another thought occurred to me, as I sat there pondering: Whoever had sent those pictures hadn't sent them to Michael—he'd sent them to me. What if I'd put

Michael and his family into real danger by showing up? What if I'd somehow reacted in exactly the way I'd been meant to react?

I grimaced around the cheerful room. So much for sleep.

I got up and padded back downstairs in my sock feet to raid the fridge, and while I was in the kitchen munching on an impromptu cold-cuts sandwich, I saw a shadow move past the back window.

I had several options, but none of them were real appetizing. I settled for the one that might accomplish the most. I turned and padded as quickly and quietly as I could to the front door, slipped out, and snuck around the side of the house in the direction that would, I hoped, bring me up behind the intruder. A quick spat of rain had made the grass wet, and the night had grown cool enough to make my instantly soaked socks uncomfortable. I ignored them, and went padding through the grass, keeping to the side of the house and watching all around me.

The backyard was empty.

I got an itchy feeling on the back of my neck and continued my circle. Had I given myself away somehow? Was the intruder even now circling just the way I was, hoping to sneak up on *me*? I took longer steps and stayed as quiet as I knew how—which is pretty darn quiet. I've developed my skulking to professional levels, over the years.

And as I rounded the corner, I spotted the intruder, a dark form hurrying down the sidewalk past Courtney's house. I couldn't follow him without being spotted pretty quickly, unless I cheated, which I promptly did. My ability to throw up a veil wasn't anything to write home about, but it ought to be good enough to hide me from view on a dark night, on a heavily shadowed street. I focused on my surroundings, on drawing the light and shadow around me in a cloak, and watched my own vision dim and blur somewhat as I did.

I half wished I'd woken Molly up. The kid is a natural at subtle stuff like veils. She can make you as invisible as Paris Hilton's ethical standards, and you can still see out of it with no more impediment than a pair of mildly tinted sunglasses. But, since it was me doing the job, I was probably just sort of indistinct and blurry, and my view of the street was like something seen through dark, thin fabric. I kept track of the pale concrete of the sidewalk and the movement of the intruder against the background of shadowy shapes and blurry bits of light, and walked softly.

The intruder crept down the street and then quickly crouched down beside my old Volkswagen, the *Blue Beetle*. It took him maybe five seconds to open the lock, reach into the car, and draw out the long, slender shape of a sheathed sword.

He must have come to the house first, and circled it to determine where I was. He could have spotted my staff, which I'd left resting against the wall by the front door, when he looked into the kitchen window. And I was pretty sure it was a him I was dealing with, too. The movement of his arms and legs was brusque, choppy, masculine.

I took a few steps to one side and picked up Courtney's soccer ball. Then I approached to within a few yards and tossed it up in a high arc. It came down with a rattling thump on the *Blue Beetle*'s hood.

Lurky-boy twitched, twisting his upper body toward the sound and freezing, and I hit him in a diving tackle with my body as rigid as a spear, all of my weight behind one shoulder, trying to drive it right through his spine and out his chest. He was completely unprepared for it and went down hard, driven to the sidewalk with a "whuff" of expelled air.

I grabbed him by the hair so that I could introduce his forehead to the sidewalk, but his hair was cut nearly military-short, and I didn't have a good grip. He twisted and got me in the floating rib with an elbow, and I wasn't in a good enough position to keep him from getting out from under me and scrambling away, the sheathed weapon still in hand.

I focused my will, flicked a hand at him and spat, *"Forzare!"* Unseen force lashed out at the back of his knees—

—and hit the mystic equivalent of a brick wall. There was a burst of twinkling, shifting lights, and he let out a croaking sound as he kept running. Something that glowed like a dying ember fell to the sidewalk.

I pushed myself up to pursue him, slipped on the wet grass next to the sidewalk, and rolled my ankle painfully. By the time I'd gotten to my feet again, he was too far away for me to catch, even if my ankle had been steady. A second later, he hopped a fence and was out of sight.

I was left there, standing beside my car on one foot, while neighborhood dogs sent up a racket. I gimped forward and looked down at the glowing embers of the thing he'd dropped. It was an amulet, its leather cord snapped in the middle. It looked like it had been a carving of wood and ivory, but it was scorched almost completely black, so I couldn't be certain. I picked it up, wrinkling my nose at the smell. Then I turned back to the car and closed the open door. After that, I untwisted the piece of wire that holds the trunk closed, picked up a blanket-wrapped bundle, and went back to Michael's place.

Morning on a school day in the Carpenter household is like Southampton, just before June 6, 1944. There's a lot of yelling, running around, and organizing transport, and no one seems to be exactly sure what's going on. Or maybe that was just me, because by a little before eight, all the kids were trooping out to their bus stop, led by Alicia, the senior schoolchild.

"So he grabbed the sword and ran?" Molly asked, sipping coffee. She apparently had a cold, and her nose was stuffy and bright pink. My apprentice was her mother's daughter, tall and blond and too attractive for me ever to be entirely comfortable—even wrapped up in a pink fluffy robe and flannel PJs, with her hair a mess.

"Give me some credit," I said, unwrapping the blanket-wrapped bundle and producing *Amoracchius*. "He *thought* he took the sword."

Michael frowned at me as he put margarine on his toast. "I thought you told me that the sword was best hidden in plain sight."

"I've been getting paranoid in my age," I replied, munching on a bit of sausage. I blinked at the odd taste and looked at him.

"Turkey," Michael said mildly. "It's better for me."

"It's better for everyone," Charity said firmly. "Including you, Harry."

"Gee," I said. "Thanks."

She gave me an arch look. "Can't you just use the amulet to track him down?"

"Nope," I said, putting some salt on the turkey "sausage." "Tell her why not, grasshopper."

Molly spoke through a yawn. "It caught on fire. Fire's a purifying force. Wiped out whatever energy was on the amulet that might link back to the owner." She blinked watery eyes. "Besides, we don't need it."

Michael frowned at her.

"He took the decoy," I said, smiling. "And I know how to find that."

"Unless he's gotten rid of it, or taken steps to make it untraceable," Michael said in a patient, reasonable tone. "After all, he was evidently prepared with some sort of defensive measure against your abilities."

"Different situation entirely," I said. "Tracking someone by using one of their personal possessions depends upon following a frequency of energy that is inherently unstable and transient. I actually have a piece of the decoy sword, and the link between those two objects is much more concrete. It'd take one he—uh, heck of a serious countermeasure to stop me from finding it."

"But you didn't trail him last night?" Charity asked.

I shook my head. "I didn't know where I'd have been going, I wasn't prepared, and since apparently someone is interested in the swords, I didn't want to go off and leave . . ."

You.

". . . the sword . . ."

Unprotected.

". . . here," I finished.

"What about the other one?" Michael asked quietly.

Fidelacchius, brother-sword to Michael's former blade, currently rested in a cluttered basket in my basement—next to the heavy locked gun safe that was warded with a dozen dangerous defensive spells. Hopefully, anyone looking to take it would open the safe first and get a face full of boom. My lab was behind a screen of defensive magic, which was in turn behind an outer shell of defensive magic that protected my apartment. Plus there was my dog, Mouse, two hundred pounds of fur and muscle, who didn't take kindly to hostile visitors.

"It's safe," I told him. "After breakfast, I'll track buzz-cut guy down, have a little chat with him, and we'll put this whole thing to bed."

"Sounds simple," Michael said.

"It could happen."

Michael smiled, his eyes twinkling.

Buzz, as it turned out, wasn't a dummy. He'd ditched the decoy sword in a Dumpster behind a fast-food joint less than four blocks from Michael's place. Michael sat behind the wheel of his truck, watching as I stood hip-deep in trash and dug for the sword.

"You sure you don't want to do this part?" I asked him sourly.

"I would, Harry," he replied, smiling. "But my leg. You know."

The bitch of it was, he was being sincere. Michael had never been afraid of work. "Why dump it here, do you think?"

I gestured at a nearby streetlight. "Dark last night, no moon. This is probably the first place he got a good look at it. Parked his car here, too, maybe." I found the handle of the cheap replica broadsword I'd picked up at what had amounted to a martial arts trinkets shop. "Aha," I said, and pulled it out.

There was another manila envelope duct-taped to the blade. I took the sword and the envelope back to the truck. Michael wrinkled up his nose at the smell coming up from my garbage-spattered jeans, but that expression faded when he looked at the envelope taped to the sword. He exhaled slowly.

"Well," he said. "No use just staring at it."

I nodded and peeled the envelope from around the blade. I opened it and looked in.

There were two more photos.

The first was of Michael, in the uniform shirt he wore when he coached his daughter's softball team. He was leaning back on the bleachers, as he had been when I'd first walked up to speak to him.

The second picture was of a weapon—a long-barreled rifle with a massive steel snout on the end of it, and what looked like a telescope for a sight. It lay on what looked like a bed with cheap motel sheets.

"Hell's bells," I muttered. "What is that?"

Michael glanced at the picture. "It's a Barrett," he said quietly. "Fifty-caliber semiautomatic rifle. Snipers in the Middle East who use them are claiming kills at two kilometers, sometimes more. It's one of the deadliest long-range weapons in the world." He looked up and around him at all the buildings. "Overkill for Chicago, really," he said with mild disapproval.

"You know what I'm thinking?" I said. "I'm thinking

we shouldn't be sitting here in your truck right next to a spot Buzz expected us to go while he and his super-rifle are out there somewhere."

Michael looked unperturbed. "If he wanted to simply kill me here, he's had plenty of time to make the shot."

"Humor me," I said.

He smiled and then nodded. "I can take you to your place. You can get some clean clothes, perhaps."

"That hurts, man," I said, brushing uselessly at my jeans as the truck moved out. "You know what bugs me about this situation?"

Michael glanced aside at me for a second. "I think I do. But it might be different than what you were thinking."

I ignored him. "Why? I mean sure, we need to know who this guy is, but *why* is he doing this?"

"It's a good question."

"He sends the pictures to me, not you," I said. I held up the new photo of the sniper rifle. "I mean, this is obviously an escalation. But if what he wanted was to kill you, why . . . ? Why document it for me?"

"It looks to me," Michael said, "as if he wants you to be afraid."

"So he threatens *you*?" I demanded. "That's stupid."

He smiled. "Do people threaten you very often?"

"Sure. All the time."

"What happens when they do?" he asked.

I shrugged. "I say something mouthy," I said. "Then I clean their clocks for them at the first opportunity."

"Which is probably why our photographer here—"

"Call him Buzz," I said. "It will make things simpler."

"Why Buzz hasn't bothered threatening you."

I frowned. "So you're saying Buzz knows me."

"It stands to reason. It seems clear that he's trying to push you into some sort of reaction. Something he thinks you'll do if you're frightened."

"Like what?" I asked.

"What do you think?" he replied.

I put my hand on the hilt of *Amoracchius*. The sword's tip rested on the floorboards of the truck, between my feet.

"That would be my guess, too," he said.

I frowned down at the blade, and nodded. "Maybe Buzz figured I'd bring you the sword if you were in danger. So that . . ." I didn't finish.

"So that I'd have some way of defending myself," Michael said gently. "You can say it, Harry. You won't hurt my feelings."

I nodded at the true sword. "Sure you don't want it?"

Michael shook his head. "I told you, Harry. That part of my life is over."

"And what if Buzz makes good?" I asked quietly. "What if he kills you?"

Michael actually laughed. "I don't think that's going to happen," he said. "But if it does . . ." He shrugged. "Death isn't exactly a terrifying proposition for me, Harry. If it was, I could hardly have borne the sword for as long as I did. I know what awaits me, and I know that my family will be taken care of."

I rolled my eyes. "Yeah, I'm sure everything will be fine if your younger kids have to grow up without a father in their lives."

He winced, and then pursed his lips thoughtfully for a few moments before he replied. "Other children have," he said, finally.

"And that's it?" I asked, incredulous. "You just surrender to whatever is going to happen?"

"It isn't what I'd want—but a lot of things happen that I don't want. I'm just a man."

"The last thing I would expect from you," I said, "is fatalism."

"Not fatalism," he said, his voice suddenly and unexpectedly firm. "Faith, Harry. Faith. This is happening for a reason."

I didn't answer him. From where I was standing, it looked like it was happening because someone ruthless and fairly intelligent wanted to get his hands on one of the swords. And worse, it looked like he was probably a mortal, too. If what Charity had said was accurate, that meant that Michael didn't have a heavenly insurance policy against the threat.

It also meant that I would have to pull my punches—the First Law of Magic prohibited using it to kill a human being. There was some grey area involved with it, but not much, and it was the sort of thing that one didn't play around with. The White Council enforced the laws, and anyone who broke them faced the very real possibility of a death sentence.

"And that's all I need," I muttered.

"What?"

"Nothing."

Michael pulled the truck into the gravel parking lot of my apartment, in the basement of a big old boarding-house. "I need to drop by a site before we go back to get your car. Is that all right?"

I took the sword with me as I got out of the truck. "Well," I said, "as long as it's all happening for a reason."

Michael's small company built houses. Years of vanishing at irregular intervals to battle the forces of evil had probably held him back from moving up to building the really expensive, really profitable places. So he built homes for the upper couple of layers of the middle class instead. He probably would have made more money if he cut corners, but it was Michael. I was betting that never happened.

This house was a new property, down toward Wolf Lake, and it had the depressing look of all construction sites—naked earth, trees bulldozed and piled to one side, and the standard detritus of any such endeavor: mud, wood, garbage discarded by the workers, and big old boot tracks all over the ground. Half a dozen men were at work, putting up the house's skeleton.

"Shouldn't take me long," Michael said.

"Sure," I said. "Go to it."

Michael hopped down from the truck and gimped his way over to the house, moving with an energy and purpose I'd seldom seen from him. I frowned after him, and then pulled the first envelope out of my pocket and started looking at the photos inside.

The photo of Michael at a building site had been taken at this one. Buzz had been here, watching Michael.

He might still be here now.

I got out of the car and slung the sword's belt over my shoulder, so that it hung with its hilt sticking up next to my head. Photo in hand, I started circling the site, trying to determine where Buzz had been standing when he'd taken his picture. I got some looks from the men on the job—but like I said before, I'm used to that kind of thing.

It only took me a couple of minutes to find the spot Buzz had used—a shadowed area of weeds and scrub brush behind the pile of felled trees. It was obscured enough to offer a good hiding spot, if no one was looking particularly hard, but far enough away that he had to have used a zoom lens of some kind to get those pictures. I had heard that digital cameras could zoom in to truly ridiculous levels these days.

I found footprints.

Don't read too much into that. I'm not Ranger Rick or anything, but I had a teacher who made sure I spent my share of time hiking and camping in the rugged country of the Ozarks, and he taught me the basics— where to look, and what to look for. The showers last night had wiped away any subtle signs, but I wouldn't have trusted my own interpretation of them in any case. I did find one clear footprint, of a man's left boot, fairly deep, and half a dozen partials and a few broken branches in a line leading away. He'd come here, hung around for a while, then left.

Which just about anyone could have deduced from the photo, even if he hadn't seen any tracks.

I had this guy practically captured already.

There weren't any bubble-gum wrappers, discarded cigarettes, or fortuitously misplaced business cards that would reveal Buzz's identity. I hadn't really thought there would be, but you always look.

I slogged across the muddy ground back toward the truck, when the door of one of the contractors' vans opened, and a prematurely balding thin guy with a tool belt and a two-foot reel of electrician's wire staggered out. He had a shirt with a name tag that read, "Chuck." Chuck wobbled to one side, dragging the handles of some tools along the side panel of Michael's truck, leaving some marks.

I glanced into the van. There was an empty bottle of Jim Beam inside, with a little still dribbling out the mouth.

"Hey, Chuck," I said. "Give you a hand with that?"

He gave me a bleary glance that didn't seem to pick up on anything out of the ordinary about me or the big old sword hanging over my shoulder. "Nah. I got it."

"It's cool," I said. "I'm going that way anyhow. And those things are heavy." I went over to him and seized one end of the reel, taking some of the weight.

The electrician's breath was practically explosive. He nodded a couple of times, and shifted his grip on the reel. "Okay, buddy. Thanks."

We carried the heavy reel of wire over to the house. I had to adjust my steps several times, to keep up with the occasional drunken lurch from Chuck. We took the wire to the poured-concrete slab that was going to be the garage at some point, it looked like, and dropped it off.

"Thanks, man," Chuck said, his sibilants all mushy.

"Sure," I said. "Look, uh. Do you really think you should be working with electricity right now, Chuck?"

He gave me an indignant, drunken glare. "What's that supposed to mean?"

"Oh, you just, uh. Look a little sick, that's all."

"I'm just fine," Chuck slurred, scowling. "I got a job to do."

"Yeah," I said. "Kind of a dangerous job. In a big pile of kindling."

He peered at me. "What?" It came out more like *Wha?*

"I've been in some burning buildings, man, and take it from me, *this* place . . ." I looked around at the wooden framework. "Fwoosh. I'm just saying. Fwoosh."

He worked on that one for a moment, and then his face darkened into a scowl again. He turned and picked up a wrench from a nearby toolbox. "Buzz off, freak. Before I get upset."

I wasn't going to do anyone any favors by getting into half of a drunken brawl with one of Michael's subcontractors. I looked around to see if anyone had noticed, but they were all at other parts of the house, I guessed. So I just held up one hand in front of me and said, mildly, "Okay. I'm going."

Chuck watched me as I walked out of the garage. I looked around until I spotted the power lines running into the house, and then followed the trench they were buried in back to the street, until I got to the transformer. I looked up at it, glanced around a little guiltily, and sighed. Then I waved my hand at the thing, exerted my will, and muttered, *"Hexus."*

Wizards and technology don't get along. At all. Prolonged exposure to an active wizard has really detrimental effects on just about anything manufactured after World War II or so, especially anything involving electricity. My car breaks down every couple of weeks, and that's when I'm not even trying. When I'm making an effort?

The transformer exploded in a humming shower of blue-white sparks, and the sound of an electric saw, somewhere on the site, died down to nothing.

I went back to the truck, and sat quietly until Michael returned.

He gave me a steady look.

"It was in the name of good," I said. "Your electrician was snockered. By the time the city gets by to repair it, he'll have sobered up."

"Ah," Michael said. "Chuck. He's having trouble at home."

"How do you know?"

"He's got a wife, a daughter," Michael said. "And I know the look."

"Maybe if he spent less time with Jim Beam," I said, "it'd go better."

"The booze is new," Michael said, looking worriedly at the house. "He's a good man. He's in a bad time." He glanced back at me a moment later. "Thank you. Though perhaps next time . . . you could just come tell me about it?"

Duh, Harry. That probably would have worked, too. I shook my head calmly. "That's not how I roll."

"How you roll?" Michael asked, smiling.

"I heard Molly say it once. So it must be cool."

"How you roll." Michael shook his head and started the truck. "Well. You were trying to help. That's the important thing."

Harry Dresden. Saving the world, one act of random destruction at a time.

"Okay," I said to Molly, as I prepared to get into my car. "Just keep your wits about you."

"I know," she said calmly.

"If there's any trouble, you call the cops," I said. "This guy looks to be operating purely vanilla, but he can still kill you just fine."

"I know, Harry."

"If you see him, do not approach him—and don't let your dad do it, either."

Molly rolled her eyes in exasperation. Then she muttered a quick word and vanished. Gone. She was standing within an arm's length of me, but I couldn't see her at all. "Let's see the bozo shoot this," said her disembodied voice.

"And while we're at it, let's hope he isn't using a heat-sensitive scope," I said drily.

She flickered back into sight, giving me an arch look. "The *point* is that I'm perfectly capable of keeping a lookout and yelling if there's trouble. I'll go with Dad to softball, and you'll be the second person I call if there's a whiff of peril."

I grunted. "Maybe I should go get Mouse. Let him stay with you, too."

"Maybe you should keep him close to the swords," Molly said quietly. "My dad's just a retired soldier. The swords are icons of power."

"The swords are bits of sharp metal. The men who hold them make them a threat."

"In case you hadn't noticed, my dad isn't one of those men anymore," Molly said. She tucked a trailing strand of golden hair behind one ear and frowned up at me worriedly. "Are you sure this isn't about you blaming yourself for what happened to my dad?"

"I don't blame myself," I said.

My apprentice arched an extremely skeptical eyebrow.

I looked away from her.

"You wanna talk to me about it?"

"No," I said. I suddenly felt very tired. "Not until I'm sure the swords are safe."

"If he knew where to send the pictures," Molly said, "then he knows where your house is."

"But he can't get inside. Even if he could get the doors or one of the windows to open, the wards would roast him."

"And your wards are perfect," Molly said. "There's no way anyone could get around them, ever. The way you told me those necromancers did a few years ago."

"They didn't go around," I said. "They went through. But I see your point. If I have to, I'll take one of the Ways to Warden's command center at Edinburgh and leave the swords in my locker."

Molly's eyes widened. "Wow. A locker?"

"Technically. I haven't used it. I've got the combination written down. Somewhere. On a napkin. I think."

"Does it hurt to be as suave as you, boss?"

"It's agonizing."

"Looks it." Her smile faded. "What are you going to do after you're sure the swords are safe?"

She hadn't thought it through. She didn't know what was going to happen in the next few minutes. So I gave her my best fake grin and said, "One step at a time, grasshopper. One step at a time."

I began pouring my will into my shield bracelet about half a mile from home. That kind of active magic wasn't good for the *Beetle*, but having a headless driver smash it into a building would be even worse. I fastened closed the buttons on my leather duster, too. The spells that reinforced the coat were fresh, and they'd once stood up to the power of a Kalashnikov assault rifle—but that was a world of difference from the power of a fifty-caliber sniper round.

Buzz had missed his shot at the sword at Michael's house. It's really hard to tail someone without being noticed, unless you've got a team of several cars working together—and this had all the earmarks of a lone-gunman operation. Buzz hadn't been tailing me today, and unless he'd given up entirely—sure, right—that could only mean that he was waiting for me somewhere. He'd had plenty of time to set up an ambush somewhere he knew I'd go.

Home.

The sword was my priority. I wasn't planning on suicide or anything, but at the end of the day, I'm just one guy. The swords had been a thorn in the side of evildoers for two thousand years. In the long term, the world needed them a lot more than it needed one battered and somewhat shabby professional wizard.

As I came down the street toward my apartment, I stomped on the gas. Granted, in an old VW Beetle, that isn't nearly as dramatic as it sounds. My car didn't roar as much as it coughed more loudly, but I picked up speed and hit my driveway as hard as I could while keeping all the wheels on the ground. I skidded to a stop outside my front door as the engine rattled, pinged, and began pouring out black smoke, which would have been totally cool if I'd actually made it happen on purpose.

I flung myself out of the car, the sword in hand, and into the haze of smoke, my shield bracelet running at maximum power in a dome that covered me on all sides. I rushed toward the steps leading down to the front door of my basement apartment.

As my foot was heading down toward the first step there was a flash of light and a sledgehammer hit me in the back. It spun me counterclockwise as it flung me down, and I went into a bad tumble down the seven steps to my front door. I hit my head, my shoulder screamed, and the taste of blood filled my mouth. My shield bracelet seared my wrist. Gravity stopped working, and I wasn't sure which way I was supposed to be falling.

"Get up, Harry," I told myself. "He's coming. He's coming for the sword. Get *up.*"

I'd dropped my keys in the fall. I looked for them.

I saw blood all over the front of my shirt.

The keys lay on the concrete floor of the stairs. I picked them up and stared stupidly at them. It took me a minute to remember why I needed them. Then another minute to puzzle out which of the five keys on the ring went to my front door. My head was pounding and I felt sick, and I couldn't get a breath.

I tried to reach up to unlock the door, but my left

shoulder wouldn't hold my weight and I almost slammed my head against the concrete again.

I made it up to a knee. I shoved my key at the door.

He's coming. He's coming.

Blue sparks flew up, and a little shock lit up my arm with pain.

My wards. I'd forgotten about my wards.

I tried to focus my will again, but I couldn't get it to gel. I tried again, and again, and finally I was able to perform the routine little spell that disarmed them.

I shoved my key into the lock and turned it. Then I leaned against the door.

It didn't open.

My door is a heavy steel security door. I installed it myself, and I'm a terrible carpenter. It doesn't quite line up with the frame, and it takes a real effort to get it open and closed. I had grown used to the routine bump and thrust of my shoulders and hips that I needed to open it up—but like the spell that disarmed my wards, that simple task was, at the moment, beyond me.

Footsteps crunched in the gravel.

He's coming.

I couldn't get it open. I sort of flopped against it as hard as I could.

The door groaned and squealed as it swung open, pulled from the other side. My huge, shaggy grey dog, Mouse, dropped his front paws back to the ground, shouldered his way through the door, and seized my right arm by the biceps. His jaws were like a vise, though his teeth couldn't penetrate the leather. He dragged me indoors like a giant, groggy chew toy, and as I went across the threshold, I saw Buzz appear at the top of the stairs, a black shadow against the blue morning sky.

He raised a gun, a military sidearm.

I kicked the door with both legs, as hard as I could.

The gun barked. Real guns don't sound like the guns in the movies. The sound is flatter, more mechanical. I couldn't see the flash, because I'd moved the door into the way. Bullets pounded the steel like hailstones on a tin roof.

Mouse slammed his shoulder against the door and rammed it closed.

I fumbled at the wards, babbling in panicked haste, and managed to restore them just in time to hear a loud popping sound, a cry, and a curse from the other side of the door. Then I reached up and snapped the dead bolt closed for good measure.

Then I fell back onto the floor of my apartment and watched the ceiling spin for a while.

In two or three minutes, maybe, I was feeling a little better. My head and shoulder hurt like hell, but I could breathe. I tried my arms and legs and three of them worked. I sat up. That worked, too, though it made my left shoulder hurt like more hell, and it was hard to see straight through the various pains.

I knew several techniques for reducing and ignoring pain, some of them almost too effective—but I couldn't really seem to line any of them up and get them working. My head hurt too much.

I needed help.

I half crawled to my phone and dialed a number. I mumbled to the other end of the phone, and then lay back on the floor again and felt terrible. Buzz must have fallen back by now, knowing that the sound of the shots could attract attention. Now that the sword was behind the protection of my wards, there was no reason for him to loiter around outside my apartment. I hoped.

The next thing I knew, Mouse was pawing at the door, making anxious sounds. I dragged myself over to it, disarmed the wards, and unlocked it.

"Are these shell casings on the ground? Is this blood?" sputtered a little man in pale blue hospital scrubs and a black denim jacket. He had a shock of black hair like a startled haystack, and black wire-rimmed spectacles. "Holy Hannah, Harry, what happened to you?"

I closed the wards and the door behind him. "Hi, Butters. I fell down."

"We've got to get you to a hospital," he said, turning to reach for my phone.

I slapped my hand weakly down onto it, to keep him from picking it up. "Can't. No hospitals."

"Harry, you know that I'm not a doctor."

"Yes, you are. I saw your business card." The effort of vocalizing that many syllables hurt.

"I'm a medical examiner. I cut up dead people and tell you things about them. I don't do live patients."

"Hang around," I said. "It's early yet." Still too many syllables.

"Oh, this is a load of crap," he muttered. Then he shook his head and said, "I need some more light."

"Matches," I mumbled. "Mantel." Better.

He found the matches and started lighting candles. "Next, I'll be getting out a big jar of leeches."

He found the first aid kit under my kitchen sink, boiled some water, and came over to check me out. I sort of checked out for a few minutes. When I came back, he was fumbling with a pair of scissors and my duster.

"Hey!" I protested. "Lay off the coat!"

"You've dislocated your shoulder," he informed me, frowning without stopping his work with the scissors. "You don't want to wriggle it around trying to take your shirt off."

"That's not what I—"

The pin that held the two halves of the scissors together popped as Butters exerted more pressure on their handles, and the two halves fell apart. He blinked at them in shock.

"Told you," I muttered.

"Okay," he said. "I guess we do this the hard way."

I won't bore you with the details. Ten minutes later, my coat was off, my shoulder was back in its socket, and Butters was pretending that my screams during the two failed attempts to put it back hadn't bothered him. I went away again, and when I came back, Butters was pressing a cold Coke into my hand.

"Here," he said. "Drink something. Stay awake."

I drank. Actually, I guzzled. Somewhere in the middle, he passed me several ibuprofen tablets, and told me to take them. I did it.

I blinked blearily at him as he held up my coat. He turned it around to show me the back.

There was a hole in the leather mantle. I flipped it up. Beneath the hole, several ounces of metal were flattened against the second layer of spell-toughened leather, about three inches below the collar and a hair to the right of my spine.

That was chilling. Even through my best defenses, that was how close I'd come to death.

If Buzz had shot me six inches lower, only a single layer of leather would have been between the round and my hide. A few inches higher, and it would have taken me in the neck, with absolutely no protection. And if he'd waited a quarter of a second longer, until my foot had descended to the first step leading down to my door, he would have sprayed my brains all over the siding of the boardinghouse.

"You broke your nose again," Butters said. "That's where some of the blood came from. There was a laceration on your scalp, too, which accounts for the rest. I stitched it up. You're holding your neck rigid. Probably whiplash from where the round hit you. There are some minor burns on your left wrist, and I'm just about certain that you've got a concussion."

"But other than that," I muttered, "I feel great."

"Don't joke, Harry," Butters said. "You should be under observation."

"Already am," I said. "Look where it got me."

He grimaced. "Doctors are required to report gunshot wounds to the police."

"Good thing I don't have any gunshot wounds, eh? I just fell down some stairs."

Butters shook his head again and turned toward the phone. "Give me a reason not to do it, or I call Murphy right now."

I grunted. Then I said, "I'm protecting something important. Someone else wants it. If the police get involved, this thing would probably get impounded as evidence. That's an unacceptable outcome, and it could get a lot of people hurt."

"Something important," Butters said. "Something like a magic sword?"

I scowled at him. "How do you know that?"

He nodded at my hand. "Because you won't let go of it."

I looked down to find the burn-scarred fingers of my left hand clutching *Amoracchius*'s hilt in a white-knuckled grasp. "Oh," I said. "Yeah. Kind of a tip-off, isn't it?"

"Think you can let it go now?" Butters asked quietly.

"I'm trying," I said. "My hand's kind of locked up."

"Okay. Let's just go one finger at a time, then." Butters peeled my fingers off the sword, one at a time, until he had removed it from my grasp. My hand closed in on itself, tendons creaking, and I winced. It sort of hurt, but at the moment it was a really minor thing.

Butters set the sword aside and immediately took my left hand in his, massaging brusquely. "Murphy's going to be pissed if you don't call her."

"Murphy and I have disagreed before," I said.

Butters grimaced. "Okay. Can I help?"

"You are helping."

"Besides this," Butters said.

I looked at the little M.E. for a moment. Butters had been my unofficial doctor for a long time, never asking a thing in return. He'd waded into some serious trouble with me. Once, he'd saved my life. I trusted his discretion. I trusted him, generally.

So, as the blood started returning to my hand, I told

him more or less everything about Buzz and the swords.

"So this guy, Buzz," Butters said. "He's just a guy."

"Let's don't forget," I said. "Despite all the nasties running around out there, it's just guys who dominate most of the planet."

"Yeah, but he's just a guy," Butters said. "How's that?"

I flexed my fingers, wincing a little. "It's good. Thanks."

He nodded and stood up. He went over to the kitchen and filled my dog's water bowl, then did the same for my cat, Mister. "My point is," he said, "that if this guy isn't a super-magical something, he had to find out about the swords like any other guy."

"Well," I said. "Yeah."

Butters looked at me over his spectacles. "So," he said. "Who knew that you had the swords?"

"Plenty knew I had Shiro's sword," I said. "But this guy tried to get to me through Michael. And the only ones who knew about *Amoracchius* were me, a couple of archangels, Michael, Sanya, and . . ."

Butters tilted his head, looking at me, waiting.

"And the Church," I growled.

St. Mary of the Angels is just about as big and impressive as churches get. In a city known for its architecture, St. Mary's more than holds its own. It takes up most of a city block. It's massive, stone, and as Gothic as black frosting on a birthday cake.

I'd watched my back all the way there, and was sure no one was following me. I parked behind the church and marched up to the delivery door. Twenty seconds of pounding brought a tall, rather befuddled-looking old priest to the door.

"Yes?" he asked.

"I'm here to see Father Forthill," I said.

"Excuse me," he said.

" 'S okay, padre," I told him, clapping his shoulder and moving him aside less than gently. "I'll find him."

"Now, see here, young man—"

He might have said something else, but I didn't pay much attention. I walked past him, into the halls of the church, and headed for Forthill's room. I rapped twice on the door, opened it, and walked in on a priest in his underwear.

Father Forthill was a stocky man of medium height, with a fringe of white hair around his head, and his eyes were the color of robins' eggs. He wore boxers, a tank top, and black socks. A towel hung around his neck, and what hair he had left was wet and stuck to his head.

A lot of people would have reacted to my entrance with outrage. Forthill considered me gravely and said, "Ah. Hello, Harry."

I had come in with phasers set on snark, but even though I'm not particularly religious, I do have *some* sense of what is and isn't appropriate. Seeing a priest in his undies just isn't, especially when you've barged into his private chamber. "Uh," I said, deflating. "Oh."

Forthill shook his head, smiling. "Yes, priests bathe. We eat. We sleep. Occasionally, we even have to go to the bathroom."

"Yeah," I said. "Um. Yeah."

"I do rather need to get dressed," he said gently. "I'm giving Mass tonight."

"Mass?"

Forthill actually let out a short belly laugh. "Harry, you didn't think that I just sit around in this old barn waiting my chance to make you sandwiches, bandage wounds, and offer advice?" He nodded to where a set of vestments was hung up on the wall. "On weeknights they let the junior varsity have the ball."

"We've got to talk," I said. "It's about the swords."

He nodded and gave me a quick smile. "Perhaps I'll put some pants on first?"

"Yeah," I said. "Sorry." I backed out of the room and shut the door.

The other priest showed up and gave me a gimlet eye a minute later, but Forthill arrived in time to rescue me, dressed in his usual black attire with a white collar. "It's all right, Paulo," he told the other priest. "I'll talk to him."

Father Paulo harrumphed and gave me another glare, but he turned and left.

"You look terrible," Forthill said. "What happened?"

I gave it to him unvarnished.

"Merciful God," he said, when I'd finished. But it wasn't in an "oh, no!" tone of voice. It was a slower, wearier inflection.

He knew what was going on.

"I can't protect the swords if I don't know what I'm dealing with," I said. "Talk to me, Anthony."

Forthill shook his head. "I can't."

"Don't give me that," I said with quiet heat. "I need to know."

"I'm sworn not to speak of it. To anyone. For any reason." He faced me, jaw outthrust. "I keep my promises."

"So you're just going to stand there," I snapped. "And do nothing."

"I didn't say that," Forthill replied. "I'll do what I can."

"Oh, sure," I said.

"I will," he said. "You have my word. You're going to have to trust me."

"That might come easier if you'd explain yourself."

His eyes narrowed. "Son, I'm not a fool. Don't tell me that you've never been behind this particular eight ball before."

I looked for something appropriately sarcastic and edgy to say in response, but all I came up with was, "Touché."

He ran a hand over his mostly bald scalp, and I suddenly saw how much older Forthill looked than he had when I met him. His hair was even more sparse and brittle-looking, his hands more weathered with time. "I'm sorry, Harry," he said, and he sounded sincere. "If I could . . . is there anything else I could do for you?"

"You can hurry," I said quietly. "At the rate we're going, someone is going to get killed."

At the rate we'd been going, probably me.

I approached the park with intense caution. It took me more than half an hour to be reasonably sure that Buzz wasn't there, somewhere, lurking with another fifty-caliber salutation for me. Of course, he could have been watching from the window of one of the nearby buildings—but none of them were hotels or apartments, and none of the pictures taken in the park had been shot from elevation. Besides. If I avoided every place where a maniac with a high-powered rifle might possibly shoot me, I'd live the rest of my life hiding under my bed.

Still, no harm in exercising caution. Rather than walking across the open ground of the park to the softball field, I took the circuitous route around the outside of the park—and heard quiet little sobs coming from the shade beneath the bleachers opposite the ones where I'd sat with Michael.

I slowed my steps as I approached, and peered under the bleachers.

A girl in shorts, sneakers, and a powder-blue team jersey was huddled up with her arms wrapped around her knees, crying quietly. She had stringy red hair and was skinny, even for someone her age. It took me a minute to recognize her as Alicia's teammate, the second basem—person.

"Hey, there," I said quietly, trying to keep my voice gentle. "You all right?"

The girl looked up, her eyes wide, and immediately

began wiping at her eyes and nose. "Oh. Oh, yes. I'm fine. I'm just fine, sir."

"Right, right. Next you'll tell me you've got allergies," I said.

She looked up at me with a shaky little smile, huffed out a breath in the ghost of a laugh—and it transformed into another sob on her. Her face twisted up into an agonized grimace. She shuddered and wept harder, bowing her head.

I can be such a sucker. I ducked down under the bleachers and sat down beside her, a couple of feet away. The girl cried for a couple more minutes, until it began quieting down.

"I know you," she said a minute later, between sniffles. "You were talking to Coach Carpenter yesterday. A-Alicia said you were a friend of the family."

"I'd like to think so," I agreed. "I'm Harry."

"Kelly," she said.

I nodded. "Shouldn't you be practicing with the team, Kelly?"

She shrugged her skinny shoulders. "It doesn't help."

"Help?"

"I'm hopeless," she said. "Whatever it is I'm doing, I just screw it up."

"Well, that's not true," I said with assurance. "Nobody can be bad at *everything*. There's no such thing as a perfect screwup."

"I am," she said. "We've only lost two games all year, and both of them were because I screwed up. We go to the finals next week and everyone's counting on me, and I'm just going to let them down."

Hell's bells, what a ridiculously tiny problem. But it was obvious that it was real to Kelly, and that it meant the world to her. She was just a kid. It probably looked like a much larger issue from where she was standing.

"Pressure," I said. "Yeah, I get that."

She peered at me. "Do you?"

"Sure," I said. "You feel like people's lives depend on you, and that if you do the wrong thing they're going to be horribly hurt—and it will be your fault."

"Yes," she said, sniffling. "And I've been trying so hard, but I just can't."

"Be perfect?" I asked. "No, of course not. But what choice do you have?"

She looked at me uncertainly.

"Anything you do, you risk screwing up. You could do a bad job of crossing the street one day and get hit by a car."

"I probably could," she said darkly.

I held up my hand. "My point," I told her, "is that if you want to play it safe, you can stay at home and wrap yourself up in bubble wrap and never do anything."

"Maybe I should."

I snorted. "They still make you read Dickens in school? *Great Expectations*?"

"Yeah."

"You can stay at home and hide if you want—and wind up like Miss Havisham," I said. "Watching life through a window and obsessed with how things might have been."

"Dear God," she said. "You've just made Dickens relevant to my life."

"Weird, right?" I asked her, nodding.

Kelly let out a choking little laugh.

I pushed myself up and nodded to her. "I never saw you hiding over here, okay? I'm just gonna go do what I gotta do, and leave you to make the choice."

"Choice?"

"Sure. Do you want to put your cap back on and play? Or do you want to wind up an old maid wandering around your house in the rotting remains of a wedding dress and thirty yards of bubble wrap, plotting heartlessly against some kid named Pip?" I regarded her soberly. "There's really no middle ground."

"I'm pretty sure that's not right," she said.

"See there? I'm not much good at offering wise counsel, but that didn't stop me from trying." I winked at her and walked on, around behind the backstop to where Michael sat on the bleachers on the far side of the field.

Molly sat on a blanket underneath a tree maybe ten yards away, with earbuds trailing wires down into her shirt's front pocket, as if she was listening to a digital music player. It was an effort to blend into the background, I supposed, since she couldn't have been listening to one of those gizmos any more than I could have. She was wearing sunglasses, too, so I couldn't tell where her focus was, but I was sure she was being alert. She gave me the barest trace of a nod as I approached her father.

I sat down next to him and waited for it.

"Harry," Michael said. "You look awful."

"Yes, I do," I said. I told him about the attempted assassination and about my discussion with Forthill.

Michael frowned out at the children practicing, his expression quietly disturbed. "The Church wouldn't do something like that, Harry. It isn't how they operate."

"People are people, Michael," I said. "People do things. They make mistakes."

"But it isn't the Church," he said. "If this person is part of the Church, he isn't acting with their blessing or under their instructions."

I shrugged. "Maybe. Maybe not. I don't think they were too happy with me when I was a couple of days late turning over the Shroud."

"But you did return it, safe and sound," Michael said.

"How many people know about the swords? How many knew that I had *Amoracchius*?"

He shook his head. "I'm not certain. Given the sorts of foes they contend with, the knowledgeable people within the Church are more than mildly secretive and security-conscious."

I gestured around us. "Ballpark it for me."

He blew out a breath. "Honestly, I just don't know. I've personally met perhaps two hundred priests who understood our mission, but it wouldn't shock me if there were as many as six or seven hundred, worldwide. But among them, that kind of important information would be closely kept. Four or five, at most. Plus the Holy Father."

"I'm going to assume that Il Papa didn't personally attempt to blow me away," I said gravely. "How do I find out about the others?"

"You might talk to Father For—"

"Been there, did that. He isn't talking."

Michael grimaced. "I see."

"So, other than him—"

He spread his hands. "I don't know, Harry. Forthill was my primary temporal contact."

I blinked. "He never talked to you about your support structure in the Church?"

"He was sworn to secrecy," Michael said. "I just had to trust him. Excuse me." He stood up and called to the softball team, "Thank you, ladies! Two laps of the park and we'll call it a day!"

The team began discarding gloves and such, and fell into a line to begin jogging around the exterior of the park, in no great hurry, talking and laughing as they went. I noticed that Kelly was among them and felt a little less like a complete incompetent.

"I'd really like to keep my brains on the inside of my skull," I told him when he sat down again. "And if one of the Church's top guys is leaking information or has sprung a gear, they need to know it."

"Yes."

I stared out at the now-empty softball diamond for a minute. Then I said, "I don't want to kill anybody. But Buzz is playing for keeps. I'm not going to pull any punches."

Michael frowned down at his hands. "Harry. You're talking about murder."

"What a shock," I said, "after taking one of those monster rounds in the back."

"There must be some way to end this without bloodsh—"

Over his shoulder, I saw Molly abruptly spring to her feet and whip off her sunglasses, staring across the park with a puzzled frown on her face. Then the girls from the team appeared from the direction Molly had been staring. The girls were running as fast as they could, screaming as they came.

"Coach!" screamed Kelly. "Coach! The man took her!"

"Easy, easy," Michael said, rising. He put his hands on Kelly's shoulders as Molly came hurrying over. "Easy. What are you talking about?"

"He came out of the van with one of those electric stunner things," Kelly babbled, through her panting. "He zapped her and then he put her in the van and drove away."

Molly drew in a sudden breath and almost seemed to turn green.

Michael stared at the girl for a second, and then glanced at me. His eyes widened in horror. "Alicia!" he called, stepping past Kelly and looking wildly around the park. "Alicia!"

"He took her!" sobbed Kelly, her tears making her face blotchy. "He took her!"

"Kelly," I said, to get her attention. "What did he look like?"

She shook her head. "I don't, I can't . . . White, not really tall. His hair was cut really short. Like army haircuts."

Buzz.

He'd threatened Michael to get me to bring a sword out in the open, where it was vulnerable. Then he'd tried to kill me before I locked it away again. And when that failed, he tried something else.

"Molly," Michael said quietly. "Take the truck. Drive

Sandra and Donna home. Call your mother on the way and tell her what's happened. Stay at the house."

"But—" Molly began.

Michael turned hard eyes to her and said, "Now."

"Yes, sir," Molly said, instantly.

Michael tossed her the keys to the truck. Then he turned to a nearby equipment bag and smoothly withdrew an aluminum bat. He whipped it around in a flowing *rondello* motion, nodded as if satisfied, and turned to me. "Let's go. You're driving."

"Okay," I said. "Where?"

"St. Mary's," Michael said, his tone positively grim. "I'm going to talk to Forthill."

Forthill had just finished giving evening Mass when we showed up. Father Paulo greeted Michael like a long-lost son, and how was he doing, and of course we could wait for Forthill in his chambers. I suspected Paulo held deep reservations in regards to me. But that was okay. I wasn't feeling particularly trusting toward him, either.

We'd been waiting in Forthill's quarters for maybe five minutes when the old priest came in. He took one look at Michael and got pale.

"Talk to me about the order," Michael said quietly.

"My son," Forthill said. He shook his head. "You know that I—"

"He's taken Alicia, Tony."

Forthill's mouth dropped open. "What?"

"He's taken my daughter," Michael roared, his voice shaking the walls. "I don't care what oaths you've sworn. I don't care what the Church thinks needs to be kept secret. We have to find this man and find him now."

I blinked at Michael and found myself leaning a little away from him. The heat of his anger was palpable, a living thing that brought its own presence, its own gravity, into the room.

Forthill faced that anger like an old rock thrusting up

stubbornly through a turbulent sea—worn and unmoving. "I will not break my oaths, Michael. Not even for you."

"I'm not asking you to do it for me," Michael said. "I'm asking you to do it for Alicia."

Forthill flinched. "Michael," he said quietly. "The order maintains security for a reason. Its enemies have sought to destroy it for two thousand years, and in that time the order has helped hundreds of thousands, even millions. You know that. A breach could put the entire order at risk—and that means more than my life, or yours."

"Or an innocent child's, apparently," I said. "I guess you're going to take that 'suffer the little children to come unto Me' thing kind of literally, eh, padre?"

Forthill looked from Michael to me, and then to the floor. He took a slow breath, and then smoothed his hands over his vestments. "It never gets any easier, does it? Trying to work out the right thing to do." He answered his own question. "No. I suppose it's often simpler to determine the proper path than it is to actually walk it."

Forthill rose and walked over to a section of the wood-paneled wall. He put his hands at the top right and lower left section of the panel, and with a grunt, pushed it in. It slid aside, revealing a space the size of a closet, filled with file cabinets and a small bookshelf.

I traded a glance with Michael, who raised his eyebrows in surprise. He hadn't known about the hidey-hole.

Forthill opened a drawer and started thumbing through files. "The Ordo Malleus has existed, in one form or another, since the founding of the Church. Originally, we were tasked with the casting out of demons from the possessed, but as the Church grew, it became clear that we needed to be able to counter the threats from other enemies as well."

"Other enemies?" I asked.

"Various beings who were masquerading as gods," Forthill said. "Vampires and other supernatural predators. Wicked faeries who resented the Church's influence." He glanced at me. "Practitioners of witchcraft who turned their hand against the followers of Christ."

"Hell's bells," I muttered. "The Inquisition."

Forthill grimaced. "The Inquisition has become the primary reason Malleus maintains itself in secrecy—and why we very seldom engage in direct action ourselves. It's all too easy to let power go to your head when you're certain that God is on your side. The Inquisition, in many ways, attempted to bring our struggle into the light—and because of the situation it helped create, more innocent men and women died than centuries of the most savage supernatural depredation.

"We support the Knights of the Cross and do whatever we can to counsel and protect God's children against supernatural threats—the way we protected the girl you brought to me the year Michael's youngest was born. Now the order recruits people singly, after years of personal observation, and maintains the highest levels of personal, ethical integrity humanly possible." He turned to us, with a file folder in his hands. "But as you pointed out earlier, Harry. We're only human."

I took the folder from him, opened it, and found Buzz's picture. I recognized the short haircut, and the severe lines of his chin and jaw. His eyes were new to me, though. They were as grey as stone, but less warm and fuzzy.

"Father Roarke Douglas," I read. "Age forty-three. Five eleven, hundred eighty-five. Sniper for the Rangers, trained in demolitions, U.S. Army Chaplain, parish priest in Guatemala, Indonesia, and Rwanda."

"Good Lord preserve us," Michael said.

"Yeah. A real holy warrior," I said. I eyed Forthill. "And this guy was brought in?"

"I've met Roarke on several occasions," Forthill said. "I was always impressed with his reserve and calm in the face of crisis. He repeatedly distinguished himself by acts of courage in protecting his parishioners in some of the most dangerous locations in the world." He shook his head. "But he ... changed, in the last few years."

"Changed," Michael said. "How?"

"He became a strong advocate for ... preemptive intervention."

"He wanted to hit back first, eh?" I asked.

"You wouldn't say that if you'd seen what life can be like in some of the places Father Douglas has lived," Forthill said. "It's not so simple."

"It never is," I said.

"He was, in particular, an admirer of Shiro's," Forthill continued. "When Shiro died, he was devastated. They had worked together several times."

"The way you worked with Michael," I said.

Forthill nodded. "Roarke was ... not satisfied with the disposition of *Fidelacchius*. He made it known to the rest of Malleus, too. As time went by, he became increasingly frustrated that the sword was not being put to use."

I could see where this one was going. "And then I got hold of *Amoracchius*, too."

Forthill nodded. "He spent the last year trying to convince the senior members of Malleus that we had been deceived. That you were, in fact, an agent of an enemy power, who had taken the swords so that they could not be used."

"And no one thought to mention the way those archangels gave orders that I was supposed to hold them?"

"They never appear to more than one or two people at a time—and you *are* a wizard, Harry," Forthill said. "Father Douglas hypothesized that you had created an illusion to serve your purpose, or else had tampered directly with our minds."

"And now he's on a crusade," I muttered.

Forthill nodded. "So it would seem."

I kept on reading the file. "He's versed in magic—well

enough, at least, to be smart about how he deals with me. Contacts in various supernatural communities, like the *Venatori Umbrorum*, which probably explains that protective amulet." I shook my head. "And he thinks he's saving the world. The guy's a certifiable nightmare."

"Where is he?" Michael asked quietly.

"He could be anywhere," Forthill replied. "Malleus sets up caches of equipment, money, and so forth. He could have tapped into any one of them. I tried his cell phone. He's not returning my calls."

"He thinks you've been mindscrambled by the enemy," I muttered. "What did you expect to accomplish?"

"I had hoped," Forthill said gently, "that I might ask him to be patient and have faith."

"I'm pretty sure this guy believes in faith through superior firepower." I closed the file and passed it back to Forthill. "He tried to kill me. He abducted Alicia. As far as I'm concerned, he's off the reservation."

Forthill's expression became distressed as he looked at me. He turned to Michael, beseeching.

Michael's face was bleak and unyielding, and quiet heat smoldered in his eyes. "The son of a bitch hurt my little girl."

I rocked a step backward at the profanity. So did Forthill. The room settled into an oppressive silence.

The old priest cleared his throat after a moment. He put the file back in the cabinet and closed the door. "I've told you what I know," he said. "I'm only sorry that I can't do more."

"You can find her, can't you?" Michael asked me. "The way you found Molly?"

"Sure," I said. "But he's bound to be expecting that. Magic isn't a cure-all."

"But you can find her."

I shrugged. "He can't stop me from finding her, but he can damn well make sure that something happens to her if I do."

Michael frowned. "What do you mean?"

"Maybe he stashes her in a box that's being held fifty feet above the ground with an electromagnet, so that when I get close with an active spell up and running, it shorts out and she falls. The bastard is smart and creative."

Michael's knuckles popped as his hands closed into fists.

"Besides," I said. "We don't need to find him."

"No?"

"No," I said. "We've got the swords. He's got the girl." I turned to go. "He's going to find us."

Father Douglas called Michael's house later that night, and asked for me. I took the call in Michael's office.

"You know what I want," he said, without preamble.

"Obviously," I said. "What do you have in mind?"

"Bring the swords," he said. "Give them to me. If you do so without attempting any tricks or deceptions, I will release the girl to you unharmed. If you involve the police or attempt anything foolish, she will die."

"How do I know you haven't killed her already?"

The phone rustled, and then Alicia said, "H-Harry? I'm okay. H-he hasn't hurt me."

"Nor do I want to," Father Douglas said, taking the phone back. "Satisfied?"

"Can I ask you something?" I said. "Why are you doing this?"

"I am doing God's work."

"Okay, that doesn't sound too crazy or anything," I said. "If you're so tight with God, can you really expect me to believe that you'll be willing to murder a teenage girl?"

"The world needs the swords," he replied in a level, calm voice. "They are more important than any one person. And while I would never forgive myself, yes. I will kill her."

"I'm just trying to get you to see the fallacious logic you're using here," I said. "See, if I'm such a bad guy to have stolen the swords, then why would I give a damn whether or not you murder some kid?"

"You don't have to be evil to be ambitious—or wrong. You don't want to see the girl harmed. Give me the swords and she won't be."

There clearly wasn't going to be any profitable discussion of the situation here. Father Douglas was going to have his way, regardless of the impediments of trivial things like rationality.

"Where?" I asked.

He gave me an address. "The roof. You come to the east side of the building. You show me the swords. Then you come up and make the exchange. No staff, no rod. Just you."

"When."

"One hour," he said, and hung up.

I put the phone down, looked at Michael, and said, "We don't have much time."

The building in question stood at the corner of Monroe and Michigan, overlooking Millennium Park. I had to park a couple of blocks away and walk in, with both swords stowed in a big gym bag. Father Douglas hadn't specified where I was supposed to stand and show him the swords, but the streetlights adjacent to the building were all inexplicably dark except for one. I ambled over to the pool of light it cast down onto the sidewalk, opened the bag, and held out both swords.

It was hard to see past the light, but I thought I saw a gleam on the roof. Binoculars?

A few seconds later, a red light flashed twice from the same spot where I'd thought I had seen something.

This would be the place, then.

I'd brought my extremely illegal picklocks with me, but as it turned out, I didn't need to use them. Father

Douglas had already circumvented the locks and, presumably, the security system. The front door was open, as was the door to the stairwell. From there, it was just one long, thigh-burning hike up to the roof.

I emerged into cold, strong wind. You get up twenty stories or so and you run into that a lot. It ripped at my duster, and sent it to flapping like a flag.

I peered around the roof, at spinning heat pumps and AC units and various antennae, but saw no one.

The beam of a handheld floodlight hit me, and I whirled in place. The light was coming from the roof of the building next to mine. Father Douglas flipped it off, and after blinking a few times, I could see him clearly, standing in the wind in priestly black, his white collar almost luminous in the ambient light of the city. His grey eyes were shadowed, and he was maybe a day and a half past time to shave. A long plank lay on the rooftop at his feet, which he must have used to move over.

Alicia sat in a chair next to him, her wrists bound to its arms, blindfolded, with a gag in her mouth.

Father Douglas lifted a megaphone. "That's far enough," he said. I could hear him over the heavy wind. "That's detcord she's tied up with. Do you know what that is?"

"Yeah."

He held up his other hand. "This is the detonator. As long as it's sending a signal, she's fine. It's a dead man switch. If I drop it or let it go, the signal stops and the cord goes off. If the receiver gets damaged and stops receiving the signal, the cord goes off. If you start using magic and destroy one of the devices, it goes off."

"That's way better than the electromagnet thing," I muttered to myself. I raised my voice and bellowed, "So how do you want to do this?"

"Throw them."

"Disarm the explosives first."

"No. The girl stays where she is. Once I'm gone, I'll send the code to disarm the device."

I considered the distance. It was a good fifteen-foot jump to get from one rooftop to the other. An easy throw.

"Douglas," I shouted. "Think about this for a minute. The swords aren't just sharp and shiny. They're symbols. If you take one up for the wrong reasons, you could destroy it. Believe me, I know."

"The swords are meant for better things than to molder in a dingy basement," he replied. He held up the detonator. "Surrender them now."

I stared at him for a long second. Then I tossed the entire bag over. It landed at his feet with a clatter. He bent down to open it.

I steeled myself. This was about to get dicey. I hadn't counted on the dead man switch or a fifteen-foot-long jump.

Father Douglas opened the bag and the smoke grenade Michael had rigged inside it in his workshop went off with a heavy thud. White smoke billowed back into his face, and I took three quick steps and hurled myself into the air. For an awful portion of a second, twenty stories of open air yawned beneath me, and then I hit the edge of the other roof and collided with Father Douglas. We went down together.

I couldn't think about anything but the detonator, and I clamped down on that with my left hand, crushing his fingers beneath mine so that he couldn't release it. He jabbed his thumb at my right eye, but I ducked my head and he got nothing but bone. He slammed his head against my nose—*again* with the nose, Hell's bells that hurt—and drove a knee into my groin.

I let him, seizing his arm with both hands now, squeezing, trying to choke off the blood to his hand, to weaken it so that I could take the detonator from him. His left fist slammed into my temple, my mouth, and my neck. I bent my head down and bit savagely at his wrist, eliciting a scream of pain from him. I slammed my weight against him, slipping some fingers into his grasp, and got one of them over the pressure trigger. Then I wrenched with my whole body, twisting my shoulders and hips for leverage, and ripped the detonator away from him.

He rolled away from me instantly and seized the bag. Then he was up and running for a doorway leading down into the building.

I let him go and rushed over to Alicia. The dark-haired girl was trembling uncontrollably.

Detcord is basically a long rubber tube filled with explosive compound. It's a little thicker than a pencil, flexible, and generally set off by an electrical charge. Wrap detcord around a concrete column and set it off, and the explosion will cut through it like a piece of dry bamboo. Alicia was tied to the chair with it. If it went off, it would cut her to pieces.

The detonator was a simple setup—a black plastic box hooked to a twelve-volt battery, which was in turn connected to a wire leading to the detcord. A green light on the detonator glowed cheerily. It matched a cheery green light on the dead man switch transmitter in my hand. If what Douglas had said was accurate, then if the light went out, things wouldn't be nearly so cheery.

If I let go of the switch, it would stop the signal to the detonator, which would then complete the circuit, send current to the detcord, and boom. In theory, I should be able to cut the wire leading from the battery and render it harmless—as long as Douglas hadn't rigged the device to detonate if that happened.

I didn't have much time. The electronics of the transmitter wouldn't last long around me, even though I hadn't used any magic around them. I had to get the girl out now.

I made the call based upon what I knew about Father Douglas. He seemed like he might have good intentions, despite all his shenanigans. So I gambled that he wouldn't want the girl to die by any means other than a conscious decision from someone—either him letting go of the trigger or me blowing the transmitter by using magic.

I took out my pocketknife, opened it with my teeth, and slashed at the heavy plastic tubing that held her tied down. I cut through the tube once, unwound it from first one arm, then the other, and she was free. She clawed away the blindfold and gag, her fingers still clumsy from being bound.

"Come on!" I said. I grabbed her arm and hauled her out of the chair and away from the explosives. She staggered, leaning against me, and I ran for the stairs.

As we got to the first landing, my ongoing presence apparently became too much for the transmitter. Something sparked and crackled inside the plastic case, the cheery green light went out, and there was a huge and horrible sound from above and behind us. I managed to get between Alicia and the stairwell wall as the pressure wave caught us and threw us into it. It slammed my already abused head into the wall.

I staggered under the pain for a minute, and forced my way through it, like a drowning man clawing for the surface.

"Come on," I croaked to Alicia. "Come on. We have to go."

She looked at me with dull, stunned eyes, so I just grabbed her hand and started down the stairs with her, stuffing the heavy transmitter into my duster pocket with the other hand. We only had a few minutes before the place would be swarming with police and firefighters. I didn't particularly feel like answering their questions about why my fingerprints were on an expensive transmitter and showed trace evidence of explosive residue.

Going down all those stairs was only slightly less taxing than going up had been, and my legs were going to be complaining at me for days. We got to the bottom and I led Alicia out into an alley, then out to Monroe. I looked wildly up and down the street. Michael's truck was there waiting right where it was supposed to be, out in front of the original building. I put my fingers to my lips and let out a shrill whistle.

Michael's truck pulled into the street and stopped in front of us. I hurried Alicia forward. The door swung open, and Molly leaned out, taking Alicia's hand and pulling her in. I went in right behind her, though it made things awfully cozy in the pickup's cab.

"He's loose with the swords," I said. "Did you do it?"

"Did it," Molly replied, and promptly handed me a dashboard compass with one of her own golden hairs stuck to it with clear tape. The needle pointed firmly to the east, instead of to the north. The grasshopper had set up a basic tracking spell, one of the handier tricks I know.

"He's probably moving on foot through the park," I told Michael. "Circle around to Lakeshore, get us in front of him."

"Are you all right, baby?" Michael asked.

Alicia fumbled for his hand and squeezed it tight. Then she leaned against Molly and started crying.

"Hurry," I told Michael. "He's got to know we've bugged the swords somehow. If he finds those hairs Molly tied onto the hilts, we're done."

"He won't get away," Michael said with perfect confidence, and slammed the accelerator down as we approached an intersection sporting a bright red light. Maybe it was divine intervention, or fate, or just good driving, but the truck shot through the intersection, missing two other cars by inches, and sailed on forward.

The needle on the compass pointed steadily toward the park as we went, but then abruptly began to traverse from one side to the other. I looked up ahead of me and saw a dark form sprinting across the road that separated the park from Lake Michigan.

"There!" I shouted, pointing. "There he is!"

Michael pulled over to the side of the road, and I hit the ground before the truck had stopped moving, sprinting after Father Douglas. He was in good shape, covering the ground in long, loping strides. Normally it wouldn't have been a contest to catch him. I run three or four days a week, to train for situations exactly like this one. Of course, when I practice I'm not generally concussed, weary, and sporting a recently dislocated shoulder. Douglas was holding his lead as we sprinted down the beach, and I was tiring more rapidly than I should have.

So I cheated.

I reached into my pocket, drew out the heavy transmitter, and flung it at him as hard as I could. The black plastic device struck him on the back of the head, shattering, and sending several heavy batteries flying.

Father Douglas staggered, and couldn't keep his balance at the pace he was moving. He went down in the sand. I rushed over to him and seized the bag with the swords, only to have him sweep one leg out in a martial arts move, and kick my legs out from beneath me. I went down, too.

Father Douglas ripped at the bag, but I clung grimly, while we fought and kicked at each other—until the bag tore open under the strain and spilled the swords onto the sand.

He seized the hilt of *Fidelacchius*, a katana-type sword that was built to look like a simple, heavy walking stick, until you drew the blade. I seized *Amoracchius*, scabbard and all, and barely brought the sheathed broadsword up in time to deflect a sweeping slash from Father Douglas.

He gained his knees and swung again, and I had all I could do to lift the sheathed sword and fend off the strike. Blow after blow rained down on me, and there was no time to call upon my power, no opportunity to so much as rise to my knees—

Until a size-fourteen work boot hit Father Douglas in the chest and threw him back.

Michael stood over me, aluminum baseball bat in his right hand. He put out the other one, and I slapped *Amoracchius* into it. He gripped it mid-blade, like some kind of giant crucifix, and limped toward Father Douglas with his bat held in a guard position.

Father Douglas stared at Michael with wide eyes. "Stay back," he said. "I don't want to hurt you."

"Who says you're able to?" Michael rumbled. "Put down the sword, and I'll let you go."

Douglas stared at him with those cold grey eyes. "I can't do that."

"Then I'll put you down and take the sword anyway. It's over, Roarke. You just don't realize it yet."

Father Douglas wasted no more time on talk, but came at Michael, the katana whirling.

Michael batted (no pun intended) the attack aside like a cat swatting down moths, the baseball bat spinning.

"Slow," he said. "Too slow to hit a half-blind cripple. You don't know the first thing about what it means to bear a sword."

Douglas snarled and came at him again. Michael defeated this attack, too, with contemptuous ease, and followed it by smacking Douglas across one cheek with the hilt of the sheathed sword.

"It means sacrifice," Michael said as Douglas reeled. "It means forgetting about yourself, and what you want. It means putting your faith in the Lord God Almighty." He swung a pair of blows, which Douglas defended against, barely—but the third, a straight thrust with the baseball bat's tip, drove home into his solar plexus. Douglas staggered to one knee.

"You *abandoned* your duty," Douglas gasped. "The world grows darker by the day. People cry out for our help—and you would have the swords sit with this creature of witchcraft and deceit?"

"You arrogant child," Michael snarled. "The Almighty Himself has made His will known. If you are a man of faith, then you must abide by it."

"You have been lied to," Douglas said. "How could God ignore His people when they need his protection so badly?"

"That is not for us to know!" Michael shouted. "Don't

you *see*, you fool? We are only men. We only see in one place at one time. The Lord knows all that might be. Would you presume to say that you know better than our God what should be done with the swords?"

Douglas stared at Michael.

"Are you stupid enough to believe that He would want you to cast aside your beliefs to impose your will upon the world? Do you think He wants you to murder decent men and abduct innocent *children*?" The bat struck *Fidelacchius* from Douglas's hands, and Michael followed it with a pair of crushing blows, one to the shoulder and one to the knee. Douglas went down to the sand in a heap.

"Look at yourself," Michael said, his words hard and merciless. "Look at what you have done in God's name. Look at the bruises on my daughter's arms, at the blood on my friend's face, and then tell me which of us has been deceived."

Again, the bat swept down, and Douglas fell senseless to the sand.

Michael stood over the man for a moment, his entire body shaking, the bat still upraised.

"Michael," I said quietly.

"He hurt my little girl, Harry." His voice shook with barely repressed rage.

"He isn't going to hurt her now," I said.

"He hurt my little girl."

"Michael," I said, gently. "You can't. If this is how it has to be, I'll do it. But you can't, man."

His eyes shifted back toward me for just a second.

"Easy, easy," I told him. "We're done here. We're done."

He stared for another long, silent moment. Then he lowered the bat, very slowly, and bowed his head. He stood there for a minute, his chest heaving, and then dropped the bat. He settled down onto the sand with a wince.

I got up and collected *Fidelacchius*, returning it to its sheath.

"Thank you," Michael said quietly. He offered me *Amoracchius*'s hilt.

"Are you sure?" I asked.

He nodded, smiling wearily. "Yes."

I took the sword and looked at Douglas. "What do we do with him?"

Michael stared at him silently for a moment. In the background, we could hear emergency vehicles arriving to attend to the aftermath of the rooftop explosion. "We'll bring him with us," Michael said. "The Church will deal with its own."

I sat in the chapel balcony at St. Mary's, staring down at the church below me and brooding. Michael and Forthill had been seeing to Father Douglas, who wasn't going anywhere under his own locomotion for a while. They had him in a bed somewhere. It had hurt to watch Michael, moving in what was obviously great pain, hobble around the room helping to make Douglas feel better. I'd have been content to dump the asshole in an alley somewhere and leave him to his fate.

Which might, just possibly, be one reason I was never going to be a Knight.

I had also swiped Forthill's flask of scotch from his room, and it was keeping me company in the balcony. Two more reasons I was never going to be a Knight.

"Right at the end, there," I said to no one in particular, "those two started speaking a different language. I mean, I understood all the words, and I understood the passion behind them, but I don't get how they connect. You know?"

I sipped some more scotch. "Come to think of it, there are a lot of things I don't get about this whole situation."

"And you want an explanation of some kind?" asked a man seated in the pew beside me.

I just about jumped out of my skin.

He was an older man. He had dark skin and silver-white hair, and he wore a blue workman's jumpsuit, like you often see on janitors. The name tag read "Jake."

"You," I breathed. "You're the archangel. You're Uriel."

He shrugged. The gesture carried acknowledgment, somehow.

"What are you doing here?" I asked—maybe a bit blearily. I was concussed and half the flask was gone.

"Perhaps I'm a hallucination brought on by head trauma and alcohol," he said.

"Oh," I said. I peered at him, and then offered him the flask. "Want a belt?"

"Very kind," he said, and took a swig from the flask. He passed it back to me. "I don't exactly make it a habit to do this, but if you've got questions, ask them."

"Okay," I said. "Why did you guys let Michael get so screwed up?"

"We didn't let him do anything," Jake replied calmly. "He chose to hazard himself in battle against the enemy. The enemy chose to shoot him, and where to point the gun and when to pull the trigger. He survived the experience."

"So in other words, God was doing nothing to help."

Jake smiled. "Wouldn't say that. But you got to understand, son. God isn't about making good things happen to you, or bad things happen to you. He's all about you making choices—exercising the gift of free will. God wants you to have good things and a good life, but he can't gift wrap them for you. You have to choose the actions that lead you to that life."

"Free will, huh?"

"Yes. For example, your free will on that island."

I eyed him and sipped more scotch.

"You saw the Valkyrie staring at Michael. You thought he was in danger. So even though it was your turn, you sent him up to the helicopter in your place."

"No good deed goes unpunished," I said, with one too many "sh" sounds. "That's where he got hurt."

Jake shrugged. "But if you hadn't, you'd have died in that harness, and he'd have died on that island."

I scowled. "What?"

Jake waved a hand. "I won't bore you with details, but suffice to say that your choice in that moment changed everything."

"But you lost a Knight," I said. "A warrior."

Jake smiled. "Did we?"

"He can barely walk without that cane. Sure, he handled Douglas, but that's a far cry from dealing with a Denarian."

"Ah," Jake said. "You mean warrior in the literal sense."

"What other kind of warrior is there?" I asked.

"The important kind."

I frowned again.

"Harry," Jake said, sighing. "The conflict between light and darkness rages on so many levels that you literally could not understand it all. Not yet, anyway. Sometimes that battlefield is a literal one. Sometimes it's a great deal more nebulous and metaphorical."

"But Michael and me are literal guys," I said.

Jake actually laughed. "Yeah? Do you think we angled to have you brought into this situation because we needed you to beat someone up?"

"Well. Generally speaking. Yeah." I gestured with the flask. "Pretty much all we did was beat up this guy who had good intentions and who was desperate to do something to help."

Jake shook his head. "The real war happened when you weren't looking."

"Huh?"

"Courtney," Jake said. "The little girl who almost got hit by a car."

"What about her?" I asked.

"You saved her life," he said. "Moreover, you noted the bruise on her cheek—one which she acquired from her abusive father. Your presence heightened her mother's response to the realization that her daughter was being abused. She moved out the next morning." He spread his hands. "In that moment, you saved the child's life, prevented her mother from alcohol addiction in response to the loss, and shattered a generational cycle of abuse more than three hundred years old."

"I . . . um."

"Chuck the electrician," Jake continued. "He was drunk because he's fighting with his wife. Two months from now, their four-year-old daughter is going to be di agnosed with cancer and require a marrow transplant. Her father is the only viable donor. You saved his life with what you did—and his daughter's life, too. And the struggle that family is going to face together is going to leave them stronger and happier than they've ever been."

I grunted. "That smells an awful lot like predestination to me. What if those people choose something different?"

"It's a complex issue," Jake admitted. "But think of the course of the future as, oh, flowing water. If you know the lay of the land, you can make a good guess where it's going. Now, someone can always come along and dig a ditch and change that flow of water—but honestly, you'd be shocked how seldom people truly choose to exercise their will within their lives."

I grunted. "What about second baseperson Kelly? I save her life, too?"

"No. But you made a young woman feel better in a moment where she felt as though she didn't have anyone she could talk to. Just a few kind words. But it's going to make her think about the difference those words made. She's got a good chance of winding up as a counselor to her fellow man. The five minutes of kindness you showed her is going to help thousands of others." He spread his hands. "And that only takes into account the past day.

Despair and pain were averted, loss and tragedy thwarted. Do you think that you haven't struck a blow for the light, warrior?"

"Um."

"And last but not least, let's not forget Michael," he said. "He's a good man, but where his children are involved he can be completely irrational. He was a hairbreadth from losing control when he stood over Douglas on the beach. Your words, your presence, your will helped him to choose mercy over vengeance."

I just stared at him for a moment. "But ... I didn't actually mean to do any of that."

He smiled. "But you chose the actions that led to it. No one forced you to do it. And to those people, what you did saved them from danger as real as any creature of the night." He turned to look down at the church below, and pursed his lips. "People have far more power than they realize, if they only choose to use it. Michael might not be cutting demons with a sword anymore, Harry. But don't think for a second that he isn't still fighting the good fight. It's just harder for you to see the results from down here."

I swigged more scotch, thinking about that.

"He's happier now," I said. "His family, too."

"Funny how making good choices leads to that."

"What about Father Douglas?" I asked. "What's going to happen?"

"For the most part," Jake said, "that will be up to him. Hopefully, he'll choose to accept his errors and change his life for the better."

I nodded slowly. Then I said, "Let's talk about my bill."

Jake's eyebrows shot up. "What?"

"My bill," I said, enunciating. "You dragged me into this mess. You can pay me, same as any other client. Where do I send the invoice?"

"You're ... you're trying to bill the Lord God Almighty?" Jake said, as if he couldn't quite believe it.

"Hel—uh, heck no," I said. "I'm billing *you*."

"That isn't really how we work."

"It is if you want to work with me," I told him, thrusting out my jaw. "Cough up. Otherwise, maybe next time I'll just stand around whistling when you want me to help you out."

Jake's face broadened into a wide, merry grin, and laughter filled his voice. "No, you won't," he said, and vanished.

I scowled ferociously at the empty space where he'd been a moment before. "Cheapskate," I muttered.

But I was pretty sure he was right.

THE DIFFERENCE A DAY MAKES

SIMON R. GREEN

ONE

It was three o'clock in the morning, in the oldest bar in the world, and I was killing time drinking with a dead man. Dead Boy is an old friend, though he's only seventeen. He's been seventeen for some thirty years now, ever since he was mugged and murdered for the spare change in his pockets. He made a deal to come back from the dead and take his revenge on his killers; but he should have read the small print. He's been trapped inside his dead body ever since, searching for a way out. He's surprisingly good company, for a man with so many strikes against him.

I'm John Taylor, private investigator. I don't do divorce work, I don't chase after the Maltese Falcon, and I am most definitely not on the side of the angels. Either variety. I do, however, wear a white trench coat, get in over my head more often than not, and get personally involved with my female clients far more often than is good for me. I have a gift, for finding things and people.

I'd just finished a case that hadn't ended well. A man hired me because his imaginary friend had gone missing, and he wanted me to find out why. Apparently this man's imaginary friend had been his constant companion since childhood, and had never gone off on his own before. The client got quite tearful about it, so I gave him my best professional look, and my most reassuring smile, and promised him I would waste no time in tracking down his imaginary friend. As cases go, it wasn't that difficult. I found the imaginary bastard in the first place I looked. He was having an affair with the client's wife. I put the three of them together in the same hotel room, and left them to it, knowing there was no point in even sending in my bill.

It was all the client's fault, really. Far too imaginative, except when it came to his wife.

And there I was, consoling myself with a large glass of wormwood brandy, while Dead Boy made heavy going of something that heaved back and forth, and looked like it was trying to eat its way through the glass. Being very thoroughly dead, though not in the least departed, Dead Boy doesn't need to eat or drink, but he likes to pretend. It makes him feel more real. And since his taste buds are quite definitely damaged, it takes more than the usual hard stuff to hit his spot. Dead Boy knows this appalling old obeah woman who whips up pills and potions especially for him, potent enough to make a corpse dance and a ghoul show you her underwear. God alone knows what it would do to the living; certainly I've never been tempted to find out. For the moment, Dead Boy was drinking a graveyard punch, made with ingredients from real graveyards. I just hoped it was no one I knew.

For once, Dead Boy was in a better financial state than me, so he was paying for the drinks. He'd just started a new job, as doorman for Club Dead, the special club for zombies, vampires, mummies, and all the other forms of the mortally challenged. (Club motto: *We Belong Dead.*) I didn't see the job lasting. Dead Boy has all the social graces of a lemming in heat or a sewer rat with bleeding haemorrhoids. But, since he was in the money, I was ordering the best of everything, in a big glass.

The oldest bar in the world is called Strangefellows, these days. You get all sorts in here, the living and the dead and those who haven't made their minds up yet, along with gods and monsters, aliens and shapeshifters, and a whole bunch of things that shouldn't exist but unfortunately do. Something from a Black Lagoon was sitting slumped in one corner, big and green and mossy and stinking of brine, drinking whiskey sours one after the other and mourning over *the one that got away*. The Tribe of the Gay Barbarians, tall muscular fellows resplendent in fringed leather chaps, nipple piercings, and tall ostrich feather headdresses, were challenging all comers to a game of Twister. A dancing bear was giving it his best John Travolta moves. He looked pretty silly in the white jacket, but given his size no one felt like telling him. And a group of rather disreputable-looking dwarves were selling tickets to see The Incredible Sleeping Woman. (I'd seen her. Forty years of catatonia had not been kind, which was why the dwarves were no longer allowed to bill her as The Incredible Sleeping Beauty.)

One of Frankenstein's female creations was singing a torch song, the transvestite superheroine Ms. Fate was reading a gossip tabloid with great concentration, to see if he was in that week, and Harry Fabulous was doing his rounds, selling chemical adventures, knockoff Hyde formula, and short-time psychoses, for really quite reasonable prices.

Just another night, at Strangefellows.

But while the oldest bar in the world has few rules and even fewer standards, we do draw the line at weeping women. So when the tall slender brunette in the expensive outfit came stumbling into the bar, crying her eyes out, everyone fell quiet and turned to look. Weeping women always mean trouble, for someone. She lurched to a halt in the middle of the room and looked about her, and I quickly realised that she was crying hot angry tears of rage and frustration, rather than sorrow. The tears ran jerkily down her cheeks, the sheer force of them shaking her whole body. Something about her gave me the feeling she wasn't a woman who often gave in to tears. She sniffed them back with an effort, and glared about her as defiantly as her puffy eyes and streaked makeup would allow. And then she looked in my direction, and my heart sank as she fixed her attention on me. She pushed her way quickly through the packed tables, and marched right up to me. The bar's normal bedlam resumed, as everyone celebrated someone else getting hit by the bullet. I sighed inwardly, and turned unhurriedly on my bar stool to nod politely to the woman as she crashed to a halt before me and fixed me with dark, haunted eyes.

She was good-looking enough, in an undemanding way, her long lean body positively burning with thwarted nervous energy. Her clothes were expensive, though somewhat dishevelled. She was clutching a white leather shoulder bag as though she would never let it go, and her whole stance screamed stress and tension. Her mouth was compressed into a thin dark red line, and she held herself very stiffly, as though she might fall apart if her control lapsed for just one moment. And yet, behind the clear anger in her eyes, I could see an awful, unfocused fear.

"Hi," I said, as kindly as I could. "I'm John Taylor."

"Yes," she said jerkily, the words coming out clipped, in sudden bursts. "I know. You were described to me. The man in the white trench coat. The knight in cold armour. He said you'd help me. Sorry. I'm not making myself clear . . . I've had something of a shock. My name is Liza Barclay. I'm lost. I don't know what I'm doing here. I've lost all memory of the last twenty-four hours of my life. I want you to find them for me."

I sighed again, still inwardly, and handed her my glass. "Take a sip of brandy," I said, doing my best to sound kind and helpful and not at all threatening.

She grabbed the brandy glass with both hands, took a good gulp, and immediately pulled a face and thrust the glass back into my hand.

"God, that's awful. You drink that for fun? You're tougher than you look. But then, you'd have to be. Sorry. I'm rambling."

"It's all right," I said. "Take your time, get your breath back. Then tell me how you got here. This isn't an easy place to get to."

"I don't know!" she said immediately. "I've lost a day. A whole day!"

I slipped off my bar stool and offered her a seat, but she shook her head quickly. So I just leaned back against the long wooden bar and studied her openly as she looked around Strangefellows, making it very clear with her face and body language that not only had she never seen anything like it, but that she was quite definitely slumming just by being there. I was impressed. The oldest bar in the world isn't for just anyone. Most people take one look and run away screaming, and we like it that way. Strangefellows is a place of old magic and all the very latest sins and indulgences. This is not the kind of bar where everyone knows your name; it's the kind of bar where you can wake up robbed and rolled in someone else's body.

Liza Barclay deliberately turned her back on the disturbing sights and the appalling patrons, and fixed her full attention on me. I did my best to look tall, dark, and handsome, but I couldn't have been that successful because after only a moment she nodded briskly, as though I'd passed some necessary test, but only just. She switched her gaze to Dead Boy, who smiled vaguely and toasted her with his glass. The graveyard punch made a valiant attempt to escape, and he had to push the stuff back in with his fingers.

Dead Boy was tall and adolescent thin, wrapped in a long purple greatcoat spotted with various food and drink stains, and topped with a fresh black rose on his lapel. Scuffed black leather trousers over muddy calfskin boots completed the ensemble. He let his coat hang open, to reveal a bare torso covered with old injuries, bullet holes, and one long Y-shaped autopsy scar. Dead Boy might be deceased, but he still took damage, even if he couldn't feel it. He was mostly held together with stitches and staples and superglue, along with a certain amount of black duct tape lashed around his middle. His skin was a pale gray, and dusty-looking.

He had the face of a debauched and very weary Pre-Raphaelite poet, with dark fever-bright eyes, a sulky mouth with no colour in it, and long dark curly hair crammed under a large floppy hat. He didn't smile at Liza Barclay. He didn't care. Her tears hadn't touched him at all.

Liza shuddered, but didn't look away. She was impressing me more and more. Most people can't stand being around the dead, and that goes double for Dead Boy. Liza glanced around the bar again, at its various strange and unnatural patrons, and rather than being scared or appalled, she just sniffed loudly and turned her back on them again. They were no help to her, or her problem, so they didn't matter. Liza Barclay, it seemed, was a very single-minded lady.

"How can you stand being in a place like this?" she said to me, quite seriously.

"What, Strangefellows?" I said. "There are worse places to drink in. The ambience isn't up to much, I'll grant you, but ..."

"I don't mean just here! I mean ... everywhere! This whole area!" A tinge of hysteria had entered her voice. Liza heard it, and clamped down hard on it. She hugged herself suddenly, as though a cold wind had blown over her grave. "I've been walking back and forth in the streets for ages. This *terrible* place. I've seen things ... awful things. Creatures, walking right out in the open, with normal people, and none of them batted an eye! Where am I? Am I dead? Is this Hell?"

"No," I said. "Though on a good day you can see Hell from here. As far as I can tell, you are a perfectly normal woman who has had the misfortune to somehow find her way into the Nightside."

"The Nightside." She grabbed on to the word, considered it, and then looked to me for more information.

And it wasn't a request; it was a demand. I was liking her more and more.

"The Nightside," I said, "the dark secret hidden in the heart of London. The longest night in the world, where the sun has never shone and never will. Where it's always three o'clock in the morning, and the hour that tries men's souls. This is where all the secret people come, in search of forbidden knowledge and all the pleasures people aren't supposed to want, but still do. You can pursue any dream here, or any nightmare. Sell your soul or someone else's. Run wild in the streets and satisfy any fantasy you ever had. As long as your credit holds out. This is the Nightside, Liza Barclay, and it is not a place for normal people like you."

"It's not an easy place to find your way into," said Dead Boy. "How did you get here?"

"I don't know! I can't remember!" Her shoulders slumped, and her strength seemed to seep out of her. I understood. She was having to take in a lot at one go. And the Nightside does so love to break people ... I thought for a moment she might start crying again, but her chin lifted, her eyes flashed, and just like that she was back in control again. "I live in London, have done all my life. And I never heard of the Nightside. I just ... came to, and found myself here. Lost, and alone."

"And now you're among friends," I said.

"More or less," said Dead Boy.

"I am John Taylor," I said, ignoring Dead Boy with the ease of long practice. "And I'm a private eye. Yes, really."

Her mouth twitched in a brief smile. "I suppose I shouldn't be surprised, to find one more mythical creature, among so many."

"And my appalling friend here is Dead Boy. Yes, really."

"Hi," said Dead Boy, leaning forward and offering a pale dead hand for her to shake. "Yes, that is formaldehyde you're smelling, so get used to it. I'm dead, I'm wild and exciting and extraordinarily glamorous, and you're very pleased to meet me."

"Don't put money on it," said Liza. "What's it like, being dead?"

"Cold," said Dead Boy, unexpectedly. "It's getting hard for me to even remember what being warm feels like. Though I think I miss sleep the most. Never being able to just lie down and switch off. No rest, no dreams . . ."

"Don't you get tired?" said Liza, fascinated despite herself.

"I'm always tired," Dead Boy said sadly.

"Cut it out," I said firmly. "You think I don't know you mainline that synthetic adrenaline when no one's looking?" I shrugged apologetically at Liza. "Sorry, but you mustn't encourage him. He's not really as self-pitying as he likes to make out. He just thinks it makes him more attractive to women."

"Never dismiss the pity factor," Dead Boy said easily. "Suicide girls go crazy for dead flesh."

"That's disgusting," said Liza, very firmly.

He leered at her. "You haven't lived till you've rattled a coffin with someone on graveyard Viagra."

"Changing the subject right now," I said loudly. "Tell me about your memory loss, Liza. What's the last thing you do remember, before waking up here?"

She frowned, concentrating. "The last twenty-four hours are just gone. A whole day. The last thing I'm sure of, I was in London. The real London. Down in Tottenham Court Road Underground station . . . though I can't quite seem to remember why . . . I think I was looking for someone. The next thing I knew, I was here. Running through the streets. Crying as though my heart would break. I don't know why. I'm not the crying kind, usually. I'm just not."

"It's all right," I said. "What happened next?"

"I was attacked! They came out of nowhere . . . Tall

spindly men in top hats and old-fashioned clothes, with great smiling faces, and ... knives for hands."

"Scissormen," I said. "Always looking for someone weaker to prey on. They can home in on guilt and horror like sharks tasting blood in the water."

"I haven't done anything to feel guilty about," said Liza.

"As far as you know," said Dead Boy, reasonably. "Who knows what you might have done, in the missing twenty-four hours? It's amazing how much sin a determined person can cram into twenty-four hours. I speak from experience, you understand."

"Ignore him," I said. "He's just boasting."

"But ... Scissormen?" said Liza.

"Everything comes to the Nightside," I said. "Especially all the bad things, with nowhere else to go. Still, it's always a shame when childhood characters go bad. How did you get away from them?"

"I didn't," said Liza, her eyes and her voice becoming uncertain again as she remembered. "They were all around me, smiling their awful smiles, opening and closing their ... scissorhands, chanting something in German in shrill mocking voices. They cut at me, always drawing back at the very last moment, and laughing as I jumped this way and that to avoid them. Scuttling round and round me, always pressing closer, smiling and smiling ... And nobody did anything! Most people didn't even stop to watch! I was screaming by then, but no one helped. Until this ... strange man appeared out of nowhere, and the Scissormen stopped, just like that. They huddled together, facing him like a pack of dogs at bay. He said his name, and the Scissormen just turned and ran. I couldn't believe it."

"What was his name?" I said.

"Eddie. He was very sweet, though he looked like some kind of vagrant. And from the smell of him, he'd been sleeping rough for some time. I tried to give him some money, but he wasn't interested. He listened to my story, though I don't know how much sense I made, and then he brought me here. Told me to look for you. John Taylor. That you'd be able to help me. Do you know this man?"

"Oh, sure," said Dead Boy. "Everyone here knows Razor Eddie. Punk God of the Straight Razor. No wonder the Scissormen cut and ran. Most people do."

Liza looked at me, and I nodded. "Eddie's a good man, in his own disturbing way. And he's right; I can help you. I have a gift for finding things."

"Even missing memories?" Liza managed a real, hopeful smile for the first time.

"Anything," I said. "But I have to ask . . . are you sure you want to remember? A lot of the time, people forget things for a reason."

She looked at me steadily. "Of course I want to remember. I think I need to. I think . . . something bad happened."

"In the Nightside? I can practically guarantee it," said Dead Boy.

"You're really not helping," I said. "Liza, you're sure you've never even heard of the Nightside before? It's not unheard of for innocents to wander in by accident, but usually you have to want it pretty bad."

"I never knew places like this existed," Liza said stubbornly. "I never knew monsters were real."

"The world is a much bigger place than most people realise," I said. "Magic still exists, though it's grown strange and crafty and maybe just a bit senile."

"Magic?" she said, raising one perfectly plucked eyebrow.

"Magic, and other things. Time isn't as firmly nailed down in the Nightside as it might be. We get all sorts turning up here, from the Past and any number of alternate Futures. Not to mention all kinds of rogues, adventurers, and complete and utter scumbags from other worlds and dimensions, all looking for a little excitement, or a nice bit of sin that isn't too shop-soiled." I stopped, and considered her thoughtfully. "You really don't care about any of this, do you? It doesn't interest or attract you in the least."

"No," said Liza. "I don't belong in a madhouse like this. I have no business being here."

"I could just take you home," I said. "Back to the safe and sane London you've always known."

"No," she said immediately. "There's a whole day of my life missing. It's mine, and I want it back."

"But what if you've done something really bad?" said Dead Boy. "Most people come to the Nightside to do something really bad."

"It's always better to know," Liza said firmly.

"No," I said. "Not always. And especially not here. But if that's what you want, then that's what you get. The client is always right. Now, the odds are you came here looking for something. Or someone. So let's take a look in that shoulder bag of yours. The way you've been clinging to it since you got here, it must hold something important."

She looked down at the bag as though she'd honestly forgotten it was there. And when I reached out a hand to take it, she actually shrank back for a moment. But once again her stern self-control reasserted itself, and she made herself hand over the bag. But there was a subtle new tension in her that hadn't been there before.

I hefted the bag. It wasn't that large, and it didn't feel like there was that much in it. Nothing obviously special about it. Expensive, yes; white leather Gucci without a mark on it. I opened the bag, and spilled the contents out onto the wooden bar top. All three of us leaned in for a closer look. But it was just the usual feminine clutter, with nothing out of the ordinary. Apart from a single colour photograph, torn jaggedly in two. I fitted the pieces together as best I could, and we all studied the image in silence for a while. The photo showed a somewhat younger Liza Barclay in a stylish white wedding dress, hugging a handsome young man in a formal suit. They were both laughing at the camera, clearly caught a little off guard. They looked very happy. As though they belonged together, and always would. Someone had torn the photo fiercely in two, right down the middle, as though trying to separate the happy couple.

"That's Frank," said Liza, frowning so hard her brow must have ached. "My husband, Frank. That's our wedding day, just over seven years now. I was never so happy in my life, the day we got married. Poor Frank, he must be worried sick by now, wondering where I am. But . . . this is my favourite photo ever. I must have worn out half a dozen copies, carrying it around in my bag and showing it to people. Who could have torn it like this?"

"Maybe you tore it," said Dead Boy. "Been having problems recently, have you?"

"No! No . . ." But even as she objected, I could practically see the beginnings of memories resurfacing in her. She concentrated on the two pieces of the photo, speaking only to them. "We were always so much in love. He meant everything to me. Everything. But . . . I followed him. All the way across London, on the Underground. He never saw me. He'd been so . . . preoccupied, the last few months. I could tell something was wrong. I was worried about him. He'd been keeping things from me, and that wasn't like him. There were letters and e-mails I wasn't allowed to read, phone calls he wouldn't talk about. He'd never done that before. I thought he might be in some kind of trouble. Something to do with his business. I wanted to help. He was my love, my life, my everything. I was so worried . . ."

"Sounds like another woman," Dead Boy said wisely, and was genuinely surprised when I glared at him. "Well, it does."

But Liza was smiling, and shaking her head. "You don't know my Frank. He loves me as much as I love him. He's never even looked at another woman."

"Come on," said Dead Boy. "Every man looks at other women. When he starts pretending he doesn't, that's when you know he's up to something."

"You followed Frank through the Underground," I said to Liza, ignoring Dead Boy. "What happened then?"

"I don't know." Liza reached out to touch the photo, but didn't, quite. "The next thing I remember, I'm here in the Nightside, and there's no sign of Frank anywhere. Could we have been kidnapped, dragged here against our will, and I somehow escaped?"

"Well," I said diplomatically, "it's possible, I suppose."

"But you don't think so."

"It's not the way I'd bet, no. But at least now we know you're not here alone. If you're here, then the odds are Frank is too. I can find him with my gift, and see if perhaps he holds the answer to your missing memories."

"No!" said Liza. "I don't want my Frank involved in all this . . . madness."

"If he's here, he's involved," said Dead Boy. "If only because the Nightside doesn't take kindly to being ignored."

She shook her head again, still smiling. "You don't know my Frank."

"And you don't know the kind of temptations on offer here," said Dead Boy. "Sex and love and everything in between, sweet as cyanide and sprinkled with a little extra glamour to help it go down easier. Sin is always in season in the Nightside."

"And you followed him here," I said.

She glared at me. "How could he know the way to a place like this?"

"Because he'd been here before," said Dead Boy. "Sorry, but it's the only answer that makes sense."

Liza glared at him, and then looked me right in the eye. "Find him. Find my Frank for me. If only so he can tell us the truth, and throw these lies back in your faces."

"I'll find him," I said. "Anything else . . . is up to you, and him."

I picked up the two pieces of the photo, holding them firmly between thumb and forefinger, and held them up before me. I took a deep breath and concentrated, reaching deep inside myself for my gift, my special gift, that allowed me to find anyone or anything. I concentrated on the photo until I couldn't see anything else, and then slowly, my inner eye opened; my third eye, my private eye . . . from which nothing can hide. With my inner eye all the way open, I could See the world as it really was, every last bit of it. All the things that are hidden from Humanity, because if we could all See the true nature of this world, and the kinds of things we share it with, Humanity would go stark staring mad with horror.

I can only bear to See it for a little while.

I sent my Sight soaring up out of my body, shooting up through the roof of my skull and the roof of Strangefellows, until I was high in the star-speckled sky, looking down on the Nightside spread out below me, turning slowly, like the circles of Hell. Hot neon burned everywhere, like balefires in the night. Sudden bright glares detonated in this place or that; as souls were bartered, great magical workings rewrote the world, or some awful new thing was born to plague Mankind. There were great Voices abroad in the night, and terrible rumblings deep in the earth, as Powers and Dominations went about their unknowable business.

Ghosts howled in the streets, trapped in moments of Time like insects in amber. Demons rode their human hosts, whispering in their ears. And vast and powerful creatures walked the night in majesty, wonderful and terrible beyond human ability to bear.

I dropped down from my high vantage point, sending my Sight flashing through the packed narrow streets, slamming in and out of buildings with the quickness of thought, following a trail only I could See. The photo of Frank Barclay had let me sink my mental hook in his consciousness, if not his soul, and I could See the ghost of him still striding purposefully through the streets. Semi-transparent and fragile as a soap bubble, the mark he'd made in the Nightside was still clear, his imprint on Time itself, still walking the streets that he had walked not so long ago . . . and would do until the last vestiges of it faded away.

Frank Barclay showed no interest in any of the usual pleasure joints or temptations. The open doors of night-clubs where the music never ends, the heavy-lidded glances from dark-eyed ladies of the twilight, had no attraction for him. He never hesitated once, or paused to check directions. He knew where he was going. And from the increasingly intense, almost desperate anticipation in his face, wherever he was going promised something none of the usual temptations could hope to satisfy. I could See him clearly now, and he was smiling. And something in the smile chilled me all the way to my soul.

I pulled back, as I realised where he was going. There are some places you just don't go into with your spirit hanging out. Some parts of the Nightside are hungrier than others. I slowly closed my third eye, my inner eye, until I was safely back inside my own head again. And then I dropped the two pieces of the photo back onto the bar top as though they burned my fingers. I looked at Liza.

"Good news and bad news," I said. "I've found him. I've found husband Frank."

"Then what's the bad news?" said Liza, meeting my gaze unflinchingly.

"He's in the badlands," I said. "Where the really wild things are, and hardly anyone gets out alive. You only go into the badlands in search of the pleasures too sick, too twisted, and too nasty for the rest of the Nightside."

"If that's where he is," Liza said steadily, "then that's where I have to go."

"You can't go there alone," I said. "They'd eat you up and chew on the bones."

"But I have to know!" said Liza, her chin jutting stubbornly. "I have to know what's wrong with him, what could possibly bring him to an awful place like this. And I have to know what, if anything, this has to do with my missing memories. I have to go there."

"Then I guess I'll have to take you," I said.

"I . . . don't have much money on me, at the moment," said Liza. "Is my credit good?"

"Put the plastic away," I said. "No charge, this time. Razor Eddie owes me a favour, for dumping you on me, and that's worth more than you could ever pay."

I leaned over and nudged Dead Boy, who'd lost interest in all this long ago. His eyes snapped back into focus.

"What is it, John? I have some important existential brooding I need to be getting on with."

"I'm taking Liza into the badlands in pursuit of her missing husband, and her missing memories," I said briskly. "Bound to be some trouble. Interested?"

"Oh, sure," said Dead Boy. "You can't get too much excitement, when you're dead. How much are you offering?"

"Tell you what," I said. "You can have half of my fee. But only if we can use your car."

"Done!" said Dead Boy.

"Why do we need his car?" said Liza.

"Because we have to travel all the way across town," I said. "And the rush hour can be murder."

TWO

She'd never seen the sky before. Preoccupied with so much new sin and strangeness right before her, it had never even occurred to her to stop and look up. Now, on the rain-slick pavement outside the oldest bar in the world, Liza Barclay followed my pointing finger and stood very still, held to the spot by awe and enchantment, quite unaware of all the people, and others, hurrying by on every side. In the Nightside, the sky is full of stars, thousands and thousands of them, burning bright and sharp in constellations never seen in the outside world. And the moon . . . ah, the moon is big and bright indeed in the Nightside, unnaturally luminous and a dozen times larger than it should be, hanging over us all like a great mindless eye, like an ancient guardian that has quite forgotten its duty and purpose. Seeing all, judging nothing.

I often think that it isn't a matter of where the Nightside is, so much as when.

Meanwhile, all kinds and manner of Humanity, and many things not in any way human, pushed past with brisk impartial haste, intent on their own personal salvations and damnations. No one got too close, though. They might not give a damn about Liza, clearly just another starstruck tourist, but everyone in the Nightside knows me. Or knows enough to give me plenty of room. Liza finally tore her gaze away from the overcrowded heavens, and gave her attention to the crowds bustling around us. The street, as always, positively squirmed with life and energy and all manner of hopes, the pavements packed with desperate pilgrims come in search of sin and temptation and the kinds of love that might not have a name but most certainly have a price. Hot neon blazed and burned up and down the street, gaudy as a hooker's smile, signposts to all the most succulent hells. If you can't find it in the Nightside, it doesn't exist.

Liza clung to my arm like a drowning woman, but to her credit she never flinched or looked away. She took it all in, staring grimly about her, refusing to allow the strange sights and tacky glamour to overwhelm her. She pressed a little more closely to me, as a bunch of eight-foot-tall insect things paused to bow their devilish heads before me. Bones glowed through their flesh, filmy wings fluttered uncomfortably on their long chitinous backs, and their iridescent compound eyes didn't blink once. Their absurdly jointed legs lowered them almost to the ground as they abased themselves, speaking in unison with urgent breathy children's voices.

"All hail to thee, sweet prince of a sundered line, and remember us when you choose to come into your kingdom."

"Move on," I said, as kindly as I could.

They waited a while, antennae twitching hopefully, until they realised I wasn't going to say any more, and then they moved on. Liza watched them go, and then looked at me.

"What the hell was that all about? Who . . . what were they?"

"They are all that remains of the Brittle Sisters of the Hive," I said. "They were just being polite."

"So you're . . . someone special here?"

"I might have been, once," I said. "But I abdicated."

"So what are you now?"

"I'm a private investigator," I said. "And a bloody good one."

She favoured me with another of her brief smiles, and then looked out at the traffic, thundering ceaselessly through the Nightside. There was a lot of it to look at. Vehicles of all kinds and natures flashed past, never slowing, never stopping, jockeying endlessly for position and dominance. Some of them carried goods and some of them carried people, and many of them carried things best not thought about at all. Most were just passing through, on their way to somewhere more interesting; mysteries and enigmas, never to be understood.

A horse-drawn diligence from the eighteenth century clattered past, overtaken by a lipstick red Plymouth Fury with a dead man grinning at the wheel. An articulated rig bore the logo of a local long-pig franchise, while a motorcycle gang of screaming skeletons burning forever in hellfire chased something very like a tank crossed with an armadillo. The Boggart On Stilts, one of the Lesser Atrocities, strode disdainfully down the middle of the road, while smaller vehicles nipped in and out of its tall bone stilts. A great black beauty of a car cruised past, driven by an Oriental in black leathers, and the man in the back in the green face mask and snap-brimmed hat nodded respectfully to me in passing. Liza turned and looked at me speechlessly, demanding an explanation.

"In the Nightside, the traffic comes and goes, but not everything that looks like a car is a car," I explained patiently. "Here, ambulances run on distilled suffering, motorcycle couriers snort powdered virgin's blood for that extra kick, and sometimes the bigger vehicles sneak up behind the smaller ones and eat them. Pretty much everything passes through the Nightside, at one time or another and sometimes simultaneously, and it's always in a hurry. Foot down, everything forward and trust in the Lord, and Devil take the hindmost. That isn't traffic out there; that's evolution in action. Which is why we can't get where we're going by just hopping on the cross-town bus. We are waiting for Dead Boy, and his marvellous car of the future."

"The sky, the traffic, creatures and demons walking openly in the street . . ." Liza shook her head just a bit dazedly. "Where is this place, John?"

"Good question," I said. "Of this world, but not necessarily in it. Halfway between Heaven and Hell, but beholden to neither. A place of infinite jest and appalling possibilities. But don't let it get to you. The Nightside is just a place where people go, in search of all the things they're not supposed to want. Forbidden knowledge, forgotten secrets, and all the nastier kinds of sex. A place where the shadows are comfortably deep, and the sun never rises because some things can only be done in the dark.

"It's the Nightside."

Liza looked at me. "You do like the sound of your own voice, don't you?"

"You asked," I said.

Perhaps fortunately, Dead Boy arrived at that moment in his fabulous futuristic car, and Liza had something else to stare at. Dead Boy's car is always worth a good look. It glided silently to a halt before us, hovering a few feet above the ground. A car from the future, so stylish it didn't even bother with wheels anymore. It originally arrived in the Nightside through a Timeslip, from some future time line, and adopted Dead Boy as its driver. Bright gleaming silver, long and sleek and streamlined to within an inch of its life, the car hovered arrogantly before us, looking like it ran on distilled starlight. The long curving windows were polarised so no one could see in, and the mighty engines didn't so much as deign to murmur.

The driver's door swung open, to reveal Dead Boy lounging languidly behind the steering wheel. He had a half-empty bottle of vodka in his hand.

"All aboard for the badlands, boys and girls! Feel free

to admire my beautiful ride's elegance and style. This is what every car would be, if they only had the ambition."

"You're late," I said sternly.

"I'm always late. I'm the late Dead Boy." He sniggered at his own joke, and took a healthy pull from his vodka bottle.

"I am not getting into that!" Liza said firmly. "It hasn't got any wheels. It looks like something from a bad seventies sci-fi movie."

"Hush, hush, my beauty!" Dead Boy said soothingly to his car. "She is an uneducated barbarian, and doesn't mean it." He appeared to listen for a moment. "All right, yes, she probably did mean it, but you mustn't take it personally. She is a mere tourist, and knows nothing of cars. Please let her in. And please don't activate the ejector seat, no matter how annoying she gets."

There was a pause, and then the other doors opened, slowly enough to express a certain reluctance. Liza looked at me.

"Does he often have conversations with his car?"

"Oh, yes," I said. "Only he can hear her, though."

"I see. And does this car really have an ejector seat?"

"Oh, yes. More than powerful enough to blast you into a whole different dimension."

"I'll be more polite to the car from now on," said Liza.

"I would," I said.

"But I'm still not sitting next to Dead Boy."

So we both got in the back. Liza jumped just a bit as the door shut itself behind us. The seats were bloodred leather, and very comfortable. There was a faint perfume of crushed roses on the slightly pressurised air. There were no seat belts, of course. Their very existence would have been an insult to the car's driving skills. Liza leaned forward and stared openly at the frankly futuristic display screens where the dashboard dials should have been. In fact, there were enough screens and displays and flashing lights to suggest anything up to and including warp speed.

"Can you get warp speed on this thing?" said Liza, proving that great minds think alike.

"Only in emergencies," said Dead Boy. He didn't seem to be kidding.

Liza took in the whiskey, brandy, and gin bottles lined up on top of the monitor screens, all of which showed signs of extensive sampling, and sniffed loudly. Dead Boy took this as a hint, and gestured generously at the bottles, and the open dashboard compartment full of honeyed locusts, spiced potato wedges, and assorted chocolate biscuits.

"Help yourself," he said, around a mouthful of chocolate hobnob. Liza declined. Dead Boy shrugged, finished his biscuit, knocked back a handful of glowing green pills, finished off the last of the vodka, and slung the bottle through the window, which didn't happen to be open. The bottle passed right through the glass without stopping. They really have thought of everything, in the future.

"Where to, John?" Dead Boy said easily. "My car requires directions. She is powerful and lovely and full of surprises, but she is not actually prescient. Apparently that only came as an optional extra."

"Head for the badlands," I said. "I should be able to provide more specific directions once we get there."

"I love mystery tours," Dead Boy said happily. "Off you go, girl."

The futuristic car moved smoothly out into the vicious traffic, and absolutely everything slammed on the brakes or changed lanes in a hurry, to give us plenty of room. Everybody knew Dead Boy's car, and the awful things it could and would do if it got even slightly annoyed.

"I can't help noticing you're not even touching the steering wheel," Liza said to Dead Boy.

"Oh, I wouldn't dare," he said. "My sweetie's a much better driver than I'll ever be. I don't interfere."

Liza leaned back in her seat, watched the traffic for a while, and then looked thoughtfully at me. "Why are you helping me, John? It's not like I'm even paying you for your services."

"I'm curious," I said honestly. "And ... I don't like to see an innocent caught up and crushed under the Nightside's wheels. There's enough real evil here, without adding cruel and casual stuff. Good people shouldn't end up here, but if they do, they need to be protected. Just on general principles."

"If this is such a bad place," she said, "what are you doing here?"

"I belong here," I said.

She settled for that, and went back to watching the traffic. I took out the two pieces of her photo, fitted them together, and concentrated on the image of her husband. My gift barely stirred, manifesting just enough to keep a firm hold on Frank's location. Husband Frank. He'd better be worth all this trouble. Liza clearly loved him with all her heart; but women have been known to fall for complete bastards before now. His face in the photo didn't give anything away. The smile seemed genuine enough, but I wasn't so sure about the eyes.

Frank hadn't moved since I first sensed his location, and I got the feeling he hadn't moved in some time. As I concentrated on his image, I began to get a feel for his surroundings, and the first thing I felt was the presence of technology. Advanced, future tech, not from this time and place. Frank seemed to be surrounded by it, fascinated by it ... and the more I concentrated, the more my images of this future technology were tainted by distinctly organic touches.

Sweating steel and cables that curled like intestines; lubricated pistons rising and falling, and machines that murmured like people disturbed in their sleep. Strange nightmare devices, performing unnatural tasks, with hot blood coursing through their systems.

What had Frank got himself into?

I was beginning to get a really bad feeling about this. Especially when Frank's image in the photo suddenly turned its head to look right at me. His face was drawn, tired, and burning with a strange delirium. His eyes were dark and fever-bright ... and he never even glanced at his wife, Liza, sitting right next to me. He locked his gaze onto mine, and his faraway voice sounded in my head.

Go away. I don't want you here. Don't try and find me. I don't want to be found.

"Your wife's here," I said silently to the photo. "Liza's here, in the Nightside. Looking for you. She's very worried about you."

I know. Keep her away. For her sake.

And just like that, the photo was only a photo, and his face was just an image from the past. I didn't tell Liza what had just occurred. It didn't matter to me whether Frank wanted to be found or not; I was working for his wife. And she wanted to know what her husband was up to, even if she hadn't actually put it that way. This is why I don't do divorce work. No matter what the client says, they never really want the truth. Still, the unexpected contact with Frank, brief as it was, had given me a more definite fix on his position.

"I've found Frank," I announced, to Liza and Dead Boy. "He's on Rotten Row."

"Ah," said Dead Boy, sucking noisily on his whiskey bottle. "That is not good."

"Why?" Liza said immediately. "What happens on Rotten Row? What do people do there?"

"Pretty much everything you can think of, and a whole lot of things most people have never even contemplated," said Dead Boy. "Rotten Row is for the severely sick and disturbed, even by the Nightside's appalling standards."

Liza turned to me. "What is he talking about?"

"Rotten Row is where people go to have sex with the kind of people, and things, that no sane person would want to have sex with," I said, just a bit reluctantly. "Sex with angels, or demons. With computers or robots, slumming gods or other-dimensional monsters; worms from the earth or some of the nastier versions of the living dead. Rotten Row is where you go when the everyday sins of the flesh just don't do it for you anymore. Where men and women and all the many things they can do together just don't satisfy. Sex isn't a sin or a sacrament on Rotten Row; it's an obsession."

Liza looked at me, horrified. "Sex with . . . how is any of that even *possible*?"

"Love finds a way," Dead Boy said vaguely.

Liza shook her head stubbornly, as though she could prove me a liar if she was just firm enough. "No. You must be wrong, John. My Frank would never . . . never lower himself to . . . He just wouldn't! He's always been very . . . normal. He'd never go to a place like that!"

"We all find love where we can," said Dead Boy.

"You're talking about sex, not love!" snapped Liza.

"Sometimes . . . you have to go a little off the beaten path to get what you really need," said Dead Boy philosophically. "There's more to life than just boy meets girl, you know."

And that was when all the car's alarms went off at once. Flashing red lights, followed by a rising siren, and the sound of an awful lot of systems arming themselves. Dead Boy sat bolt upright, tossed his whiskey bottle onto the passenger seat, and studied his various displays with great interest. Dead Boy lived for action and adventure.

"All right, car, turn off the alarms, I see them. Proximity alert, people. We are currently being boxed in by three, no four, vehicles. In front and behind, left and right. Look out the windows, see if you can spot the bastards."

It wasn't difficult; they weren't being exactly furtive

about it. Four black London taxicabs were forcing their way through the crowded lanes of traffic to surround us on every side, positioning themselves to cut off all possible exits and escapes. The cabs bore no name or logo on their flanks, just flat black metal, like so many malignant beetles. They all had cyborged drivers, human only down to the waist. The head and torso hung suspended in a complex webbing of cables, tubes, and wires that made them a part of their taxis. The car was just an extension of its tech-augmented driver, so it could manoeuvre as fast as they could think. Human consciousness given inhuman control and reaction times. By the time I'd finished peering out of every window, there were black cabs speeding in perfect formation all around us.

And long machine-gun barrels protruded from each and every one of them, covering us.

"Put your foot down," I said to Dead Boy. "Try and lose them."

"You go, girl, go!" said Dead Boy, and the futuristic car surged forward.

The back of the taxicab in front of us loomed up disturbingly fast, and for a moment I thought we were going to ram it, but the taxi accelerated too, maintaining its distance. The other cabs swiftly increased their speed too, suggesting the cyborged drivers and the protruding machine guns weren't the taxis' only special features. These black cabs had been seriously souped up. We were all moving incredibly fast now, hurtling through the Nightside at insane speed, streets and buildings just gaudy blurs of colour. All around us, traffic hurried to get out of our way. Vehicles that didn't, or couldn't, move quickly enough were slammed and shunted aside by the taxis. Cars ran careering off the road, into defenceless storefronts, or smashed into one another, crying out like living things. Screams and shouts of outrage rang briefly behind us, Dopplering away into the distance.

The cabs decided enough was enough, closed in on us from every side, and slammed on their brakes simultaneously. We had to slow down with them or risk a collision, and the futuristic car was clearly cautious enough not to want to risk direct contact until it had to. Just because they looked like cabs, it didn't mean they were. Protective camouflage is a way of life in the Nightside.

Why do you think I work so hard to look like a traditional private eye?

Dead Boy beat on the steering wheel with his pale fists, hooting with the excitement of the chase and shouting helpful advice that the car mostly ignored. Liza peered out of one window after another, her small hands unconsciously clenched into fists. I wasn't that worried, yet. The car could look after itself.

One cab pressed in from the left, trying to pressure us into changing lanes. The cyborged driver wasn't even looking at us. The other cabs gave way a little, to entice us, trying to persuade us away from the badlands exit, some way up ahead. To keep us away from Frank . . . and probably to herd us into a previously chosen killing zone where they'd have all the advantages. The futuristic car swayed back and forth, looking for a way out between the cabs, but they constantly manoeuvred with their more than human reflexes to block our way. And then, without warning, all four sets of machine guns opened fire on us. The sound was painfully loud, as bullets raked our car from end to end, and slammed viciously into front and back. Liza cried out, but quickly calmed down again as she realised I wasn't even ducking. The machine-gun fire roared and stuttered, but none of it could touch us. Whatever Dead Boy's car was made of, it wasn't just steel. Bullets ricocheted harmlessly away in flurries of sparks and metallic screeches, but the futuristic car didn't even shudder under the impact. The gunfire continued, as though the taxis thought they could break through our defences through sheer perseverance.

"Time for Puff the Magic Dragon, I think," Dead Boy said cheerfully, entirely unmoved by the massed firepower aimed at him from all sides.

"What?" said Liza. "What did he just say? He's got a bloody dragon in here somewhere?"

"Not as such," I said. "More of a nickname, really. Because it breathes fire and makes problems disappear. Go for it, Dead Boy."

Lights gleamed brightly all across the display screens, and there was the sound of something large and heavy moving into position. To be exact, a large gun muzzle was slowly protruding from the car's radiator grille. Puff the Magic Dragon fired two thousand explosive fléchettes a second, pumping them out at inhuman speed and with appalling vigour. Puff is a gun's gun. The futuristic car opened up on the taxicab in front of us, and the whole back of the cab just exploded, black steel disintegrating under the impact, throwing ragged shrapnel in all directions. The cab surged wildly back and forth, but Puff moved easily to follow it, tearing the cab apart with invisible hands. The cab burst into flames, and was thrown this way and that by a series of explosions, before the endless stream of explosive fléchettes picked the cab up and threw it end over end across several lanes of traffic, leaving a trail of blazing debris and drifting smoke behind it. I caught a brief glimpse of the cyborged driver, trapped behind his wheel in his ruptured webbing, screaming horribly as he burned alive in the wreckage.

I couldn't bring myself to care, much. He would have done worse to us, if he could.

The taxi to our left accelerated wildly, forcing its way in front of us to block our escape, machine guns blazing fiercely from its rear. A brave and determined move, but the driver really shouldn't have taken his eyes off the main threat. The other traffic.

A long dark limousine with dull unreflective black windows moved effortlessly in beside the cab, having sneaked up in the driver's blind spot while he was concentrating on us. I winced, despite myself. I'd seen the limousine in action before. It moved in beside the taxicab, matching speeds perfectly until it was right opposite the driver's window; and then the black window surface erupted into dozens of long grasping arms with clawed hands. Hooked fingers sank deep into the steel side of the cab, holding it firmly in place, while powerful black arms smashed through the window to get at the cyborged driver. The limousines can smell human flesh, and they're always hungry. The cyborged driver screamed horribly as a dozen clawed hands gripped him fiercely, long barbed fingers sinking deep into flesh and bone, and then they hauled the driver right out of his webbing, tearing the human torso free from its rupturing tubes and cables. They dragged the screaming head and torso out through the shattered window, and into the interior of the limousine. The driver's mouth stretched wide in an endless howl of horror, his eyes almost starting from his head at what he saw waiting for him. He disappeared inside the limousine, there was a brief spurt of blood out the window, and then the black arms snapped back in, the window re-formed itself, and the dark limousine accelerated smoothly away. The empty taxicab shot across the lanes, traffic diving every which way to avoid it, until finally it ran off the road and crashed.

That left just two taxicabs, running now on either side of us, still firing their guns and trying to herd us away from the badlands.

Puff the Magic Dragon had fallen silent. At two thousand rounds a second, it runs out of ammo pretty fast. The taxi guns fell silent too, either because they'd realised their inventory was getting low as well, or perhaps because they'd finally realised the guns weren't doing any damage. The taxis pressed in close on either side, and a dozen long steel blades protruded from the sides of the cabs, aimed right at our windows. Long blades, with strangely blurred edges, and a chill ran through me as I realised what they were.

"Dead Boy," I said, doing my best to sound calm and concerned and not at all like I was filling my trousers, "do you see what I see?"

"Of course I see them," he said, entirely unconcerned. "The car's computers are already running analysis on the blades. Monofilament edges, one molecule thick. Cut through anything. Someone really doesn't want us going wherever it is we're going. Which means . . . they must be protecting something really interesting, and I want to know what it is more than ever. We're going to have to do something about those blades, John. The car says her exterior is no match for them, and while she does have a force shield, maintaining it for any length of time will put a serious strain on the engines. I think we're going to have to do this old school. In their face, up close and personal. Just the way I like it. Sweetie, lower the window, please."

His window immediately disappeared, and Dead Boy calmly climbed out the window. It took a certain amount of effort to force his gangling body through the gap, and then he braced himself in the window frame before throwing himself at the taxicab. It jerked away at the last moment, as the cyborged driver realised what Dead Boy was planning, but the unnatural strength in Dead Boy's dead muscles propelled him through the air, across the growing gap, until he slammed into the side of the cab, and his dead hands closed inexorably onto the cab's steel frame. He clung to the side of the cab as it lurched back and forth, trying desperately to shake him off. His purple greatcoat streamed out behind him, flapping this way and that in the slipstream. I couldn't hear Dead Boy above the roar of the traffic, but I could see he was laughing.

He drew back a gray fist, and drove it right through the cab's window. The cyborged driver cried out as the reinforced glass shattered, showering him with fragments. The cab was all over the place now, trying to throw Dead Boy off, but he held his balance easily, the fingers of one hand thrust deep into the steel roof, his feet planted firmly on the wheel arch. He leaned in through the empty window, and punched the cabdriver repeatedly in the head with his free hand. Bone shattered and blood flew, and the driver screamed as the force of the blows slammed him all around the cab's interior. Dead Boy grabbed a handful of tubes and cables and pulled them free. Sparks flew and hot fluids spurted, and the driver's face went slack and empty. He collapsed forward across the jerking steering wheel, and Dead Boy threw the cables aside. He checked to make sure he'd done all the damage he could, and then backed out of the cab window. He turned and braced himself, his back pressed against the empty window frame. The cab was a good ten feet away now, but he jumped the increasing gap like he did it every day, and landed easily on the futuristic car's roof. I heard the thud above me, followed by whoops and cheers as Dead Boy applauded himself and challenged all comers to come and have a go, if they thought they were hard enough.

The futuristic car was still driving itself. It didn't need Dead Boy, and it certainly didn't need me, so I gave my full attention to the one remaining taxicab, closing in really fast from the right. Its vicious steel blades were now only a few inches away. One good sideswipe and those blades would punch right through the car's side and gut Liza and me. We'd already retreated as far back as we could, pressed up against the far door; but those blades looked really long . . . Dead Boy came suddenly swinging in through the driver's window, and dropped back into his seat. He grinned widely, and started to beat a victorious tattoo on the steering wheel before he realised one hand still had bits of glass sticking out of it. So he leaned back in his seat, and set about removing them one at a time from his unfeeling flesh.

"Hi!" he said cheerfully. "I'm back! Did you miss me?"

"You're a lunatic!" said Liza.

"Excuse me," Dead Boy said coldly. "But I wasn't talking to you." And he spoke loving baby talk to his car until I felt like puking.

I did point out the nearness and threat of the remaining taxi, but Dead Boy just shrugged sulkily, suggesting through very clear body language that he felt he'd done his bit, and it was now very definitely my turn. So I very politely asked the car to lower the window facing the taxi, and it did. I peered out into the rushing wind, concentrating on the distance between us as the rushing wind blew tears from my eyes. We were still both moving at one hell of a speed, but the taxi was having no trouble keeping up. The blurry-edged blades were almost touching the car. The cyborged driver glared at me, his lips pulled back in a mirthless grin. His tubes and cables bobbed around him as he stuck close to the futuristic car, despite all it could do to lose him. I leaned out through the car's window and smashed the driver's window with the knuckle-duster I'd slipped on my fist while he wasn't looking.

I always make it a point to carry a number of useful objects in my coat pocket. Because you never know . . .

The taxi window shattered, glass flying everywhere, and the cyborged driver ducked, yelling obscenities at me as I leaned farther through the empty window and grabbed on to his door frame. I hung in midair between the two vehicles, very much aware that if they pulled apart, I'd very probably be torn in two. And I would have overbalanced and fallen, if Liza hadn't been clinging desperately to my legs in the back of the car. I hauled myself inside the cab, and the taxi driver pointed his arm at me. A dull gray metal nozzle protruded from his wrist, pointing right at my face. I really hadn't expected the driver to have an energy gun implant, but I still knew one when I saw one, and my mind raced for something to do. Time seemed to slow right down, to give me plenty of time to consider the possibilities; but since they all seemed to end with my face being shot off, that didn't help much. I was just about to try a really desperate lunge, when Liza let go of my legs.

I could feel myself sliding out of the car, only a few

moments from falling and almost certainly dying, when Liza appeared suddenly beside me, forcing herself into the remaining gap in the car window. The cyborged driver hesitated, as surprised as I was, and while he tried to decide which of us to shoot first, Liza surged forward and grabbed his arm, forcing it to one side. She was more than half out of the car now, and only our two bodies wedged in the car window stopped her from falling.

The cabdriver struggled to bring his gun hand to bear on either of us, while Liza fought to control his flailing arm. I tried to reach him with my knuckle-duster, but I was too far away, and I couldn't risk trying to wriggle farther out the window. And all the time the taxicab and the futuristic car were hurtling through the Nightside at terrible speed, the ground rushing by only a few feet below us.

"Whatever you're planning on doing," Liza yelled to me, "now would be a really good time to do it!"

So I gave up trying to reach the driver, and wriggled back through the car window. Liza clung fiercely to the driver's arm, as she started to fall. He brought his energy gun to bear on her. And I pulled a small blue sachet from my coat pocket, ripped it open, and threw the contents into the driver's face.

Vicious black pepper filled his eyes, blinding him in a moment, shocked tears streaming down his face. He was just starting to sneeze explosively as I pulled Liza away from him, and both of us wriggled back through the window into the backseat of the futuristic car. We sprawled together on the bloodred leather seat, breathing harshly as we struggled to get our breath back.

The taxicab swayed away from us, the driver utterly blind and unable to control his cab for the force of his sneezing. The cab fell away behind us, and a fifty-foot articulated rig ran right over it from behind.

And that was very definitely that.

Liza looked at me speechlessly for a long moment, and then . . .

"Pepper? That was your great idea? Pepper?"

"It worked, didn't it?" I said reasonably. "Condiments are our friends. Never leave home without them."

Liza shook her head slowly, and then sat up straight, pushing herself away from me, and adjusting her clothes as women do. "Was that ... All that just happened, was that normal for the Nightside?"

"Not really, no," I had to admit. "Most people have the sense to leave Dead Boy's car strictly alone. And they certainly should have known better than to take on Dead Boy and myself. We have ... reputations. Which can only mean it has to do with your Frank. Someone knows we're coming. Someone who really doesn't want us to know what's happened to Frank. And to justify this kind of open attack ... whatever's going on, it must be something really out of the ordinary."

"Which means," Dead Boy said cheerfully, "it must be something new! And I'm always up for something new! On, my lovely car, on to Rotten Row!"

"You're weird," said Liza.

THREE

And so we headed into the badlands. Where the neon gets shoddier and the sins grow shabbier, though no less dangerous or disturbing. If the Nightside is where you go when no one else will have you, the badlands is where you go when even the Nightside is sick of the sight of you. The badlands, where all the furtive people end up, pursuing things even the Nightside is ashamed of . . . because some things are just too tacky.

The traffic thinned out more and more as we left the major thoroughfares behind, dying away to just the occasional tattooed unicorn with assorted piercings and a Prince Albert, a stretch hearse with the corpse half out of its coffin and beating helplessly against the reinforced windows, and a headless bounty hunter on horseback. The flotsam and jetsam of the Nightside, all hot in pursuit of their own private destinies and damnations. The streets grew narrower and darker, and not only because maybe half the streetlights were working. The shadows were darker and deeper, and things moved in them. More and more buildings had boarded-up windows and broken-in doors, and where lights did sometimes glow in high-up windows, strange shadows moved behind closed blinds. The neon signs remained as gaudy as ever, like poisonous flowers in a polluted swamp. A few people still walked the rain-slick streets, heads down, looking neither left nor right, drawn on by siren calls only they could hear.

Homeless people lurked in the shadows, broken men in tattered clothes. Mostly they moved in packs, because it was safer that way. There are all kinds of predators, in the badlands. And a few good people, fighting a losing battle and knowing it, but fighting on anyway, because they knew a battle is not a war. I saw Tamsin MacReady, the rogue vicar, out in her rounds, determined to do good in a bad place. She recognised Dead Boy's car, and waved cheerfully.

The night grew quieter and more thoughtful, the deeper into the badlands we went, a shining silver presence in a dark place. Working streetlights grew few and far between, and the car cruised quietly from one pool of light to another. Dead Boy tried the high beams, but even they couldn't penetrate far into the gloom, as though there was something in this new darkness that swallowed up light. The roar and clamour of the Nightside proper seemed far away now, left behind as we moved from one country to another. The few people we passed ignored us, intent on their own business. This wasn't a place to draw attention to yourself; unless, of course, you had something to sell.

A tall and willowy succubus, with dead white skin, crimson lingerie, and bloodred eyes, loped along beside the futuristic car for a while, easily matching its speed. She tapped on our polarised windows with her clawed fingertips, whispering all the awful things she would let us do. Liza shrank back from the succubus, her face sick with horror and revulsion. When the succubus realised we weren't going to stop, she increased her speed to get ahead of us and then stepped out into the middle of the road, blocking our way. Dead Boy told the car to put its foot down, and the car surged forward.

The succubus ghosted out, becoming immaterial, and the futuristic car passed right through her. A spectre, tinted rose red and lily white, the succubus drifted at her own pace through the car, ignoring Dead Boy, her inhuman gaze fixed on Liza. A succubus always has a taste for fresh meat. She reached out a ghostly hand to Liza, but I grabbed her wrist and stopped her. It was like holding the memory of an arm, cold as ice, soft as smoke. The succubus looked at me, and then gently pulled her arm free, the ghostly trace passing through my mortal flesh in an eerily intimate moment. She trailed the fingertips of one hand along my face, winked one bloodred eye, and then passed on through the car and was gone.

The badlands grew grimly silent, abandoned and forsaken, as we closed in on Rotten Row. We had left civilisation behind, for something else. Here buildings and businesses pressed tight together in long ugly tenements, as though believing there was strength, and protection, in numbers. Windows were shuttered, doors securely locked, and none of these establishments even bothered to look inviting. Either you knew what you were looking for, or you had no business being here. Enter at your own risk, leave your conscience at the door, and absolutely no refunds.

Welcome, sir. What's your pleasure?

Few people walked the gloomy, desolate streets, and they all walked alone, despite the many dangers, because no one else would walk with them. Or perhaps because the very nature of their needs and temptations had made them solitary. And though most of the figures we passed looked like people, not all of them walked or moved in a human way. One figure in a filthy suit turned suddenly to look at the car as it drifted past, and under the pulled-down hat I briefly glimpsed a face that seemed to be nothing but mouth, full of shark's teeth stained with fresh blood and gristle.

It's all about hunger, in the badlands.

Glowing eyes followed the progress of the futuristic car from shadowy alley mouths, rising and falling like bright burning fireflies. They didn't normally expect to see such a high-class, high-tech car in their neighbour-hood. They could get a lot of money, and other things, for a car like ours. And its contents. In the quiet of the street, a baby began to cry; a lost, hopeless, despairing sound. Liza leaned forward.

"Stop. Do you hear that? Stop the car. We have to do something!"

"No, we don't," said Dead Boy.

"We keep going," I said, and turned to Liza as she opened her mouth to protest. "That isn't a baby. It's just something that's learned to sound like a baby, to lure in the unsuspecting. There's nothing out there that you'd want to meet."

Liza looked like she wanted to argue, but something in my voice and in my face must have convinced her. She slumped back in her seat, arms folded tightly across her chest, staring straight ahead. I felt sorry for her, even as I admired her courage and her stubbornness. She was having to take an awful lot on board, most of which would have broken a weaker mind, but she kept going. All for her dearest love, Frank. Husband Frank. What kind of man was he, to inspire such love and devotion . . . and still end up here, in Rotten Row? I would see this through to the end, because I had said I would; but there was no way this was going to end well.

Interesting, that Dead Boy hadn't even slowed the car. Perhaps his dead ears heard something in the baby's cry that was hidden from the living.

"This is it, people," he said abruptly, as the car turned a tight corner into a narrow, garbage-cluttered cul-de-sac. "We have now arrived at Rotten Row. Just breathe in that ambience."

"Are you sure?" Liza said doubtfully, peering through the car window with her face almost pressed to the glass. "I can't see . . . anything. No shops, no businesses, no people. I don't even see a street sign."

"Someone probably stole it," Dead Boy said wisely. "Around here, anything not actually nailed down and guarded by hellhounds is automatically considered up for grabs. But my car says this is the place, and my sweetie is never wrong."

Someone in the tattered remains of what had once been a very expensive suit lurched out of a side alley to throw something at the futuristic car. It bounced back from the car's windscreen, and exploded. The car didn't even rock. There was a brief scream from the thrower as the blast threw him backwards, his clothes on fire. He'd barely hit the ground before a dozen dark shapes came swarming out of all the other alleys to roll his still twitching body back and forth as they robbed him of what little he had that was worth the taking. They were already stripping the smouldering clothes from his dead body as they dragged it off into the merciful darkness of the alley shadows. Liza looked at me angrily, more disgusted than disturbed.

"What kind of a place have you brought me to, John? My Frank wouldn't be seen dead in an area like this!"

"The photo says he's here," I said. "Look."

I held up the two jaggedly torn pieces, pressed carefully together, and concentrated my gift on them. The image of Frank jumped right out of the wedding photo, to become a flickering ghost in the street outside. He was walking hurriedly down Rotten Row, a memory of a man repeating his last journey, imprinted on Time Past. His palely translucent form stalked past the car, his face expectant and troubled at the same time. As though he was forcing himself on, towards some long-desired, long-denied consummation that both excited and terrified him. His pace quickened until he was almost running, his arms flailing at his sides, until at last he came to one particular door, and stopped there, breathing hard. The badly hand-painted sign above the door said simply Silicon Heaven.

Frank smiled for the first time at the sight of it, and it was not a very nice smile. It was the smile of a man who wanted something men are not supposed to want, not supposed to be able to want. This was more than need, or lust, or desire. This was obsession. He raised a trembling hand to knock, and the door silently opened itself before him.

The doors of Hell are never bolted or barred, to those who belong there.

Frank hurried inside, the door closed behind him, and our glimpse into Time Past came to an end. I busied myself putting the torn pieces of photo away, so I wouldn't have to see the disappointment and betrayal of trust in Liza's face. Dead Boy turned around in his seat to look at us, calmly munching on a chocolate digestive. He didn't care about where we were, or what we were doing here. He was just along for the ride. Apparently when you're dead you only have so much emotion in you, and he doesn't like to waste it. He would go along with whatever I decided. But this wasn't my decision; it was Liza's.

"We don't have to do this," I said, as gently as I could. "We can still turn the car around, and go back."

"After coming all this way to find Frank?" said Liza. "Why would I want to leave, when all the answers are in there waiting for me? I need to know about Frank, and I need to know what happened to my memories."

"We should leave," I said, "because Frank has come to a really bad place. Trust me; there are no good answers to be found in Silicon Heaven."

Liza looked from me to Dead Boy and back again. She could see something in our faces, something we knew and didn't want to say. Typically, she became angry rather than concerned. She wasn't scared and she wasn't put off; she wanted to know.

"What is this place, this Silicon Heaven? What goes on behind that door? You know, don't you?"

"Liza," I said. "This isn't easy . . ."

"It doesn't matter," she said firmly, resolutely. "If Frank's in there, I'm going in after him."

She wrestled with the door handle, but it wouldn't turn, no matter how much strength she used.

"No one's going anywhere, just yet," Dead Boy said calmly. "We are all staying right here, until John has worked out a plan of action. This is not your world, Liza Barclay; you don't know the rules, how things work, in situations like this."

"He's right, Liza," I said. "This is a nasty business, even for the Nightside, with its own special dangers for the body and the soul."

"But ... look at it!" said Liza, gesturing at Silicon Heaven, with its boarded-up window and its stained, paint-peeling door. "It's a mess! This whole street would need an extreme makeover before it could be upgraded enough to be condemned! And this ... shop, or whatever it is, looks like it's been deserted and left empty for months. Probably nobody home but the rats."

"Protective camouflage," I said, when she finally ran out of breath. "Remember the baby that wasn't a baby? Silicon Heaven set up business here, because only a location like this would tolerate a trade like theirs; but even so, it doesn't want to draw unwelcome attention to itself. There are a lot of people who object to the very existence of a place like Silicon Heaven, for all kinds of ethical, religious, and scientific reasons. We like to say anything goes in the Nightside, but even we draw the line at some things. If only on aesthetic grounds. Silicon Heaven has serious enemies, and would probably be under attack right now by a mob with flaming torches, if they weren't afraid to come here."

"Are you afraid?" said Liza, fixing me with her cold, determined eyes.

"I try very hard not to be," I said evenly. "It's bad for the reputation. But I have learned to be ... cautious."

Liza looked at Dead Boy. "I suppose you're going to say you're never afraid, being dead."

"There's nothing here that bothers me," said Dead

Boy, "but there are things I fear. Being dead isn't the worst thing that can happen to you."

"You really do get off on being enigmatic, don't you?" said Liza.

Dead Boy laughed. "You must allow the dead their little pleasures."

"Talking of fates worse than death," I said, and Liza immediately turned back to look at me, "you have to brace yourself, if we're going in there. Just by coming to an establishment like this, Frank is telling us things about himself, and they're things you're not going to want to hear. But you have to know, if we're going in there after him."

"Tell me," said Liza. "I can take it. Tell me everything."

"Silicon Heaven," I said carefully, "exists to cater to people with extreme desires. For men, and women, for whom the ordinary pleasures of the flesh aren't enough. And I'm not talking about the usual fetishes or obsessions. You can find all of that in the Nightside, and more. In Silicon Heaven, science and the unnatural go hand in hand like lovers, producing new forms of sexuality, new objects of desire. They're here to provide extreme and unforgivable outlets for love and lust and everything in between. This is the place where people go to have sex with computers."

Liza looked at me for a long moment. She wanted to laugh, but she could see the seriousness in my face, hear it in my voice, telling her that there was nothing laughable about Silicon Heaven.

"Sex . . . with computers?" she said numbly. "I don't believe it. How is that even possible?"

"This is the Nightside," said Dead Boy. "We do ten impossible things before breakfast, just for a cheap thrill. Abandon all taboos, ye who enter here."

"I won't believe it until I see it," said Liza, and there was enough in her voice beyond mere stubbornness that I gave the nod to Dead Boy. We were going to have to go all the way with this, and hope there were still some pieces left to pick up afterwards. Dead Boy spoke nicely to his car, and the doors swung open.

We stepped out onto Rotten Row, and the ambience hit us like a closed fist. The night air was hot and sweaty, almost feverish, and it smelled of spilled blood and sparking static. Blue-white moonlight gave the street a cold, alien look, defiantly hostile and unsafe. I could feel the pressure of unseen watching eyes, cold and calculating, and casually cruel. And over all, a constant feeling that we didn't belong here, that we had no business being here, that we were getting into things we could never hope to understand or appreciate. But I have made a business, and a very good living, out of going places where I wasn't wanted, and finding out things no one wanted me to know. I turned slowly around, letting the whole street get a good look at me. My hard-earned reputation was normally enough to keep the flies off, but you never knew what desperate acts a man might be driven to, in a street like Rotten Row.

The futuristic car's doors all closed by themselves, and there was the quiet but definite sound of many locks closing. Liza looked back at the car, frowning uncertainly.

"Is it safe to just leave it here, on its own?"

"Don't worry," said Dead Boy, patting the bonnet fondly. "My sweetie can look after herself."

Even as they were speaking, a slim gun barrel emerged abruptly from the side of the car, and fired a brief but devastating bolt of energy at something moving not quite furtively enough in the shadows. There was an explosion, flames, and a very brief scream. Various shadowy people who'd started to emerge into the street, and display a certain covetous interest in the futuristic car, had a sudden attack of good sense and disappeared back into the shadows. Dead Boy sniggered loudly.

"My car has extensive self-defence systems, a total lack of scruples about using them, and a really quite appalling sense of humour. She kept one would-be thief locked in the boot for three weeks. He'd probably still be there, if I hadn't noticed the flies."

In his own way, he was trying to distract Liza and make her laugh, but she only had eyes for Silicon Heaven. So I took the lead, and strolled over to the door as though I had every right to be there. Liza and Dead Boy immediately fell in beside me, not wanting to be left out of anything. Up close, the door didn't look like much; just an everyday old-fashioned wooden door with the paint peeling off it in long strips . . . but this was Rotten Row, where ordinary and everyday were just lies to hide behind. I sneered at the tacky brass doorknob, sniffed loudly at the entirely tasteless brass door knocker, and didn't even try to touch the door itself. I didn't want the people inside thinking I could be taken out of the game that easily.

I thrust both hands deep into my coat pockets, and surreptitiously ran my fingertips over certain useful items that might come in handy for a little light breaking and entering. A private investigator needs to know many useful skills. In the end, I decided to err on the side of caution, and gave Dead Boy the nod to start things off, on the grounds that since he was dead, whatever happened next wouldn't affect him as much as the rest of us. He grinned widely, and drew back a gray fist. And the door swung slowly open, all by itself. I gestured quickly for Dead Boy to hold back. A door opening by itself is rarely a good sign. At the very least, it means you're being watched . . . and, that the people inside don't think they have anything to fear from you entering. Or it could just be one big bluff. The Nightside runs on the gentle art of putting one over on the rubes.

"Are we expecting trouble?" said Liza, as I stood still, considering the open door.

"Always," Dead Boy said cheerfully. "It's only the threat of danger and sudden destruction that makes me feel alive."

"Then by all means, you go in first and soak up the punishment," I said generously.

"Right!" said Dead Boy, brightening immediately. He kicked the door wide open and stalked forward into the impenetrable darkness beyond. His voice drifted back to us: "Come on! Give me your best shot, you bastards! I can take it!"

Liza looked at me. "Is he always like this?"

"Pretty much," I said. "This is why most people won't work with him. Personally, I've always found him very useful for hiding behind when the bullets start flying. Shall we go?"

Liza looked at the open doorway, and the darkness beyond, her face completely free of any expression. "I don't want to do this, John. I just know something really bad will happen in there; but I need to know the truth. I need to remember what I've forgotten, whether I want to or not."

She stepped determinedly forward, her small hands clenched into fists at her sides, and I moved quickly to follow her through the doorway. My shoulder brushed against hers, and I could feel the tension in her rock-hard muscles. I thought it was something simple: fear or anticipation. I should have known better.

The darkness disappeared the moment the door closed behind us, and a bright, almost painful glare illuminated the room we'd walked into. Solid steel walls surrounded us, a good forty foot a side, and even the floor and the ceiling were made from the same brightly gleaming metal. Our own distorted images stared back at us from the shining walls. Dead Boy stood in the middle of the room, glaring pugnaciously around him, ready to hit anything that moved or even looked at him funny, but we were the only ones there. There was no obvious way out, and when I looked back, even the door we'd come through had disappeared.

"I don't understand," said Liza. "This room is a hell of a lot bigger than the shop front suggested."

"In the Nightside, the interior of a building is often much bigger than its exterior," I said. "It's the only way we can fit everything in."

There was no obvious source for the sharp, stark light that filled the steel room. The air was dry and lifeless, and the only sounds were the ones we made ourselves. I moved over to the nearest wall, and studied it carefully without touching it. Up close, the metal was covered with faint tracings, endless lines in endless intricate patterns, like ... painted-on circuitry. The patterns moved slowly, changing subtly under the pressure of my gaze, twisting and turning as they transformed themselves into whole new permutations. As though the wall was thinking, or dreaming. I gestured for Dead Boy and Liza to join me, and pointed out the patterns. Dead Boy just shrugged. Liza looked at me.

"Does this mean something to you?"

"Not ... as such," I said. "Could be some future form of hieroglyphics. Could be some form of adaptive circuitry. But it's definitely not from around here. This is future tech, machine code from a future time line ... There are rumours that Silicon Heaven is really just one big machine, holding everything within."

"And we've just walked right into it," said Dead Boy. "Great. Anyone got a can opener?"

He leaned in close to study the wall tracings, and prodded them with a long pale finger. Blue-gray lines leapt from the wall onto his finger and swarmed all over it. Dead Boy automatically pulled his finger back, and the circuitry lines stretched away from the wall, clinging to his dead flesh with stubborn strength. They crawled all over his hand and shot up his arm, growing and multiplying all the time, twisting and curling and leaping into the air. Dead Boy grabbed a big handful of the stuff, wrenched it away, and then popped it into his mouth. Dead Boy has always been one for the direct approach. He chewed thoughtfully, evaluating the flavour. The blue-gray lines slipped back down his arm and leapt back onto the wall, becoming still and inert again.

"Interesting," said Dead Boy, chewing and swallowing. "Could use a little salt, though."

I offered him some, but he laughed, and declined.

Liza made a sudden pained noise, and her knees started to buckle. I grabbed her by one arm to steady her, but I don't think she even knew I was there. Her face was pale and sweaty, and her mouth was trembling. Her eyes weren't tracking; her gaze was fixed on something only she could see. She looked like she'd just seen her own death, up close and bloody. I held her up, gripping both her arms firmly, and said her name loudly, right into her face. Her eyes snapped back into focus, and she got her feet back under her again. I let go of her arms, but she just stood where she was, looking at me miserably.

"Something bad is going to happen," she said, in a small, hopeless voice. "Something really bad . . ."

A dozen robots rose silently up out of the metal floor, almost seeming to form themselves out of the gleaming steel. More robots stepped out of the four walls, and dropped down from the ceiling. It seemed Silicon Heaven had a security force after all. The robots surrounded us on every side, silent and implacable, blocky mechanical constructs with only the most basic humanoid form. Liza shrank back against me. Dead Boy and I moved quickly to put her between us.

For a long moment the robots stood utterly still, as though taking the measure of us, or perhaps checking our appearance against their records. They were roughly human in shape, but there was nothing of human aesthetics about them. They were purely functional, created to serve a purpose and nothing more. Bits and pieces put together with no covering, their every working open to the eye. There were crystals and ceramics and other things moving around inside them, while strange lights came and went. Sharp-edged components stuck out all over them, along with all kinds of weapons, everything from sharp blades and circular saws to energy weapons and blunt grasping hands. They had no faces, no eyes, but all of them were orientated on the three of us. They knew where we were.

Many things about them made no sense at all, to human eyes and human perspectives. Because human science had no part in their making.

They all moved forward at the same moment, suddenly and without warning, metal feet hammering on the metal floor. They did not move in a human way, their arms and legs bending and stretching in unnatural ways, their centres of gravity seeming to slip back and forth as needed. They reached for us with their blocky hands, all kinds of sharp things sticking out of their fingers. Buzz saws rose out of bulking chests, spinning at impossible speeds. Energy weapons sparked and glowed, humming loudly as they powered up. The robots came for us. They would kill us if they could, without rage or passion or even satisfaction, blunt instruments of Silicon Heaven's will.

I've always prided myself on my ability to talk my way out of most unpleasant situations, but they weren't going to listen.

Dead Boy stepped forward, grabbed the nearest robot with brisk directness, picked it up and threw it at the next nearest robot. They both had to have weighed hundreds of pounds, but that was nothing to the strength in Dead Boy's unliving muscles. The sheer impact slammed both robots to the steel floor, denting it perceptibly, the sound almost unbearably loud. But though both robots fell in a heap, they untangled themselves almost immediately and rose to their feet again, undamaged.

Dead Boy punched a robot in what should have been its head, and the whole assembly broke off and flew away. The robot kept coming anyway. Another robot grabbed Dead Boy's shoulder from behind with its crude steel hand, the fingers closing like a mantrap. The purple greatcoat stretched and tore, but Dead Boy felt no pain. He tried to pull free, and snarled when he found he couldn't. He had to wrench himself free with brute strength, ruining his coat, and while he was distracted by that, another robot punched him in the back of the head.

I'm sure I heard bone crack and break. It was a blow that would have killed any ordinary man, but Dead Boy had left ordinary behind long ago. The blow still sent him staggering forward, off balance, and straight into the arms of another robot. The uneven arms slammed closed around him immediately, forcing the breath out of his lungs with brutal strength. But Dead Boy only breathes when he needs to talk. He broke the hold easily, and yanked one of the robot's arms right out of its socket. He used the arm as a club, happily hammering the robot about the head and shoulders, smashing pieces off and damaging others. But even as bits of the robot flew through the air, it kept coming, and Dead Boy had to back away before it. And while he was concentrating on one robot, the others closed in around him.

. They swarmed all over him, clinging to his arms, beating at his head and shoulders, trying to drag him down. He struggled valiantly, throwing away one robot after another with dreadful force, but they always came back. He was inhumanly strong, but there were just so many of them. He disappeared inside a crowd of robots, steel fists rising and falling like jackhammers, over and over again, driving Dead Boy to his knees. And then they cut at him, with their steel blades and whirring buzz saws and vicious hands.

While the majority of robots were dealing with Dead Boy, the remainder closed in on me, and Liza. She'd frozen, her face utterly empty, her body twitching and shaking. I gently but firmly pushed her behind me, out of the way. Our backs were to the nearest wall, but not too close.

I was thinking furiously, trying to find a way out of this. Most of my useful items were magical in nature, rather than scientific. And while I knew quite a few nasty little tricks to use against the living and the dead and those unfortunate few stuck in between . . . I didn't have a damned thing of any use against robots. Certainly throwing pepper into their faces wasn't going to work. I don't carry a gun. I don't usually need them.

I backed up as far as I dared, herding Liza behind me, and fired up my gift. My inner eye snapped open, and immediately my Sight found just the right places for me to stand, and where and when to dodge, so that the robots couldn't touch me. Their blocky hands reached for me again and again, but I was never there, already somewhere else, one step ahead of them. Except the more they closed in, the less room there was for me to move in. I managed to be in the right place to trip a few and send them crashing into one another, but all I was doing was buying time.

I knew what was happening to Dead Boy, but there wasn't a damned thing I could do.

One robot aimed an energy weapon at me. I waited till the very last moment, and then sidestepped, and the energy beam seared past me to take out the robot on my other side. It exploded messily, bits and pieces flying across the room. They ricocheted off the other robots harmlessly, but one piece of shrapnel passed close enough to clip off a lock of my hair. Liza didn't react at all.

The robots had discovered they couldn't hurt Dead Boy, so they decided to pull him apart. They grabbed him by the arms and legs, stretched him helpless in midair between them, and did their best to tear him limb from limb. He struggled and cursed them vilely, but in the end, they were powerful machines and he was just a dead man.

Liza darted suddenly forward from behind me, grabbed up the robot arm that Dead Boy had torn off, and used it like a club against the nearest robot. She swung the arm with both hands, using all her strength, her eyes wide and staring, lips drawn back in an animal snarl. She wasn't strong enough to damage the robot, but I admired her spirit. We weren't in her world anymore, but she was still doing her best to fight back. But she still couldn't hope to win, and neither could Dead Boy, so as usual it was down to me.

I concentrated, forcing my inner eye all the way open, till I could See the world so clearly it hurt. I scanned the robots with my augmented vision, struggling to understand through the pain, and it didn't take me long to find the robots' basic weakness. They had no actual intelligence of their own; they were all receiving their orders from the same source, through the same mechanism. I moved swiftly among the robots, dancing in their blind spots, yanking the mechanisms out, one after another. And one by one the robots froze in place, cut off from their central command, helpless without orders. They stood around the metal room like so many modern art sculptures . . . and I sat down suddenly and struggled to get my breathing back under control, while my third eye, my inner eye, slowly and thankfully eased shut.

I have a gift for finding things, but it's never easy.

Dead Boy pulled and wriggled his way free from the robots holding him, looked in outrage at what they'd done to his purple greatcoat, and kicked some of the robots about for a bit, just to ease his feelings. Liza looked about her wildly, still clutching her robot arm like a club. I got up from the floor and said her name a few times, and she finally looked at me, personality and sanity easing slowly back into her face. She looked at what she was holding, and dropped it to the floor with a moue of distaste. I went over to her, but she didn't want to be comforted.

A voice spoke to us, out of midair. A calm, cultured voice, with a certain amount of resignation in it.

"All right, enough is enough. We didn't think the se-

curity bots would be enough to stop the famous John
Taylor and the infamous Dead Boy ... or should that be
the other way round ... but we owed it to our patrons to
try. You might have been having an off day. It happens.
And the bots were nearing the end of their warranty ...
Anyway, you'd better come on through, and we'll talk
about this. I said Liza Barclay would come back to haunt
us if we just let her go, but of course no one ever listens
to me."

"I've been here ... before?" said Liza.

"You don't remember?" I said quietly.

"No," said Liza. "I've never seen this place before."
But she didn't sound as certain as she once had. I remembered her earlier premonition, just before the robots appeared, when she'd known something bad was
about to happen. Perhaps she'd known because something like it had happened the last time she was here.
Unless she was remembering something else, even worse,
still to come ...

A door appeared in the far wall, where I would have
sworn there was no trace of a door just a moment before.
A section of the metal just slid suddenly sideways, disappearing into the rest of the wall, leaving a brightly lit
opening. I started towards it, and once again Dead Boy
and Liza fell in beside me. You'd almost have thought I
knew what I was doing. We threaded our way through
the motionless robots, and I held myself ready in case
they came alive again; but they just stood there, in their
stiff awkward poses, utterly inhuman even in defeat.
Dead Boy pulled faces at them. Liza wouldn't even look
at the robots, all her attention focused on the open door,
and the answers it promised her.

We passed through the narrow opening into a long
steel corridor, comfortably wide and tall, the steel so
brightly polished it was like walking through an endless
hall of mirrors. It occurred to me that none of our reflec-
tions looked particularly impressive, or dangerous. Dead
Boy had lost his great floppy hat in his struggle with the

robots, and his marvellous purple greatcoat was torn and tattered. Some of the stitches on his bare chest had broken open, revealing pink-gray meat under the torn gray skin. I keep telling him to use staples. Liza looked scared but determined, her face so pale and taut there was hardly any colour in it. She was close to getting her answers now; but I think, even then, she knew this wasn't going to end well. And I . . . I looked like someone who should have known better than to come to a place like Rotten Row, and expect any good to come of it.

The corridor finally took a sharp turn to the left, and ushered us into a large antechamber. More steel walls, still no furnishings or comforts, but finally a human face. A tall, slender man in the traditional white lab coat was waiting for us. He had a bland forgettable face, and a wide welcoming smile that meant nothing at all. Slick, I thought immediately. That's the word for this man. Nothing would ever touch him, and nothing would ever stick to him. He'd make sure of that. He strode briskly towards us, one hand stretched out to shake, still smiling, as though he could do it all day. The smile didn't reach his eyes. They were cold, certain, the look of a man utterly convinced he knew important things that you didn't.

Fanatic's eyes. Believer's eyes. Such men are always dangerous.

He dropped his hand when he realised none of us had any intention of shaking it, but he didn't seem especially upset. He was still smiling.

"Hi!" he said brightly. "I'm Barry Kopek. I speak for Silicon Heaven. I'd say it's good to see you, but I wouldn't want to start our relationship with such an obvious lie. So let's get right down to business, shall we, and then we can all get back to our own lives again. Won't that be nice?"

He tried offering us his hand again, and then pulled it back with a resigned shrug, as though he was used to it. And if he was the official greeter for Silicon Heaven, he probably was. Even a ghoul in a graveyard would look down on a computer pimp like him.

"Come with me," he said, "and many things will be made clear. All your questions will be answered; or at least, all the ones you're capable of understanding. No offence, no offence. But things are rather . . . advanced, around here. Tomorrow has come early for the Nightside, and soon there'll be a wake-up call for everyone. Slogans are such an important part for any new business, don't you agree? Sorry about the robots, but we have so many enemies among the ignorant, and our work here is far too important to allow outside agitators to interfere with it."

"Your work?" I said. "Arranging dates for computers, for people with a fetish for really heavy metal, is important work?"

He looked like he wanted to wince at my crudity, but was far too professional. The smile never wavered for a moment. "We are not a part of the sex industry, Mister Taylor. Perish the thought. Everyone who finds their way here becomes part of the great work. We are always happy to greet new people, given the extreme turnover in . . . participants. But they all understand! They do, really they do! This is the greatest work of our time, and we are all honoured to be a part of it. Come with me, and you'll see. Only . . . do keep Mrs. Barclay under control, please. She did enough damage the last time she was here."

Dead Boy and I both looked at Liza, but she had nothing to say. Her gaze was fixed on the official greeter, staring at him like she could burn holes through him. She wanted answers, and he was just slowing her down.

"All right," I said. "Lead the way. Show us this great work."

"Delighted!" said Barry Kopek. I was really starting to get tired of that smile.

He led us through more metal corridors, turning this way and that with complete confidence, even though there were never any signs or directions on the blank steel walls. He kept up an amiable chatter, talking smoothly and happily about nothing in particular. The light from nowhere became increasingly stark, almost unbearably bright. There was a sound in the distance, like the slow beating of a giant heart, so slow you could count the moments between each great beat, but they all had something of time and eternity in them. And there was a smell, faint at first, but gradually growing stronger ... of static and machine oil, ozone and lubricants, burning meat and rank, fresh sweat.

"You said Liza's been here before," I said finally, after it became clear that Kopek wasn't going to raise the subject again himself.

"Oh, yes," he said, carefully looking at me rather than at Liza. "Mrs. Barclay was here yesterday, and we let her in, because of course we have nothing to hide. We're all very proud of the work we do here."

"What work?" said Dead Boy, and something in his voice made Kopek miss a step.

"Yes, well, to put it very simply, in layman's terms ... We are breaking down the barriers between natural and artificial life."

"If you're so proud, and this work so very great, why did you send those cyborged taxis to attack us?" I said, in what I thought was really a quite reasonable tone of voice. Kopek's smile wavered for the first time. He knew me. And my reputation.

"Ah, yes," he said. "That. I said that was a mistake. You must understand, they were some of our first crude attempts, at melding man with machine. Those men paid a lot of money for it to be done to them, so they could operate more efficiently and more profitably in Nightside traffic. We were very short of funds at the beginning ... When they found out you were coming here, Mister Taylor, well, frankly, they panicked. You see, they relied on us to keep them functioning."

"Who told them I was coming?" I said. "Though I'm pretty sure I already know the answer."

"I said it was a mistake," said Barry Kopek. "Are they all . . . ?"

"Yes," I said.

He nodded glumly. Still smiling, but you could tell his heart wasn't in it. "I'm not surprised. Your reputation precedes you, Mister Taylor, like an attack dog on a really long leash. It's a shame, though. They only wanted to better themselves."

"By having their humanity cut away?" said Dead Boy, just a bit dangerously.

"They gave up so little, to gain so much," said Kopek, just a bit haughtily. "I would have thought you of all people would appreciate . . ."

"You don't know me," said Dead Boy. "You don't know anything about me. And no one gets away with attacking my car."

"Being dead hasn't mellowed you at all, has it?" said Kopek.

"Is Frank here?" I said. "Frank Barclay?"

"Well, of course he's here," said Kopek. "It's not like we're holding him prisoner, against his will. He came to us, pursuing his dreams, and we were only too happy to accommodate him. He is here where he wanted to be, doing what he's always wanted to do, happy at last."

"He was happy with me!" said Liza. "He loves me! He married me!"

"A man wants what he wants, and needs what he needs," said Kopek, looking at her directly for the first time. "And Mister Barclay's needs brought him to us."

"Can we see him? Talk to him?" I said.

"Of course! That's where I'm taking you now. But you must promise me you'll keep Mrs. Barclay under control. She reacted very badly to seeing her husband last time."

"She's seen him here before?" I said.

"Well, yes," said Kopek, looking from me to Liza and back again, clearly puzzled. "I escorted her to him myself. Didn't she tell you?"

"No," Liza said quietly, though exactly what she was saying no to, I wasn't entirely sure. She was all drawn up in herself now, looking straight ahead, her gaze fixed, almost disassociated.

The corridor finally ended in a flat featureless wall, in which another door appeared. Kopek led us through, and we all stopped dead to look around, impressed and overwhelmed despite ourselves by the sheer size of the glass-and-crystal auditorium spread out before us. It takes a lot to impress a native of the Nightside, but the sheer scope and scale of the place we'd been brought to took even my breath away. Bigger than any enclosed space had a right to be, with walls like frozen waterfalls of gleaming crystal, set so far apart the details were just distant blurs, under tinted glass ceilings so high above us clouds drifted between us and them. Like some vast cathedral dedicated to Science, the auditorium was so enormous it had generated its own weather systems. Kopek's smile was openly triumphant now, as he gestured grandly with outstretched arms.

"Lady and gentlemen, welcome to Silicon Heaven!"

He led the way forward, between massive machines that had shape and form, but no clear meaning or significance. So complex, so advanced, as to be incomprehensible to merely human eyes. There were components that moved, and revolved, and became other things even as I watched; strange lights that burned in unfamiliar colours; and noises that were almost, or beyond, voices. Things the size of buildings walked in circles, and intricate mechanisms came together in complex interactions, like a living thing assembling itself. Gleaming metal spheres the size of sheepdogs rolled back and forth across the crystal floor, sprouting tools and equipment as needed to service the needs of larger machines. Dead Boy kicked at one of the spheres, in an experimental way, but it dodged him easily.

Kopek led the way, and we all followed close behind. This wasn't a place you wanted to get lost in. It felt . . .

like walking through the belly of Leviathan, or like flies crawling across the stained-glass window of some unnatural cathedral ... So of course I strolled along with my hands in my coat pockets, like I'd seen it all before and hadn't been impressed then. Never let them think they've got the advantage, or they'll walk all over you. Dead Boy seemed genuinely uninterested in any of it, but then he died and brought himself back to life, and that's a hard act to follow. Liza didn't seem to see any of it. She had a hole in her mind, a gap in her memories, and all she cared about was finding out what had happened the last time she was here. Did she care at all about husband Frank, anymore? Or was she remembering just enough to sense that her quest wasn't for him, and never had been, but only to find the truth about him and her, and this place ...

There was a definite sense of purpose to everything happening around us, even if I couldn't quite grasp it, but I was pretty sure there was nothing human in that purpose. Nothing here gave a damn about anything so small as Humanity.

"I was here before," Liza said slowly. "There's something bad up ahead. Something awful."

I looked sharply at Kopek. "Is that right, Barry? Is there something dangerous up ahead, that you haven't been meaning to tell us about?"

"There's nothing awful here," he said huffily. "You're here to see something wonderful."

And finally, we came face-to-face with what we'd come so far to see. A single beam of light stabbed down, shimmering and scintillating, like a spotlight from Heaven, as though God himself was taking an interest. The illumination picked out one particular machine, surrounded by ranks and ranks of robots. They were dancing around the machine, in wide interlocking circles, their every movement impossibly smooth and graceful and utterly inhuman. They moved to music only they could hear, perhaps to music only they could hope to understand, but there was nothing of human emotion or sensibility in their dance. It could have been a dance of reverence, or triumph, or elation, or something only a robot could know or feel. The robots danced, and the sound of their metal feet slamming on the crystal floor was almost unbearably ugly.

Kopek led us carefully through the ranks of robots, and at once they began to sing, in high chiming voices like a choir of metal birds, in perfect harmonies and cadences that bordered on melody without ever actually achieving it. Like machines pretending to be human, doing things that people do without ever understanding why people do them. We passed through the last of the robots and finally . . . there was Frank, beloved husband of Liza, having sex with a computer.

The computer was the size of a house, covered with all kinds of monitor screens and readouts but no obvious controls, with great pieces constantly turning and sliding across each other. It was made of metal and crystal and other things I didn't even recognise. At the foot of it was an extended hollow section, like a large upright coffin, and suspended within this hollow was Frank Barclay, hanging in a slowly pulsing web of tubes and wires and cables, naked, ecstatic, transported. Liza made a low, painful sound, as though she'd been hit.

Frank's groin was hidden behind a cluster of machine parts, always moving, sliding over and around him like a swarm of metallic bees, clambering over themselves in their eagerness to get to him. Like metal maggots, in a self-inflicted wound. Thick translucent tubes had been plugged into his abdomen, and strange liquids surged in and out of him. Up and down his naked body, parts of him had been dissected away, to show bones and organs being slowly replaced by new mechanical equivalents. There was no bleeding, no trauma. One thigh bone had been revealed from top to bottom, one end bone and the other metal, and already it was impossible to tell where the one began and the other ended. Metal rods plunged in and out of Frank's flesh, sliding back and forth, never stopping. Lights blinked on and off inside him, briefly rendering parts of his skin transparent; and in that skin I could see as many wires as blood vessels.

The computer was heaving and groaning, in rhythm to the things going in and out of Frank's naked body, and the machine's steel exterior was flushed and beaded with sweat. It made ... orgasmic sounds. Frank's face was drawn, shrunken, the skin stretched taut across the bone, but his eyes were bright and happy, and his smile held a terrible pleasure. Cables penetrated his skin, and metal parts penetrated his body, and he loved it. One cable had buried itself in his left eye socket, replacing the eyeball, digging its way in a fraction of an inch at a time. Frank didn't care. He shuddered and convulsed as things slid in and out of him, changing him forever, and he loved every last bit of it.

Liza stood before him, tears rolling silently and unheeded down her devastated face.

I turned to Barry Kopek. "Is he dying?"

"Yes, and no," said Kopek. "He's becoming something else. Something wonderful. We are making him over, transforming him, into a living component capable of being host to machine consciousness. A living and an unliving body, for an Artificial Intelligence from a future time line. It came to the Nightside through a Timeslip, fleeing powerful enemies. It wants to experience sin, and in particular the hot and sweaty sensations of the flesh. It wants to know what we humans know, and take for granted; all the many joys of sex. Together, Frank and the computer are teaching each other whole new forms of pleasure. He is teaching the machine all the colours of emotion and sensuality, and the very subtle joys of degradation. In return, the machine is teaching him whole new areas of perception and conception. Man becomes machine, becomes more than machine, becomes immortal living computer. A metal messiah for a new Age ..."

Kopek's face was full of vision now, a zealot in his

cause. "Why should men be limited to being just men, and machines just machines? Human and inhuman shall combine together, to become something far superior to either. But like all new life, it begins with sex."

"How many others have there been?" said Dead Boy. "Before Frank?"

"One hundred and seventeen," said Kopek. "But Frank is different. He doesn't just believe. He wants this."

"Oh, yeah," said Dead Boy. "Looks like he's coming his brains out."

Liza collapsed, her knees slamming painfully onto the crystal floor. Her face was twisted, ugly, filled with a horrid knowledge, as all her repressed memories came flooding back at once. She pounded on the floor with her fist, again and again and again.

No! No, no, no! I remember . . . I remember it all! I came here, following Frank. Following my husband, into the Nightside, and through its awful streets, all the way here . . . Because I thought he was cheating on me. I thought he had a lover here. He hadn't touched me in months. I thought he was having an affair, but I never suspected this . . . Never thought he wanted . . . *this*."

"She talked her way in, yesterday," said Kopek. "Determined to see her husband. But when we brought her here, and showed her, she went berserk. Attacked the computer. Did some little damage, before the robots drove her off. We wouldn't let her hurt Frank, or herself, and after a while she left."

"And she blocked out the memories herself," I said. "Because they were unbearable."

"How could you?" Liza screamed at Frank. "How could you want *this*? It doesn't love you! It can't love you!"

Frank stirred for the first time, his one remaining eye slowly turning to look down at her. His face showed no emotion, no compassion for the woman he'd loved and married, not so long ago. When he spoke, his voice already contained a faint machine buzz.

"This is what I want. What I've always wanted. What I need ... And what you could never give me. I've dreamed of this for years ... of flesh and metal coming together, moving together. Thought it was just a fetish, never told anyone ... Knew they could never understand. Until someone told me about the Nightside, the one place in the world where anything is possible; and I knew I had to come here. This is the place where dreams come true."

"Including all the bad ones," murmured Dead Boy.

"What about us, Frank?" said Liza, tears streaming down her face.

"What about us?" said Frank.

"You selfish piece of shit!"

Suddenly she was back on her feet again, heading for Frank with her hands stretched out like claws, moving so fast even the robots couldn't react fast enough to stop her. She jumped up and into the coffin, punched her fist into a hole in Frank's side, and thrust her hand deep inside him. His whole body convulsed, the machines going crazy, and then Liza laughed triumphantly as she jerked her hand back out again. She dropped back down onto the crystal floor, brandishing her prize in all our faces. Blood dripped thickly from the dark red muscle in her hand. I grabbed her arms from behind as she shouted hysterically at her husband.

"You see, Frank? I have your heart! I have your cheating heart!"

"Keep it," said Frank, growing still and content again, in the metal arms of his lover. "I don't need it anymore."

And already the machines were moving over him, mopping up the blood and sealing off his wound, working to replace the heart with something more efficient. While the computer heaved and groaned and sweated, Frank sighed and smiled.

It was too much for Liza. She sank to her knees again, sobbing violently. Her hand opened, and the crushed heart muscle fell to the crystal floor, smearing it with blood. She laughed as she cried, the horrid sound of a woman losing her mind, retreating deep inside herself because reality had become too awful to bear. I gave her something to breathe in, from my coat pocket, and in a moment she was asleep. I eased her down until she was lying full length on the floor. Her face was empty as a doll's.

"I don't get it," said Dead Boy, honestly puzzled. "It's just sex. I've seen worse."

"Not for her," I said. "She loved him, and he loved *this*. To be betrayed and abandoned by a husband for another woman or even a man is one thing, but for a machine? A thing? A computer that meant more to him than all her love, that could do things for him that she never could? Because for him, simple human flesh wasn't enough. He threw aside their love and their marriage and all their life together, to have sex with a computer."

"Can you do anything for her?" said Dead Boy. "We've got to do something, John. We can't leave her like this."

"You always were a sentimental sort," I said. "I know a few things. I'm pretty sure I can find a way to put her back the way she was, when she came to us, and this time make sure the memories stay repressed. No memory at all, of the Nightside or Silicon Heaven. I'll take her back into London proper, wake her up, and leave her there. She'll never find her way back in on her own. And in time, she'll get over the mysterious loss of her husband, and move on. It's the kindest thing to do."

"And the metal messiah?" said Dead Boy, curling his colourless lip at Frank in the computer. "We just turn our back on it?"

"Why not?" I said. "There's never been any shortage of gods and monsters in the Nightside; what's one more would-be messiah? I doubt this one will do any better than the others. In the end, he's just a tech fetishist, and it's just a mucky machine with ideas above its station. Everything to do with sex, and nothing at all to do with love."

You can find absolutely anything in the Nightside; and every sinner finds their own level of Hell, or Heaven.

THE THIRD DEATH OF THE LITTLE CLAY DOG

KAT RICHARDSON

FOR TEAM SEATTLE AND THE DENVER MOB

Trouble radiated from the black figurine like some kind of dark neon at the Devil's own fairground. Not that I could actually see any such thing even in the Grey, but an electric prickling sensation zipped up my arms and down my spine when I touched it and that was close enough; I know human hair can't literally stand on end like a dog's, but I would have sworn mine was trying to.

Nanette Grover was still standing at the side of her desk, looking at me and the little statue. Her fanatically neat office flickered silver, smudged with red and orange and sad shades of green she would never see—the emotional and energetic leftovers of her clients still hanging in the Grey like smoke. A ghost or two lingered in the corners with sour, accusing faces and the odor of misery, muttering their cycles of frustration. They weren't interested in me, so I ignored them and put my attention back on Nan.

She was impeccable as always: her straightened, java-brown hair was smoothed into a perfect French twist, her stylish tweed skirt suit was unwrinkled even after she'd been behind her desk since five a.m., and her smooth, dark skin was highlighted by delicate makeup that didn't show a single crease. Even her energy corona was cool and constrained to a narrow bright line, except when she stepped onto the stage of the courtroom floor, where it alternated between hypnotic pall and legal scalpel. In spite of her beauty she had all the warmth of a copper pipe in the snow—which was part of her appeal as a litigator, but not as a human being. One of her opponents in court had referred to her as "the Queen of Nubia," and it wasn't hard imagining Nan on a war elephant chasing off Alexander the Great—even her allies found her intimidating. "Well?" she asked, the word leaving amber ripples in the air.

"Well what?" I responded, shrugging off the commanding effect of her voice.

"You're supposed to accept or reject the conditions."

"What happens if I say no?"

Her energy closed back down to an icy line. "Then I have instructions regarding the disposition of the item."

"What are those?"

"None of your business. Yes, or no, Harper."

"What was it the client wants done with this, again?"

Nan sat down on the other side of the desk, the mistiness of the settling Grey giving her a deceptively soft appearance, and blinked once, long and slow—like some kind of reset—and explained again, with no heat or change of inflection from the first time. "A colleague of mine in Mexico City forwarded this item to me upon the death of his client. His client, Maria-Luz Arbildo, left you a bequest in her will, with conditions. Namely, to personally hand-carry the statuette—this little dog figurine—to Oaxaca City in Oaxaca state in Mexico, and place it on the grave of Hector Purecete on the night of November first and attend the grave as local tradition dictates until daybreak of November second. Additional specific instructions for the preparation of the grave will be provided. All this to be done in the first occurrence of November first following his client's death. Ms. Arbildo died earlier this month."

"The twentieth of October," I added. "A week ago."

Nan nodded.

"November first is the day after Halloween. Doesn't that seem strange to you?" I asked.

Nan's ice-smooth expression didn't change. "No."

"And I never met this woman, never heard of her, but she sends this thing all the way to Seattle so I can take it all the way back to Mexico—the far end of Mexico, I might add. Still not sounding kind of weird?"

"I don't question the conditions of clients."

"Is this sort of thing even legal?"

"Perfectly. If it flew in the face of public interest, then it would be illegal, but this does not. The conditions also do not require you to do anything illegal either here or there, nor to violate your professional ethics, nor take on unreasonable expenses—everything will be paid for by Ms. Arbildo's estate. If you choose to follow the conditions of Ms. Arbildo's bequest, you will receive the thirty thousand dollars, once the conditions have been completely and correctly met. Sum to be paid through this office."

I was raised in Los Angeles County, California, so I'm not totally ignorant of Mexican culture—just mostly. I knew the first of November was the Mexican equivalent of Halloween, but I didn't know the details. My experience as a Greywalker, however, makes me wary of any date on which the dead are said to go abroad among the living. I know that ghosts—and plenty of other creepy things—are around us all the time, it's just that most people don't see them. I do more than just see them; I live with them and I've discovered that days associated with the dead are usually worse than most people imagine—they're veritable Carnivales of the incorporeal, boiling pools of magical potential. So being asked to take a folk sculpture to a Mexican graveyard on the Day of the Dead sounded like a dangerous idea to me. Especially when the client is deceased.

On the other hand, I can at least see what's going on.

As someone who lives half in and half out of the realm of ghosts, monsters, and magic, I stand a chance against whatever strange thing may rear its head in such a situation. And the money was attractive. The work I regularly did for Nan, investigating witnesses and filling in the details of her cases prior to trial, paid the majority of my bills, but it wasn't an extravagant living. Even with all the rest of my work added in, thirty thousand dollars was a major chunk of what I usually made in a year and it would only take about four days.

I looked back down at the statuette. It was a hollow clay figure of a dog, about a foot tall and long—give or take—and about four inches wide. The shape was simplified, not realistic, with stumpy legs and tail, a cone-shaped muzzle, and a couple of pinched clay points for ears. It had been painted with a gritty black paint and decorated with dots and lines of red and white that made rings around the limbs and a lightning bolt on the dog's side. It also had two white dots for eyes, but no sign of a mouth.

Peering at it, I could see the little clay dog had been cracked and repaired at some point, the casting hole in its belly covered up with an extra bit of clay and painted over with more of the black paint. A hint of Grey energy gleamed around the repair seam, but beyond that, I couldn't tell anything about what might be inside the dog. The statue itself had only a thin sheen of Grey clinging to its surface like old dirt, as if whatever magical thing it came from had withered long ago. There wasn't any indicative cloud of color or angry sparks around it as I'd seen with other magical objects, yet I was sure there was something more to it than met the eye.

I looked back up at Nan, who hadn't moved so much as an eyebrow. The silence in her office would have unnerved some people, but I found it pleasant in contrast to the incessant mutter and hum of the living Grey and its ghosts.

"What about the lawyer?" I asked.

"What about him?"

"Is he legit?"

Nan didn't crack either a smile or a frown. "Yes. His name is Guillermo Banda. He does a lot of maritime and international work."

I admit I had some reservations, but I was also a little intrigued by the mystery of it—I'm a sucker for mysteries—and the money was pretty good, so I shrugged and said, "All right, I'll take the thing to Mexico."

Nan waved to the small shipping carton from which she'd originally removed the dog at the start of our conversation. "You can put it back in its box while I get the papers ready. I'll need your signature on a receipt to prove that you picked it up and I have a copy of the instructions for you as well."

I nodded and wiggled the little clay dog back into the snowstorm of paper shred that had sprung from the box when Nan had opened it. We finished up quickly and I left with the papers in my pocket and the box full of probable trouble under my arm.

The aluminum and glass tower that houses Nan's office has lousy cell reception, so I had to wait until I was just outside the lobby doors to make a call.

"King County Medical Examiner's office. May I help you?"

"I'd like to speak to Reuben Fishkiller, please," I replied.

I was put on hold for a few moments while someone located the forensic lab technician for me. I'd met him during an investigation into the deaths of homeless people in Pioneer Square and Fish's connections to the local Salish Indians had certainly come in handy. But he'd been a bit upset when one of his ancestral legends tried to kill us and I hoped he wasn't still too freaked out to talk to me.

"This is Fish, what can I do for you?"

"Hi, Fish, it's Harper Blaine."

He paused. "Oh. Hi, Harper. You, uh . . . need something?"

"I do, if you're willing to do it for me."

"Does it have anything to do with monsters in the sewer this time? Or Salish holy ground? Because I really didn't enjoy the last time."

"No monsters, no Salish, no sewers. I promise. I just need an X-ray."

"We only X-ray the dead."

"This thing is inanimate, is that close enough?"

"What is it?" he asked. I could almost see him narrowing his eyes with suspicion.

"It's a clay statue of a dog."

"You're sure it's inanimate? Things act weird around you. . . ."

"I promise it's just a hollow lump of baked clay, totally incapable of movement or pretty much anything else. I just want to know if there's anything inside it."

Fish sighed. "Okay. . . . I can take a look, but it'll have to be quick. Get here at lunchtime and I'll see what I can do."

I agreed to come while most of the staff was occupied with food, and thanked Fish before hanging up.

It would be just my luck to spark off an international incident and get arrested for drug smuggling if the dog had anything significant in its hollow innards. I hoped Fish and his X-ray machine would tell me if there was anything to fear. The easy-money aspect of the situation bothered me; I don't believe in harmless, eccentric benefactors. There was a sting of some kind in the little dog's tail—or belly—and I wanted to figure it out before I got hit by it.

I killed some time at the library before heading down to Pill Hill, where the major hospitals cluster like concrete trees. Fish met me at the front desk of the morgue and we walked back through the chilly chambers in the basement of Harborview to the X-ray room. His shaggy dark hair with premature streaks of white, hanging over his square face, still reminded me of a badger, but a more wary and grumpy badger than he'd been before. He'd become a bit nervous since our run-in with living myths, as if he, too, could now see the steam-billow shapes of the dead that wandered through the old hospital, or sense the tingling power that thrummed in the neon-bright lines of magical power that shot through the Grey.

"What have you got?" he asked as we pushed through the door to the X-ray machine and other lab paraphernalia.

I put the white cardboard box down on the machine's table and carefully removed the little dog statue. He started to reach for it, then stopped.

"You—um . . . it's OK to touch it without gloves, isn't it?"

"I think so. I've been handling it bare-handed all morning." I had supposed I'd know if there was anything toxic on the figure's surface, but there really wasn't any way that I would. I looked at the small black dog as I clutched it by its middle and hoped it wasn't dusted with anthrax or the like.

Fish paused to pull on a pair of purple gloves before he took the figurine from me. Then he scraped a bit of the black paint into a glass tube and repeated the scraping on the bottom of the dog's foot, where the mellow orange clay was bare of glaze or paint. The sheen of Grey on the sculpture's surface rippled and squirmed as he scraped, but it didn't flare or change color—either of which would have been bad signs. He added some chemicals to the tubes and put them aside in a large white machine.

"I'll run a couple of tests on those while we're at it," he said. He poked some buttons on the machine. Then he turned back to the X-ray table. "Now, let's look at this little guy. . . ."

Altogether, Fish took three views of the dog. Since the morgue had updated to digital X-ray, we didn't have to wait for the pictures to be developed, but just viewed them on the computer screen behind the radiation barrier. There was indeed something inside the clay dog.

"What's that?" I asked, pointing to a bundle of faint lines that showed on every picture. It was in a different spot each time.

"Something loose in the hollow interior. Let's crank up the resolution. . . ."

Fish poked a few keys and the image of the bundle got larger and more clear.

"Looks like hair or threads knotted together. Whatever it is, there's not much of it," Fish observed. "I could pull it out and examine it if you didn't mind reopening that hole in the dog's belly."

One condition of the bequest was that the dog statue be put on the grave intact by me and only me. I didn't think it would qualify as "intact" if part of its secret bundle were missing, not to mention the plug of clay in the figure's belly. And I didn't have much time to sit around in Seattle: it was already October twenty-eighth, the trip was going to be a long one, even by air, and I didn't know where in Oaxaca City Hector Purecete was buried. I wasn't fool enough to think there was only one cemetery in town, so I'd have to do some investigating in Oaxaca before I could complete the conditions of the bequest, as Nan insisted on calling them.

"I don't think it should be removed, unless you suppose it's something illegal," I said, frowning at the picture.

"That small? Nah, not likely to be anything drug-related, or human remains. Unless it's hair, like I said, in which case it probably got in there while the dog was being painted. It's too fine to be plant matter and there's not enough of it to be worth much if it's any other fiber. It's not dense enough to be metal strands, either. Without actually seeing it with my own eyes and running tests, my best guess is still human hair." Then he shrugged and added, "Or a few strands of some really long-haired animal's fur or tail. Maybe horse tail . . ."

Noises in the hallway and a sudden agitation among the ghosts indicated the post-lunch return of Fish's coworkers. We packed up the figurine and Fish led me back out, promising to call when he had the result of the tests on the clay and paint. I headed back to my office to clear off my schedule and check on the flights Nan had promised to book for me on behalf of the estate.

Only Nan's work had any specific deadlines on it, so it wasn't difficult to rearrange my meetings and appointments—I don't make that many anyhow. The biggest hurdle was finding someone to look after my pet ferret while I was gone, and that was taken care of by tracking down Quinton and depositing the tube rat with him. I suspect Chaos prefers him over me, since he will happily carry her around with him all day in one deep pocket or another, while I usually have to leave her at home. Anyhow, she didn't look grieved to see me go, even if Quinton did.

We sat in the glass picnic shelter beside Ivar's Acres of Clams on the waterfront and talked while we ate our fish and chips. Chaos helped us with the chips and ignored the gulls screaming outside, even in the late-October chill, for their tithe of greasy fast food. Ivar Haglund may have loved those damned birds, but to me they were a nuisance worse than persistent spooks: ghosts don't poop on you.

"Oaxaca?" Quinton questioned. "Why?"

"Some nonsense with a bequest. There's a set of instructions—sorry: conditions—that have to be fulfilled."

"Like in one of those movies where you have to stay in the haunted house overnight or change your name to Gaggleplox?" he asked. "Those usually don't work out well—most of the cast ends up dead or the inheritance turns out to be a stash of counterfeit bills."

I made a face. "That's in the movies. This is just a job. Find the right grave, put the dog on it, and wait for daybreak."

"And in between is when all hell could break loose. Which seems pretty likely considering your talents."

"It's possible," I conceded, "but the money is pretty attractive and I don't get a sense of danger from the statue—just trouble."

He snorted. "Just trouble . . . And why did this woman pick you? Did you know her?"

I shook my head and pinched off a bit of fried potato for the ferret. "No. I didn't know her and I don't know why she picked me for this job. I assume she somehow knew what I can do, but how she knew, that's the big mystery. And why I agreed to go. Maybe there's some clue to be found about why this happened to me and not to every person who's ever had a near-death experience. There must be someone who knows more about all of this than I do, or the Danzigers do, or every vampire from here to Vancouver seems to." I felt a flush on my face that didn't come from the space heater overhead and realized I was getting angry. Not at Quinton, but at the shifty fate that had yanked the rug out from under me when I'd died only long enough to have my life wrenched into a shape beyond my control.

"But if it was this Arbildo woman, she's already dead," Quinton said.

"Then I'll hunt her down in the Grey." At least my change of life had come with useful skills. I was still figuring them out more than a year later, but I no longer hated and resented them.

My flight was set for 11:40 that evening with a five-hour layover in Dallas before I could fly on to Mexico City and from there to Oaxaca, but even with the delay, I'd still have a few hours once I got to Oaxaca City to find the records office and start looking for the grave of Hector Purecete.

I finished up my food and gave Chaos a final scratch around the ears. Quinton got a lot more than an ear scratch, which annoyed the ferret, judging by the way she kept pushing herself in between us and snagging our kisses for herself. Jealous little furball.

*   *   *

The trip was smooth. Right up to Mexico City, where they broke the dog.

The customs agent was going through my bag when it happened. There was the box with the little clay dog inside. He held it up.

"Is this a gift?" he demanded in a crabby, tired voice.

I'd have guessed he was near the end of his shift if it wasn't quite noon, but maybe he was aware in his own way of the cranky, dispirited, overexcited motion of the Grey as much as I was. The customs area was aroil in the flashes and clouds of hundreds of passengers' emotional energy giving shape and color to the loose power of the magical grid. It chafed and roared and twisted through the space around us like angry lions in a too-small cage. The sound of the Grey was a strong, steady hum with a sharp edge, like barbed wire under silk.

That sharpness was probably why my response was inappropriately flippant: "No. It's a dog," I said.

One really shouldn't joke with security people of any kind while they are on the job; most have had to leave their sense of humor in their locker with their civilian clothes. He raised his eyebrow and opened the box, rooting inside with his blue-gloved hand—every employee at airport security looks like they're about to play doctor in some very unpleasant way these days. He snorted in surprise and jerked his hand out with the figurine not quite gripped in his sweat-sticky glove. You'd have thought the little dog had bitten him from the way he moved. His hand yanked back, jerking upward a little as the statuette cleared the edge of the box. The black object moved up, popping out of his loose grip, and arced into the air, ripping a slice of glove with one pointed ear as it went. It was like slow-motion film, watching it rise from safety and crash to the hard linoleum beneath our feet.

As it hit the floor, it flashed a panic-bolt of silver white into the Grey. The little clay dog shattered, a tiny bundle of dark fibers bouncing onto the floor amid the terra-cotta shards. With a silvery gasp, the flash rushed back toward the broken figurine and coalesced into the ghost of a dog.

The ghost dog looked around, then looked at me, and whined piteously. It was a rangy, mongrel beast with the shape of a stunted greyhound and the coat of a shaggy pony. It sidled up to me and leaned against my legs and I felt its cold Grey shape press against me with its memory of weight.

The customs agent looked at the smashed figurine and bent to pick the tiny knot from the wreckage. "Eh?" he mumbled. "What is this?"

I shrugged. "Hair?" I guessed.

He looked at it, rubbed it between his fingers, sniffed it. Then he motioned to one of his coworkers, who walked over and rubbed a small cloth swab over the little bundle. He put the swab into a machine while the first man moved me and my bags to another table deeper inside the security zone. Someone else swept up the bits of clay and put them in a plastic bag. The dog stuck to me like a shy toddler.

"*Nada,*" said the man with the machine. "*Este es pelo.*"

They put a little of the clay dust from the broken figurine into the machine, but that also yielded "nada." The customs agent looked sad as he finished inspecting my bag and closed it up, handing it and the bag of shards back to me with what almost looked like a contrite bow, and an apology for breaking my dog.

"*De nada,*" I replied. Then I asked for the knot of fluff back, which he thought was odd, but he dug into the trash and retrieved it for me anyhow. I dropped it into the bag of broken ceramic—it wasn't intact anymore, but better to keep it all together, just in case, I thought.

He handed me a claim form to fill out if the dog had been insured, and I took it, even though I doubted the figurine was valuable. I was sure it was the ghost that was the important thing.

The spirits of Mexico hummed and roared. The ghost dog pasted itself to my heels and shadowed me around the halls of the Mexico City airport as I tried to find a place to put down my bags and make a phone call. Of course, the place I found was a bar.

I threw myself and my bags down and ordered a beer while I called Nan on my cell phone. Seattle being close to the other border, I'd had international calling added to my service long ago. Sometimes I wondered how I'd managed without a cell phone so long. Other times I wished I still had my pager.

It took a few minutes to get connected to Nan.

"Hello, Harper."

"Hello, Nan. Mexican customs broke the dog."

"Is it reparable?"

"No. But I have a major part of it," I added, looking at the cowering ghost at my ankles.

"Where are you?"

"Mexico City airport."

"Banda is located there. He may have instructions for that contingency."

She gave me his number. I wrote it on my cocktail napkin, as is traditional in that sort of situation. "If I call this guy, I may miss my connection to Oaxaca," I warned her. "I'm already running tight because of the mess at customs."

"I'll have Cathy reschedule you to a later flight and call you back with the information. Is there anything else?"

"No. I'll let Cathy know if anything is still out of whack when she calls."

"Good. Stay in touch." And she was off the phone as fast as that.

I finished my Negra Modelo and called the number on the napkin. I felt itchy from annoyance and lack of sleep—I don't get more than a fitful doze on planes, since my long legs end up cramped and headrests are never in the right place for me. I always longed to upgrade to first class, but the PI business usually comes with a tourist-class budget.

Guillermo Banda answered his own phone. He spoke English like a New Yorker as soon as he heard how bad my Spanish was.

"Miss Blaine! You're here! This is excellent! How is the perrito? The little dog?"

"Customs broke it."

"Fuck! Pardon me. My client would be very upset to hear it. If she weren't dead."

"Which is why I'm here at all." Talking to this guy was like talking to Lou Costello, and I was afraid I might start laughing. "I do have part of the dog and I could take that up to Oaxaca, if you think that would be in the spirit intended."

"I don't know. . . ." There were noises in the background and he muttered away from the receiver something about Puerto Vallarta, which was rejoined by a feminine giggle.

I tried to keep him on track. "Well, if you could tell me what it was your client had in mind with this condition, I'm sure we can figure out a way to satisfy the spirit, if not the letter, of her request."

"That I also don't know. Miss Arbildo wasn't very . . . forthcoming."

"How long had she been your client, Mr. Banda?"

"Oh, years! Years and years! But we never spoke. She came in to update her will last year and before that we'd only seen each other twice. I inherited her account from my partner, who died a few years back in a plane crash. Horrible."

"Did your firm do any work for her aside from the will?"

"Well, the specifics are confidential, but yes. We did a little background investigative work for her and for her father—mostly routine checks. We managed her estate—her father's estate—and of course we'd been doing work for his company for many years. We work primarily with international and maritime law and his company was involved in quite a bit of international shipping. Handling Miss Arbildo's will and so on was more in line of a . . . courtesy."

"I see. Do you have any idea what her relationship was to Hector Purecete? The guy on whose grave the dog was supposed to be put."

"None at all."

"Damn. I wish I knew what she expected. This is kind of a pain in the butt. You don't have any idea what her intentions were in the will instruction?"

"No. Like I said, the woman was very strange."

I sighed. "Maybe if I could see the will itself we could figure this out. May I come to your office?"

"Oh, no," he said. "You'd never get here and back before your flight."

"I've already called Nan to change it."

"No, no . . . you don't understand—the traffic. Here's what I'll do. I'll bring it to you at the airport, if you have time."

"I'll make the time." I told him where I was and that he should bring as much of the paperwork as he had. He said it would take him an hour to get to the bar and I said that was fine. After all, I was still waiting for Nan's secretary to call me back.

I was thinking about ordering food when the phone went off, showing me Nan's office number on the ID. It was Cathy with my flight change and some additional information.

"Nan's booked you into a guesthouse in Oaxaca City—it's one she's used before. The owner speaks English and can help you with the records search if you need it."

"Thanks. I only hope I'll get there before the offices close."

"I think you're going to have to rearrange your schedule. The earliest flight I could get you was five fifty. I'm sorry. But the provincial offices should be open Friday."

Terrific. My two days for research was now down to one. I'd have to hope I got what I wanted the first time or could work up some local contacts very fast. "I'll make it work," I said, then continued, "Umm ... I talked to Banda.... Nan said he was reputable, but he seems a little ... skittish. Is there anything I should know about him?"

"About Guillermo? I don't know much except that he's the biggest New York Yankees fan in Mexico. And I'm not even sure that's unusual."

"Baseball?"

"Yup. Baseball is big in Mexico City. A few years ago he had season tickets and flew up to watch the games— I swear that's why he took his international courses at Columbia; so he could go to Yankees games—he even tried to take Nan out to one, but she's not a sports fan. Don't get him started on any conversation about baseball or you'll miss your plane."

I said my good-byes and started thinking while I waited for Banda. It was after one o'clock already. I'd have to get lunch at the airport and see what I could do by phone. I'd miss the open hours in person today at whatever government office might have the burial records and I'd only have Friday to do records searches before the holiday weekend hit—if they didn't close early or not open at all. I'd have to get to that office first thing on the thirtieth if I was going to stand much chance of finding the right grave. I only hoped that whatever I could turn up about Hector Purecete in that time would help me get information from Maria-Luz Arbildo. If she showed up at his grave. Definitely no time for "Who's on First" discussions with Guillermo Banda that afternoon— I hoped he didn't look as much like Lou Costello as he sounded or I might lose it.

Fish called me before I could get anything done with directory assistance, saying there was not much to report on the scrapings he'd taken from the clay dog, except that the black paint was colored with crushed charcoal and volcanic sand, with just a touch of human blood. Not your average pottery glaze. No sign of dread diseases or drug residue. No unusual clay substrate, just plain terra-cotta. I mentioned that the dog had broken and dropped the bundle of hair out.

"So it is hair?" he asked.

"It looks like it. My Spanish is lousy, but I heard the inspector call it *pelo*—which I recognize from my shampoo bottle as the Spanish word for 'hair,' " I replied, gazing into the plastic bag of shards. "Five or six strands here, dark brown and black, with a red thread holding them together."

"Two different kinds of hair?"

"Two different colors, but they have the same look and texture."

"Interesting. I wonder if the DNA matches the blood in the paint. . . . I'd love to take a look at it when you get back—if you're game."

"I don't know if I'll be able to bring it back. It might have to stay here," I added, glancing down again at the phantom hound. Once the knot of hair had come free, so had the dog, and I wasn't sure if it was the hair or the sculpture that had held the spirit in the clay shell, but I wanted to know more before I let any of the parts out of my hands.

The ghost dog leaned against me and seemed to doze. I envied it; the beer had made me feel more tired than ever. Resigned, I stuffed the bag of pottery bits into my purse and went back to fruitless phone calls for the next hour. Outside of Mexico City directory assistance, most of the people I talked to had no better English than I had Spanish—and my Spanish was embarrassingly poor. The dog stirred and I could feel its low growl as it pressed against my leg.

A man of medium height with short black hair stopped beside me and looked me over as I tried to make myself clear—without much success—to a clerk in a provincial office somewhere in Oaxaca. The man carried a leather briefcase. He wore a gray suit, had a bland, oval face made interesting only by a boxer's crooked nose and basset-hound eyes. He smelled of laundry starch. The aura around him jittered and jumped in flickers of vibrant orange and blue as his eyes moved over everything, evaluating, cataloging. . . . He seemed to have a hot-sauce stain on his tie, but it could have been part of the pattern.

His eyes flicked down toward my feet and he blinked, but I wasn't sure if he saw the ghost dog or if he just didn't like my boots. He turned his restless gaze back to me, waited until I hung up in frustration, and said, "You gotta be Harper Blaine."

He didn't look at all like Lou Costello, not even a Hispanic version. He didn't look like an international law practitioner with an advanced degree from Columbia, either. He looked like a guy who worked in an office eight to five, like an insurance adjuster or a midlevel manager in a very expensive suit.

"You must be Guillermo Banda," I replied.

"Willy. You can call me Willy." He hoisted himself onto the bar stool next to mine, keeping his feet away, as if I might kick him without warning.

Considering my ex-boyfriend was named Will, that particular first name didn't sound like a good idea. "I'd rather not," I said and wondered if he could see the ghost dog—he seemed a little wound up.

He shrugged. "I'm sorry if I offended you, Miss Blaine." He put the briefcase on the bar and snapped it open. It held a single manila folder and a business-size envelope. Banda picked up the folder. "These are the last three versions of Miss Arbildo's will. I don't have to show them to you, but since a will in probate is a public record here, just as it is in the U.S., you could get most of this information by searching the district probate records—"

I cut him off. "Mr. Banda, I'm not offended with you and I'm not trying to put your back up. I'm just at a loss to understand this. I don't know why I was named in your client's will—I've never met her or heard of her. I just want to understand what I'm doing. I don't want to be stuck with some creepy mystery for the rest of my life." I did not look at the dog, but I could feel it still rumbling and pressing to me. "The conditions say I'm to put the dog on the grave intact. What am I supposed to do, now that the statue is broken?"

He put the folder down in the case and picked up the envelope, offering it to me. "That's easy. You take the money and run. I'm sure Miss Arbildo won't even know. She inherited a truckload. Thirty thousand U.S. is a drop in the bucket."

I was sure she would mind. Very much. I shook my head and didn't touch the envelope. "I can't do that. Maybe if I knew why she wanted the dog put on Purecete's grave, I could agree, but I don't. What is with the dog?"

Banda laughed—a tired laugh but genuinely amused. "It's a tradition. A really old one. You don't see it around here much anymore—up in the mountains around Michoacan and Yunuen, maybe in Oaxaca, but even there it's dying out. It's from the Aztecs. They used to sacrifice a dog and burn the body on the funeral pyres because they believed the dog could lead the spirit of the dead to Mictlan. Now we just use a statue.

"See, the Mexican Land of the Dead is kind of like Dante's geography of Hell—it's got rings, only nicer. In the middle is Mictlan—where the dead live just like we do and from which they can someday be reborn. But it's a long way for a soul to go and there's a river you have to cross as well, so you need a guide: the dog, because tradition says dogs can always find the way home. Every year, the dead come back to visit us during el Día de los Muertos. The really traditional people put a statue of a dog on the *ofrenda*—the offerings on the family altar—so their dead relatives don't get lost coming and going."

"OK, I get the dog, but why me? Why would your client want a perfect stranger from two thousand miles away to take the dog to Purecete's grave?"

Banda shrugged again and dropped the envelope back into the briefcase, glancing down. "I don't know. Before you ask, I don't know who Purecete was or what his connection was to Miss Arbildo, either. You want to see the will for yourself?" he asked, looking back up at me.

I nodded. He pulled a draft copy of the will from the folder and handed the long pages to me. He pointed as he talked.

"See how she left her money to all these charities? That was pretty much unchanged from the first version I ever saw—one Jimenez, my partner, drew up for her. You can tell she was kind of an oddball when you look at the list." He pulled out another version of the document. "In an earlier draft of this will, she'd designated Jimenez's grave as the recipient of the dog, as you can see. She did it right after he died and she was very upset with him. Then she changed her mind—out of the blue— and named Purecete. Just a few months ago, she marched into the office and she handed me this."

He fished a creased scrap of paper out of the file. It was the hard white of a cheap notepad, torn along one side to make a ragged square from a longer piece of paper. The handwriting was similar to the signature on the will, but more crabbed and wandering:

Harper Blaine

Seattle Wash USA

The letters were cramped up against the left edge, but became more expansive and arched as they moved to the right, as if she hadn't thought she'd have enough space when she started and tried to stretch the words out to fill the page as she finished each line. It looked odd.

"She just held it out to me and said 'this is the one' and I knew better than to argue with Maria-Luz. So I wrote you in." He offered me the collection of drafts.

"Take a look, you can see she had pretty definite—if crazy—ideas about her money. The woman was kind of loopy."

I glanced at the will again, making mental notes of the recipients of her bequests. They were mostly church charities for the unfortunate, the homeless, the poor, the dispossessed. There were a few odd animal charities as well, such as support for retired racing greyhounds, a rabbit shelter, llama farms, and care for retired circus elephants. None of them had conditions. And there were no individuals named other than me and Purecete.

"Didn't she have any family, or friends . . . employees even?" I asked.

Banda laughed and pretended he was coughing. "Miss Arbildo? No. She was the last of a literally dying breed—the Arbildo family died with her. And as I said, she was pretty strange and she wandered around a lot, didn't settle down much after a certain age, didn't make a lot of friends. She was kind of fond of Jimenez once—like I said, she put him in the will at one point—but about the time he died she was furious with him. She stormed into the office screaming about it: 'Why did he do it? Why, why?' I almost thought that she would have dragged him back out of his grave and killed him if she could."

"What was she so mad about?"

"Well . . . his dying on her. She worked Jimenez pretty hard—he used to say if he died suddenly it would be her fault. His death shook her up. She was irrational. You know how some people get mad instead of grieving. . . ."

I nodded; I was familiar with that phenomenon. Arbildo sounded like a difficult client, and I could understand not wanting to argue with—or console—one like her. But there was something incredibly strange about both the wills and Banda himself. I just couldn't pin down what was bugging me. . . .

As I pondered the problem, under cover of checking the wills, the ghostly dog at my feet began whimpering and moving restively, then it got up and walked a few feet away from the bar, toward a column of thick mist that was forming in the Grey between the bar and the doorway. I adjusted my position on the bar stool so I could watch the dog and still seem to be reading the documents. The dog stopped near the smoky mass, then looked back at me with that pleading look dogs have. It looked at the ill-defined shape, whimpered, then glanced back to me.

The form that interested the dog was vaguely human in size and shape, but it had no features. There was no face, and after a few moments the dog turned and trotted back to me, whimpering and scratching at my legs with its cold, incorporeal paws. The specter drifted out the door. I didn't know what it was or where it was going, but the dog seemed to be urging me to follow it—or at least humor the dog's desire to do so. Banda would still be in Mexico City in a day or an hour, but whatever the ghost dog was after might not last another five minutes.

I wanted to ask him more about Arbildo, but I excused myself from Banda and said I'd be right back. Let him assume I needed the washroom, if he liked. I stood up and the dog darted out of the bar and into the main concourse. I hoped my luggage would be all right with the lawyer for the time it would take to chase the dog.

And it was fine, since the dog only got a few feet farther into the concourse before the shape seemed to fall apart and drift into the clutter of thousands of passengers' energy coronas moving through the silvery space of the air terminal. A few shapes had no living person within them, but most of those were simple repeating ghosts or fogs of happenstance and emotion left over from some altogether human interaction. The shadowy dog trotted back to me and pushed against my legs again.

Banda was looking impatiently at his watch when I returned to the bar.

"I can't stay longer. Have some clients to meet in

twenty minutes and the traffic is getting bad. I have to go." He took a card from his inner jacket pocket and offered it to me. "If you have any more questions, call me. My cell phone number is on here. Good luck, Miss Blaine," he added, picking up his briefcase and heading for the door.

"Hey," I called. "Aren't there any other documents? And what am I supposed to do about the dog?"

"Any other documents in Miss Arbildo's file are none of your business, Miss Blaine. As to the dog, the check is right here—you could just turn right around with it in your hand and call this thing done, as far as I'm concerned. But if you feel you have to, take the broken bits up to Oaxaca and leave 'em. Stick 'em back together with superglue if you want."

"What about the grave? Where is it?"

"Damned if I know," he called back. "Pick one!"

He waved and ducked out before I could ask him anything more. It appeared that Guillermo Banda just wanted shut of Maria-Luz Arbildo and her nutty will and I was as convenient a way as any. I followed him a few paces out the door, saw him duck past the customs area, waving to the guards on the other side as he went past—old friends? Something odd was going on with Banda, but I wasn't entirely sure what. I did pause to wonder if the breaking of the dog was entirely an accident. . . . I shook off that thought and went back to my seat, the Grey dog scampering along in my wake.

I ordered some food and ate in a hurry before heading to the Mexicana Airlines desk to pick up my new boarding passes and check my luggage for the flight to Oaxaca. The phantom dog stuck to my side the whole time, casting glances around the room and sniffing for signs—of what I didn't know.

For just a moment as I boarded the little prop plane I wondered what to do with the dog before I remembered that no one but me would even be aware of it. It huddled under my feet the whole hour we were in the air and again on the ride from the airport, which reminded me of the regional airports I'd grown up near in Los Angeles County with their pushcart stairs and windblown tarmac. A white van was standing at the curb outside, offering rides to downtown Oaxaca City, and the ghost dog and I shared the vehicle with a family of six and two couples who all seemed excited beyond my ability.

The van driver dropped each group off, leaving me at a tall, Spanish colonial building on the edge of the downtown core. As far as I could tell, the whole area was late Spanish colonial, though at that elevation, darkness had already fallen and it was hard to see details beyond the streetlamps. The road was layered thickly with silvery ghosts and loops of memory, playing like old movies in a two-dollar theater. I saw a discreet sign on the buttercup-colored plaster wall that indicated the carved wooden door before me led to my guesthouse. I pulled the bell handle as instructed and was greeted with a flood of light and the odors of spicy cooking as the door was opened wide.

"*Soy* Harper Blaine—" I started.

"Oh! Miss Blaine! *Sí!* Come in! You were bumped to a later flight?" the dark-haired woman in the doorway asked, snatching my bag indoors with one hand as she waved me in with the other. "We have dinner for you if you like it."

She turned her head and called for "Miguelito!" who proved to be a teenager as tall as a professional basketball player and as dramatically emo as a Cure album cover. "You are in *manos de leon*," she continued to me while pointing at my suitcase without shifting her gaze from my face. "My nephew will take your bag. You can wash and come back down to the *sala* for some food."

I was almost dizzy with exhaustion by then, but I know better than to argue with whirlwind women. I followed "little Miguel" up the tiled stairs and around an open gallery to a door with a painting of a magenta coxcomb flower on it. Miguelito unlocked the door for me and put the suitcase just inside before handing me my key and slouching off with an insouciant nod.

I glanced down over the railing before I went into the room. In the courtyard below I could see people gathered around a ceramic firepit that gleamed with heat, serving themselves from a nearby table laden with food. The cool mountain air settled gently from above through the open center of the building's roof, drifting down to meet the swirl of sparks and heat that rose from the gathering below.

I was so tired I didn't make it back down that night. I woke up in the morning on October thirtieth with one boot on and one off and the ghost dog running in and out through the closed door, whining. Someone was tapping on my door. Groggily, I stumbled to it and opened up.

Miguel-the-not-so-small was slouching there—clad in black jeans, black T-shirt, and black boots with his naturally dark hair hanging over his eyes—probably hoping I hadn't heard his timid tapping and he could lope off to whatever he'd rather do than wait on me. The energy around him was a dun-colored cloud shot with red lightning bolts of annoyance—or something short-tempered and pissy—while thin gold lines trailed off his fingertips in a way I'd never seen before. In the face of his determined gloom, I smiled at him with perverse malice, in spite of being still half asleep.

"*Buenos días*, Miguel!" I chirped—fairy-tale princesses had nothing on me for chipper.

"Yeah, yeah ... good morning to you, too." His accent was still pretty strong, but his English was clear. And abrasive. I could almost see the expletive deleted from that sentence still hanging in the air in all its F-bomb glory. "Tía Mercedes said I'm supposed to show you around the city 'cause you have some kind of business thing. . . ."

"Yup! Busy-ness. Busy, busy! Gotta find a grave."

He frowned at me. "Grave?" he asked, as if I surely didn't know what I'd just said.

"Yup. I have a mission to do something with a grave and I don't know where it is."

"Today?"

"No. On Sunday, November first."

"Oh." Was that disappointment? "Día de los Muertos. Yeah."

"Is today special or something?" I asked as he started to turn away.

"Yeah. There's, like, a whole series of Days of the Dead. Todos Santos—November first—is just the big one the tourists are all crazy for. Today's, like, the day for the spirits that died by violence. Tía Mercedes doesn't celebrate that in the house—we have to go outside so the mad ghosts don't come in and mess stuff up." He shrugged and started to turn away, having lost all interest in me, now that I was no more interesting than the average tourist.

I grabbed his arm. "Hey, where y'going, Miguel?"

He huffed his hair out of his face and glared at me. "Call me Mickey."

"Not Mike?"

"No." Like, duuuuh, I thought facetiously. Was I this snotty as a teenager?

"Mickey Mouse fan, then? Mickey Mantle?"

He snorted, and pulled his arm out of my grasp. "Tía Mercedes has breakfast downstairs in twenty minutes. Then we can go look for your grave. OK?"

I didn't miss the implication of whose grave, but I did ignore it. "OK. Be right down. Thank your aunt for me."

He skulked away as I retreated into my room. I took a very fast shower and threw on clean clothes.

I'd been given a room with its own bath, which I suspected was an unusual luxury in an antique house. And there was no denying the building—some wealthy man's town home originally, I'd have bet—was exactly as old as its style indicated. It didn't mimic Spanish colonial, it *was* Spanish colonial.

Downstairs the food was endless and lush: eggs scrambled with corn tortillas, green salsa, and cheese; fried plantains; grilled tomatoes; bread and sweet pastries only distantly related to the greasy churros found in American malls. Coffee, chocolate, and milk were all available as well as horchata and fruit juice. My hosts, the Villaflores family, felt that their guests during the holiday should be well fed before they faced a day of hiking up and down the mountainous elevations of Oaxaca City and its environs. Midday meal would be on our own, but dinner with the family was open to all, Mercedes informed me—she was the proprietress I'd met the previous night. I thought I'd have to find an excuse to dodge it or I stood a good chance of gaining five pounds before November second, hiking or no.

Miguel-call-me-Mickey was not so enthusiastic, picking at his food and jumping up the moment I was finished, telling his aunt we had to leave and get to the *"palacio de gobierno"* that morning or we'd never get in before they closed. He sloped off to wait for me outside while I thanked Mercedes for breakfast.

She smiled. "Gracias. I hope you won't mind Miguelito too much—he is bored here. I don't know why he came at all—such an odd boy—but at least he can be some help to you. If he doesn't make you scream and leave him in a ditch by the road."

"Oh . . . I think we'll be OK," I replied, thinking there would be ample opportunities to knock a hole in Mickey's attitude if I wanted to. Angsty teens aren't much of a challenge after vampires and vengeful ghosts and monsters in the sewer.

Stepping through the door, the sound of the Grey really hit me. Where Mexico City had been a strong, steady song of steel and silk, Oaxaca was a wild roar. It sounded like the Battle of the Bands in which someone had forgotten to tell the musicians not to play all at once. Layers of contrasting melody and meter, song and noise flooded the mist-world and made the lines of energy around me spark and throb. Strata of time and memory seemed to juggle and flow, like Einstein's river. It was tiring just to stand in it.

Mickey lounged against the wall outside, smoking a noxious-smelling cigarillo and shifting his fake-sleepy gaze around the street like a hoodlum looking for a chump in a black-and-white film. I stood on the doorstep for a minute while he ignored me. Then I tapped his foot with mine to get his attention—OK, maybe a little more insistent than a tap, but not a full-on kick. He jerked upright and muttered a phrase under his breath even I knew was an insult.

"Hey, I thought you were in a hurry," I said.

He grunted and threw down his smoke, grinding it out under his toe with more malice than the horrid thing deserved. "Yeah, right." A sentence that seemed to mean nothing when he said it.

He gathered himself after a final glance around and turned his back to me, heading out into the street. "This way."

I wondered if his shoulders got tired carrying the weight of that chip.

I was there because of the holiday, yet I hadn't thought of some of the implications of its presence beyond the possibility of office closures and an increased presence of the dead. Once out on the street with Mickey, it became obvious that el Día de los Muertos was a much bigger thing than Halloween and there was more to contend with, both living and dead, than bureaucrats on holiday. We walked down the wide, gray-bricked road, hemmed in by a mix of adobe and buildings of pale green stone, none newer than the late 1920s, many painted, like the Villaflores house, in rich shades of red, yellow, orange, or the native pale green. The bricked street boiled with ghostly traffic on foot, in cars, on horse- and donkey-back, even a group of ancient Spanish soldiers marching with pikes pointing at the sky.

I was startled to note that unlike the ghosts of Seattle, most of these looked like skeletons in clothing and not like the remembered shapes of live people. Skulls grinned and empty eye sockets gleamed with only the memory of eyes. They were completely aware of us, too, watching us as we went and seeming amused. It was unsettling to be observed through eyeless, unblinking sockets, and so much more closely than I was used to.

We scuffed through the legions of phantoms without talking for a while, to a huge central plaza. Miguel paused and pointed into it, saying in a bored voice, "That's our famous *zócalo*. Where the Federales shot all those teachers a couple of years ago. That was in front of the old palacio de gobierno, but it's a museum now. We'll have to go through the market to get to the new one—I hope you don't want to stop and go shopping," he added with a sneer. He didn't know me very well. . . .

I rolled my eyes and ignored the jab—for now. "I'm not much of a shopper. I just need to find this guy's grave by November first."

"You know which cemetery?"

"Nope, just have a name and a date of death."

"Yeah, right. We'll go to the Registrar of Deaths." He said it with such relish I had to stifle a giggle. "We have to move it, though, 'cause they'll close early. Día de los Muertos is a major holiday. It's like your Christmas, only with dead guys. The market's crazy full with old ladies like Tía Mercedes and all their kids doing the shopping for the ofrendas and all that. And tourists. And you want to get inside before the ghosts of the violently dead return." He gave me a sly glance from the corner of his eye to see if I'd bite, but I didn't.

"Then we'd better get going," was all I said.

We continued down the street to the market with the

ghost dog tagging at our heels and the gold threads that
dragged from Mickey's fingertips spinning out through
the crowds of spirits that thronged the streets already
crowded with the living. He seemed unaware of the vibrant threads spooling from his hands. I wished I knew
what that shiny energy strand was all about, but I'd have
to wait and see.

We threaded our way through the periphery of the
market crowd and cut across the corner of the *zócalo*—
partially "opened" by the ruthless removal of towering
trees, the memories of which still threw phantom shade
over the raised, central "kiosk" where the state band
played on Tuesdays, according to a notice nearby.

I could see the memory of the original plaza like a
projection over the new design, with huge, thick-trunked
trees and Victorian iron benches set along the narrower,
shadier paths, and the not-so-long-ago stench of tear gas
floating on the warm breeze and an echo of screams.
Shadows of the dead protesters glimmered over the
memory of blood on the stones in front of the old government building. I could hear the shouts and the shots
mingled with the scent of flowers and fresh, spiced bread
from the market nearby. The combination made me
queasy. No one in their right mind would want to linger
there that night.

We turned from the market, the shops, and the cafes
that lined the sun-baked *zócalo* and headed down to the
government offices a few blocks away. We entered the
usual bureaucratic maze of once-grand rooms chopped
into offices and cubicles with flimsy, movable walls, re-
pulsively out of place in the building that predated World
War I.

The man behind the registrar's desk, however, fit in
perfectly. He had a small mustache with waxed points
and wore his shirt collar buttoned up tight under his con-
servative tie.

"Hi," I started, hoping I could manage to make myself
understood in English. "I need to locate a grave. . . ."

The clerk's nostrils pinched in annoyance and he shook his head. *"No habla inglés, Señora."*

I cast a glance at Mickey, who was leaning against a wall again. He shot me back a snotty look. This was going to be fun. . . .

"Mickey, would you translate for me?" I asked.

With a sigh, the teenager heaved himself upright and ambled to the desk.

He made a gesture at the clerk, who gave him a look nearly as disdainful as the one Mickey had given me.

"La gringa busca un sepulcro," he said.

"La gringa" . . . well, at least I wasn't *"puta"* this time.

The clerk heaved a shrug and spat back something that I imagined was, "Yeah, aren't they all?"

There was a bit more wiseass chitchat before I put a restraining hand on Mickey's arm.

"Mickey. Just translate. Commentary isn't required."

He rolled his eyes. "Yeah, right." Then he gave me a blank look.

"What?" I asked, feeling the ghost dog brush past me to lie down on the floor near the door. I didn't look down, just stared at Mickey.

"So . . . ? What am I supposed to translate?"

Maybe I should have kicked him harder. . . .

"Ask him if there's a form I need to fill out and what it will cost for him to find the information right now."

Mickey made with the rolling eyes again and looked back to the clerk, who was glaring at us, even though there was no one else waiting in his cubbyhole. Mickey seemed to be repeating my request, but this time in a slightly singsong, high-pitched voice.

The man frowned at him. *"Forma? Para qué?"*

"He says, 'A form for what?'"

"Yeah . . . I figured that part out, Mickey. I need to know if there is a form I am required to fill out in order to find out where a certain person is buried here in Oaxaca. If so, I need that form and I wish to know what fee I have to pay to get that information immediately—while I stand here and wait. Now, you think you can be that specific with him, Mickey?"

He huffed and turned back to the clerk, parroting my request in his mocking voice.

The clerk was annoyed by it, too, but he grunted an affirmative and handed over a form and said something about pesos.

"He says it'll cost a hundred dollars to do it right now."

"No, he didn't, Mickey. He said *'cinco cientos pesos.'* That's about fifty bucks. My Spanish sucks, not my math."

"Yeah, right." And the eye roll. I was getting too familiar with the routine already.

I filled in the form as best I could with Mickey's non-help and fished a thousand pesos from my wallet. I put it down with the form, saying, *"Apesadumbrado,"* and jerking my head toward Mickey. Even as bad as it is, I can manage a few important words in Spanish: please, thank you, beer, toilet, keys, and sorry.

A smile almost cracked the man's wooden face as he accepted the form and the overpayment, with an amused snort. *"Momentito,"* he said, taking the form away behind a screen.

I sat down on one of his two cracked green vinyl-covered chairs to wait.

"He only goes back to the computer," Mickey groused. "He just wants to make it look important."

I shot him a quelling glance, but said nothing.

The phantom dog got up to chase a phantom cat around the room. I ignored their antics and so did almost everyone else, except a skeletal clerk, who tried to give the dog one of his finger bones to dissuade it from barking. The dog wasn't having anything to do with the clerk's finger and backed away, bristling, leaving the ghost cat free to dash out of the room to the relative safety of the hall.

The flesh-and-blood clerk, who looked nothing like his bony predecessor, returned with a sheet of paper. "Hmph," he coughed, then launched into a rattling discourse aimed somewhere in between me and Mickey, as if he couldn't decide which of us he was supposed to talk to—Mickey the brat or the illiterate gringa.

Finally the clerk let out an impressively heavy sigh, shrugged, and shoved the paper forward for one of us to take. *"Buenos días,"* he added, turning his back and stomping off to his sanctum in the back.

Mickey grabbed the sheet and held it out to me after a second's perusal. "You're fucked. There are three graves for your guy."

"Three? Not for the same date."

"Yeah. Look."

I took the page and looked it over. And there were three grave sites given for Hector Purecete, all with the same death date in 1996. "That's gotta be wrong—it's not a common name, is it?"

"No."

"Great," I muttered. "I guess I'll have to go look at all of them and see what shakes loose."

I stood up and walked out of the government offices with Mickey and the dog trailing me.

We'd started back across the *zócalo*, passing closer to the site of the teachers' fatal protest than I liked, when Mickey finally decided to talk again.

"What do you want to find this guy's grave for anyway?" Mickey asked. "Some kind of creepy ritual or something?"

My turn to sigh. "No. I told you before, I just need to find it and leave something on it. On November first."

"Yeah, right."

I stopped, burning in the high-altitude sun and the hot Grey energy of the massacre. "Mickey, is it just for me, or do you always have a bad attitude?"

He turned his head and muttered under his breath, starting to walk on. I snatched his arm and dragged him back to me, through a red blotch of remembered blood and pain. He flinched a little and tried to wrench himself out of my grip, spitting nasty Spanish words.

"Damn, that's a lot of endearing little nicknames you have for me. How 'bout we make this easier on both of us. You can just call me the GP—"

"Huh? The what?"

"The gringa puta. And I'll just call you brat-boy. It'll be so much easier, don't you think?"

He glowered at me and pulled against my hold. I let him go and sighed.

"Mickey, look: I appreciate the offer of help, but your attitude is just not flying with me. You can straighten up and stop acting like a punk, or I can do without you. What's it going to be?" My ghostly dog companion circled around us, growling as if to keep something unpleasant at bay.

Mickey seemed to consider my statement seriously, sidling into the sun and away from the crying red energy of the teachers' deaths. "OK . . . GP. We'll have to get to the *panteones* soon. It'll be a lot busier tomorrow. And you really don't want to be out tonight."

"You're serious about that ghosts of the violent dead thing?"

He nodded. "You *norteamericanos* think el Día de los Muertos is just a funny tradition—not real—but we don't. Not up here. This is the ghost country. We're not afraid of death—not like you. We live with it."

"You might be surprised. . . ."

He ignored me. "But we don't do foolish things like stand where people were murdered on their day to return from Mictlan. That's just fucking stupid."

I nodded. "All right. Let's get someplace better then. Like the panteon—a panteon is a cemetery, right?"

"Yeah. It's actually pretty safe right now. But we should get the car. Those three aren't close to each other."

I was surprised at his change of attitude. He was still

kind of surly, but at least he seemed to be helping me instead of making more work. We walked back to the house and Mickey borrowed his aunt's car—a dusty silver Chevy, which amused me.

I took the passenger seat and held the door open for a moment. The ghost dog stopped at the car's doorsill and sat on the ground, looking pathetic and thumping its stumpy tail, but wouldn't step up into the car.

Mickey looked at me. "Something wrong?"

"No . . . no, I'm fine." I closed the door and the dog vanished from view. We drove away without any sign of the phantom canine until we got out at the first panteon on the list.

The first stop was the municipal cemetery of San Miguel. We drove around a small carnival that was setting up in a courtyard in front and walked across drifts of flowers and greenery that had escaped from the bundles carried by a stream of people entering the panteon ahead of us. The dog trotted up, materializing out of the road dust and Grey mist to rub against my legs and bump its head against me impatiently until we walked through the cemetery gates. The dog ran ahead, into the crowd of animate skeletons and live humans who filled the graveyard.

Everyone was busy, the living and the dead, and I paused to stare. "There are . . . a lot of people here . . . ," I said.

"Yeah. The graves have to be cleaned and decorated, the family ofrendas made, and the cooking has to be done before Todos Santos on November first. It's a Sunday this year, so they gotta be done today and tomorrow— or the Church might be offended. Most of these guys won't bring their feasts until after sundown on Sunday."

I glanced at him with a curious frown. "Feasts? In a graveyard?"

He snorted something that was almost a laugh. His tone still left a bit to be desired, however. "Yeah. I keep trying to tell you: it's like a party. El Día de los Muertos is a cycle-of-life thing. We have all this stuff at home— the ofrendas and stuff—but we come to the panteon in the evening to party with the family ghosts. We know death, but we don't worship it or freak out about it. It's just … part of life. We aren't afraid of the old bony woman. Just look at the skeletons," Mickey added, pointing at a pair of children waving paper skeleton puppets at each other in an elaborate pantomime punctuated with much chattering and laughing.

The puppets had jointed legs and arms controlled with strings the children pulled with their fingers while clutching the sticks to which the paper skeletons were mounted. One was a musician with a guitar and a top hat, while the other was a girl singer with a fur stole and long skirt. The kids pranced ahead with their puppets. The ghosts of several other children tagged behind, giggling, as the impromptu cabaret act headed for the family plot. The group was herded along by an aging man carrying an elaborate ironwork cross under his arm and followed by a cold boil of silver and red energy—the imminence of those who died by violence, perhaps.

"Those guys are gonna clean the graves of their family and put that new cross up," Mickey lectured me; he was almost spitting. "They're not sad—they're happy. They work hard today. They remember the dead. 'Cause they know we're all gonna die. That's the big deal you norteamericanos don't get. You can't 'cheat' death. You just have to know it's there and remember. We all got a skeleton inside us."

The skeletons. As I looked around the panteon, I saw few ghosts of the type I was most familiar with—the memory manifestations of the dead. Nearly all the ghosts in this cemetery were skeletal with only the barest hint of faces or flesh, a few were purely bones, while a smaller handful had the shape of the living people they had once been. These were the only ghosts I saw that seemed distressed or confused, wandering among the raised graves as if desperate to find something they'd misplaced, blind to the throngs of living and dead around them.

I got it: the manifestations of the Grey depended upon the minds of those who shaped it. Here, where skeletons were the symbol of the dead, embraced, even beloved in all their bony glory as just another part of the cycle of life, most of the spirits of the dead looked like skeletons. In the U.S., where death was the end of life, most ghosts manifested with the memory-shape of their formerly living bodies. But they could have been anything, like the discorporate entities I'd met once or twice, manifesting as changing shapes, or inconclusive features on a mutable column of fog, or the roiling anger of the slaughtered.

The ghost dog trotted back from its peregrinations through the crowd and sat at my feet, tongue lolling, looking happy for the first time since it had appeared. I almost reached to pat its head before I remembered that most people don't see ghosts. Even as comfortable with death as the Oaxaqueños were, I doubted they would understand my stooping to pet a spectral hound. Mickey would probably think I was crazy and say so. I didn't believe he'd suddenly decided to respect me; he just didn't want me to kick his ass. But he wasn't above a few more needling comments.

I cleared my throat. "Where do you think we'll find the grave? This is a big place...."

"Caretaker will have a list of the plots and tombs." He was pretty savvy about graveyards, but I supposed that wasn't unusual for the goth-inclined.

We pushed through the crowds to a large stone building with colonnades filled with niches on one side and open to a large courtyard on the other. The patio of the mausoleum was full of people walking or crawling on the paving stones to lay out pictures in mounds of colored sand: cavorting skeletons, Virgins of Guadalupe, flowers and crosses and skulls. Mickey called these "sand carpets." We found one of the caretakers assisting a sand painter, laying out a border of small bricks to keep the moist, colored sand from dribbling into the walkways. We picked our way closer, careful not to disturb the developing sand carpets. Mickey called out to the caretaker as we got near.

The woman looked up from her bricks and said something I couldn't follow. The caretaker was darker-skinned and had a more pronounced nose and cheekbones than Mickey—probably related to some local Indian group. Mickey replied in a language I knew wasn't Spanish. The kneeling woman stood and began to talk very fast. Mickey pointed to the paper we'd gotten from the Registrar of Births and Deaths. The woman frowned and pointed off across the cemetery, making motions with her hands to indicate turns. Mickey nodded and seemed to be thanking her, then turned and tugged me back into the mausoleum's colonnade.

"She says it's out in the edge, near the back fence, but she thinks this is wrong. The grave's been around a long time. You *sure* 1996 is right?" he added with a touch of sneering doubt at my brainpower.

"Yup."

Mickey shrugged so hard his eyes rolled. "All right. Let's go look at it."

We set out through the graveyard, trailed by the dog. Distracting myself from Mickey's volatility, I tried to imagine the scruffy mongrel as a skeleton. I didn't succeed, to my relief.

We found the grave under a pile of people who were busily scrubbing the headstone and stone fence clean of dirt with stiff-bristled brushes. As we watched the inscription came clear: Hector Purecete, died 1888. Not even close.

Mickey grunted and shot me a smug look. Oh, yeah . . . that showed me, all right.

He started to turn back, but before he could move away I waved to the oldest woman in the grave-cleaning group. She peered up at me and I tried to ask her if she knew of Maria-Luz's Hector Purecete, but her English was nonexistent. Groaning in disgust, Mickey stepped in.

After a rapid exchange, he held her off with a gesture and glanced back at me, his face creased with curiosity. "This is Señora Acoa. She says this is the only Hector Purecete she knows about. But she says a man came asking the same question a few years back. Señora Acoa couldn't help him, either. She says Hector, here, was a soldier. Sounds like a real *pendajo.* She's his, like, great-, great-, great-niece. She doesn't live here anymore and is going back to Coyoacán tomorrow, but she figured they should come and clean up Hector's grave every year. She didn't even know where he was buried until that guy showed up."

"Does she remember the man's name?" I asked, looking at the elderly woman who stood by her ancestor's grave.

Mickey translated for me and this time he was dead serious.

The elderly Señora Acoa replied in a streak of words I couldn't begin to follow, her voice wavering. Then she swayed, putting her hand to her chest. The energy around her shut down to a thin, white line that grew more and more translucent, then began to shift and rise away from her as a messy skein of gold and white light.

I started to jump between them, knowing that the old woman was dying right in front of us, overcome by heat and excitement, her mortality rising off her corporeal form. But Mickey kept talking, his tone going gentle and cajoling, as the gold strands at his fingertips waved and stroked at the old woman, calming her down, smoothing the rising knot of her soul back into its body, easing her back into herself. It was an eerie effect coming from such a determined jerk, and he didn't know he was doing it. Finally the old woman plumped herself down on the edge of the grave with a huff of breath, and fanned herself with her hands until one of her staring family handed her a paper fan shaped like a grinning skull. She cooled herself, catching her breath and settling her life back into her oblivious body as my reluctant assistant returned his attention to me. Nothing in his demeanor showed he knew what had just happened, any more than her family did. He didn't know he'd saved her life, or that he seemed to have some kind of power. He was just Mickey the jerk again.

"She wants to know why you want to know, but I told her you're doing a family a favor. I think she said the other guy's name was Jimenez. A lawyer maybe? She's kinda confused. And a little loco—she thought she had seen this Jimenez guy just today."

I gazed at the tired old woman who was still living in spite of everything. I blinked slowly, getting my thoughts back to the case. "Maybe she did. He died a few years ago in a plane crash," I said. "And yes, he was a lawyer." Hadn't Banda said he knew nothing about Purecete? But his partner had been to this grave. . . .

Mickey's eyes flashed wider. The word that dropped from his mouth was unknown to me, but it was inflected just like "Cool!" He had no idea what was really cool here.

I wondered if Señora Acoa had actually seen Jimenez; maybe her proximity to death had made it possible—this was the day for the violently dead to return, and I couldn't imagine a death much more violent than his. "What else did she have to say?" I asked, trying not to stare too much at the old woman.

"Not much. She said Hector didn't have any kids, so there's only her and her family to look after his grave. She's worn out, but she's afraid her family will forget him after she dies. So she makes them come here every year so he doesn't die the third death."

"Excuse me. What's the third death?"

The lecturing tone was back as he explained. "The first death is the death of the body. The second is when they put us in the ground. Then we can go to Mictlan—

the Land of the Dead—and, y'know, live among the dead. But we can come back for the Día de los Muertos feast with our families, so long as they remember us. That's the third death—being forgotten. That's the real end, when we don't come back 'cause there's no one here for us. But we can be reborn once everyone forgets, so it's not so bad. That's the three deaths."

"How do you know all this stuff?" I asked.

He shrugged. "It's tradition around here. I'm kind of into the death-magic thing. And my, like, great-uncle was supposed to be a black sorcerer or something. It's cool."

Typical goth fascination, though I suspected his went a little deeper and from a more personal angle, whether he understood that or not. To me, the life-magic "thing" he'd just done was a lot cooler.

We both looked at the family, who had returned to sprucing up the grave of Hector number one. We watched in silence a while. Then we turned away, letting them get on with their task as we headed back to the car with the ghostly dog in tow.

"You said Mexicans were not afraid of death," I said. I didn't want to ask him about what he'd done yet, that would only get us off our track, but I hadn't forgotten it.

"We aren't. But no one wants to be forgotten. That's why we have all these parties in the graveyard. We bring the dead all the stuff they loved in life so they can party with us, and that way we remember them like they really were. Not like a body in a casket. Or some saint. It's kind of funny: you're keeping the third death away, but you didn't even know Hector Purecete."

"I'm not sure Maria-Luz did, either."

"Who's Maria-Luz?"

"She's the woman who wanted a dog laid on Hector Purecete's grave."

We were nearly back to the cemetery gates, deep in the twining, boiling mess of the carnival and the confluence of the living and the dead. Mickey wheeled and stared at me. "Not that dog!" he asked, pointing right at the canine phantom panting at my heels.

Startled, I turned and looked for another, corporeal dog, just in case. But there was no animal near enough to be the one he meant. I pointed at the ghost. "This one?"

Mickey nodded. "Yeah."

"Umm . . . this dog's already dead."

He peered at it and the ghost dog let its tongue loll out in a huge yawn. I could see right through its transparent, silver-mist skull to the ground below. Apparently Mickey could, too, because he jumped a little and then looked back to me.

"Fuck me! Where did it come from?"

"I'll tell you in the car on the way to the next cemetery."

We climbed back into the Chevy and again the dog refused to come in. We drove away, the dog vanishing into the misty Grey as we pulled out of the lot.

"How is it that you can see the dog?" I asked as he started the car.

"I just—I just can." He looked a little uncomfortable and hunched his shoulders. "Why are you taking it to this guy's grave?"

I told him about the dog statue—after all, there was no seal of secrecy or confidentiality on the bequest— how it had come to me and what had befallen it at customs. I told him about Maria-Luz Arbildo's odd last request that the statue containing the dog's spirit was to be placed on the grave for which we were searching on November first.

"Weird," he said as we wound onto a narrow road. "Why did she wait so long to give him the dog? He's been dead since 1996."

"She didn't seem to know where he was buried."

Mickey shook his head. "Weird," he repeated. "Hey, at least we've narrowed the search to just two graves.

That Jimenez guy must have done the same thing . . . so why didn't he put the dog on Hector's grave?"

I shook my head. "I don't know. Miss Arbildo was still alive then, so I assume she wanted to do it, but didn't get around to it for some reason." But if she had known which grave to put it on, wouldn't she have given that information in the will? I guessed that Jimenez hadn't told her. But why not?

Mickey scowled. "That's messed up." But he didn't say any more and we reached the next panteon in silence. The dog greeted us at the gate to the cemetery of San Antonio and ran ahead, barking like a puppy chasing butterflies. Mickey watched it dash into the bustling crowds in the graveyard and shook his head.

"Maybe the dog knows where the grave is," he suggested, "but it runs so fast. . . ."

"I'm not even going to try to follow it," I said. "If the grave is here, maybe we'll find the dog nearby when we get there."

"Yeah, right."

The courtyard of Panteon San Antonio was filled with people building elaborate table displays.

"Competition ofrendas," Mickey explained. His sneer wasn't quite as pronounced now. "Each group makes an offering in a traditional style and they compete to see whose is the most authentic, or whatever. Home ofrendas are more plain, they usually have more food and personal stuff. This is mostly for the tourists." He pointed at one table where a pair of men were lashing tall, dusty green plants into a seven-foot-tall arch attached to the front legs. "That's sugarcane—it's traditional. Those guys are Purepeche Indians. See the little clay dog? That's really old school." He stared at me. "Hey . . . was your statue like that one?"

I glanced at the table and saw a small black figurine, much like the one I'd started off with. I walked closer and the men stopped work and stared at me. One of them said something I couldn't translate.

"He says, 'Can I help you?'" Mickey supplied.

"Ask him about the dog," I replied, pointing to the small clay figure sitting on the table with a pile of other items waiting for its place. "Where did it come from? Are all the little dog statues the same?"

Mickey asked and translated his reply. "It's from Mita—that's a village near here. It's a traditional design."

"May I look at it?"

The man listened to Mickey, then shrugged and picked up the clay dog. He offered it to me with a half smile.

I smiled back and took the dog, turning it over and studying the rough shape and paint. It was the same shape, but the black glaze was very ordinary—I'd bet there was no blood or volcanic sand in this one's finish. The lines around the legs were the same, but there was no lightning bolt on this one. The hole in its belly was unpatched, open, and had a fine lip where the glaze had tried to drip around the rim. I handed the dog back to the man, who grinned at me, showing gapped teeth stained by tobacco and coffee.

"Could you ask him if he ever met Maria-Luz or Hector Purecete?"

Both men frowned and shook their heads, apparently telling Mickey they'd never heard of either. We thanked them and headed off to find the caretaker and look for grave number two.

"That statue is almost identical to the one I had that broke," I said as we walked away. "But mine had a white lightning bolt on the side."

"A glyph to keep the spirit inside the dog. Someone worked magic on it."

"I guessed that, but how do you know?"

Mickey shrugged. "Like I said, magic is kind of interesting. . . ."

Mickey seemed to have been studying more than he admitted. I decided to fish a bit. "I was thinking that the bit of hair that fell out was part of the magic, too."

Mickey shot a startled glance at me. "Hair? There was hair inside the dog?"

"Yeah, a little bundle of five or six strands tied with red thread. It looked like human hair, not animal."

"Tied with red thread? Inside the dog? With the light-ning bolt?" He looked both excited and scared. "That's witchcraft."

I frowned at him. The only witch I knew was good, but Mickey was plainly not acquainted with the same sort of witch—and like a lot of young morons, he seemed to think it was kind of sexy.

"It's death magic," he explained. "The dark-side stuff."

"I thought you guys weren't into that death-worship thing."

"Not normal death, the cycle-of-life stuff. Death-cult stuff. It's black magic from the colonial days—half native magic, half Christian mysticism stuff. It's all about *Santísima Muerte*—Most Holy Death, the reaper of souls, Death triumphant over Man." Frightened rever-ence resounded in his tone and set his aura sparking red and gold. "Your Maria-Luz used black magic to hold the dog's spirit inside the statue. Trust me: I know this shit."

"It didn't feel like evil magic when it broke," I said.

He shrugged, pretending sudden disinterest he then undermined by saying, "I wonder why she wanted to put that thing on this guy's grave."

I didn't know, but I wanted to. If I knew who Hector Purecete was to Arbildo, maybe I could figure it out. But we'd have to find his grave first.

Once again we were directed to a grave and picked our way through the people who were cleaning and dec-orating throughout the cemetery. Here, the families and friends of the dead were making sandcastle coffins over the graves, mounding the wet sand up into caskets and even the archetypal long pentagon. Some were bordered with cement block or brick to retain the wet sand, others were freestanding. Other groups were just beginning the process of clearing off the weeds and grasses that had invaded the cemetery during the year, attacking the plants with hoes and hands and, in one case, a big knife, to get down to raw earth.

Panteon San Antonio bore no resemblance to the carefully manicured cemeteries of Seattle, with their endless lawns, or Victorian markers. This was a place of gritty brown earth, punctuated with riots of gold and purple flowers and green foliage. The plants and flowers were being arranged into patterns or pictures on the sand coffins, or lashed into little huts and ofrendas that would straddle the graves when finished. The scent of marigolds was thick and spicy on the air along with the smell of turned earth and green sap.

Once we had cut a path through the crowd, we found a short stone obelisk with a list of names carved on it. Hector Purecete's was there, but listed as one of a dozen men lost at sea in 1982. No grave, wrong date, wrong Hector. The Grey was thick as oatmeal and the ghost dog gamboled around the base of the stone, snapping at the marigold petals floating on the breeze. It glanced up at me and seemed to laugh, giving me a doggy smile.

Mickey glowered and the energy around him pinwheeled orange sparks that looked just like the flower petals. "That guy at the registrar's office just took the money and gave us a list of all the Hector Purecete graves he had," he groused. "He didn't even try to get the right one!"

"Yeah, because your attitude was just so endearing," I reminded him, but I was looking at the dog, which was now pawing around the base of the obelisk with incorporeal paws.

I crouched down to get a look at whatever had caught the dog's attention and saw a loop of blue energy protruding from the ground. Warily, I caught it on my fingers and pulled it up. It came like a long-rooted weed from a flower bed and popped out of the ground with a small crackle of electricity.

A skeletal man wearing a yellow fisherman's coat appeared where the blue bit of energy had left a hole in the ground. I had the impression that he was blinking, even though he had no eyelids or eyes to cover with them.

Mickey stared and jerked back half a step, but the skeleton man didn't notice. He let out a glad exclamation I heard in my head and bent down to ruffle the ghost dog's fur. "Iko! Look how big you got!" He wasn't really speaking English, but the words seemed to come clearly into my head.

The dog frisked around and whined in glee, taking slobbery licks at the skull in between joyous wiggles.

"Is that your dog?" I asked.

The skeleton in the slicker glanced at me. "He was the cook's dog, but we all liked him. He was just a puppy when the old *Dulcia* went down."

"So . . . was Hector Purecete the cook?"

"Hector? No. Hector was a deckhand. I suppose he must have saved Iko. Neither of them drowned."

"His name's on the memorial," I said.

The skeleton looked at the obelisk and laughed, clacking his teeth. "It's wrong. Martin Ramirez got off in Bermuda and was replaced by an American named Lofland. And see, there I am, but they spelled my name wrong," he added, pointing to the name Ernesto Sanchez. "It should say Santara, but my writing on the contract was so bad, they had to guess. No, they must have just taken the crew list from Señor Arbildo and assumed we all died."

"Arbildo?" I asked, surprised.

"*Sí*, he owned the boat."

So there was a connection, but not a clear one. . . . "What became of Hector, then?"

The bony shoulders under the slicker shrugged. "I don't know. He must have been picked up by someone.

He came and looked at the memorial once or twice and used to clean it up for us every year, but then he stopped and people began to forget about us. Most of the crew are gone now, since no one comes to remember us. I have a sister who is building the ofrenda right now at home. I can feel her thinking about me and I can go soon and see all my nieces and nephews. . . ." He trailed off, his empty eye sockets directed just over my shoulder, as if he could really see them, just there, in the field of graves behind me.

"Ernesto," I said, hoping to recapture his attention just a little longer. "Hey, did Hector have a family? Was he married? Had kids?"

"Eh? Oh, Hector? No. He was our Don Juan—always charming the ladies—he couldn't make himself get married and settle down, he said. His family here was all gone. He said. I don't know. We were shipmates, and you know how sailors are with stories. . . ." Now he was pulled away, drifting into the air like a dandelion puff and wafting toward the cemetery gates. "Good-bye, Iko," he called, without looking back. "Be a good dog. . . ."

He vanished into the crowd of living and dead, heading for home, I supposed. I stood up, dusting off my knees and butt, thinking that the memorial must have been raised before anyone realized Hector wasn't dead, so it wasn't really wrong, just premature. I wondered how long he'd been "lost at sea" before he'd shown up again in Oaxaca. . . .

Mickey was gaping at me, but I'm used to that. Most people give me strange looks when they catch me talking to ghosts. But Mickey had seen Ernesto, also, as well as the dog, Iko. "How long have you been seeing ghosts?" I asked.

He was too shaken to lie. "Me? I've always seen them, but only during Día de los Muertos. You too?"

"No. I see them all the time. They aren't usually so helpful, though."

"He didn't seem very helpful. . . ."

"He identified the dog and it seems like a safe bet Iko was rescued and raised by Purecete. But that doesn't really answer how Arbildo had the dog's spirit or why she put it in the statue."

"Yeah, maybe...."

I agreed and started for the car.

Mickey caught my arm. "Hey ... how come you see ghosts? *Mi madre* says it's because my birthday is Todos Santos. Are you ... ?"

I shook my head, slipped his grasp, and kept walking for the car. I wasn't sure this was a good conversation. Or that I liked the sudden avid expression in Mickey's eyes.

"C'mon! Tell me!" he yelled. "Please!"

"I'll tell you in the car. This isn't a good place for it," I conceded.

Mickey nearly dragged me back to the parking lot, flinging open the doors for both of us and sliding behind the wheel clumsily in his frenzy.

As soon as the doors were closed he turned to me again, but I shut him down with a look. "Start the car and drive. It's getting dark and I want to get inside before it's full night."

"But—"

"I'll tell you as you drive. If you don't kill us."

He ground the car to life and drove like Mario Andretti to get us out of the parking lot.

"OK," I started. "I died. That's why I see ghosts."

"Died? No way!"

"Yeah, way. Don't ask why, 'cause I don't know. It just is what it is."

He muttered, prayers or curses, I didn't know. "You don't look dead."

"It was only two minutes. But it was enough. Trust me."

"But you didn't just talk to him. What were you doing? Magic?"

"No. I just ... pull them out. If they want to talk, they

do. Sometimes they don't. Sometimes they try to kill me. Most of them are useless."

"Yeah. I see those, too! They don't really know we're here."

I nodded. "Somehow she must have known. . . ."

"Who? Knew what?"

"Maria-Luz Arbildo. She never met me, but she put me in her will to do this job. She must have known about me, but I don't know why or how or what she expected me to do. I hope I can figure it out before Todos Santos."

"She must have been a *bruja*," Mickey muttered. "Doing black magic and stuff. I'll bet she scryed you out somehow because of the ghost thing."

"Maybe," I conceded. "How would I know?"

"Umm . . . the *Santísima Muerte* magic goes backward. Y'know: right to left and down to up. Counterclockwise and stuff like that."

"But I never saw the woman do any magic," I reminded him. "I didn't know her."

Big-eyed, Mickey nodded and drove. But I could see his thoughts grinding and the gold strands from his fingertips wrapped the steering wheel like a frantic vine.

We approached the last grave on the list as the sun was beginning to paint its farewell on the slice of sky above Oaxaca's mountains. We'd taken a long drive into the hilly countryside to find the small panteon of San Felipe del Agua and then trudged through the crowds and the boiling Grey to discover an abandoned burial plot far in the back, under a stunted tree. Grass and weeds had grown over it undisturbed for years and no one was making an effort to clear it. I heaved a sigh of annoyance and got down on my knees to rip up the corn stalk–like growths obscuring the memorial stone. Mickey knelt down and helped brush the dirt aside, scraping the carving clear enough to read in the dimming light.

This time the list was right: Hector Purecete, born 1929, died 1996. Sixty-seven years old.

Mickey sat back on his heels and studied the filth-crusted memorial stone. "He's been forgotten here."

"Maria-Luz remembered him," I said. I didn't know with what emotion she recalled Hector, however, or what she'd been up to with the dog and its black-magic spirit bundle. I'd have to take a look and see if the red thread wound counterclockwise around it.

"That's an irony," I said, looking at the stone and thinking aloud. "The only person who seems to remember this guy is already dead and has been for years."

"You mean that other ghost? Ernesto? Yeah. And Iko."

I nodded. "Yeah, that's a problem. Iko seems like a nice dog, but who knows what will happen—if there really is black magic involved here? I was hoping to find Hector's family or someone who knew him or Maria-Luz. But the registrar will be closed tomorrow and it's not likely I'll find anyone who knew what their relationship was at this point."

"The ghosts know."

I rubbed my face, breathing in the scent of the broken grasses, the turned earth, and the spicy odor of the marigolds that had already been placed onto the grave decorations and ofrendas proliferating throughout the burial ground. I didn't enjoy interviewing ghosts, even when I knew where to find them. Obstinate, limited beings—when they qualified as beings at all—with axes to grind and personal quirks more annoying and unhelpful than a ward full of recovering heroin addicts. "Yeah, but how would I find the right ghosts?" I asked, tired and, I admit, disappointed. "This is going to suck. Purecete's grave wasn't even in Oaxaca proper but way out in this little mountain village."

Mickey jumped up, beaming in the sudden magenta flare of mountain sunset. "You can call them here! You know how and the ghosts will find you if you make the right offerings—it's the Day of the Dead! The living have forgotten this guy, but the dead haven't!"

I stared at him. "I'm not sure I'm following you.... The instructions just said to clean the grave and put the dog on it."

"Yeah, yeah. Clean the grave, but you should do the whole thing. Decorate, make an ofrenda. Put out food and drink and stuff—throw a party for old Hector Purecete, and the ghosts of his friends will show up for it! It's not just the living who come visiting the grave-yard, you know. Tomorrow is for the *angelitos*—the little kids. We can make an ofrenda and bring it here for them. If he ever had any kids, or if his family ever had any that haven't died the third death, they'll come. Then on Sun-day we can make the party for the rest of 'em—and Hec-tor. I'll have to hang out with Tía Mercedes, but I can help you first and come back later. Tía's big on this stuff, she'll understand—she'll probably even cook extra food for you if we go shopping early enough."

I tried not to groan at the thought. "What about the dog?" I asked.

He frowned. "I'm not sure. Maybe if you don't bring the clay bits and hair, it won't matter, even if his ghost comes along."

The ghost dog had come back from a nose-guided tour of the graveyard to sit down beside me and pant through his doggy grin. He looked increasingly like a real dog and less like the remnant of one. I wondered what he'd be like come Sunday night.

I looked around and saw the deepening colors of the sky. Shadows writhed with the spirits of the violently dead waiting to emerge once darkness fell. I shuddered and hoped we wouldn't have to go past the *zócalo* to-night and its slaughtered teachers.

"Let's get out of here," I suggested.

Mickey jumped up and we nearly ran back to the car. Once in it, he chattered half in excitement and half in relief of terror, trying to persuade me his plan was solid. I would never have thought of throwing a party for ghosts. Mickey waxing enthusiastic over it was downright creepy to watch. He dodged silvery clots of horror as we barreled through the falling twilight.

Back in the guesthouse, normalcy reigned and most people would have no idea of the gruesome sights and sounds playing out in the night beyond the doors. Over dinner Mickey wheedled his aunt into agreeing to cook extra food for my ghost party. He finally let me go at the door of my room with a warning to be up early for our shopping trip. I hate shopping ... especially in the morning. The surreal quality of the whole day left me dizzy and grateful to crawl into bed.

Bundled up against the chilly morning, we had to shed our coats by the time we were carrying home the third load of the stuff on which Mickey had insisted: colored paper and strings of paper banners; armfuls of flowers; incense cones; food; sweets; candles; tiny toys; papier-mâché skeletons going about their daily business, including one lady called Catrina in an elaborate hat; and a set of combs and brushes for the dead to tidy themselves with, once they arrived for the party. If I didn't know better, I'd have thought he was enjoying himself, but of course Mickey managed to drag me thither and yon with disgusting amounts of energy, while still slouching, glowering, and shooting barbed comments, though almost none of them were now directed at me. I bought him a sugar skull with his name on it as a birthday present, getting a twisted, uncertain smile in return.

Iko followed us back and forth, barking and running through the stalls, playing with skeleton children and chasing skeleton rats. The odors of food and flowers and cones of copal incense waiting to be burned mingled with the odor of wet streets and warm bodies. Color rose in dust devils from the power grid of the Grey and spun off Mickey's shape like the golden spines of a religious icon. I felt light-headed and found it difficult to tell the Grey from the real, if not for the hard shapes of skulls and bones where I would normally expect flesh. More than once I excused myself to a specter after stepping on it and each time they nodded to me as any living person would. Mickey stared at me with a strange yearning expression that disappeared under the glower as soon as he noticed my attention.

I wasn't sure this crazy plan was going to work, but it was the best thing either of us had come up with. And frankly, it was nice to get out of the guesthouse before the smells of food overwhelmed me. Mercedes Villaflores and her daughters had been cooking since before dawn, starting with the *pan de muerto*—traditional loaves of bread that smelled of orange and spices and had dough bones crossed on top. By the time I'd gotten up, there'd already been half a dozen of them set on the patio counter to cool; excess seemed to run in the family.

After our shopping, Mickey dropped me off at the cemetery in San Felipe del Agua to clean the grave site, promising to come back with the ofrenda supplies later. Then he dashed back down the hill to join his family for their own work party. As I crossed the cemetery gate, Iko the ghost dog appeared and followed me to Hector Purecete's plot, making scent-led loops and discursions across the path as we went.

The morning was giving way to afternoon and in the thin air at fifty-five hundred feet, the sun warmed the graveyard and set the odors of earth and work, flowers and food toward the blue crown of the heavens above. Iko performed an inspection of the site and gave it his doggy approval as I rolled up my sleeves and began clearing weeds, hearing the chatter of others working at family plots, or setting up vendor booths in the square and street nearby. Some musicians started practicing in the distance, serenading our labors in fits and starts. After a while, the ghost dog hied off to hunt ghost rodents, leaving me alone with the weeds.

A while later, I paused to wipe the sweat off my face and found an old man in a wide-brimmed hat squatting at the edge of my efforts, grinning at me. I had to look hard through the thickened and colorful Grey to be sure he was no ghost, for he looked more like a vision than a man. But that might have been the elevation and my own sleep-deprived brain talking.

He held out a clear glass bottle. "Agua?"

I took the bottle gratefully, muttering my "gracias," and sipped the warm water. It tasted of deep rock wells.

"I never see a gringa working out here before," he said, watching me drink.

"Never been here before," I replied, pushing my clinging hair back and returning the bottle to him.

He put the bottle down, digging its bottom into the dirt I'd softened with my weeding at the edge of the grave. "You come for this man's angelitos?"

"I don't know if he had any. Did you know him?"

The dark-tanned old man shook his head. "No. I live here all my life and I never hear of him until they bury him here. And no one comes to this grave for a long time. Until you. Why?"

"A woman named Maria-Luz Arbildo died last week and she wanted me to come here and take care of the grave."

"Huh. But she never come here. I never see any woman here before."

"No. She didn't know where the grave was. I had to find it. You ever heard of her?"

He narrowed his eyes and searched the ground for his memory, brushing pebbles and bits of weed away from the headstone. "No. Antonio Arbildo lived here, long time ago, but he moved away. Old man, then. He get rich, the whole family go to the D.F.—Distrito Federal, Mexico City," he explained with a nod. "I'm a little boy, then—so tall," he added, holding his hand up about two feet from the ground, and cackling. He shot an amused glance at me from the corner of his yellowed eyes. The ghost of Iko trotted back from his hunting and threw himself down in the dirt about two feet from the old man with a contented dog sigh. The old man made no comment.

I nodded. Another interesting connection, but not complete. "Are there Arbildos buried in this panteon? Maybe Maria-Luz?"

Again he shook his head, his gnarled stick fingers digging into the ground to pull a weed. "Not her. Some a long time ago, *sí*. Not now." He pointed to a group of equally abandoned graves nearby. "There."

Hector Purecete had been buried within sight of the Arbildos of San Felipe, yet it seemed Maria-Luz had never found him on her trips to Oaxaca. But with the two false graves Mickey and I had found, maybe that wasn't so strange. Of course the Arbildos of San Felipe and those of Mexico City weren't necessarily the same family, but I doubted it.

I nodded to the old man and got up, unkinking my work-stiff knees and back, to go look at the graves of the Arbildos. The most recent had been buried in 1943. When I got back to Purecete's grave, the old man was gone, but his water bottle still stood in the soft earth between the gravestone and Iko's napping form sprawled in the dirt. I looked around for the man. A dozen hats identical to his bobbed in the field of graves, but I couldn't spot the old man under one. I took another sip of the water and went back to work, thinking Iko had it good.

By two o'clock I'd gotten the weeds cleaned up and the plot squared away. Some helpful live children helped me find stones to replace the missing border around the grave, begging, in return, for *"mi calavera,"* which confused me until Mickey showed up.

He made a face at them and started digging into one of the boxes of ofrenda decorations. "They want these," he explained, dragging out a box of small sugar skulls, coffins, and lambs we'd purchased in the market that morning. "Like your trick or treat, but with skulls."

He handed me the box and snapped at the kids to go away as soon as they had their "calavera" in their sticky fists.

"Need to work, here!" he added to me, unfolding a small card table he'd snatched from the guesthouse. "Usually the ofrenda's at home, but yours will have to be here."

The ghost dog sat up and watched us work. We got a few odd looks from the humans, too, as we put up the decorations, but no one came to ask what we were doing. Mickey helped me bend long, slender poles into arches over the table and attach them to the legs. Then we put colored paper over it all and hung up the paper banners, which were decorated with punched silhouettes of skeletons dancing, riding bicycles, eating, and generally carrying on. We made patterns on the grave with the marigolds, magenta cockscomb flowers, and greenery, edging it all with white candles in tiny glass jars.

Mickey looked around. "You should go wash while I put out the food—and bring back water in the big bowl for the spirits to wash in, too."

I shrugged, not minding a pause to clean the dirt and sweat off my face and hands while Mickey took over—he had managed to avoid the really filthy work of weeding, edging, and shoring up the grave, after all. Iko dogged me to a standpipe where a few other people were washing up and filling containers with water for flowers or washing. The old man was standing near the water spigot and grinned at me as I approached.

"It is going well, your ofrenda?"

"I think so. Does it look OK?"

He glanced toward Purecete's grave. "Sí. Is very nice for the angelitos—white is good."

"Mickey picked the color."

"Really?" the old guy said, raising his eyebrows. "Surely for him, red is more likely."

I turned to glance back at Mickey. He did have a lot of red in his aura. . . .

"You mean Mickey?" I asked.

"Your *amigo joven, sí*. So very angry . . ." He shook his head.

I stared at the old man. "What is it about Oaxaca? Is everyone around here tuned in to the freaky frequency?" I asked.

His laugh was like sandpaper. "Only you, *pequeña faisán*. But, you are staying to see the angelitos?"

"Sí," I answered, turning back to the immediate task, putting my hands under the cold water that streamed from the pipe, and then throwing several handfuls onto my sticky face. Iko stuck his muzzle into the water and tried to drink it, but I wasn't sure any was making it down his ghostly throat, no matter how fast his spectral tongue was going. "Maybe it's not so bad that Mickey's supposed to be home with his family tonight."

"Maybe." The old man nodded. "I also must go tonight, so I bid you *buenas noches*. Dress warm—the night takes the heat away. And give your amigo good wishes from Tío Muñoz, eh?"

"I will, *gracias*," I replied, filling the washbowl for the spirits of dead children. My hands full, I nodded again to him and turned to head back to the plot, wondering what Mickey was up to.

"Buena suerte," the man said with a chuckle as I started off.

I turned my head to look back at him over my shoulder and saw him scratch Iko's head, smiling. I guess I wasn't even surprised. Then he turned and walked away, vanishing into the crowd with a golden glitter in his wake. I stood a moment staring after him, not sure what he was; nothing about him seemed ghostly, yet in the mess of the active Grey of Oaxaca, I hadn't noticed he had no aura. What was he? I frowned, holding the heavy bowl of water. Iko pawed at my knee and barked, prancing impatiently on the path.

I shook off my surprise and walked to rejoin Mickey.

While I'd been gone, Mickey had laid out a small feast of sweets, soda pop, and pan de muerto as well as some more substantial food—all provided by his aunt. Small plastic toys were scattered among the cockscomb flowers that we'd piled up around a stack of empty boxes at the back of the table and an arc of small teacups and saucers surrounded a dish for the copal incense. A dozen more white candles now stood on the boxes. It looked like an album cover for something gothic and creepy.

"Nice, huh?"

"Umm . . . yeah. These ghosts eat a lot. . . ."

Mickey shrugged. "They eat the spirit of the food. My cousins say the food they leave behind has no calories." He barked a derisive laugh. He pointed to the end of the table. "Put the water, comb, and towel where the hot bottle is."

I saw a large vacuum flask where he pointed.

"Tía Mercedes made hot chocolate. You can put it on the ground till you need it," he said. "Pour some for the angelitos after you light the candles and the incense— they should come when they smell it. And there's a box under the ofrenda with some food and a blanket and stuff for you. Think you can make it?"

"It's not as cold as a stakeout during a Seattle winter."

He snorted. "Gonna be empty up here. Most people do this at home." Mickey gave me an assessing look that clearly found me a bit wanting.

"I think I can handle it," I said.

Yet another shrug as he started gathering up the excess supplies. "The angelitos come at four and stay until the morning. You'll have to do it all again tomorrow for the adults, too. I'll pick you up when the sun comes up."

"Hey, Mickey, Tío Muñoz says Happy Birthday."

He jumped back from me. "What?"

"An old man near the water said I should tell you he sends his good wishes."

He stared at me. "Tío Muñoz? *Mierda!* He's a legend in my family. He's a . . . a . . ."

"Ghost? Didn't look like a ghost. . . ."

Mickey was shaking his head and gathering the excess stuff in a hurry. "No, no. . . . He's the one—you know: I said about my great-uncle? What's the word . . . a bad wizard."

"Warlock?"

He shook his head. "No. . . . Not a *brujo*. He's . . . a black sorcerer. Undead." He threw the last of the materials into a box and snatched it up against his chest, eyes wild—which was not what I'd have expected. "I'm going back to Tía Mercedes. You'll be fine, yeah?"

"Yeah . . . ," I said, not sure why he was freaking so thoroughly, since his Tío Muñoz wasn't any kind of undead I knew.

"Yeah, right. OK. I'll be back for you in the morning. Don't go talking to Tío Muñoz! Don't believe what he says!"

Iko and I followed him with the rest of the boxes and loaded them into the Chevy under the weight of Mickey's red-and-orange brooding. Then we watched him drive away, leaving the ghost dog and me in the emptying panteon as the hour of dead children approached.

The last of the homeward-bound walked out of the gate—two small children in slightly rumpled clothes—strewing a path of marigold petals for the dead. I watched them lay the deep orange line down the road until they disappeared around a bend in a mood of strange solemnity. I walked back to the grave, Iko dancing before me all the way.

The ghost dog seemed more real than ever, if still a bit translucent. As the long shadow of the mountain began to steal the light, that became less apparent, but a new oddity began to show around him: a blue glow like marshlight that flickered over the dog shape and cast it into strange silhouette against the pockets of twilight forming in the cemetery as night crept forward.

I unfolded a camp stool from the box and set it aside, paused to put on my coat, and dug deeper for a box of kitchen matches. As the church bell began pealing four, I lit the candles and the copal, sending the sweet, musky scent into the cooling air. The breeze stirred the grasses near the fence to rattling. Smoke and Grey mingled, sparking with gold and white lights, and I could hear the Grey humming, the shapes of the mountains glowing in the silvery mist as great bulks of power.

Something splashed into the water bowl and I turned with a jerk to see nothing, no small shape lurking near the table end, as I'd half expected. I shivered as my skin prickled with a premonition of movement nearby. The darkness was still only a threat, but a presence seemed to gather with it, though nothing stepped forth. Yet.

I poured hot chocolate into one of the teacups and sat down to wait while afternoon advanced toward evening. The ghost dog lay down beside me and smiled with secret thoughts. We waited, swirled in the dizzying odors of the night and the sound of distant music from houses just out of sight, alone in the hush of sacred anticipation in the doorway to the Land of the Dead.

Something brushed past me, giggling. Iko barked and chased the formless whisper of laughter across the burial ground toward the iron gates. Then nothing. The ghost dog returned and threw himself down on the ground with a dog sigh. Candles smoked and the stream of incense swayed upward like a charmed cobra. The muttering emptiness of the cemetery held sway long past sunset, past the eight o'clock peal from the church tower.

I renewed the hot chocolate in the cup and sipped a little myself, finding it more bitter and spicy than American chocolate. It went better with the sandwich Mickey's aunt had packed for me than the coffee did, but I thought I'd better save it in case of tiny haunts. Maybe it was because I was thinking of it, but that was when a little cup of chocolate on the table rattled and I looked again at the ofrenda.

One of the cups was moving in its saucer, tilting forward and back. Tiny silver-mist hands clutched for it and missed again and again. I stood up and picked up the cup, saying, "Here, let me help you."

I held the cup low and filled it to the brim. Then I offered it down around my knees, holding it still until I felt something tug on it. I let myself slip all the way into the Grey, looking for whatever was pulling on the cup.

A skeleton child, barely as tall as the table, reached for the cup. Its bony, incorporeal hands met the porcelain, but couldn't grip. I tipped the cup and watched the steaming chocolate dribble onto the ground while the foggy skeleton seemed to nibble at the edge of the cup. It pushed the cup away and clacked its teeth in satisfaction.

The toys on the table moved. Smears of color hovered around the ofrenda, lined up in front of the other, empty, cups. I poured chocolate into all of them and watched shadows of the cups tilt and rise as spectral hands reached for the sweets. There was a burst of chatter— like radio static—and a dozen small skeletons dressed in the memories of their best clothes appeared around the table. They weren't as well formed as the adult ghosts I'd seen—as if they hadn't had time to get the knack of being alive before they were dead. None of the chatter was quite understandable to me—unlike the adult ghosts I'd talked to—coming through to my mind only in Spanish.

Iko jumped to his feet again and began trotting around the little ghosts, sniffing them, but he returned disgruntled and disappointed to my side and sat down with a huff of breath. Apparently none of the skeletal kids was familiar.

I felt small hands on my knees and plucking at my sleeves. I looked down and found two small skeletons dressed in cloudy white dresses looking back up at me with empty eye sockets.

I'm not much of a kid person, so I never know what

to say or do when faced with children. I had no idea if the ghosts of children knew any more than they had when alive, but even children have information. I squatted down, feeling my bad knee pop.

"No hablo español muy bien," I said, probably mangling what little I remembered from years living in Los Angeles. With my luck they didn't speak anything else, but sometimes ideas came through with ghosts, even when the language was foreign, as they had with the ghost of Ernesto Santara. *"Ustedes habla inglés?"*

They turned their skulls on their slender spines in unison: no. They didn't bother to talk at all, but, with a shiver, I knew they were twins then, and they wanted to know why I was in their graveyard. No one had come for them in a long time and they were lonely—was I a relative of theirs? How I knew these thoughts I couldn't begin to tell you.

I shook my head and pointed to Purecete's memorial stone. "I'm looking for him. And for Maria-Luz Carmen Arbildo. Maria-Luz y Hector."

Two skulls tilted in curiosity as if to say, "Why those two?" while a toy truck pushed its way across the dirt nearby guided by a misty skeletal boy.

"Umm . . . ," I started, not sure how to explain. *"Como* Maria-Luz . . . umm . . . knows?" I stumbled through the language, tapping the side of my head and hoping the sign translated somehow. "Hector?"

The skulls consulted each other with a glance of unseen eyes. They turned back to me and spoke as one. The words pushed the concept into my head, naked and complete, but not in English. *"Él es su padre."*

Her father. Whose burial place she did not seem to know, whose name she did not have. "Oh," I breathed, the situation both more clear and less. Why the black-magic present, then? What was the nature of that paternity that she sent such a dubious gift?

The twin ghosts beckoned me to follow and they drifted toward the Arbildo plot. Leaving the chocolate and the ofrenda behind, I followed them and Iko followed me.

The graves of the Arbildos were crowded with tiny skeletons and strange, half-formed shapes of silvery energy thick as clay moving in some somber dance. The two skeletal girls floated through the weird party and stopped before a grave with an unusual double cross of gilded iron from which the gold had flaked until only shreds remained. *"Nuestra madre y nosotros."*

This was the grave of Dulcia Maria-Carmen Ochoa Arbildo, wife of Antonio, and her two daughters, Carmen and Lucia, who had all died in April of 1936. The girls had been four years old. Dulcia had been twenty-five.

"Por qué—" I started, but the ghosts of Carmen and Lucia pointed their bony fingers at the crowd of small spirits.

"Vea: nuestros hermanos y hermanas."

I looked. Beside the grave huddled a knot of unformed shapes, the features of lives they never lived flickered and changed, fluid as water, over half faces the size of my fist. I'd seen this before; they were transient souls, in flux between one life and the next. Grave upon grave across the plot was littered with the reminders of children who had never been born, or died while still infants and toddlers. They were everywhere, generation after generation of the family's bad genetic luck and horrific accident. It seemed as if the Arbildos of San Felipe had been cursed.

Maybe, against all tradition, this was something the family preferred to forget. Hardly a wonder, then, if Antonio Arbildo had removed his family from this place as soon as he had the money to do so. Not too surprising if he had named a boat for his ill-fated wife, or that the boat had been lost with everyone aboard, except a single man and a dog.

A dark shape started to push the grid into some new

form, struggling against the strength of the Grey's energy lines. Iko barked suddenly and the deep humming of the Grey hit a sour note. The ghosts flickered out with a collective gasp. The shape collapsed back into darkness and I was alone again in the graveyard.

I still didn't have all the pieces, but an idea was forming in my head. Dead children and a daughter by the wrong father ... I returned to my camp stool and sat again beside Purecete's grave, pouring out the last of the chocolate and wondering if the ghosts would return.

They didn't.

Dawn came up slowly in cold shades of blue, while I huddled, expectant and ultimately disappointed, in the empty panteon. It was still lit only by candles and drifted with copal smoke when Mickey arrived.

He avoided my glance and packed up the food and chocolate, the toys and gewgaws, in glowering silence. I let him. My body was too tired and my brain too full of strange threads weaving slowly and incompletely into a tapestry I didn't yet understand to want to add the frustration of cross-examining my volatile escort to the mix. I followed him back to the Chevy, hardly noticing that Iko had disappeared with the dawn and didn't follow us to the car this time.

Back at the guesthouse, I fell into bed and slept six hard hours. I was still a bit groggy when I turtled out of my bedroom and down to the empty sala about noon. The visitors had all gone out, most of the family was at church or in the kitchen. Mercedes Villaflores glanced out of the kitchen window and waved to me to come inside.

"*Buenos días!* Did you enjoy your evening?" she asked, immediately putting a cup of coffee and a plate of food on the counter for me.

"Yes," I replied, not sure if "enjoy" was the right word, but certain I'd learned something, if I could shake it into clarity. "Where's Mickey—Miguel?" I sipped the coffee and felt it kick my system back up to speed. I looked for Iko, but didn't see him, and was just wondering about that when Mercedes replied.

"Oh, he's still asleep." She shrugged and returned to her stove, chatting over her shoulder. "Teenagers . . . You know."

Thinking about the missing ghost dog and Mickey made me think of the cemetery. "Mercedes . . . who's Tío Muñoz?"

"Tío Muñoz? Where did you hear of him?"

"Mickey mentioned him."

"Ah! That boy . . . he's such a trouble. Muñoz is . . . the family bogeyman. You know: the crazy uncle your mama tells you will take you away in the night if you don't finish your supper. *Totalmente loco en la cabeza,*" she added, knocking a knuckle against her temple, as if sounding a melon for ripeness. "He was accused of working black magic long ago, but he run up into the hills and disappeared. I think, if he is alive, he is no trouble to anyone, just a crazy old man. If not . . . maybe he'll come to dinner tonight, eh?"

She laughed; clearly she didn't feel the same horror as her nephew, but then . . . she wasn't fascinated with black magic, as Mickey was.

"Do you know anything about the Arbildo family that used to live in San Felipe del Agua?" I asked.

She just shook her head.

I poked at my food and thought. I was seeing a picture that was not at all pretty. I wished I was sure what had turned Maria-Luz from sweet on Jimenez to sour. Why hadn't Jimenez told her where Purecete was buried? Was that the key? Or had she discovered something else?

I fished the little baggie of statue shards from my jacket pocket and stared at the bundle of hairs, tied with red thread, wound counterclockwise. The magic goes backward. . . . Like the writing on the paper. I could see the slip of notepaper clearly in my mind: the letters cramped on the left, expansive on the right, as if it had been written backward, running out of space.... She'd scryed me out through the Grey, talking to ghosts through a black-magic connection, as Mickey had described. Death magic, blood magic ... Had Maria-Luz sacrificed the dog ... ? No, Iko was dead long before she knew about me—possibly before I was a Greywalker—back when Jimencz died in a plane crash. Just how long had she had the statue waiting for the right grave? Why had she wanted to put Iko's spirit, wound in black magic, on Jimenez's grave?

Tío Muñoz seemed more interested in Mickey than in me. But if he was—or had been—a black sorcerer, maybe he was interested in the black magic I was carrying in my pocket as well as his great-nephew. You can't count on much about black magic or bogeymen, though he didn't seem to approve of Mickey's personal darkness.

I needed to talk to Maria-Luz or Hector Purecete. I hoped one or both would show up once darkness fell at San Felipe del Agua.

Mickey scuffed into the kitchen looking morose and wan.

"We still on for tonight, Mickey?" I asked.

"Huh? Tonight?"

"Yeah. My little ghost party at the panteon, remember? You're going to help me with the setup, right?"

He looked relieved I hadn't said anything about Tío Muñoz. "Yeah, right. Setup. Sure."

"What time do we need to head up the mountain? Four?"

"Dusk. Whatever. Tía Mercedes won't mind if I'm back late for the party here."

She said something in Spanish that sounded like she'd be happier the later he was.

"OK," he replied. "We can leave at four with the food and stuff."

"Cool. See you down here, then," I agreed, carrying

my empty coffee cup to the sink and allowing Mickey to escape.

I walked down to the *zócalo* and found a cafe table to occupy while I made a phone call. The layers of spirits and magic were thicker and brighter than ever, surging like an ocean in the plaza and spilling into the streets leading to it. I dialed Quinton's pager and waited for him to call me back. Quinton was still paranoid about the possibility of being rediscovered by his ex-boss, so the easily tracked technology of cell phones was one he chose to do without.

About half an hour later, as I was working on a sunburn, he returned my call.

"Hey."

"Hey, yourself. Need a favor."

"Shoot."

"I don't have Internet access here, so can you run some searches for me and get back with information before four p.m. here?"

"That's . . . two here. Yeah, I can do that. What are the search terms?"

"I need everything you can find on the death and bio of a Mexico City lawyer named Jimenez. Sorry I don't know the first name, but he was the partner of a guy named Guillermo Banda. Jimenez died in a plane crash a few years ago. Also anything on the Arbildo family that owned a ship or boat called the *Dulcia* that sunk in 1982, based out of Mexico. And look for any connections between Jimenez's firm and Arbildo—especially anything shady or questionable."

"Arbildo. That's the woman who left you the dog."

"Her family and her lawyer, yeah. There's something strange going on between them and, so far, death hasn't proved to be much of a barrier. I'm also wondering if Maria-Luz was adopted, but it's doubtful there'd be any record of that on the Internet."

"You never know. I'll see what I can get and call you back."

I thanked Quinton and hung up before going out to walk around the *zócalo* and take a closer look at the Grey grid of Oaxaca. There were a lot of things about the way energy flowed here that were different from Seattle's grid and I didn't want to be surprised that night. I needed a little local practice with the power lines before I felt comfortable about my ability to deal with the potential conflicts that might be in store. I tried a variation of the ghost-pull that had brought up Ernesto Santara and got Iko, as I'd hoped. I was pretty sure I'd be able to banish him again, if I had to. I still had no idea what part he had been intended to play at Hector's grave.

Quinton called back and I took notes about the perfidy of lawyers; hard financial times; an unhappy schoolgirl with bad, black habits; and the sinking of insured boats, while leaning against an old church wall, cooled by the shade of the stones and the ice-water feeling of the rising tide of ghosts. The ghost dog panted at my feet, tongue lolling onto the bricks of the plaza.

A silvery skeleton dressed in a dark vest and trousers paused to pet the dog and raised his head to me. *"Éste es tu perro?"*

"Hang on," I told Quinton. "My dog? No," I replied to the skeleton man. "You know this dog? Uh ... *Usted* ... uh ..." I stumbled through the language as badly as ever, but the ghost seemed to know what I meant.

He shook his skull and clacked something I didn't catch, but the meaning seemed clear enough. It wasn't his dog, but it might have been Estancio Rivera's dog. I pointed at Iko. *"Esta perro?"*

The skeleton nodded his skull vigorously. *"Sí! Es Iko!"*

Iko rolled over in the spectral dust and offered his belly for rubbing.

I returned to my phone call while the skeleton man gave Iko some attention. "Is there any mention in those files of an Estancio Rivera?" I asked Quinton.

"Not that I've seen, but Rivera is about the most common name in Mexico after Garcia. This is in Oaxaca, right . . . ?"

I could hear his fingers speeding on a keyboard. "Yeah."

"Huh. This is kind of weird. A guy named Estancio Rivera disappeared from a Mexico City hotel room in 1981, presumed dead. Wallet, ID, and clothes were found, but not his money or the man. ID was from Oaxaca. He worked in a mezcal distillery and guess who owned it."

"Arbildo?"

"Give the little lady a cigar!"

"Damn," I muttered. Did I have it? Was it that easy? Hector was the missing Estancio as well as Maria-Luz's real father. He'd vanished in Mexico City, where the Arbildos lived. Then changed his name and taken a post on an Arbildo ship that sunk. . . . He'd been "dead" twice before he died for good.

The skeleton ghost stood up, tipped his hat, and walked off after wishing me a "Buenas noches." I nodded at him and noticed the shadow of the church was nearly across the plaza now. The tower bells began tolling four.

"I have to run. Thanks for the help."

"No problem, but I would like to hear the story. . . ."

"I'll take you to dinner when I get back and tell you the whole thing. Right now I have an appointment in a graveyard."

I shut off the phone and ran back toward the Villaflores guesthouse. Iko barked and ran along beside me. We skittered into the doorway together and straight into a glowering Mickey.

"Thought you'd ditched me."

"No," I panted. "Just lost track of time. You ready to go?"

He frowned at me, clearly teetering on a decision.

"Come on, Mickey. You didn't come up here just for

the family celebration." I leaned in close to him and breathed my words into his ear. "You want the magic."

He bit his lip.

I wanted all the help I could get, and even if Mickey didn't know what he could do, he could still be useful if things went bad. And a plain "please" was not going to work with him.

He gave a sudden, hard nod. "I'm coming."

We grabbed our coats and boxes and bundled into the car as fast as possible. Iko sat and waited patiently, then vanished to meet us at the graveyard.

The sun was already gone by the time we reached the panteon at San Felipe del Agua. A procession by candlelight was wending to the cemetery, carried on a wave of music. We parked and joined the crowd that surged into the cemetery, Iko reappearing as before, just inside the gates.

The ofrenda and decorations were untouched and it took only a few minutes to put out the food and drink, trinkets, cigarettes, mezcal, and wash water, to light the candles and the copal. We both sat down to wait while the ghost dog circled the graves, sniffing.

The odors of food, flowers, incense, and alcohol floated into the air on mariachi music and the chatter of living humans while the Grey hummed like a generator nearing overload. The thin silver mist-world seemed to quake as the ghosts flooded out, eager, hungry, happy. They rushed into the gap between the worlds with a roar. I gasped at the explosive upheaval of the Grey and Mickey stared, crouching on his stool like an angular gargoyle.

"How many do you see?" I asked.

"Thousand. . . . More than ever. And there's . . . stuff. Like worms. Everywhere."

Everyone who can see it sees it differently, I guess.

"Where's our man?" Mickey looked around, shivering. "Maybe . . . the dog?"

"Yeah, maybe it's time. Iko," I called, reaching down to pat the ground on top of the grave, sending up a sudden gust of marigold scent and the odor of earth. Iko ran onto the grave and sat down. Nothing changed.

Remembering the children and their chocolate, I put out my hand. "Hand me that mezcal, Mickey."

Quivering, Mickey picked up the bottle and slapped it into my outstretched hand. "You want a drink?"

"No. But I think Señor Purecete might—or Estancio Rivera, if he prefers." I twisted the bottle open and spilled an ounce or two onto the grave next to Iko. The ground seemed to swallow it, groaning and heaving a cloud of yellow and gold sparks into the air.

Someone crawled up from the grave.

He was probably a slim man in life, judging by the narrow-cut clothes his skeletal form wore in death. He had a jaunty hat on his skull and a scarf tied around the absent circumference of his neck. A shadow of flesh clung over the skeleton, giving it a blurry, out-of-focus look. Iko whined and wriggled at the ghost's feet, rolling in the dirt and showing his belly.

"Oh . . . Iko," the shade breathed, the words coming clear into my head. "Where is your mistress?" He scratched the dog as it quivered in delight.

"Not here yet," I offered. "But I think she'll show up soon."

Mickey glanced around and I followed his lead, but no one was paying us any particular attention. They were all busy and the sounds of the fiesta ramping up to last the whole night through drowned the oddness of any conversation we might have.

I held out the bottle and the ghost took it. "*Gracias, Señora.* It is a long time since I had a drink with a lovely lady." A spectral twin of the mezcal bottle rose to his mouth and he poured a long shot down his transparent throat.

"Ernesto said you were a lady's man," I said.

The ghost of Hector Purecete belched and lowered the bottle. "Ernesto? From the *Dulcia*? Poor fellow.

Good-hearted, not so good-headed. I'm sorry about the crew. It was only me Arbildo wanted drowned."

"So it wasn't an accident that the boat sank when you were on it. Jimenez found a way to sink it for Arbildo. The insurance company wasn't sure, but they suspected it. You know they paid off, eventually, right?"

"Oh, *sí*. It was an old boat. Kill two birds with one stone—heh. Or two problems with one hole in the hull. He didn't want her to know, or he'd have just had me cut to pieces in an alley in the Distrito."

"Leon Arbildo, you mean."

"*Sí*," Hector replied, taking another gulp of ghostly mezcal. "Leon had a head for business."

"What was her name?"

"Who?"

"Leon Arbildo's wife. You met her at the mezcal distillery, didn't you?"

"Ohhhh . . . Consuela. No, we met at a party. She was very bored. So was I. But of different things." Hector drew closer to the table and looked it over, pausing to scratch Iko behind the ears and pat his sides roughly. "I imagined I was so very suave she fell at my feet, but I suppose it was truly that I was new and not like Leon." He laughed and his yellow teeth snapped together with a sound like castanets. "Youth is arrogant and full of folly."

He put out a skeleton claw for the towel and water. Mickey and I watched him in silence as the ghost washed his nonexistent face and combed his memory of hair. Then the specter straightened his scarf and resettled the hat on his head before surveying the spread of food.

Mickey's eyes couldn't stretch any wider without the orbs falling out, I thought. "They never speak," he whispered. "I never hear them speak. . . ."

"Get used to it," I muttered back. "Once they know you can hear them, they don't shut up."

The boy jerked his head toward me, drawing a breath

that shook in his throat. He was more excited than the dog.

Hector—I couldn't think of him as Estancio after all this time—had torn off a hunk of phantom bread and sat on the edge of his grave, munching it. His teeth clicked and ground together. "I thought I would never taste pan de muerto again. It's very good."

"Mi—mi tía lo hizo," Mickey stammered, replying in Spanish, since he heard Hector in that language, just as I heard him in English.

Hector looked at him for the first time and the boy flinched back at the uncanny gaze from the ghost's empty eye sockets.

"Your aunt? You must thank her for me. My Carmencita—my little girl Leon called Maria-Luz—could not bring me food and drink for these many years. She was afraid the lawyers would discover her knowledge of me and of what they would do if she came here. I left my home to be with Consuela—her mother—and I hid myself as a long-dead man, Hector Purecete, who would not mind. At first I did it to be near Consuela and later, when they thought they'd killed me, to watch over my daughter."

Bones and wings rustled in the darkness and a sigh of unearthly wind brought another ghost to the party.

"Papa."

We all turned to look at the smaller spirit that had walked up to Hector Purecete's grave. She wouldn't have been very tall in life, but she had probably had her father's build. A gleaming, oil-black nimbus surrounded her, shivering off the white surface of her dress. The memory of her face was still strong, creating a translucent veil of phantom flesh and expression over the visible bones of her skull. So this was Maria-Luz Carmen Arbildo.

The dog jumped into the air and barked in joy, running to tangle under her feet.

The ghost woman laughed and patted the dog. Then

she looked sharply at me. "You brought him. But what happened? He should not be loose already."

"The statue was broken at customs," I answered. "I think Guillermo Banda paid someone to do it."

"That bastard . . . I hate him. More than I ever hated Jimenez for what he did."

I opened my mouth to ask her how she'd known what Jimenez had done—though I thought I knew—but was cut off by a shriek of eldritch wind.

"Don't dare!"

"Dare what? To tell the truth?" Maria-Luz screamed, turning to the latest arrival.

This skeleton ghost was dressed in a suit—possibly the one he'd died in—much like Banda's suit. I guessed this must be Jimenez since he'd come when named, and he was royally pissed about it.

"*Bruja*. Your father knew what you were up to. We followed you for your own good!"

"Liar!" she shouted, smacking him across his grinning, naked jaw with her bone-claw hand. "Leon Arbildo was not my father. That's why you followed me. That's why you spied on me and my real father. You said you were looking for him, but you weren't. You tried to hide him from me—you tried to take him from me when I was still a child. That's why you wrecked the boat, why you killed all those people. To get rid of my father!" So she had known about Jimenez, about Arbildo's sinking of the boat, and about the graves Jimenez had not reported to her. No wonder she'd been mad when he died.

"You don't know the truth, Luzita. The *Dulcia* sank because it was old."

Still more ghosts flooded toward our little huddle of misery, perhaps a dozen, all drenched in seawater. I spotted Ernesto Santara, but he didn't look at me. He kept his empty gaze on the ghost of Jimenez. He was no longer a pleasant haunt, but an angry one. The drowned crew moved toward the dead lawyer and Iko stalked along with them, hackles raised, teeth bared.

"My dog!" Maria-Luz screamed at me. "Give me my dog!"

I held up the bundle of hair and pot shards. "This?" I asked.

Maria-Luz lunged at me. Mickey leapt to his feet but I'd already pulled a bit of the Grey between us and the furious woman's shade recoiled with a screech.

"Mickey, keep her back," I said, in the calmest voice I could muster.

"Me? How?"

"Just like you kept Señora Acoa from dying. Just put out your hands and send that feeling toward Maria-Luz."

Jimenez was backing away, starting to fade, but I grabbed him, sinking my fingers into the stinging electrical fire of his ghostly form.

"No, no. You have to face the music, Counselor," I said.

Mickey was talking as fast as he could, crooning, and holding his hands between himself and Maria-Luz. The gold strings spun out from his fingertips, stroking over her, making her more solid, more alive-seeming. She began to cry.

Jimenez struggled in my grip. "Let me go, *puta loca*!"

I waved the bundle of Iko's figurine at him. "You want me to give this to her? You dodged this bullet before, but I can make sure it hits you this time." I was guessing, but I knew Maria-Luz had not meant any comfort for Jimenez when she'd tried to have Iko sent to him before. Iko jumped and snapped at him, snarling.

Jimenez froze and the crew gathered tight around him. I let him go so they could hold him prisoner themselves. They muttered to him and the sound raised the hair on my arms.

Mickey shot me a panicked look over his shoulder and I stepped closer to him. Maria-Luz was still standing in front of him, looking almost solid, while Hector hovered just behind her, clucking and making the soothing noises people murmur to upset children.

"It's all right, Mickey. You can stop."

"But—I—what—?"

"Ask Tío Muñoz."

Mickey jerked his gaze back and forth, searching for the bogeyman. We were creating a ruckus. The other partiers in the cemetery were beginning to look our way with curiosity.

I sat down on my stool and tried to act like there was nothing at all strange at our feast of souls. I bobbed my head and let my feet tap in time with the brass and strings of the mariachis nearby. I motioned to Maria-Luz, who wafted closer. Jimenez was still petrified in the circle of dead sailors.

"All right," I started. "You tried to give the dog to Jimenez before, then you decided to give it to Hector, and then you gave it to me to give to Hector. Why?"

She hung her head. "At first, I was angry. Iko never liked those lawyers—"

"A good judge of character," Hector injected.

"Iko was all I had after Papa—went away. And when Iko died, that was all I knew how to do, all I could think of to keep him for a little longer—to take me to Mictlan someday."

"Some people think this is a very bad kind of magic."

"It's not. It's just . . . the dark kind. The death magic. What is death but part of life? And my dog was dead. I had done bad things with the magic when I was angry at that . . . man who called himself my father," she spat, "but I never meant harm with keeping Iko. But I found out Jimenez had lied to me. He had never tried to find out what happened to my father. He spied on me and he took the information to Leon and they tried to kill my father a third time so he had to run here and hide. I was so angry when I found out what he had done, I wanted to punish him! I thought Iko would keep him from Mictlan. Keep him in limbo and torment, forgotten but never released to the third death, wandering the way he had done to the sailors on the *Dulcia*."

"Tell the rest, *pequeña*," Hector urged.

She sobbed for a moment. Mickey sat next to me, wide-eyed and still, watching the ghostly woman weep until she raised her head and looked at him. "You understand the magic, you know how hard it is . . . to be good. It was so hard, but I thought I should do a better thing. I changed my will so Iko would go to my father, to help him find the road, and I gave all the money for the families of the sailors. Leon and the insurance company gave them nothing. I thought I could repair the wrong, even if the magic was a little . . . dark."

"But the will I saw doesn't give the money to the families of the *Dulcia*'s crew."

"No." She hung her head, ashamed. "Banda changed it. I don't know why I thought he was different than Jimenez. They were both charming liars. . . ."

"Banda forged your will."

She nodded. "He is my father's man, even after death. Just like that pig," she added, spitting in Jimenez's direction. Her spittle hissed and raised a red spark on the ground where it hit.

Jimenez recoiled, but kept silent.

Hector tapped her again and motioned her on.

Maria-Luz sighed the smell of earth and copal. "The spirits told me of you. I was sick with the cancer that killed me, but they came when I called and they said you could fix the horrible mess of this. I believed them. I told Banda to give the dog to you. I thought you could solve my puzzle of the graves, find out what had happened and make it right. And my papa and Iko could be together again."

"So . . . this bit of junk controls Iko's soul. . . ."

Maria-Luz and Hector nodded together.

I studied the bit of hair and thread. I glanced at Mickey.

"What do you think? Eternal torment for Jimenez? Or can we do something else with this?"

The boy was trembling. "Why are you asking me?" he demanded.

"Because you have the magic. And Maria-Luz doesn't anymore. She's dead, Mickey. She can't change the things she did."

"I don't have any magic! Just the ghosts! That's why I read up on the *Santísima Muerte*—so I could use the ghosts for magic," he finished in a harsh whisper.

"You already have the magic. You do. Look at your hands."

"They're just hands!"

"Look at them the way you look at the ghosts— sideways, through the worms and lights and crazy mist. Look softly."

He stared down at his gangling, oversized paws, flexing them slowly in and out of fists and turning his head side to side. Tears began to well and fall over his lower lids as he stared without blinking. "It's—there's something on my fingers. . . ."

"Yeah. That's it. That glowy stuff. Real magic, bratboy. Live magic."

He stared at me. "Do you—?"

I shook my head. "No. I don't have anything like that. I just see ghosts." That wasn't strictly true, but that wasn't the time for messy little details. "But I can tell you that's life magic, not death magic. If you die, it goes away. That's what's happened to Maria-Luz."

He glanced all around the panteon, taking note of the ghosts, the living, the dead . . . and Tío Muñoz, who sat on the ground among the tombs of the Arbildos and smiled at us, glimmering with a golden sheen.

"What do you think?" I asked again. "Should we sic Iko on Jimenez for eternity? Poor old Iko, faithful unto death and beyond. I'm not sure he deserves an eternity spent snapping at the heels of this scum."

"No," the lawyer agreed, and was silenced again by the drowned crew that surrounded him.

Maria-Luz and Hector hung on the moment, watching Mickey.

"What . . . what about the other one? The guy who faked the will?"

"Banda," I supplied. "Yeah, he's a piece of work."

"Can you—?"

"You, Mickey. I can deliver the bomb, but only you can build it. Iko hates him. All you have to do is make the magic go the right way so it's alive. If the magic is tuned for Banda, Iko will seem to be alive to him, but he'll still be a ghost dog to everyone else."

I cut a glance at Maria-Luz. "Then all we have to do is tether Iko to Banda. . . ."

She nodded. "I think . . . it can be done. If you rewind the thread just right."

"But what will happen to the dog? Will it . . . be . . ."

"Doomed to eat lawyer in hell?" I added.

Mickey nodded, but he was looking at Maria-Luz now.

"Wind the thread the other way, wind it to the life of the man," Maria-Luz whispered, beginning to fade. "Iko will come to me when his job is done. Or when you break your binding."

Was it so late . . . or so early that the night was ending already? No, I could see it was still dark. But she was tiring, her energy fading after such an evening—her first and probably last return from the Land of the Dead. Only the sailors and Jimenez were as present as ever. Hector and his daughter had started to slide away.

"You'd better start before Maria-Luz is all gone, or you might lose the chance," I prompted Mickey.

"But . . ."

"Try it. What's the worst that can happen? You let the dog go. Right?"

"Yeah. Right."

I handed Mickey the bag of Iko's shards. He took the

bundle of hair out and began picking the red thread loose. He concentrated, pulling the thread loose, unwinding it with care.

Iko began to fade with a whimper.

"No, Iko," Hector called to the dog in a singsong voice, thin as steam. "No, *perrito*, stay. Good dog...."

"Think of the man," Maria-Luz whispered. "Think of him, Jimenez's partner, Banda, the lawyer, the thief, the fraud...." She pointed toward the thread, a stream of her knowledge flowing out of her skeletal fingertips, touching the boy and the bundle of hair.

Mickey rewound the red strand the other way, muttering under his breath. The gold threads from his fingers caught on the hairs in the bundle, caught in the twist of the thread and bound up, muttering with Mickey, singing magic, alive and golden and hot as the sun.

Hector and Maria-Luz stepped backward, back, back, fading as they went, until they were only a whisper and a shred of smoke on the air. Iko stopped whining.

A hush fell, as if all the spirits of San Felipe del Agua held their breath.

Mickey tied off the string. "There. OK? You think?" he asked, holding it out. But there was no one left to see it but me and Tío Muñoz.

The old man had come up on us without any warning or apparent movement.

"*Muy bien!*" he cackled.

Mickey started with surprise, jumping to his feet. The old man backed away, chuckling.

"Where did they all go?" Mickey asked, bewildered.

"Back where they came from, I'd guess. The sailors took Jimenez—I think he may be in for some trouble in the afterlife," I said.

"Good!" Mickey spat.

"And Maria-Luz and her father went ... wherever."

"To Mictlan," Mickey corrected. "I think."

"Not so sure now?"

"I—I'm not sure about much...."

Well, that was a change. But I didn't comment. Instead I said, "I think we can go now, if you want to."

"I guess. We can leave the ofrenda. No one will steal from ghosts."

We started back through the crowds, the music and laughter jarring against the strangeness of the night. Mickey handed me the bag of clay pieces and the knotted bit of hair, magic, and string as we approached the gate.

"Where's Iko?"

I pointed at the gate, where the dog had appeared again, looking more like a real dog than ever. Mickey grinned and went to pat the little mongrel, carefully, as if he wasn't sure his hand could really touch it.

"Gracias, Señorita Blaine."

I turned, not at all surprised to find Tío Muñoz behind me.

"For what?" I asked.

"For helping him find a better path. He was headed for bad things."

"I just do what the choreographer tells me. What are you going to do now?"

He laughed. "I think that is up to Miguel. What about you? You are finished here."

I nodded. "Yeah. Here. But there's one thing left in Mexico City."

Muñoz shook his head. "Justice may be hard to serve with only the word of ghosts."

"That depends on which sort of justice you're talking about."

He seemed pleased by that and nodded his head. Then he turned and walked away into the night.

Mickey and Iko ran up to me, the dog grinning a satisfied doggy smile, not nearly as tentative as Mickey's.

We walked back to the Chevy and got in. This time, Iko jumped in and curled on the floorboards at my feet.

As we drove back down the hill, Mickey cleared his throat and glanced at me.

"What?"

"Uh . . . so. What now?"

"Now, I'm done. I get to go home. By way of Mexico City. And Mr. Banda's office. Maria-Luz and Hector still have a little payback coming."

"And the guys from the *Dulcia*."

I nodded. "I think I have a way to set things up as Maria-Luz wanted them. And I won't mind giving Banda a good scare."

"How's it going to work?"

"I'll give the bundle to Banda, so he becomes the vessel—I can figure out how. Then he'll be stuck with Iko until he dies, or you let Iko go."

"Can I do that?"

"Yeah. You'll figure it out." I had.

He made a thoughtful frown and was silent for a while. Then he said, "I think I must have missed something. Why did they kill the sailors?"

"That was an accident, but it didn't matter to Arbildo and Jimenez that they died. The boat was old and the company was in a temporary financial crisis. So Arbildo decided to sink it—have a little accident at sea—and collect the insurance. The sailors were just in the way. Except for Hector. Who'd been having an affair with Arbildo's wife."

"Yeah, I got that. Maria-Luz was Hector's daughter, really."

"That's right. He followed her mother to Mexico City. I think Arbildo must have caught on and so Hector did his first disappearing act. He abandoned his real identity as Estancio Rivera and took on the name Hector Purecete, Señora Acoa's long-lost relative. Estancio was from Oaxaca—he worked in the mezcal distillery down the mountain—and he'd seen the name on the headstone in the Panteon San Miguel just like we did. He got a job with the Arbildo shipping company as Hector so he could still be near Consuela and their daughter. While he was at sea, Consuela died and she probably let his new identity slip as she was dying. So Arbildo decided to get rid of his wife's lover once and for all."

"But . . . Hector called his daughter Carmencita. . . ."

"That was Maria-Luz's middle name: Carmen. They probably called her that so it was less likely they'd trip up in front of Leon Arbildo—but he knew."

Mickey continued to frown. "I'm still not sure I get it. . . ."

"Arbildo sank his ship with the help of his trusty henchman Jimenez, and he didn't let on to anyone that Maria-Luz was not his daughter."

"Why didn't he just . . . have another kid?"

"Last night, I saw hundreds of dead kids in the cemetery. They were all Arbildo children. I'm not sure what the problem is, genetics, bad luck, a curse . . . but whatever it is, the Arbildos don't have healthy kids. They die young. Only one or two make it to carry on the family name. Consuela had four children, but only Maria-Luz made it past the age of three. Leon Arbildo didn't have any surviving brothers or sisters, or any other kids. He had to have Maria-Luz and she had to be his daughter, unequivocally.

"He was a very proud man—a jealous man, too," I continued. "And Catholic. The illegitimacy thing was not acceptable. He had Maria-Luz watched, the same way he'd had Consuela watched. She must have known she was watched and been resentful. She started doing black magic to hurt him—she got thrown out of school for it a couple of times. When she finally met Hector and found out he was her real father, that's when the hate started. But Arbildo got even: he died and he left the estate in the hands of the lawyers who'd helped him in the past."

"And they kept on watching her and manipulating her, right?"

"Yeah. And they kept right on doing all the same things they'd done for her father and not telling her they did it. They drove Hector into hiding, and when he died, Maria-Luz had nothing left but the dog and her hate. She started trying to find out about her real father, so she went to Oaxaca a lot, looking for his family or his grave or whatever she could get. She laid that false trail for us with the Registrar of Deaths to confuse her lawyers in case they were keeping track of her. We know Jimenez had tracked the graves, but so long as she didn't show up there, he'd never know she'd discovered the truth and he'd never be able to stop her plans for revenge."

"But she changed her mind!"

"Yeah, she did. Because she found out about the *Dulcia*. She decided justice was better than vengeance and, again, she left a puzzle for someone—me—to solve that would reveal the truth."

"She was devious, that Maria-Luz."

I smiled. "Yeah."

We pulled into the tiny covered carriageway of the guesthouse and I stumbled out of the car, suddenly exhausted.

Mickey caught my arm. "Hey . . . uh . . . you leaving soon? 'Cause I still got a lot of questions."

"Sorry, Mickey. I have to go tomorrow."

"Oh."

The church bells from the *zócalo* rang the quarter hour. I checked my watch; it was still early for Oaxaca on el Día de los Muertos—only ten fifteen. But it felt like two a.m.

We walked up the stairs to my room, the house still quiet while everyone was at the cemetery. I stopped and studied Mickey as he waited for me to unlock my door. He was tired, but standing straighter. His sullen look had changed into a thoughtful frown as he tried to understand what had happened and what might happen next.

"Hey," he said again. "Is Iko . . . going to . . . chew on the lawyer in hell?"

"I don't think so. When Banda dies, the dog gets to go free."

Mickey grinned. It was really a nice grin. I smiled back.

Then I stumbled into my room and fell onto the bed and into sleep.

In the morning, I returned to Mexico City with only a short pause to lay some plans and then say good-bye to Mickey and his aunt. Mickey was grinning again, though this time there may have been more malice in it than the night before.

It was pretty early, but I managed to call Banda's office and get an appointment through his secretary. If he skipped out on me, I would hunt him down.

But he didn't. He was there when I arrived, even if he seemed a little puzzled about my appearance in his office. With a dog.

He looked at the strange dog and frowned. "Did you pick up a stray in Oaxaca?"

"No. Don't you recognize this dog, Mr. Banda? A former client of yours was sure you would."

Iko began to growl like he had at the airport and stalked toward the desk. Banda stood up, looking nervous. "I think you should call off your dog."

"He's really not mine," I said, closing the door behind me. "If you take a good look at him, I think you might recognize him. He's Maria-Luz's dog. And Hector Purecete's. Who used to be Estancio Rivera. You know: the guy your partner tried to kill by sinking the *Dulcia.*"

"I think you should be more careful what you say, Miss Blaine. That's slander." He didn't look at me, just at the dog. The dog his secretary hadn't noticed. Nor anyone else we passed on the street or at the airport.

"Truth is a complete defense, I'm told. And the insurance company was never that convinced it was an accident," I replied. "But you know that. Because you helped cover it up. And still are. Which is how a guy in a two-man office can afford to fly to New York to watch the Yankees all season, every season. Because you steal, and you blackmail, and you pay people off. Like you paid off the guy at customs to break the dog so I'd go home. Didn't you?"

He was backing up as Iko kept coming, inexorable as death.

"Don't know what you're talking about. . . ."

"Oh, yeah, you do. And so do the federal investigators who drop in to chat with you once in a while, and the petty officials, and everyone else you pay off so they won't pull your license and throw you in jail to rot. There's a long list of your transgressions if you know where to look. Like I do."

"What the hell do you want, Miss Blaine? I'm sure we can settle up and go our ways. You and your dog," he added, as if he'd like to spit, but didn't dare. He was sweating and turning pale. "Will you be happy if I admit I paid to have the dog broken? Is that it?"

"No. I do like hearing you say so, but it's not enough. What will make me happy is if you were to suddenly remember Miss Arbildo's amended will. The one where she leaves everything to the families of the sailors who died on the *Dulcia*."

"There's no such will!"

"There was."

"No, there wasn't! Just the ones I showed you. Whose word are you taking? Mine or some . . . informant living in the hills?"

I walked closer to him. Iko had backed him to the wall. "I am taking Maria-Luz's word for it. And in a few minutes, I'll take yours, because I think you'll want to make a clean breast of the whole thing."

"You're crazy! Just as crazy as she was."

I gave him a cold look. "Iko, rip his throat out."

The little dog let out a banshee howl and leapt for Banda's chest.

Banda screamed, and tried to cover his face and neck with his hands, falling over his desk chair as he flailed at the ghost dog.

The secretary pounded on the door, yelling.

I stuck my head out. "He fell. He's OK," I added, pointing to the thrashing man on the floor. "Or not." I shrugged.

The secretary stared at her boss, shrieking and writhing on the floor, and backed away muttering about the police and the doctors. I wasn't too worried. They wouldn't find a scratch on him.

Iko was biting savagely at Banda, who seemed to be feeling every snap of the little dog's incorporeal jaws. I have to hand it to Mickey and Maria-Luz: they did fine work. Iko was only "alive" to the man whose life he was tied to: Banda.

"Iko," I called. "Get off that piece of trash." I clapped my hands for the ghost dog's attention. "Iko!"

Reluctantly, the dog jumped to the ground and stood on stiff legs in front of the lawyer, growling. Banda dragged himself up the wall, panting and shaking. He stared at the apparition with horror.

"Wha—what . . . is that?"

"It's retribution, Mr. Banda. That is Iko. He was on board the *Dulcia* when it sank. But Hector Purecete saved him. I don't think there's ever been a dog in this world—or the next—who hates you the way this one does. And he's all yours."

I elbowed him sharply in the gut and he gasped. I pushed the bundle of hair into his mouth and shoved his jaw shut. Convulsively, he swallowed.

Then he gagged for a moment, staring at me, until he caught his breath again.

"Jesus. What was that?"

"It's Iko. It's the little bit of magic that was in the dog you were so scared of. And now it's yours. For the rest of your life. And maybe a little longer."

He ran for his washroom and tried to throw up, but there was nothing to toss. He shook and prayed and babbled for a moment as Iko circled him, hackles raised and teeth bared.

"Payback's a bitch, isn't it?"

He glared at me as a renewed pounding started on the door. I backed up and leaned against it. "You want to talk to these guys or do you want to get out of this mess?" I asked.

"I want to get the hell rid of you. And your damned dog!"

"Your damned dog, now, Banda. But I can tell you how to get rid of him. If you do what I want."

"I'll have you arrested," he growled, rubbing his throat as he staggered out of the washroom.

"Oh, come on. You know my lawyer. You think that's going to fly? And if you think you can arrange an accident for me like Jimenez did for Purecete, consider that you currently have a dead dog waiting for a word from me to start biting the living hell out of you. It won't kill you. But I'd bet you'll wish it would. Whoever is on the other side of this door is going to think you've gone insane when they see you rolling on the floor with an invisible dog. Because only you and I can see Iko."

If hate were a living thing it would have leapt for my throat from his eyes. *"¡Salga!"* he shouted at the door. *"¡Salga! ¡Estoy bien!"*

The knocking died away.

"What. Do you want?"

"Ms. Arbildo's real will. I want it registered and entered for probate, or whatever you need to do to execute it. Today."

"I don't have it," he spat. "It's gone. I burned it!"

"Then forge it. Like you forged the ones you showed me before. The estate is to be divided among the families of the crew of the *Dulcia*."

"There is no estate to divide! Don't you get it, *estupida gringa*? It's all gone. The estate is bankrupt. The money is gone!"

"You told me Maria-Luz was loaded. That thirty thousand U.S. was a 'drop in the bucket.' And it didn't disappear until you were the sole controller. So you can un-bankrupt it the same way you broke it in the first place, Banda. And if you don't, you won't just have an angry ghost dog on your ass. Because even you and your dead partner and your cheap secretary can't possibly have blown that much money, and certainly not without leaving a trail wide enough to march the Mexican army down. So, you still have it. Which means it can be returned to its rightful owners."

He glowered.

"Iko," I said.

He threw himself into his chair, saying, "No, no! Please." He snatched his keyboard and began to type.

I came and stood over his shoulder, watching, while Iko growled nonstop. I looked the finished document over.

"That's pretty good, Banda. I see you'll still be able to feather your own nest, if less regally than before," I added, glancing around his very nice office.

He muttered under his breath.

"Knock it off. You lost. Man up and live with it."

I hung around while he finished up, printed the forms, forged the signatures, and got warily to his feet, eyeing the threatening little hound that dogged him unceasingly. Stifling his fury, he led me on a long damned walk around downtown Mexico City to register the will and rescind the previous one.

Just outside of the courts building he stopped and turned back to me.

"Satisfied?"

"Mostly. But I know you can walk right back in there and pull that paperwork by saying you were coerced. But this is the thing you need to remember, Banda: the dog is forever. And once I'm gone, you're not off the hook, because there is someone in Oaxaca who knows all about the will, the *Dulcia*, the dog, and all the rest."

"Another of your ghosts?"

I laughed. "Oh, no. A very real, solid, living person. I

know you can find out who it is, but don't be hasty. Remember I said there was a way to get rid of the dog?"

"Yes," he snapped.

"That person knows how to set you free. But they won't if you screw over the survivors of the *Dulcia*'s crew. And they can't if you decide to kill them. That person—and powerful friends—will be keeping an eye on you. If that person dies, or if that person chooses not to help you, you and Iko get to spend this life together, and the next one and the next one, until there is no one left on the planet who remembers you, or the dog. Until the third death."

He howled and threw himself at me. I just stepped back as Iko lunged.

I walked to the edge of the plaza and flagged a cab, ignoring the crowd that had gathered around the convulsing, screaming man on the ground. "Airport," I said, turning on my cell phone.

I waited for an answer to my call and finally someone picked up. "Villaflores . . ."

"Hey, brat-boy. It's the GP. It's done."

He laughed. "I'll be on the next flight. Don't want Iko to have to chew on that lawyer for too long."

"Yeah, poor, faithful Iko."

It's rare for Justice and Vengeance to stand in the same place, but I thought this time, maybe they would. At least for a while. Until the will was executed and Banda's embezzlements were restored to the proper owners. I hadn't told Banda the truth, but that wasn't bothering me too much. Whether he lived with Iko for a day or a lifetime, whether anyone remembered Banda or gave a damn in a year's time or thirty, there was at least one thing that made me smile: it would be a long time before the third death of the little clay dog.

NOAH'S ORPHANS

THOMAS E. SNIEGOSKI

ONE

emy knew it wasn't real, the product of some
strange, dreamlike state, but he didn't mind in
the least. Seeing her this way—it was almost as
if she were still with him.

Almost as if she were still alive.

She had called to him from inside their Maine summer home, and he'd gone to her, climbing up the stairs
to the second floor.

Standing in the doorway to one of the spare rooms,
he watched her.

Her back was to him as she looked out one of the open
windows onto the expanse of backyard, verdant with grass
that would need a lawn mower's attention sooner rather
than later. She was wearing a white cotton dress that billowed and moved in the warm summer breeze coming in
through the window. And as he silently stared from the
doorway, he was reminded of how much he loved her, and
how incomplete he would be without her.

"Remy," she called out again. He answered, startling
her. She laughed that amazing laugh, and turned to face
him.

"There you are," she said, eyes twinkling brighter than
the highest spires of Heaven.

"Sorry, I didn't mean to scare you." He stepped into
the room.

"No fear," she said with a slight shake of her head as she reached out to take his hand.

Deep down he knew that this was all wrong, that Madeline had passed away three long weeks ago from cancer, but he couldn't help it, eagerly wrapping himself in the warmth of a lie.

Her hand was cold and wet and he was about to ask if everything was all right, when he realized how dark it had become in the room.

Black, like the inside of a cave.

And from outside he heard the sound of heavy rain.

A dog barking pulled Remy from his fantasy, and he left his wife, the darkness, and the rain to find himself sitting on the porch of the summer home, now in the grip of winter.

It was snowing, and the wind had carried the fluffy white stuff up onto the porch. It had even collected on him as he had sat unmoving. Remy brushed the snow from his arms and the top of his head and Marlowe barked again for his attention.

"Hey," Remy said. "Sorry about that, must've dozed off."

"No sleep," the black Labrador retriever said, reminding him that angels did not sleep.

Angels of the heavenly host Seraphim were not supposed to have human wives, summer cottages in Maine, or work as private investigators, either. But he did.

"I know, but I was dreaming," he said, remembering his wife's beautiful face and how the sudden darkness had tried to claim it.

"Rabbits?" the dog asked.

"No rabbits," Remy said. Snow had accumulated on the dog's shiny black coat and Remy started to brush it away. "Madeline."

Marlowe lowered his gaze. *"Miss,"* he grumbled in his canine tongue.

As a member of God's heavenly host, Remy was able to understand the myriad languages of every living thing on Earth. But even if he could not, there was no mistaking how the animal was feeling, for Remy felt the very same way.

"I miss her, too," he said, reaching down to rub behind one of Marlowe's velvety-soft ears.

Since Madeline's passing, Remy and Marlowe had felt more than a bit lost. Remy had hoped a trip to the house in Maine might have been good for them both, a change of scenery. A needed distraction.

He took a deep breath and gazed out over the porch rail at the falling snow. "I'm not sure how great this idea was," he said and sighed.

It had been spring the last time they'd come, before everything had been thrown on its ear.

Before the cancer.

They'd had a wonderful weekend, taking the day off from the office and driving up early Thursday afternoon. He'd felt something special even then, remembering how he'd experienced a weird kind of euphoria as he'd gotten out of the car and hauled their bags from the trunk.

Madeline had already gone inside, leaving the door to their getaway wide open. And as he had climbed the stairs to the front porch, watching his wife move about, pulling up shades and opening windows to air away the winter staleness, Remy had experienced a moment of perfect contentment.

This was what he had been waiting over a millennium for.

It wasn't as though he hadn't been happy until then. He'd been on the earth for hundreds of thousands of years, and there had certainly been moments of happiness, but right then and there, at that specific moment, Remy Chandler was fulfilled.

Since leaving Heaven after the Great War against the Morningstar, he'd been searching for something. He'd always known he would find it on the Almighty's greatest experiment, among His most complex creations.

And he did—it had just taken a little while.

It had all started to fall into place when he'd made the decision to live as a human. Suppressing his angelic nature, Remy had walked among them—learning from them—trying so desperately to *be* one of them.

But it had taken a purpose, a job, to finally set him on the right path. Choosing the name Remy Chandler, the angel Remiel now worked as a private investigator, and had at last found what he had been searching for. The job allowed him to see every facet of humanity, the depravity, the cruelty, the kindness, the passion. It allowed him to observe and to learn from them, and for three hundred dollars a day plus expenses, he helped them.

He'd been around humans for what seemed like forever, but they still had so much to teach him. And that was never more obvious than when he had first met the woman who would eventually become his wife.

Madeline.

She'd shown him what it truly meant to be human. She became the anchor that allowed him to keep the nature of the divine being he truly was at bay. After all he had lost in the Great War, Madeline had become his island. She had become his Heaven.

Now she was gone, and he feared that the skin of his humanity would begin to slip away, to slough off like that of a reptile, revealing what he had always been beneath.

"We could have stayed in Boston and been just as miserable," he said to his companion while rubbing the top of the dog's blocky head.

And as if in response, the wind picked up, blowing snow across the porch, showing that the harsh New England season still had plenty of bite left.

Marlowe turned his nose into the breeze. *"Cold,"* he said softly, but loud enough for Remy to hear.

"Is it?" Remy answered, not having allowed himself to feel much of anything since his wife had died.

The Labrador placed his face in Remy's lap.

Marlowe's pack was now incomplete, and Remy could only imagine how difficult it was for him to understand that Madeline wasn't coming home. It was like attempting to explain the concept of death to a very young child.

"Sad," the dog said, and it just about broke Remy's heart.

"I know, I'm sad, too." He bent forward to whisper softly, lovingly, into the animal's ear. "What would make you happy?"

"Madeline come back?" Marlowe lifted his head excitedly. His ears perked up, and his thick tail wagged so hard that Remy thought for sure the dog would topple over.

"No, Madeline can't come back."

He remembered the strange experience he'd just had, and the feeling of his wife's hand in his. It was almost as if she had been with him again.

He kissed the bony top of the dog's hard head. "I wish she could, but she can't. Is there anything else that would make you happy?" Remy asked his four-legged friend.

Marlowe thought for a moment. *"Pig's ear,"* he said, an excited little tremor in his voice.

"A pig's ear?" Remy asked, pretending to be surprised. "That's just gross."

"Pig's ear good," the dog answered. His muscular tail continued to wag.

"Y'think?" Remy wrinkled his nose in an expression of distaste.

"Yes!" Marlowe barked, stepping back, at full attention now.

"All right, then." Remy pushed himself up from the chair. "Let's go get you a . . ."

He sensed it at pretty much the same time that Marlowe did, and the promise of a pig's ear was momentarily forgotten.

Marlowe started to growl, low and rumbling, the thick black fur around his neck and above his tail rising in caution.

Remy walked across the porch to the top of the stairs. He looked out at the woods surrounding the property, the cold wind causing the little vegetation that was able to survive the winter to sway and rustle.

In spite of how it looked, he knew that they were no longer alone.

There was a disturbance in the air near the driveway and Remy watched as a human figure gradually materialized in a walk toward them.

The male figure was tall, dressed in a finely tailored gray suit, but wasn't a man.

Marlowe was by Remy's side now, barking crazily.

"Quiet," he ordered. "It's all right."

"Greetings, Remiel," the angel Sariel said with the slightest hint of a bow. The angel was tall, his features pale and perfect, as if sculpted by a master from the finest Italian marble. He adjusted the sleeves of his suit jacket as he looked around him.

Sariel was the leader of a host of angels called the Grigori, messengers sent by Heaven in the earliest days of humanity to guide God's latest creations. They had became corrupted by the early decadence of man, and soon found themselves on the receiving end of the Lord's wrath.

The Grigori had been robbed of their wings and banished to Earth, there to await the Almighty's forgiveness before being allowed to once more pass through the gates of Heaven.

Sariel and his brothers had been waiting for a very long time.

"What can I do for you?" Remy asked the angel.

Marlowe continued to growl, his eyes locked upon the immaculately dressed angel standing in the snow-covered pathway leading up to the house.

"Is this where you've come to mourn?" Sariel asked.

"Excuse me?" Remy felt his anger begin to rise.

"I heard about your mate's passing," the Grigori leader stated flatly. "And I wonder if this is where you've come to mourn your loss?"

The dog was becoming extremely upset, and Remy reached over to place a calming hand atop his head.

"Shhhhhhhhh, now," Remy said, hoping to quiet his own growing anger as well.

"This is a private place," Remy told the angel. "Which poses the question of how you've come to find me here."

"Forgive the intrusion," Sariel said without an ounce of sincerity.

It was very difficult for Sariel to even pretend to understand what it was like to be human. The Grigori, and many of the other angelic beings that had come to walk the Earth, viewed the human race as just one more example of the myriad animal species that existed upon the surface of the world, refusing to acknowledge how special they truly were.

Refusing to acknowledge that they had been touched by God.

Remy was a rarity among heavenly beings, one who actually embraced humanity and strived to be a part of it.

"I do not wish to intrude upon your bereavement, but a matter of grave importance has arisen since last we saw one another," Sariel continued.

Just three weeks ago, the Grigori had helped Remy to avert the Apocalypse. Although their motive was selfish—for their fate if the world should die was uncertain at best—Sariel had gathered his Grigori brothers to help Remy prevent the release of the Four Horsemen.

"A matter of grave importance," Remy repeated. "Seems to be quite a bit of that going around these days."

Sariel stared, not understanding Remy's sarcasm.

"Why are you here, Sariel?" Remy asked, not even trying to hide his exasperation.

"The old man is dead," he replied.

"The old man ... who ... what old man?" Remy was confused, but then it dawned on him, the connection with the Grigori.

The old man.

"Noah?" Remy asked. "Noah is dead? How?"

Sariel adjusted his suit jacket, again tugging on his sleeves.

The cruel winter wind blew again, and with the chilling breeze came a taint of change in the air.

A taint of something menacing.

"He was murdered, Remiel," Sariel said. "The ark builder was murdered."

TWO

Before the Flood

Unbeknownst to them, Remiel watched as they toiled, building the great wooden craft.

Day after day he observed the old man, Noah, and his sons work on what gradually took the form of an enormous, roofed ship.

An ark.

Remiel had not been on the world of man for long, and he knew there was much still to explore, but he found that he could not leave.

The angel was fascinated, that fascination becoming even more pronounced when, in the early hours before dawn, he watched the old man approach the enormous vessel and begin to paint the magickal sigils upon its hull.

Unable to contain his curiosity, Remiel drew closer. He allowed himself to be seen, approaching the old man as he wrote with crimson fingers upon the hull of the great wooden craft.

"What are you doing?" Remiel asked, studying the marks, feeling the arcane energies radiating from the strange symbols of power.

"You startled me," Noah said, and Remiel felt the man's ancient eyes scrutinizing him, peeling away the deception that he was but a nomad from the desert.

That he was but a man.

Noah dropped to his knees, and immediately averted his eyes.

"Messenger of Heaven, I have done as He has asked of me. All nears readiness," the old man professed. "As soon as I have completed the symbols, we will be ready to accept the beasts of the land."

"You mistake me for someone else, old father," Remiel said, reaching down to take the man's hand and pull him to his feet.

"Are you not one of His winged children?" Noah asked.

Remiel's suspicions were correct, the old man could see through his disguise.

"You can see me?" he asked.

Noah slowly nodded.

Truly this human has been touched by God, the angel thought.

Remiel's attention returned to the ark and the sigils that the old man was painting on its surface.

"These are powerful magicks you play with," he said as he brought his hand close to one, feeling the energy emanating from it. "And did the Almighty bestow this knowledge upon you, as well as the gift of sight?"

The old man dipped his fingers into the wooden bowl of bloodred paint and began to draw upon the ark again.

"As your brethren have brought me this most holy mission, they have also delivered unto me the means to achieve this enormous task," Noah went on, the symbols of power leaving his fingers in strange patterns of scarlet.

"My brethren," Remiel repeated thoughtfully. "Why do you do this?" he asked. He walked around to what would be the bow of the great ship. "Why have you built such a craft?"

"You test me, angel," the old man said, furiously painting. "A great storm is coming."

"A storm?" Remiel asked. He spread his wings, and floated gracefully into the air to inspect the great ship further. The magick had begun to work upon the craft. The angel flew closer to an open passage leading deep into the bowels of the ship. The darkness was limitless—the space within the belly of the ark endless.

"It is a storm to wash away that which offends Him," Noah said as the angel returned to his side.

"And the ship?" Remiel questioned, folding his powerful wings behind him.

"It is needed to hold all life that has been deemed worthy to survive," Noah said. "The beasts of the land, no matter how large or small; it is my task to be certain that they live. As they are the Lord's children, so are they mine."

Remiel was fascinated. Had this old man actually received a message from the Lord of Lords, telling him of an approaching cataclysm? Did the Almighty truly intend to wash away His own creations?

He had known his Creator as a being of intense emotions. But he questioned the notion that the Almighty could be capable of destroying what He had once been so proud of, what had been the primary reason for the Great War against the forces of the Morningstar.

Remiel pondered this quandary for many days and nights, all the while watching Noah as he and his family performed the tasks supposedly assigned by God.

Eventually, the skies grew dark and pregnant with storm.

Remiel observed the beasts, deemed worthy, herded aboard the great ark. It was the magick that called to them, drawing them to the place that would be their sanctuary against the coming doom. It seemed not to matter how many there were, the belly of Noah's craft welcomed them all and gave them safety.

It took seven days for Noah and his sons to complete their miraculous task, and when the last of the animals was finally herded aboard, there was the most awesome of sounds from the sky, a clap of thunder like nothing Remiel had ever heard before.

A sound that signaled the beginning of the end.

And then the rains began.

It was a terrible rain, the water falling so quickly, the wind blowing so fiercely, that it soon began to obscure the land. A great and terrible hand in the form of a storm had descended upon the world, to wipe away its imperfections.

Remiel stood at the foot of the gangplank used by the beasts to climb to safety aboard Noah's ark, and looked out into the storm. From the corner of his eye, he thought he'd seen something. Peering intently through the torrential downpour, he scanned what little was left of the land until he found them. Hooded shapes, their skin the color of dusk, standing perfectly still in front of the caves that spotted the hills, as the rain fell around them and the waters rose.

Within moments they were gone, swallowed up by the deluge.

Remiel turned to board the craft, and came face-to-face with one of his own.

The angel Sariel stood with his Grigori brethren. One by one they climbed the ramp to board the ark. Remiel was surprised to see that they had been found worthy.

Soon only he and the Grigori leader stood upon the gangplank.

"Did you see them?" Remiel asked above the howling storm.

Sariel did not answer. Instead he turned and began the climb to board the ark.

Remiel grabbed hold of the departing Grigori's arm.

"I asked you a question," he said sternly, turning his gaze toward the now-empty hills.

"His will be done," Sariel said, pulling his arm away.

And the rain continued to fall. Ancient teachings said it lasted for forty days and forty nights, but the angel Remiel recalled that it took far less time than that to drown the world.

THREE

Remy left the ancient memories behind, returning to the here and now.

"Murdered?" he asked. "How do you know?"

"I saw it," Sariel said, stepping closer to the porch.

Marlowe started to growl again. The Grigori leader stared at the Labrador with cold, unfeeling eyes.

"I know murder when I see it."

Remy was about to ask more questions, but stopped. *No,* he told himself. *This time I will have nothing to do with their affairs.*

The affairs of angels.

"I'm sorry," he said, slowly turning his back and walking toward the door. "C'mon, Marlowe."

"Where are you going?" Sariel asked from the foot of the porch steps.

"I'm going inside," Remy replied. "To get away from you."

"I don't understand," the Grigori leader stated.

"I'm through with this." Remy stood in front of the door, but turned slightly to address Sariel again. "I'm done with all of it . . . with murder, floods, apocalypses and angels. Just leave me alone."

He opened the screen door and then the door behind it, letting Marlowe inside first.

"You're not human," Sariel called out after him. "No matter how hard you try or how much you pretend, you will never be anything more or less than what you are.

"One of the patriarchs of humanity has been slain," Sariel continued when Remy didn't respond. "I thought this is what you do, Remy Chandler," the Grigori leader taunted. "I thought this is what you play at while living among them."

Remy remained silent, stepping into the cottage and closing the door behind him.

Marlowe waited on the rug just inside the door, square head cocked inquisitively.

"Okay?" the Labrador asked.

"Fine," Remy answered. "Why don't we see about getting you some supper?"

The dog bounded toward the kitchen, and Remy chanced a quick look through the sheer curtain over the window in the door.

Sariel was gone.

FOUR

Remy decided that he'd had more than enough distraction.

Marlowe didn't mind; it was pretty much all the same to him. As long as he was fed and got his regular walks, he could have been on the surface of the moon for all he cared.

It didn't take him long to pack into a shopping bag what little he had brought up with him. Deep down Remy had always known that he wouldn't be staying long. This was a special place he had shared with Madeline, their place to get away from it all and enjoy each other, and now it only served to remind him that that life was over. Madeline was gone.

Remy stood in the entry with Marlowe beside him, nose pressed to the front door. He took a long look around. He wasn't sure when he'd be back, and for a moment he just wanted to savor the memories of *her*. When he did return, would they still be so strong?

He could see her washing their dinner dishes at the sink in the kitchen down the hall. He'd often used that time to take the car to the tiny general store five miles down the road to buy ice cream for dessert.

"Going?" Marlowe interrupted.

"Yeah, we're going." Remy turned away from the memory and opened the door to the winter night.

The snow had slowed, leaving behind two inches or so of the fluffy stuff.

Except for the patch of ground where Sariel had been standing.

Marlowe bounded down the steps, happily frolicking in the snow, snapping at the featherlike flakes that still drifted in the air.

Remy stood over the barren spot. He reached out, passing his hand through the air above it. There was most certainly a disturbance there, the residual effects of angel magick.

He started to think of Sariel, and the disturbing news that he had delivered, but quickly pushed it from his mind. This time, he wasn't going to get involved.

Continuing on to the car, he called out for Marlowe, who had gone into the woods to relieve himself. "Let's go," he said, brushing the snow from his windshield.

Marlowe came frantically running.

"Leave me?" the dog asked, standing by the rear driver's-side door.

"I'd never leave you," Remy reassured him as he opened the door, allowing the dog to hop inside.

"Never leave," the dog repeated, settling into his place in the backseat.

The ride back to Boston was uneventful; the snow eventually turned to rain as Marlowe's snores wafted up from the backseat of the Corolla, and the talk radio hosts, enamored with the sounds of their own voices, rambled on about the topics of the day.

It was after midnight by the time they returned to Beacon Hill, but the gods of parking had decided to smile on Remy, blessing him with a parking space near the State House, only a couple of blocks from home.

"Home?" Marlowe asked, suddenly awake and sitting up, his black nose twitching in the air.

"Home," Remy affirmed. He got out of the car and

opened the back door for the dog on his way to the trunk.

"Get on the sidewalk," Remy ordered, as he removed their one bag.

The dog trotted over to a light post and lifted his leg.

Remy waited until he had finished. "Empty?" he asked.

"*Empty,*" the dog repeated, joining his master as they began their trek to Remy's brownstone on Pinckney Street.

It was quiet on the Hill, the rain and damp cold keeping anyone with an ounce of common sense inside.

Marlowe darted from lamppost to lamppost, lifting his leg and proving that he was a liar.

They reached the brownstone and Remy used his key to open the front door. The dog bounded into the foyer, and pressed his nose to the bottom of the inner door. Remy barely managed to get the door open as Marlowe pushed his way inside, nose to the floor, on the trail of a particular scent.

Remy walked down the small hall to the kitchen and set the bag down atop the counter. He saw that the mail had been left on the table and he wondered when Ashley, Marlowe's frequent babysitter, had been by.

"She's not here," Remy called out, knowing who Marlowe was searching for. He removed his leather jacket and hung it in the hall closet. "She probably stopped in just long enough to drop off the mail and . . ." He stopped and turned.

Sariel was sitting in the living room; Marlowe, standing perfectly still and silent before him, had his eyes fixed upon the intruder.

The angel held one of Remy's favorite pictures. It was of Madeline when she was a little girl. She sat atop a pony, wearing a cowboy hat, and smiling that same stunning smile he had fallen in love with.

Her secret weapon, he used to call it.

"So full of life and promise," the angel said, tapping the photo with his manicured fingertips. "But it's all so fleeting for them."

"How dare you," Remy began, feeling his anger surge and the angelic nature he worked so hard to contain setting his blood afire.

"Bite him," Marlowe growled, his jowls twitching and revealing his yellowed canine teeth.

"No," Remy ordered, managing to get his own fury in check. He snatched the frame from the Grigori leader's hand. "You have no right to be here." He returned the picture to its place on the television stand, then turned to confront the angel. "I want you to leave," Remy told him, speaking in the language of their kind . . . the language of the Messengers.

Sariel stood, adjusting his suit coat. "I'm not leaving without you."

Remy glared, feeling an unnatural heat start to burn behind his eyes.

"I don't think you understand," he said, stepping menacingly toward the Grigori.

Sariel shook his head. "No, it is you who does not understand."

The angel suddenly reached out and grabbed hold of Remy's arm. He could feel the power in the grip, the angel magick flowing from Sariel into him.

Marlowe began to bark wildly as a pool of shadow expanded beneath them and the two angels dropped.

Swallowed by the darkness.

FIVE

They emerged in the middle of a storm.

The wind roared like some angry beast as it tried to rip them from their purchase on the hard, concrete surface. And if it could not succeed with its bestial strength, it would try to destroy them with the ferocity of its tears, as each drop of rain struck their exposed flesh like the sting of a wasp.

Remy raised a hand to shield his eyes from the savagery of the cold, whipping rain, and quickly looked about. From the comforting warmth of his Beacon Hill home to this; where had Sariel brought him?

It didn't take him long to realize that they weren't on land at all. They were in the middle of the ocean; an undulating mass of white-capped gray swirled all around. His eyes darted about, taking it all in: heavy machinery and equipment, and a familiar corporate symbol, faded on the side of a forklift chained to the concrete so as not to be picked up by the wind and carried away.

An oil rig; they were on an oil rig in the middle of the ocean.

Remy looked at Sariel, who stood silently beside him. The rain pelted the angel's pale features, leaving traces of red on his face where it stung him.

The Grigori leader turned away from Remy, fighting

the wind as he began to move toward a large boxy structure rising up from the platform.

Remy had no choice but to follow, struggling against the storm that seemed to grow even more agitated now that they were moving, as if it were angry that they would even think they could escape it. He followed Sariel toward the square building, and up multiple flights of rain-slicked metal steps to a heavy metal door with the words "Level One" stenciled on it in white paint.

The Grigori leader pulled open the door, fighting the wind as it attempted to tear it from his grasp. Remy reached out, helping to hold it open as the two of them beat the fury of the ocean storm and made their way inside.

"I should kill you for this," Remy snarled as he caught his breath in the shelter of the dark corridor. He could still hear the storm outside. Its rage was muffled by the shelter of their new surroundings, but it was still out there and still very angry.

"Perhaps you should," Sariel said, disregarding Remy's threat and heading down the corridor, past large glass windows that looked into empty office space. "Then again, you may want to wait and see why it is that I felt the need to resort to such desperate measures to bring you here."

Remy remained quiet, the anger inside him churning like the storm outside. He followed the Grigori to another flight of metal stairs and the two began to climb.

"What is this place?" he asked.

"Besides an abandoned oil rig in the middle of the South China Sea?" Sariel asked. "This is his home. Noah's home."

"He traded in his ark for an oil rig?" Remy said, still climbing and starting to wonder how many floors the structure had.

They reached what seemed to be the final level; the floor was lit in the sickly yellow of emergency lights, and shadow.

"Crammed on a ship with your entire family and almost every conceivable animal for an extended period of time can have a lasting effect," the Grigori said, before proceeding down the corridor.

Remy noticed that up here he could barely hear the storm. He doubted that it had subsided, and considered then that this level had been considerably soundproofed.

Sariel had reached the end of the dimly lit length of hall and now stood before a closed door. "In here," he said, not even bothering to knock as he opened it and walked inside.

Strains of classical music wafted out into the hall. It was Berlioz, his *Symphonie Fantastique*. It had been one of Madeline's favorite pieces. Remy flashed back to lazy summer mornings, windows open wide in their kitchen as they drank cup after cup of coffee while reading the Sunday *Globe*, the *Symphonie Fantastique* the morning's soundtrack.

Remy couldn't have been further from that moment.

"In here," he heard Sariel call out.

It was dark inside the room, except for a beam of light flashing on a screen that hung from the ceiling. A slide projector whirred at the opposite end of the room, its fan humming to cool its inner workings as the next slide in the carousel dropped into place.

Remy stood in darkness as the image of a bird appeared on the screen. There was nothing special about it; it was only a bird. That slide was then replaced by the image of a frog with beautiful blue skin.

Shielding his eyes from the harshness of the projector beam, Remy searched for Sariel and found him in the far corner of the room. He was standing beside the desk. The slide projector rested on it.

"Sariel?" Remy asked quietly, crossing the room toward him.

The room itself was in a shambles. Papers and books

were scattered about as if the storm outside had touched down in the cramped confines of the office.

Sariel remained silent, unmoving, his gaze fixed to something on the floor behind the desk.

Another slide fell into place as Remy approached. Stacks of the plastic carousels littered the top of the desk, all of them loaded with slides. Remy peered over the clutter to find what he had expected.

Noah lay on the floor on his back, his ancient eyes swollen to slits, gazing up, unseeing, at the ceiling. The old man's face was badly bruised, as was his neck. Twin trails of blood from his damaged lips dried in the silver-gray hairs of his beard.

He didn't look much different than he had that day so long ago when Remy had watched him paint the mystic sigils on the ark. The only difference was that he was dressed in brown corduroy trousers and a heavy fisherman's sweater.

And he was dead.

It had been quite a few centuries since Remy had come face-to-face with the old man who had come to use the name Noah Driscoll. He'd read about him from time to time, about how he'd made his fortune as a shipping magnate before turning to oil. How the family business had been handed down through the generations, father to son. But in truth, it was Noah, assuming a new identity every few decades.

God's touch had a tendency to considerably increase the life span of a human, and for Noah, that had most certainly been the case.

"He was afraid that this might happen," Sariel said.

Another slide was projected onto the screen. Remy glanced in that direction to see a photo of some kind of worm, writhing in a patch of overturned earth.

"Maybe you should tell me what you know," Remy said, the words leaving his mouth before he had the opportunity to catch them. It was happening again, as it always did; he was inexorably pulled into the matters of the divine.

"Over the centuries he'd become obsessed," Sariel started to explain, his eyes still locked upon the battered corpse. "Fixated on the mission that God had given to him."

Another slide was projected onto the screen, and they both looked toward it—a bear in a tree, looking as though it had actually posed for the shot.

"They say he had millions of these," Sariel stated.

The bear was replaced by some kind of bright green insect.

"Photos of all the beasts that he was responsible for saving, as well as those that evolved from them."

A monkey with a strange, beaklike nose.

"But his obsession eventually took a turn down a truly disturbing path," the Grigori continued.

Remy looked away from a dolphin leaping happily in the ocean waves.

"Disturbing how?"

"He became obsessed with the things he was not able to save," Sariel explained. "The things that God had deemed unworthy; the things that were destined to die beneath the waters of the Great Flood."

Remy had never really understood why the Lord God had decided to wipe clean the slate and start again. It was almost as if He'd realized He'd made some sort of mistake, and had wanted it done away with before anyone could notice.

Whatever the reason, the Almighty had seen fit to destroy the planet, and use the beasts chosen to survive as the seeds of a second generation of life in the world.

"What kinds of things?" Remy asked, his curiosity piqued.

The slide carousel clicked past the image of a female tiger and her cubs, and the room suddenly brightened as the light of the projector reflected off of the whiteness of the screen. It continued to click away, though the remainder of the tray was empty.

"He called them his orphans," Sariel said with a sad laugh.

"Noah's orphans."

SIX

Sariel was about to continue when he suddenly turned toward the door.

"We're not alone," he snarled, and before Remy could react, Sariel had traversed half the room with one powerful leap.

Shadows shifted in the doorway, someone fleeing now that they had been discovered.

Remy followed the Grigori in a run, catching a glimpse of the fallen angel as he darted around a corner in pursuit of his prey.

The rig was a maze of winding corridors, eventually coming to a stop at a set of swinging doors. Cautiously, Remy pushed one open.

Inside was a large storage space the size of a warehouse. Ordinarily it probably housed the supplies needed to keep a rig this size in working order, but now the space was nearly empty. A few crates and pallets of machine parts were stacked about the poorly lit room. But by the looks of them, they had sat there, unused, for quite some time.

Remy listened for a sign as to where Sariel had gone, but all he could hear was the wailing of the storm outside, eager to come in.

"*Remy,*" a voice suddenly whispered from somewhere in the shadows.

His heart fluttered as he looked around. He knew that voice, and had to wonder if he'd somehow slipped into another of the bizarre, dreamlike states he'd experienced while at the house in Maine.

He blinked his eyes and shook his head. Had the chamber become darker? A damp chill seemed to be emanating from the encroaching shadows.

"Remy, I have something to show you," said the voice of his wife, and he found that he couldn't move, standing perfectly still, waiting for her to come to him.

And she did, slowly emerging from the sea of black, still wearing her flowing summer dress. She smiled as she reached for him.

Remy closed his eyes and did the unthinkable. He wished the vision of her away.

Madeline's hand was deathly cold as it snaked into his, and he started at her chilling touch. Opening his eyes, he stared into hers, feeling himself drawn into their depths.

But there was something wrong. How many times had he looked into Madeline's eyes, lost in the love that he found there? These were not those eyes, and Remy fought to be free of them.

As much as it pained him, he spoke the words as he tried to pull his hand from hers. "You're not her."

But the woman that appeared as his wife held fast, refusing to let him go.

"No," she said plaintively. *"Please, don't pull away. I have something to show you."*

The desperate look on her familiar features rendered him powerless and he allowed her to pull his hand closer.

"A gift of our union," she said, and placed his hand upon the warmth of her stomach.

Remy stumbled back with a gasp, dispelling the eerily real vision. The palm of his hand tingled strangely, and he flexed his fingers.

"A gift of our union," he heard the vision's voice say again.

But the mystery of the words was quickly dispelled by a blood-curdling cry that echoed through the storage space.

"Sariel?" Remy called out, running in the direction of the scream.

As he grew closer, he could hear the unmistakable sounds of a struggle, and the Grigori leader's voice raised in anger. He came around a pallet, stacked high with wooden boxes, to see that Sariel had caught his prey, and had driven him to the ground. The man struggled weakly as Sariel's fists rained down on his face.

"What are you doing?" Remy yelled.

Sariel raised his fist to bring it down again upon the man's swollen and bloody features, but Remy caught his wrist. The Grigori's head spun toward him, insane fury burning in his cold gray eyes.

"Enough," Remy commanded.

Sariel tried to pull free of his grasp, but Remy held fast, pulling the Grigori off of his victim.

The mysterious man moaned, bubbles of blood forming upon his lips.

"Who is he?" Remy asked, letting go of Sariel's wrist and kneeling beside the man.

"The one responsible for killing Noah, I would assume," the fallen angel answered with a snarl. He was rubbing his wrist where Remy had gripped it.

"Could he be one of Noah's employees?" Remy asked, patting the man down, looking for some form of identification.

"As far as I know, Noah had no employees," Sariel answered. "The old man enjoyed his isolation. He shut this rig down years ago."

"Who are you?" Remy asked the man, gently slapping his cheek to rouse him, but Sariel had done an exceptional job in beating him unconscious.

Some of the man's blood got on Remy's hand and he felt the divine power of the Seraphim, locked away deep inside him, stir with familiarity.

"He's one of us," Remy stated, wiping the blood on the leg of his pants. "He's an angel." He turned to look up at Sariel.

But the Grigori wasn't paying any attention. He was instead staring into the shadows around them.

"What's wrong?" Remy asked.

Sariel raised a hand to silence him, head tilted. Listening.

At first, all Remy could hear was the raging storm outside the rig, but then he, too, heard the sounds.

Something rustling in the shadows.

Sariel immediately stiffened.

"We need to go," he said, his hands already moving through the air as he began to weave a magickal passage, a means for them to escape.

Remy stood, attempting to see what was there in the darkness, half expecting his dead wife to step from the shadows.

"What is it?" he asked, as what little light they had within the warehouse space was suddenly extinguished.

Sariel didn't answer, continuing to focus on conjuring the magicks to take them away.

Remy was about to demand an answer when the passage began to open, a swirling vortex even blacker than the darkness that surrounded them.

Sariel bent down, hauled the unconscious angel up, and dove through the doorway to safety.

Remy paused. His curiosity got the better of him. He allowed the divine power within him to emerge, channeling the angel fire just enough to illuminate his hand and dispel the encompassing gloom.

Something squealed as if in pain, fleeing into a pool of shadows.

It appeared almost human.

Almost.

SEVEN

Remy exited the magickal passage into the safety of an ornate ballroom. He knew this place, the grand room where Sariel and his Grigori held their countless parties. From the outside, the building located in the area of downtown Boston known lovingly as the Combat Zone appeared abandoned, run-down and decrepit. But in actuality, it hid one of the more opulent nests that the Grigori had scattered around the world.

"What the hell was that?" he asked, stepping back from the gradually diminishing supernatural doorway, eyeing the bubbling darkness in case whatever it was he had seen on the other side decided to follow.

"Your true nature is showing," Sariel spoke.

At first Remy had no idea what the fallen angel was talking about, but then remembered his hand. Its golden flesh still burned with the power of the Seraphim.

Clenching his fist, he pulled the fire back. It didn't want to go, but Remy was persistent, and the divine power finally bent to his will. It was becoming harder to suppress his true nature since the near Apocalypse, but as of now, he was still its master.

Humanity reasserted, Remy flexed his fingers. The flesh of his hand was bright red, like the shell of a cooked lobster, but already it was beginning to heal.

"It appears what I feared most has become a reality," Sariel said ominously, wiping liquid darkness from the front of his suit jacket. His gaze was also fixed on the dissipating magickal passageway.

The unconscious angel moaned on the floor.

Remy approached him. "As soon as he comes to, we'll see what our mysterious stranger here can tell us about what Noah was up to on that rig."

The other Grigori suddenly entered the ballroom in a line, as if responding to a silent command from their leader. They pushed past Remy and swarmed around the unconscious angel.

"There you are," Remy said. "I didn't think you were home."

"We're always home," one of them growled, as they picked up the stranger from the floor and began to carry him away.

The Grigori didn't care much for Remy, and truth be told, the feeling was mutual.

He started to follow the parade, but Sariel blocked his path, placing a hand against his chest to stop him.

Remy looked down at the offending hand, and the Grigori leader quickly removed it.

"They will see to him," Sariel said. "But we must talk."

Remy watched the Grigori pass through a doorway with their burden.

"Then let's talk," he said.

At the end of the ballroom was a large wooden door leading into Sariel's sanctum.

Remy followed the fallen angel inside, the Grigori leader closing the door behind them. He gestured for Remy to take a seat in one of the high-backed leather chairs on either side of the unlit fireplace.

Remy sat, eyeing Sariel as he removed a diamond-shaped stopper from a crystal decanter.

"Scotch?" he offered.

"Sure." Remy didn't feel much like drinking with the angel, but the Grigori always had very good scotch.

Sariel poured one glass and then another, replaced the stopper, and carried the two tumblers of golden fluid to the chairs.

"Thanks," Remy said, accepting his drink.

The Grigori took the chair across from him, casually crossing his legs. He took a long sip from his scotch, then leaned his head back and closed his eyes.

Remy sipped his drink. He hadn't been wrong. The Grigori still had some of the best scotch he'd ever tasted. It made him think of Steven Mulvehill, his closest friend, and how jealous he would be right then.

But Remy doubted the homicide cop would have appreciated the company. The poor guy tried to steer clear of the *weird shit*, as he liked to call it.

"You said you wanted to talk," Remy said, breaking the eerie quiet.

"I was just appreciating the silence," Sariel said, swirling the golden liquid in his glass. "Before the impending chaos."

"Now that makes me think you know more about what's going on than you've shared," Remy said before taking another drink of scotch.

"I wasn't sure before," Sariel said apprehensively. "But now, there can be little doubt."

The angel gulped the rest of his drink, then stared into the empty glass.

"Why don't you start at the beginning," Remy suggested.

Sariel chuckled.

"Yes, the beginning."

EIGHT

"**S**o these orphans that Noah obsessed about, we're talking about the figures I saw standing in front of the mountain caves when the rains started?" Remy asked.

He stood at the liquor cart, pouring two more drinks. He thought another might help Sariel get through what he had to say, and he hated the thought of the Grigori drinking alone.

"Noah referred to any life that he was unable to bring aboard the ark as his orphans," Sariel explained. "No matter how small, or seemingly insignificant, but yes, those figures ... they are the cause for my concern."

Remy returned with the drinks.

"Go on," he said, handing Sariel his glass before sitting. "I'm listening."

"When the Earth was still young, the Lord God hadn't quite decided what would be the final model for humanity. He experimented first with a species the Grigori came to know as the Chimerian.

"They were different from the two He eventually created in the Garden, more primitive, and far more cunning." The fallen angel paused for a drink from his glass.

Remy was surprised by the Grigori's words. He had never heard of this prototype for humanity. "So you're saying that there were two designs for what would eventually become the human race?"

Sariel chuckled. "He wanted to see which one worked the best."

"Why didn't I know any of this?" Remy asked in disbelief.

"There was no need for you to know," Sariel said. "It didn't concern you. As Seraphim, yours was a more militaristic purpose. It was the Grigori who were assigned to the fledgling world, and thus we were privy to all its imperfections."

"So these . . . Chimerian were His first attempts at humanity?"

"They were, and unfortunately, they lost the contest," Sariel said flatly. "The two in the Garden, though disobedient, captured His curiosity."

Remy drank deeply from his glass. It was all a bit overwhelming as he tried to fit the pieces of the picture together inside his head.

"So God brought the rains to destroy this earlier try at humankind," he stated, part of him hoping that he was wrong.

"Yes," Sariel agreed. "But somehow the Chimerian learned of their fate and were determined to survive . . . in any way they could."

There was a soft knock at the door.

"Come," the Grigori said.

The door swung open and a blind man entered. He was elderly, his back slightly hunched, and he was dressed in a butler's garb. The Grigori used the sightless as servants. Remy wasn't sure exactly why, but the blind seemed to be drawn to these fallen angels, as if the Grigori somehow satisfied their deep yearnings to see.

"Would you and your guest enjoy a fire, sir?" the old servant inquired.

"Perhaps a fire would be just the thing to take away the chill that has settled in my bones," Sariel replied.

"Very good, sir," the servant said as he carefully

crossed the room. Gripping the marble mantel, he slowly lowered himself to his knees before the open hearth.

"We believe that the Chimerian, abandoned by their Creator, found something new to worship," Sariel continued, ignoring his servant.

"A false god?" Remy asked, running his finger along the rim of his glass.

"Of a sort," Sariel said. He leaned his head back against his chair, eyes closed. "We've surmised that they somehow managed to communicate with the nameless things that thrived in the darkness before our Lord God brought the light of creation. Things that were old before even us."

Sariel drank more.

"And in exchange the Chimerian received knowledge," he said, eyes still shut. "An understanding of dark, arcane arts. But it didn't help them."

Remy watched the servant work on the fire. Slowly, methodically, the blind man felt for the cords of dry wood that were stacked alongside the fireplace, selecting each piece carefully and laying it within the cold hearth.

"They should have all been destroyed when the rains came," Remy said. "That was the point of the flood, wasn't it?"

Sariel finished his scotch and straightened in his chair. He let the empty tumbler fall to the floor.

"It certainly was the point," he said. "And for countless millennia, we believed it successful. Then Noah brought to my attention the fact that the deluge might have failed."

Remy finished his own drink and seriously contemplated another. "How did he know?" he asked.

"The old man was a tortured soul," Sariel said. "The longer he lived, the more obsessed he became with the things he had left to die. The guilt ate at him."

"You kept in touch?" Remy asked, curious as to the Grigori's relationship with Noah.

"We saw each other from time to time," Sariel said, waving his hand vaguely. "We survivors of the deluge shared a kind of bond." The Grigori leader smiled, but there was little warmth in the expression.

"When we spoke, he told me of the expeditions that he'd undertaken, traversing the globe, sparing no expense, searching for signs of those that had been left behind . . . signs that they—his orphans—may have somehow survived."

The servant appeared to have finished preparing the wood, and leaned back as if to admire what he had accomplished.

"He said he could remember them all," Sariel said, tapping the side of his skull. "Each and every species that was deemed unworthy to board the ark. He could see them in his head. Awake or asleep, they were always with him."

"I can see how that might drive you a little . . . crazy," Remy acknowledged.

"The last time we communicated, Noah told me that of all the doomed species, he believed *they* might have survived."

"They, meaning the Chimerian."

"I tried to explain the danger if this was true, but he couldn't see it," Sariel explained. "All he cared about was the alleviation of his guilt."

The servant had found the tin of fireplace matches and was attempting to ignite the fire.

"So you think Noah found the Chimerian . . . and that they are responsible for his death."

"You saw his body," Sariel snarled. "You saw that thing scuttling away in the shadows."

"Yes." Remy nodded slowly. "I did see something, although I have no idea what it was."

Sariel's thin, bloodless lips pulled back in another attempt at a smile.

"What you saw was potential doom for humanity," the Grigori said.

Remy was surprised by the intensity of the words.

"Don't you think you're being overly dramatic?"

The servant struck the match on the rough stone surface on the side of the fireplace. It ignited with a hiss, the flame growing so large that it consumed the matchstick in an instant, leaping down to the old man's fingers, and then to his clothes. A cry of surprise and pain escaped him, as he fell backward, the sleeve of his jacket afire. Remy reacted immediately, dropping to the floor and leaning across the thrashing old man to suffocate the flames with his hands.

And all the while, Sariel sat, calmly watching it all unfold.

"*That* was dramatic," he stated. "What will happen to humanity if the Chimerian are allowed to thrive . . . that will be *tragic*."

The servant seemed to shrug off the pain of his burns, and returned to the fireplace, taking another match from the tin.

Remy couldn't believe it.

"That will be enough," Sariel ordered.

The old man stopped. "Sorry for the delay, my master, but—"

"I said that will be enough," the Grigori leader interrupted.

Without another word, the servant hauled himself to his feet using the marble mantel, and clutching his injured hand to his chest, shuffled from the room.

Remy had had just about enough of the fallen angel's company.

"Perhaps you should tell me exactly why you've decided to involve me in this," he said as he got to his feet.

"You care for them a great deal," Sariel stated. "Those outside these walls." He gestured with his chin to the world beyond his lair. "I thought you would want to save them."

"What can I do?" Remy asked. "This is much bigger than I—"

"What can I do, asks the soldier of Heaven," the Grigori mocked. "You sell yourself short, my brother."

"No," Remy stated with a definitive shake of his head. "That's not me anymore. I'm not going to allow you to drag me—"

Sariel had closed his eyes again, clearly not interested in Remy's rant.

"We must hunt and destroy them," the Grigori proclaimed. His eyes opened and held Remy in an icy stare. "We must find where they nest and finish what the deluge should have."

"You can't be serious," Remy said.

Sariel glared at him. "They were never supposed to survive. They should have died when the Earth was young and the flood waters rose."

"But you're talking about exterminating a species we know nothing about," Remy said. "We can't just . . ."

"If the current kings and queens of the world are to survive, we must."

"You don't know that."

"Do you wish to take that chance?" Sariel asked.

Remy should have known better. It always came to this—passing judgment, and death.

"I won't kill for you," he said, moving toward the door.

"But the humans . . . will you kill for them?" the Grigori leader asked.

Remy stopped and turned. "Why did you drag me into this?" he asked. "You know how I feel about you and your brethren. You know I want nothing more than to live my life peacefully and to not be bothered with . . ."

"You are the powerful Remiel," Sariel said. "A Seraphim warrior that, as much as you are loath to admit, still retains the full extent of its heavenly might."

Remy shook his head. "I told you, that's not me anymore."

Sariel smiled. "I could have sworn I saw your old self driving back the Four Horsemen of the Apocalypse a few short weeks ago, but I must have been mistaken."

Remy pulled open the door. He'd heard enough.

"This isn't just for us, Remiel," Sariel called after him. "The Chimerian will hate humankind as much as they hate us. We'll need your strength if we are to succeed."

Remy didn't even turn around, allowing the door to slam shut behind him as he strode across the ballroom. Just outside the grand room, he saw a gathered crowd of Grigori, and remembered the angel they had brought with them from the rig.

"The angel," he said to one of the Grigori. "Has he regained consciousness?" He craned his neck, trying to catch a glimpse of where they had taken him.

"He's resting," the Grigori said.

Remy tried to move past and felt a hand suddenly pressed to his chest. He glanced down at the hand.

"I said he's resting," the Grigori repeated more forcefully.

"I know your kind despises me for one reason or another, but I strongly suggest that you remove your hand from my person or I'll be more than happy to provide you with something to really hate me for."

The hand stayed there a moment longer before it was withdrawn.

He considered pushing past the Grigori lackey to find the angel and ask him what he knew, but right then, he didn't have the energy.

He gave the fallen angel a final, nasty look, then quickly turned and left.

It was cold outside on the early-morning streets of Boston, but Remy didn't feel a thing.

NINE

Remy wandered up Tremont Street, onto Arlington, ending up in the lobby of the old Ritz-Carlton Hotel, now the Taj.

He glanced at his watch and figured that Ashley would probably be up by now, getting ready for school. Finding a phone, he dialed the number and got Ashley's mom. He explained that he was working on a case, and would she or Ashley mind zipping over to the apartment to give Marlowe his breakfast and take him out.

The woman said that there would be no problem, and Remy thanked her and hung up.

Now what to do? All the way up from the Zone he'd thought about what Sariel had proposed, and how freaked he was by what the Grigori had believed he'd do.

The sad thing was that no matter how disturbed he was, he couldn't really see much of a choice. If these creatures . . . these Chimerian were as dangerous as Sariel said, there could very well be human lives at stake.

Remy headed into the Club Lounge and bought a large coffee. The scotch had worn off a while ago and he needed something more stimulating to get his brain functioning the way it should.

He took the coffee and returned to the bank of

phones in the lobby, digging through his pockets for change. In this particular instance, he didn't worry about waking anybody up—this person never slept, and was almost always home.

Wishing for his cell phone, he fed the machine with change and dialed the number, listening as it rang.

On the third ring the phone was picked up, but only silence greeted Remy.

"It's me," he said.

"Hey, me," replied a voice on the other end. "What's up?"

"I've got a bit of a problem, and I want to run it by you."

"This doesn't have anything to do with the Apocalypse, does it?" the voice asked.

"Not exactly," Remy responded.

"Good, I've pretty much had my fill of the Apocalypse."

"Meet me at the Taj for breakfast. My treat," Remy told him.

"Sounds yummy, give me about a half hour and I'll be there."

"Half hour?" Remy asked. The voice on the other end lived less than ten minutes away.

"Finishing up *Once Upon a Time in the West*," he said.

"Didn't you watch that last month?" Remy remembered their conversation about Henry Fonda's performance in the Leone masterpiece.

"New month," was the answer.

It made perfect sense.

"See you in a half hour, then," Remy said, and hung up.

The former Guardian angel said nothing as he strolled into the lobby of the Taj Hotel. With his balding head, horn-rimmed glasses, and usual gray suit, white shirt, and maroon tie, Francis looked like any other white-collar business type employed in the city of Boston.

"How was the movie?" Remy asked, getting up from the sofa where he had been awaiting his friend's arrival.

"Better with every viewing," Francis said.

Remy nodded, even though *The Good, the Bad and the Ugly* was his own personal favorite of the Leone westerns.

"Are we going to eat?" Francis asked, looking toward the cafe.

"Let's go," Remy said as the two walked toward the entrance. "I could use a pot of coffee."

"Waffles," Francis said, and Remy turned his head to look at him.

"What was that?"

"Waffles," he repeated. "I could really go for some waffles."

Knowing what Remy did about the being called Francis, statements like that only made him smile.

Francis was once the angel Fraciel of the Guardian angel host Virtues. A bad choice on his part had left him on the outs with the Lord God after the rebellion. Realizing the error of his ways, Fraciel had thrown himself at the mercy of the Almighty, begging for forgiveness. Surprisingly, the Almighty did not banish the Guardian to the Hell prison, Tartarus, but instead made him watchman over one of the gates between the earthly realm and the Hellish, a gate that just so happened to be in the basement of the Newbury Street brownstone that Francis now owned.

When he wasn't taking care of his duties to the doorway to Tartarus, the former Guardian angel worked as one of the world's most sought-after assassins. If you could afford his fee, and he decided, after careful review, that the victim did in fact deserve to be taken down, there was little that could be done to prevent the inevitable.

But this morning, the inevitable was that Francis was going to have waffles.

They were seated at a table by the window, overlooking the lower end of Newbury Street, and while the hostess went off to get coffee for Remy and tea for Francis, they quietly perused the menu.

Remy really didn't have to eat, although he often did so to maintain his guise of humanity. This morning, however, he realized he had no desire for food. Francis had already closed his menu and placed it on the table beside him, so Remy did the same.

"First off, how are you doing?" the former Guardian asked, as he straightened his silverware. Francis had always been fascinated by Remy's relationship with Madeline, observing the many facets of their marriage like a scientist watching some new kind of germ beneath a microscope.

"I'm doing," Remy replied, concerned by the bizarre visions he'd been having, but not yet ready to share. Francis already thought he was nuts to live the way he did.

"And the mutt?"

"He's doing, too."

Francis accepted that with a pause and a nod.

"So what seems to be the problem?" he asked, changing the subject.

The waitress appeared then, bringing Remy a carafe of coffee and Francis a metal pot of hot water and a small wooden box filled with flavored teas. She took their order: bagel with cream cheese for Remy, and waffles topped with strawberries and whipped cream for Francis.

"So?" Francis prodded, after she'd gone. He was dunking an English Breakfast tea bag in a cup of hot water he'd just poured.

Remy took a long drink from his coffee cup before replying. "It's getting weird again."

"Again?" Francis questioned with a laugh. He removed the tea bag and placed it on the side of his saucer.

Then he added two heaping teaspoons of sugar and a splash of milk. "Has it ever stopped? Especially since the whole Apocalypse business, the crazy train has been running flat-out."

Remy didn't like to hear that. He had hoped that once they'd driven back the Four Horsemen, the world would have settled back into some semblance of normalcy, but it really hadn't. He wondered how much that had to do with his current dilemma.

"First off, Noah's dead," he began.

Francis was stirring his tea. He removed the spoon and set it down on the white tablecloth, where it left a brownish stain.

The former Guardian took a slurping sip from the rim of his cup as he digested Remy's statement. "Why am I already guessing that he didn't die peacefully in his sleep?"

"He was murdered," Remy confirmed, remembering what he had seen aboard the oil rig, the horrible condition of the old man's body, as if he'd been beaten to death.

"Color me surprised," Francis said sarcastically.

Remy drank his coffee, allowing the caffeine to work its magic upon him.

"Sariel was the one who showed me," Remy continued.

"That one is such a creep," the former Guardian said with a nod. "But he does have some damn fine scotch."

"It seems that Noah was trying to make contact with a species called the Chimerian . . . the Lord's first attempt at creating man that were supposed to be wiped out during the Great Flood, but somehow weren't."

Francis was silent as their breakfasts were delivered.

"Is there anything else I can get you?" the waitress asked.

Remy shook his head with a smile.

"Just some syrup and I'll be good to go," Francis said.

She quickly darted away and returned with the syrup,

placing it on the table in front of Francis. "Let me know if you need anything else," she offered as she moved on to her other tables.

"There was a first attempt at humanity?" Francis asked as he poured syrup on the waffles, careful not to get any on the whipped cream.

"That's what Sariel said." Remy was relieved to know that he wasn't the only one unaware of the early prototype. "Think I might've caught a glimpse of one on Noah's oil rig."

"So that's true, then?" Francis asked, breaking off a piece of waffle with his fork. "I'd heard he was living alone in the middle of the ocean."

The former Guardian took a bite of his breakfast.

"So these . . . ," he began with a mouthful.

"Chimerian."

"Chimerian. You think they offed the old man?" Francis asked.

Remy paused to think about the question, and realized, at this stage of the game, he didn't really know. "Possibly," he answered.

"No wonder our fair-haired boy sounded like he was in such a tizzy," Francis commented, eating more of his breakfast.

Remy set his bagel down and wiped at his mouth, wanting to be sure he wasn't mistaken about what he'd just heard.

"Who, Sariel? You talked with him?"

Francis nodded as he chewed. "Called about ten minutes before you did, said he was going to need my skills for a matter of grave importance."

"Did you already know what I just told you?"

Francis shook his head. "No, when I asked him what was up, he said it was a hunting expedition."

"And you agreed to this?"

He shrugged. "Business has been sort of slow, and there are these Bavarian Warhammers coming onto the market that I'm really jonesing for. . . ."

Francis had a thing for weaponry. He collected it obsessively, like a nerdy kid and comic books.

"You agreed to this," Remy repeated, resigning himself from question to statement.

"Yeah," Francis said, breaking off another piece of waffle and shoveling it into his mouth.

"Do you understand what he wants you to do?" Remy asked. "He wants you to help them kill these creatures ... these survivors."

"He said that you were on board, too," Francis told him, reaching for his teacup.

"Of course he did." Remy had picked up the other half of his bagel, but placed it back on his plate. He couldn't even pretend to be hungry anymore. "I just can't wrap my brain around the idea of wiping them out," he said.

"Think of it this way: they're murderers," Francis said flatly. "And they shouldn't even be alive. The flood should've erased them from the world."

Remy poured himself another cup of coffee, not buying the Guardian's justification.

"Think of it as tidying up," Francis stressed. "We'd be setting things right."

"We'd be committing murder."

"Is it murder when you put a rabid animal down?" Francis asked. "These things are likely dangerous. Can we take a risk on them maybe breeding and getting around?"

Remy knew that his friend's points were accurate, but something nagged at him, something that he couldn't quite put his finger on.

"We don't know anything about them, other than what Sariel has told us."

"And?" Francis asked.

"When have we ever trusted anything Sariel has said?"

"Good point." Francis took a sip of his tea.

"I'm not comfortable with this," Remy said, removing

the cloth napkin from his lap and placing it on the table.

"So does that mean you're not in?" Francis asked.

Remy fished fifty dollars out of his wallet and put it on the table.

"I don't know what it means."

"Do you want a lift?" Francis asked. "Let me finish here and—"

"Think I'll walk," Remy told him. "It'll give me a chance to think this through. I'll call you later."

"Sounds like a plan," Francis said, as he continued to eat. "And thanks for breakfast."

"Everything all right?" the hostess asked as Remy passed her on his way out.

He smiled, tempted to tell her the truth.

No, things weren't all right.

Not in the least.

It was a nice day, not that Remy noticed at all.

He walked across Arlington Street and through the Public Garden, heading toward the Boston Common. People were just starting to hit the streets on their way to work, flowing up from the Park Street T Station and trickling down from the many small streets that made up Beacon Hill.

Remy wandered against the tide heading to Downtown Crossing, the financial district and Government Center, making his own way home up through the Common to Joy Street.

As he walked, the same thoughts bounced around inside his head. He didn't want to be like them . . . like the Grigori, and even Francis. He would have been perfectly content to live like those bustling along to work around him.

Ignorant to the matters of the preternatural.

But he wasn't, and no matter how hard he tried, he couldn't ignore what he knew.

Especially when lives—human as well as angelic— might be at risk.

To say that Marlowe was happy to see him was an understatement. But that was one of the most glorious things about dogs, they were always happy to see you.

The black Lab met Remy at the door, panting like a freight train, tail wagging so fast that Remy thought he was going to take off for sure.

"Remy!" the dog barked. *"Remy! Remy! Remy!"*

"Hello, hello," Remy said with a laugh, pushing the dog aside so that he could get in and close the door.

"Thought gone," the dog said, eagerly licking Remy's hand.

"Yep, I was gone but now I'm back," he reassured the animal.

Remy walked down the hallway, excited dog by his side.

"Did Ashley stop by to feed you?" he asked, already knowing that she had.

"No," the dog said, standing at attention in the kitchen.

The dog's answer took him by surprise.

"No?" he asked.

"No feed," he growled. *"Hungry."*

Remy glanced around the room, noticing the empty food bowl and the full water dish. He also saw the note on the counter near the coffeepot and Ashley's unmistakable scrawl telling him that Marlowe had been fed and taken out. She'd even drawn a smiley face at the bottom of the note.

"Then what's this?" Remy asked, picking up the note and showing the dog.

"Paper," the dog answered, tail wagging. *"Rip?"*

"No, you can't rip it. It's a note from Ashley telling me that you already ate," Remy said. "You've been nabbed, good sir."

"Nabbed, good sir," Marlowe repeated sadly.

Remy laughed. The Lab had a bottomless pit for a stomach and often tried this trick to get an extra meal. It had worked a few times with Madeline, but never with Remy.

His wife had been too trusting.

He flashed back to the last vision he'd had of her aboard the rig, the sensation of warmth on his hand as it was placed upon her stomach.

"A gift of our union," she had said.

What does it mean? he wondered. At first he'd believed it all part of the process of grieving, but now he was beginning to suspect otherwise. There was some kind of connection between the visions and Noah's murder, but what, he hadn't a clue.

And that was what he was going to have to find out.

He'd planned on returning home, cleaning up a bit, and heading to the office to catch up on paperwork.

But not now.

There was little chance of turning this boat around. He might as well throw himself head-on into the madness. The quicker he dealt with this business, the quicker he could return to the life he'd worked so hard to build, but now that seemed to be crumbling at the foundation.

Noah's office would be the place to start. It had been in a shambles, and he hadn't had a chance to really go through it. There might be something still lying about waiting to be uncovered.

"Shit," he muttered beneath his breath.

That meant returning to the rig, and the only way he would be able to do that would be with the help of certain skills that he had used far too freely lately. He knew that there wasn't much of a choice, but it still pissed him off.

He walked into the living room to explain to the dog that he was leaving again. Marlowe lay in the middle of the floor, Sphinx-like, tail thumping. Remy knew what that particular look meant and felt bad.

"Sorry, buddy," he said. "But I can't take you for a walk right now. I have to go to work for a while."

The dog looked as though he'd just been told that he was going to the pound. Guilt almost got the best of Remy, but then he remembered something that was even better than a walk to the park.

"Would you like a pig's ear instead?" he asked.

Marlowe jumped to his feet and bolted toward the kitchen. By the time Remy caught up to him, he was standing in front of a lower cabinet door, staring intensely as his tail wagged in anticipation.

"I guess that's a yes," Remy said as he pulled open the cabinet and reached for the bag that contained the disgusting treats. "You work on this and I'll take you for a walk when I get back," he told the dog, who wasn't even listening. Marlowe's dark brown gaze was transfixed on the bag.

Remy removed one of the greasy treats and held it out. Marlowe carefully plucked it from his hand, then darted from the kitchen to his room—his lair, as Madeline used to call it—to consume his prize.

That taken care of, Remy walked into the living room and stood on the spot where Sariel had used his unique skills to take him from his home. He closed his eyes. Carefully he stirred the angelic essence lying inside him. It didn't take more than a gentle prod to awaken it.

The divine power surged through him, coursing through his blood. His senses at once awakened, coming alive with a vengeance. His hearing became preternaturally acute, and the voices of millions in prayer assaulted his ears, as though they were all in this very room with him. And the smell.

The smell was strong, nauseating—the smell of magick.

Opening his eyes, he looked down at the spot where the passage had opened. He could see the residue of Sariel's traveling spell, wafting up from the rug on his living room floor.

Rolling his shoulder blades, he allowed his wings to emerge. He could feel the appendages moving beneath his flesh, growing in size as they worked their way toward the surface. There was a brief flash of pain, and then enormous relief as his golden wings unfurled. Gently he fanned the air as he prepared for his journey.

Now is as good a time as any, Remy thought as he pulled his wings about him, wrapping himself within the tight embrace of the golden feathers. The scent of Sariel's magick was still fresh in his nostrils, and by closing his eyes he could see the path he would need to travel.

He thought of his destination, and then he was gone.

TEN

Like electricity moving through a wire, he was there.

The heavy smell of salt in the air was the first thing he became aware of. Remy opened his wings and exposed himself to the new environment.

He had appeared exactly where Sariel's magick had dropped them before. The weather this time was far more hospitable, although the wind still whipped across the broad expanse of concrete, trying desperately to catch his golden wings.

It was pitch black on the ocean, but security lights drove back the darkness of night from the vast deck of the oil rig.

Remy pulled his wings back, then headed for the metal staircase, head bowed against the humid breeze. Once inside, it didn't take him long to find Noah's quarters.

The slide projector still hummed from the desk, but the bulb had burnt out, and the room was immersed in shadow. Allowing his eyes a moment to adjust, Remy carefully approached the desk, mapping out in his mind where he remembered most of the mess to be, as well as the old man's body.

He recalled a banker's lamp, and leaned over across the desktop until his fingers found the dangling chain and pulled it, dispelling the darkness.

The office was still in chaos, but Noah's body was gone.

Remy moved around the desk to study the spot where the body had lain; telltale spatters of dried blood proved that it had been there. He recalled the vague image of the pale-skinned thing, skittering back into the darkness of the warehouse, and wondered if that had anything to do with the body's disappearance.

Turning his attention to the desk, Remy pulled out the chair, rolling it over stray pieces of paper and slides that covered the floor.

"Where do I start?" he asked himself, staring at the disheveled surface of the desktop. Deciding that the journey of a million miles begins with the first step, Remy dove right in, selecting the first random piece of paper and giving it a once-over. It was nothing special, a bill for food supplies for the months of January and February.

There were more bills and receipts, and an amazing number of charitable mailers, all of them from animal organizations, many of which Remy had never heard of.

He found a recent fax from a shipping company confirming the pickup of four transport containers from the rig in two days' time. What in the world would an old man, alone in the middle of the ocean, have been shipping? Remy made a mental note to find them before leaving.

As the surface of the desk became organized, the paperwork he found beneath became more interesting. It appeared that Noah Driscoll had been looking into real estate in the Boston area, and had found something he liked by the looks of a recent purchase and sale agreement. The property was in Lynn, north of the city. Remy jotted down the address to check out later.

Transport containers, purchased property—the old man had certainly been up to something before his untimely demise.

Remy left the office, heading back outside to find the transport containers. He could not help but be impressed by the view from the rig, undulating gray waters in every direction as far as the eye could see. If one wanted peace and quiet, total isolation, this was certainly the place.

But if that was the case, why had Noah bought property in a North Shore city?

Curiouser, and curiouser, Remy thought.

He found the transport containers at the back of the rig, stacked one on top of the other and secured to the deck by woven steel cords. *These babies aren't going anywhere,* Remy observed as he approached one of the powder blue steel containers.

It wasn't locked. He placed his hands on the cold metal latch and pulled it up and into place so he could open the first of the two doors. The chemical smell of *new* wafted out, as the dim outside light flooded into the carrier, illuminating its contents.

The container was filled with all manner of things that would be needed to set up a living space. Remy couldn't help but think of the furnishing of a college dormitory as his eyes moved across the plastic-wrapped mattresses, chairs, and thick blankets, still wrapped in their clear packaging, stacked in the corners.

In the corner with the blankets were boxes, and as Remy moved closer he saw that they were filled with toys, picture books, and brightly colored blocks. Stuffed animals stared out at him from inside a large, clear plastic bag. In one box there was even a toy Noah's Ark. He reached down and took it from the container.

Not even close, he thought, looking at the toy mock-up of the great craft. The plastic toy rattled loudly as he moved it, and he discovered that the top of the boat could be removed to reveal plastic animals inside.

Remy put the top back on the boat and placed it with the other toys. He looked about the transport container until something caught his eye. In the far corner of the container he found an unwrapped blanket and a stuffed animal. There was also an opened package of crackers, and crumbs on the floor.

Somebody...

The image of what he had seen running from the light again appeared in his head.

... or something, has taken up residence here, he thought, looking around with a more cautious eye.

Certain that he was alone, Remy decided that he'd seen enough. He left the container and returned to the spot on the deck where he'd arrived.

Again he found the residue of Sariel's magick, opened his wings, and prepared to go home. Thinking of the place he wanted to be, Remy let the wings close, wrapping him in their natural magick.

And as he felt himself slip away, drifting between time and space, he realized that he was leaving with more questions than answers.

Remy returned with little more than a whisper. One second he was on board an abandoned oil rig in the middle of the ocean, the next, in the living room of his Beacon Hill home.

It was something he could get used to, and something that would gradually leach away his humanity, until all that remained was a cold, unfeeling instrument of violence forged in Heaven. He had escaped being that a very long time ago, and would do everything in his power to never be that way again.

The wings wanted to stay, to be part of his everyday attire, but Remy told them no. This was how the divine nature that he kept locked away worked, reminding him of what he had once been, trying to tempt him with memories of a glorious time when he soared above the spires of Heaven.

But those times were gone, sullied by the violence of war.

Remembering what he did, could any of them—these

so-called creatures of Heaven—even remotely be considered divine?

Remy didn't think so, and exerting his will upon the wings, he forced them away, burying the nature he had come to abhor, and assuming the guise of humanity.

"Marlowe, I'm back," he announced, glancing at the clock on the DVD player. He'd been gone for close to two hours.

Odd, he thought, as the normally curious beast did not come to see him.

"Hey, Marlowe?" Remy called out again, leaving the living room and heading down the hallway to the dog's lair.

"Do you want to go out?" Remy asked, then stopped as he saw that Marlowe was not alone.

The creature appeared human, almost childlike, its body pale, hairless, and incredibly thin. It was dressed in swaths of filthy cloth that hung in tatters from its scarecrowlike frame.

Remy had no idea what it was. It bore no resemblance to the indigo-skinned figures he'd seen perched on the rocks so long ago. It squatted on its haunches in front of Marlowe. Toys were scattered about the floor, and the two were staring at each other intensely, eyes locked as if playing a game, victory going to the one who managed not to blink first.

The tension in the air was palpable, like an elastic band just about stretched to capacity before . . .

Marlowe barked, slapping his paws on the hardwood floor, and all hell broke loose.

The trancelike state between the two beasts suddenly broken, the creature reacted, pulling its pale lips back in a catlike hiss.

Remy was afraid, and as if suddenly catching the scent of his fear, the white-skinned being turned its gaze to him.

Its eyes were black, like shiny pools of oil, and Remy felt himself drawn toward their inky depths.

"Marlowe . . . run," he managed, looking away before the intruder sprang.

It moved incredibly fast, and collided with Remy, knocking him back against the wall as it tried to escape down the hall.

The dog was barking like crazy now.

Remy dove, wrapping his arms around the creature's thin waist, driving them both to the floor.

The invader let out an unpleasant squeal, a strange mixture of a baby's cry and the screech of brakes, as it struggled in his grasp.

"Stay back," Remy commanded the dog, as the Labrador started to slink from the room. Marlowe retreated.

The strange beast was much stronger than it appeared, easily breaking Remy's grip and scrabbling to its bare feet in a frantic run. It skidded around the corner into the living room, and Remy was right behind it. But it was waiting for him. The creature charged, slashing at him with razor-sharp claws. Remy leapt back, feeling the claws snag the front of his shirt and graze the smooth flesh beneath.

The beast had retreated deeper into the living room and crouched there, watching him.

Remy was about to charge after it, but something stopped him. Something in the monster's gaze.

Is that fear?

Still crouched on the living room rug, the creature let out another of its disturbing cries, and Remy watched in surprise as it began to convulse, hunching its back as if bending over to vomit. But instead, the pale flesh on its bony back tore with a wet, ripping sound, and two leathery batlike wings popped from beneath the skin.

Remy watched, dumbfounded, as the creature cloaked itself in its new leathern appendages, then squeezed itself smaller and smaller, until it was no longer there, leaving behind only the telltale scent of magick.

Angel magick.

Remy was still staring at the spot where the intruder had been, trying to understand what was going on, when he heard a soft whimper behind him. He turned to see a trembling Marlowe standing in the hallway, clutching a filthy stuffed monkey in his mouth.

"Hey," Remy said, going to the shaking animal. "Are you all right?" he asked, running his hands over the black Labrador's body, searching for injuries. "Did he hurt you?"

Marlowe let the toy drop to the floor, licking the side of Remy's face affectionately.

"No hurt," Marlowe said. *"Nice."*

Remy stopped inspecting the dog and looked into Marlowe's dark brown eyes. "What do you mean, nice?"

"Nice, no hurt," Marlowe explained. *"Give toy."* The dog pawed the filthy stuffed monkey. *"Nice. Give toy."*

Remy reached down to pick up the monkey.

"This isn't yours?" he asked the dog.

"Mine now," the dog said, playfully snatching it from Remy's hands and giving it a savage shake.

Images filled Remy's head as things became more clear, like jagged rocks suddenly visible through wafting holes in thick, ocean fog.

Terribly clear.

He remembered the contents of the transport containers on the oil rig, furnishings for a home, blankets and toys.

Stuffed animals peering out at him from their clear plastic packaging.

"Nice," Marlowe said again, happily tossing the new toy into the air. *"No hurt.*

"Friend."

ELEVEN

Remy called Francis on the way to Lynn.

The former Guardian angel turned assassin wasn't home, so he left a message.

"Hey, it's me. Heading to Lynn on the North Shore to check out a piece of property that the old man purchased a few weeks ago," he told his friend, debating if he should explain further or wait until things had crystallized a little bit more.

"Give me a call when you get this. There are some things I need to run by you before you accept the Grigori's offer. Later." Remy ended the call and slipped the phone into the pocket of his leather jacket.

He'd reached the rotary in Revere, and veered right onto the Lynn Marsh Road. It was a straight shot from there, across the long stretch of causeway that connected Revere to Lynn.

His thoughts were wandering again to the pale-skinned creature sprouting wings in his living room. He remembered its eyes, moist, dark, and shiny, like the cold ocean water of the marshlands he was passing by now.

But there had been something else in the blackness of its stare, ferocity, fear. . . .

Intelligence.

He passed over the Foxhill Bridge into the city of Lynn.

The sprawling General Electric jet engine plant was to his right, the city's major employer since it lost the shoe industry to foreign shores back in the 1920s.

Remy fished the piece of paper he'd written the address on from his pocket and gave it another glance. According to MapQuest, he wasn't too far away.

He continued on down Western Avenue, thinking of the silly little rhyme that just about everybody on the North Shore seemed to know.

Lynn, Lynn, the city of sin, you never go out the way you came in.

It wasn't long before he found River Street. It wasn't one of the city's better neighborhoods. Most of the buildings were boarded up and empty, many blackened and charred as if by fire.

He parked his car beneath the dim light thrown by the single working streetlight, and stepped out onto the street. He could still catch the musty smell of smoke in the air.

Most of the buildings were missing numbers, and it took a little while to figure out where he needed to be looking and on what side, but as he walked the lonely stretch of River Street, it soon became obvious where he was heading.

He could see it ahead of him, the tall spire reaching up into the dingy night sky, the abandoned remains of Saint Mathias Church. She appeared to have been let go quite some time ago, the cruel years having their way with her.

Remy always felt a tinge of sadness when he saw buildings like this, places of worship no longer carrying the prayers of the devoted faithful up to the heavens. It was a sign of the times, he told himself, but it didn't make it any less sad to see.

Saint Mathias was more than just a church; it was a sort of compound. An alley separated the church from a run-down rectory and an old brick elementary school.

It seemed that Noah had bought it all.

At the back of the church, a frame from one of the elaborate stained-glass windows depicting the Stations of the Cross had fallen away, allowing Remy to look inside.

The building was empty. Anything that would have made it recognizable as a place of worship had pretty much been removed; the only things serving as a slight reminder were wooden pews, stacked in a far, dark corner, as if waiting to be used as kindling.

He saw nothing out of the ordinary, nothing to pique his curiosity, so he turned his attention to the rectory, directly across from the church. Remy climbed the three chipped and broken concrete steps to the side door. It appeared that new locks had been recently installed.

Remy knew how to do the whole lock-picking thing, but seldom remembered to bring his tools. Looking around—as if there'd be anyone around here to raise an alarm—he placed his hand against the door. He utilized a little bit of his divine strength to force it open, and went inside.

He pulled a small flashlight from his jacket pocket and turned it on, the thin beam of light cutting through the murk. He was in a small hallway that led to a kitchen.

The room appeared clean—too clean. It had been used recently, not like the rest of what was around him. Covered in thick dust, the place looked to have been abandoned more than a few years ago.

Across the kitchen was a swinging door, and he went through into a corridor. There was a flight of stairs leading up to the next level on his right, and a short hallway that led to the rectory's main office. He checked out the office next. All he found was an old grime-covered desk and a broken wooden chair.

Remy returned to the stairs and climbed to the next floor. He stood on the landing, shining his light across closed doors to rooms that would have once housed the priests of the Saint Mathias parish. There was a strong, musty smell of dampness on the second floor—and something else.

As Remy approached the first door, he tried to convince himself that in a building this old, and in such disrepair, the offending smell could have come from a number of sources: a dead mouse or rat, maybe even a pigeon.

He turned the old-fashioned metal knob. The first door swung open. A rusty box spring lay on the floor in the room's center. There was a clean spot on the yellowed wallpaper where a crucifix had once hung.

At the next door, the smell was stronger, and Remy prepared himself. He opened the door and found a rat, its withered carcass caught in a trap. He let the beam of light linger on the desiccated rodent corpse, surprised at the amount of stink that still emanated from the remains.

The third room proved to be the charm. This knob was warm to the touch, but he barely noticed as he swung the creaking door wide, moving the beam of his light around the nearly empty room.

Nearly empty.

At first he thought it was a sleeping bag, the encampment of some vagrant who found shelter from the harsh New England cold. But then he realized otherwise.

Remy entered the room, his light trained upon the unmoving shape on the bedroom floor. It took him a moment to process what it was that he was looking at. It was a body, wrapped up in strips of heavy cloth like a mummy. Only the face was left exposed.

A face that Remy knew.

He held the light on Noah's face. Somebody had cleaned him up, washing the dried blood from his battered face and white beard.

Preparing him for burial.

Around the old man's body, somebody had dropped slides, as if in some sort of tribute, pictures of all the animal species the old man had saved escorting him on his way to the afterlife.

The sudden sound of a floorboard creaking behind him caused him to spin around, his flashlight beam searching out the source. But he found only an empty doorway, the door slowly closing on its own.

The ringing of his cell nearly gave him a heart attack.

He lowered his flashlight and fished the phone from his pocket. It was Francis.

That was when the creatures chose to make their move. There were three of them. Their pale flesh glowed translucently in the darkness of the room as they emerged from the shadows. They were lightning quick, swatting his cell from his hand. Remy could hear the faint voice of Francis, calling out his name as the phone slid across the floor.

Remy opened his mouth to try and communicate, to experiment with the theory that perhaps these creatures—these Chimerian, which he was pretty convinced they were—were not as threatening as Sariel had painted them to be.

But he didn't get the chance. Their strikes against him were savage, relentless, driving him to the floor beside the wrapped corpse of Noah. Just as he was about to call on the destructive forces that resided within him, he felt a taloned hand grip his hair. Savagely, the creature slammed his head back against the hardwood floor.

And as the flood of darkness rushed in to drag Remy down, he heard a voice cry out.

"No, do not harm this one," it said. "He isn't one of them."

A mysterious voice that saved his life.

TWELVE

I *have something to show you,* said the whispering voice, sounding very much like his Madeline, but he knew that it wasn't.

Something . . . *someone* was attempting to communicate with him, to show him something of great importance. All he had to do was accept the offer.

"Show me," Remy said aloud, suddenly finding himself awake.

At once he realized that he was no longer in the dusty old room of the Saint Mathias rectory.

There was cold stone beneath him, numbing his human flesh with its freezing temperature. Remy climbed to his feet, squinting in the darkness. He did not want to do it, but no longer in possession of his flashlight, he had no real alternative. Carefully he called upon the power of the divine once more, igniting his hand with the fires of Heaven.

In the illumination of its golden flame, he found that he was in some sort of vast underground chamber, its walls covered in thick glacial ice.

"Are you cold?" asked a voice from somewhere close by.

Remy directed the light of his hand toward an outcropping of jagged rock. A figure wrapped in a blanket sat on the ground, leaning back against a wall of ancient stone.

"You're welcome to share my blanket," he offered.

Remy walked toward the man, and the light thrown from his hand revealed a somewhat familiar face. "I know you," he said as the identity of the stranger came to him. "You're the angel we brought from the rig."

"Were you there?" the angel asked. "I thought Sariel had returned alone." The angel was a mess, looking worse even than he had after Sariel's beating.

"Did he do that to you?" Remy asked.

The angel brought broken and scabbed fingers to his horribly bruised and swollen face. "He did," the angel said. "For not telling him what he wanted to know."

"Who are you?" Remy asked. "And what's your part in all of this?"

"I am Armaros," the angel said, pushing himself up, using the stone wall for support. "And I was supposed to be Sariel's spy."

The angel stepped closer, and the light from Remy's hand showed him the extent of how badly he'd been beaten. Remy hadn't seen injuries this savage since . . .

Noah.

"When Noah started talking about how the Chimerian had survived, Sariel became worried. He assigned me to be the old man's assistant, to help him with the search."

Armaros pulled the blanket tighter around his shoulders.

"But I was really there to keep tabs on Noah's expeditions, and to alert Sariel and my brothers if anything was ever found."

"Which it was," Remy stated.

A strange, almost beatific expression came over the fallen angel's bruised face. "Yes," he said. "Yes, we found a small number of them, but I couldn't bring myself to tell Sariel. I knew why he wanted to know if the Chimerian had survived."

Remy stared, already guessing the answer.

"He wanted to destroy them," Armaros stated, his

voice trembling with emotion. "He wanted to complete what the deluge had failed to."

Something moved in the darkness behind them and Remy turned toward the sound, pushing back the darkness with the light of the divine.

Three of the Chimerian hissed angrily, scurrying back to the protection of the shadows.

"They don't mean you any harm," Armaros reassured him, moving around Remy to get to the creatures. "They're just afraid."

Armaros knelt down, calling them to him.

Remy had lowered his hand, the light thrown now at a minimum. He watched as they emerged, cautiously moving toward Armaros at his urgings.

They came to the Grigori, and he put his arms around the pale-skinned creatures. They clung to him with their clawed hands, nuzzling in the crook of his neck.

Remy's suspicions had been right; these weren't savage beasts to be put down.

"How could I tell Sariel about them?" Armaros asked, kissing one of them atop its bald, veiny head.

"They're only children."

Armaros hugged the children lovingly, and they hugged him back.

"We were going to try to save them—Noah and I," he explained. "Transporting them to a place in the modern world where they could learn, and adapt."

Remy recalled the transport containers, and the abandoned church property in Lynn.

"Noah had it all worked out," the angel continued. As soon as he spoke the old man's name, the Chimerian children immediately reacted. They became very still, throwing back their overly large heads, their mouths emitting a strange ululating howl that echoed through the vast chamber.

"I know, I know," Armaros said, pulling them closer to him.

"They miss him," the angel explained. "They loved their Noah very much."

It was the most heartbreaking sound Remy had ever heard, triggering some bizarre paternal instinct. He wanted to go to them, to hold them in his arms as Armaros did, and comfort them from the pain of the world.

"He had returned to the rig for some final preparations when Sariel found him," the angel explained, drawing the Chimerian children closer to him.

The scene of the crime flashed before Remy's eyes, Noah's beaten and battered body lying on his office floor.

"And for what he was going to do, Sariel killed him," Remy said.

Armaros nodded. "I'm not sure if that was his intention . . . but he was so enraged that Noah could even consider what he was doing . . ."

The angel looked at Remy. "But how could we not?" he asked. "Somehow they had survived the deluge . . . survived all the years following . . . doesn't it mean that they'd earned their right to live?"

Remy stepped closer, keeping his burning hand at his side.

The children grew nervous at his approach.

"Shhhhh," Armaros comforted. "He means you no harm."

One of the Chimerian looked at him with deep, cautious eyes, and Remy knew that this was the one that had found its way to his home.

Remy knelt down near Armaros, reaching out with the hand that did not burn with the fire of Heaven. The child at first studied what was offered, and then cautiously reached for it, gripping one of Remy's fingers in his.

"That's it," Armaros said. "He's our friend."

With the child's touch the images flowed through his brain, and his suspicions were confirmed. He knew these children of the flood, and why the Grigori were so desperate for them to be gone.

"The bastards," Remy whispered. "The miserable, coldhearted bastards."

Seeing that he wasn't a threat, the two other children became interested in him, leaving Armaros's arms to come to him. And with each touch of their clawed hands, or the feel of their warm breath on his cheek, Remy knew them more, and what they had gone through to live.

"I couldn't let Noah's death be in vain," Armaros went on. "I was going to try and accomplish our goals alone . . ." The Grigori laughed. "But I was sloppy and Sariel caught me. I tried to tell him that they meant us no harm, that they only wanted to live, but he would hear nothing of it. I'm surprised that I didn't share Noah's fate right then and there, but that must be where you came in."

The Chimerian children were crawling all over Remy now, completely unafraid.

Armaros chuckled. "They know you," the fallen angel said. "They know what you are."

Remy laughed, the first real laugh that he'd had since his wife had died.

With the thought of Madeline, the Chimerian children stopped. They stared at him with their intense dark eyes. And one by one, they drew back their heads and sang their sad, sad song for him.

"Sariel tried to make me talk," Armaros explained defiantly. "But I wouldn't tell him." He shook his head from side to side. "I thought I would die, but still I kept their secret. He wanted to know about this place, but I held my tongue."

Remy was holding the children now, each of them completely comfortable with the other.

"How did you escape?" he asked.

"There are some among them—the Grigori—that feel as I do. They let me go so that I could try and get the children to safety before . . ."

Remy felt it inside his head, like fingers gently running across the surface of his brain. It wasn't an entirely unpleasant sensation.

Angel of Heaven, said the voice like a gentle summer breeze tickling inside his ear. *I have something to show you.*

Armaros must have heard it as well, because he smiled.

"She wants to talk with you," the fallen angel said. He opened his arms, calling the children to him. "Go to her."

"Who?" Remy asked, feeling a psychic tug upon him, turning in the darkness like the needle of a compass, pointed toward where he needed to go.

"The Mother," Armaros said.

There wasn't a moment's hesitation; this was what he had been waiting for. Remy headed off into the vast underground cave system.

She was calling to him.

The Mother was calling, and he had no choice but to answer.

THIRTEEN

It felt as though he'd been walking for days, but he knew that wasn't the case.

The chamber went on, and on, up and over hills of ice older than recorded history, the only source of illumination being the divine fire that burned around his hand.

Dripping stalactites, like the teeth of a giant beast, hung over his head as he slid down from the other side of a black rock wall and onto a path that seemed to be taking him even deeper into the cavernous surroundings.

At first he had not the slightest idea what it was that loomed out of the darkness in front of them, believing it to be another enormous wall of rock and ice, an obstruction that could very well prevent him from going any farther.

Remy lifted his burning hand, staring at the obstruction, and realized that he was looking at something else altogether.

That he had reached his destination.

Remy nodded in satisfaction, taking it all in, absorbing the sight of the ancient craft that appeared to have become part of its rocky underground surroundings.

It must've been swallowed up by changes in the Earth's surface. Pulled farther and farther beneath the ground as time passed, he thought as he looked upon what was left of the ark.

The remains of Noah's ark.

Over the passage of time the wood had ossified, becoming like stone, blending with its geological surroundings. The front of the once gigantic ship protruded from the stone as if sailing through a monstrous ocean swell that had been frozen in time.

It made sense that this was where they'd be, Remy thought as he was drawn toward the ancient transport. Denied passage on the great craft, but now ...

Wedging his fingers deep into cracks between the rock and ice, Remy started to climb, the gentle voice of the Mother driving him on.

The answers are inside, Remy told himself, the all-too-human flesh of his fingers feeling the rigors of the harsh elements.

And Remy needed answers.

From the beginning, when Sariel had first come to him, he had sensed that something wasn't right, that he wasn't getting the entire picture.

It was all so much bigger than what the Grigori leader had cared to share.

Remy reached the top of the ark, jumping from an icy ledge to the side of the craft, and climbing over onto what had once been the deck. Countless millennia of shifting, geological change had done its job on the ship, holding the vessel in its cold, rocky clutches like a prized toy in the mouth of a playful dog.

There were gaping holes in the surface of the deck, and Remy could feel the tingle of something ancient and magickal wafting up from the darkness below.

Moving toward one of the holes, he peered down into the ship's hold. Memories from days long past exploded inside his head, of the ship's bowels filled to bursting with life of every conceivable size and shape.

Life that had been deemed worthy to survive the coming storm.

No real thought went into his next action. The Mother was waiting for him, and he simply lowered himself through the hole and into the waiting darkness below. Using protrusions of rock and ancient, ossified wood, Remy climbed down into the ship's limitless hold.

Touching bottom was like being on the ocean floor, not a lick of light to be found. He let the fire of divinity burn brighter from his hand to light the way.

He walked where they had kept the animals, remembering how it had looked then: the pens, primitive tanks, corrals and stalls, as far as the eye could see, built to hold the myriad varieties of life that the old man and his family had been instructed to save.

Remiel, whispered the voice of the Mother.

"Yes," he said aloud, walking farther into the cavernous belly of the ark.

Remember the days long past, when the Maker's world was young.

As he trudged along, images flooded his mind, rapid-fire pictures across the surface of his brain as the Mother began to show him.

He saw the world as it had been, young and vibrant, fertile with life. A dark, indigo-skinned people—*the Chimerian*—made their homes among the rocky hills of the primordial world. They were a beautiful people, their skin the bluish color of dusk.

Somehow they knew that the Maker did not favor their continued survival, and they begged Him to have mercy on them, but the All Powerful had already made up His mind, already created something to replace them.

But the Chimerian did not give up hope, continuing to pray, and to make sacrifices in hopes that their Maker would not forsake them, that He would see that they were worthy to live.

And they believed themselves saved when the emissaries came, living among them. Living *like* them.

Teaching them.

But the emissaries had come only for their own selfish reasons, immersing themselves in the earthly pleasures of food, drink and carnal acts, knowing that it was only a matter of time before the Chimerian were extinct.

Remy saw the emissaries inside his mind, saw their leader in the midst of revelry as he and his brethren partook of all mortal excesses.

He saw Sariel and his Grigori.

And then he saw a Chimerian woman, her belly swollen with life.

The fallen angel became enraged.

It cannot be, the Grigori leader ranted, and the woman cowered. *Your kind were supposed to be barren.*

And she looked to him with hope in her eyes, hope for her and all her kind, as well as the children to be born of Chimerian women and fallen angels.

A gift of our union, the beautiful woman with the night-colored skin said to Sariel.

She reached out, took Sariel's hand, and placed it on her stomach.

A gift to show the Maker we are worthy to live.

A final image was burnt into Remy's mind: it was of the Chimerian women, clad in hooded cloaks stitched from animal skins, clutching bellies swollen with life.

They stood upon the rocky hills as the rain fell in torrents, and the waters rose, watching as those deemed worthy to live filed aboard the ark.

Unworthy to exist.

Forsaken.

Remy came away from the sad vision in an area of the ark darker than even the light of the divine could illuminate.

He knew that she was here, somewhere in the ocean of night, hiding herself away.

"How?" he asked the darkness. "How did you survive?"

The feeling inside his head was immediate, like a long, sharp finger slowly pushing into the soft gray matter of his brain, but he did not fight it. Remy let the answers come.

It was like looking out through dirt-covered windows, the scenes unfolding, desperate to find a place inside his already crowded skull.

Remy stumbled and fell to the ground, fighting to stay conscious.

The Chimerian people bobbed upon the waters, one by one taken by the merciless sea. But some survived, the women of the tribe, those who had been *touched* by the Grigori. Somehow they had been changed by their experiences with the fallen ones, their bodies evolving, making them able to endure the catastrophe.

The impregnated women clung to the side of the great ark, their bodies enshrouded—*protected*—by thick cocoons made from magick and sorrow.

And they survived like that, hiding from those who wished them gone, sleeping through the passage of ages, waiting for a time—a *safe* time—to emerge.

Through a thick gauze of webbing Remy watched as a man clad in heavy winter garb, protected from the harshness of the elements, moved toward them.

Noah.

Sensing changes in the world, and in him, they had reached out, drawing him to their hiding place. And begging their forgiveness, he pulled them from their womb of shadow.

Noah at last finding his Chimerian orphans.

Remy felt the hold on him released, and he peered again into the limitless depths of the darkness, searching for the one who had called to him.

He got to his feet and moved farther into the nebulous embrace, the light of his hand nearly useless in the supernatural environment.

"Are you here?" he asked. "Show yourself to me."

The Mother responded to Remy's request; her form, as well as the forms of the other Chimerian survivors, gradually moved into focus.

It was as if they were lying in a great nest crafted from the stygian gloom, six of them, several still pregnant with the fruit of their union with the emissaries. They appeared to be asleep, but their minds were active.

Remy could feel them all reaching out to him, attempting to communicate, but one voice remained the loudest.

The Mother.

Remiel, she spoke inside his mind.

He looked down into the nest, and for a moment he saw the love of his life as he had watched her so many times, fast asleep.

The picture of a sleeping Madeline quickly changed to that of the Chimerian Mother. She appeared smaller than the others, having already borne her young.

The children that he'd encountered.

I felt you out there, the Mother whispered wearily. *A compassionate consciousness to hear our plea.*

"What would you have me do?" Remy asked, kneeling down beside the nest.

Will you speak for us, warrior of Heaven? she asked. *When we are at last gone, driven from existence, will you remember us?*

"I'll help Armaros," Remy told her. "We'll continue what Noah began and—"

Too late for that, she said resignedly. *Our time draws near. Tell me that you will remember us for what we were, and not as some blight upon the early land.*

"I'll help you," he said, the words leaving his mouth just as the Mother began to scream.

Remy didn't know what to do. Reaching down, he took her hand in his. "What's happening?" he asked.

It has begun. The end of us . . .

"What can I do?" he demanded. There had to be something.

The other women began to moan and writhe, as if held in the grip of some terrible nightmare. The smell of magick was suddenly in his nostrils, and Remy turned in the darkness.

Something was appearing behind him, a jagged, lightning-bolt tear was ripped in the shroud of shadow that had protected the Chimerian women. Remy sensed the danger at once, rising to his feet and allowing the warrior side of him to bubble to the surface.

The Grigori spilled from the open wound into the chamber, their eyes gleaming with bloodlust.

"No!" Remy screamed in the voice of the Messengers, his wings of feathered gold spreading from his back, forming a barrier between them and the Chimerian women.

And then he felt her touch again, pulling him back. Drawing him down.

The Mother had brought him into a vision.

They were at the Maine cottage, standing inside the extra room. Wearing the image of his wife, she attempted to console him.

"There's nothing that you can do," she said, standing before the open window, the wind pulling at her clothes. It had become like night outside, the air electric with the coming storm.

"Don't let them do this," Remy said, unable to keep the tremor of emotion from his voice.

"We always suspected that it could end this way," the Mother, wearing the guise of Madeline, said. She reached out and cupped the side of his face.

"Remember."

Then the storm was upon them, and the rain began to fall.

Remy awoke to the smell of blood. He could still feel the Mother's touch, restraining him from the inevitable.

There is nothing you can do.

But Remy did not want to believe it, fighting the grip

that held him. In the womb of darkness, he heard the sounds of their excitement, and looked to see the Grigori attackers, their fine Italian suits spattered black with blood as they murdered the defenseless survivors of the Great Deluge.

Something snapped inside Remy, and the power of Heaven rushed forward with a terrible fury. He let it come, letting it trample his humanity in its excitement to emerge.

The light thrown from his body burned like the heart of the sun, and he heard the Grigori squeal like frightened animals as they were driven back, away from their murderous acts.

But it appeared he was too late. The Chimerian women were dead, their defenseless bodies bearing the bloody wounds of the fallen angels' shame.

"Remiel," a voice called from behind him.

He turned to see Sariel coming toward him through the darkness, a pale hand raised to shield his eyes from the heavenly light.

"We feared for your safety."

In his other hand the Grigori held a sword, an ancient blade that had been forged in the fires of the Lord God's love, and had once glowed like a star, but now was only a thing of metal, tarnished and stained by needless violence.

"What have you done, Sariel?" Remy asked, barely able to contain his emotion as he looked upon the women savagely brutalized by the Grigori.

"We suspected you might be in danger," Sariel spoke. "And came at once to your aid."

The Seraphim laughed, a low, rumbling sound more like a growl.

"Your concern for my well-being ... is touching," Remy said.

And then he turned his cold gaze upon the Grigori leader.

"You used me, Sariel," he said, repressed fury dripping from every word.

"I have no idea what you're talking about," the Grigori leader responded indignantly.

"You made me part of this," Remy hissed. The glow from his body had dwindled, the darkness of what had transpired draining away the intensity of his light.

"Don't you see, Remiel?" Sariel asked. "You were part of our test."

All Remy could do was stare at the sight of something once holy, now but a twisted reflection.

"The Almighty provided you for us to complete our penance," the Grigori leader went on. His brothers stepped cautiously into the light to join their leader. "You were a tool of our redemption."

"Redemption," Remy said, the word like poison on his lips. "You actually believe that after all you've done . . ."

His eyes were pulled to the Chimerian bodies and he stopped.

"The Lord God provided us with a way to consummate a task that had remained incomplete for countless millennia," Sariel continued to explain. "How could we not respond?"

"And Noah?" Remy asked.

"He has been avenged," Sariel proclaimed, raising his sword as if in victory.

"You murdered him," Remy raged. He turned his gaze back to the Grigori master; the fire of Heaven burned in his stare.

Sariel started to speak, but Remy did not want to hear it. He charged at the fallen angel, grabbing the lapel of his suit jacket and pulling him closer.

"You killed him in a fit of rage," Remy accused, his teeth clenched in anger. "You beat a defenseless old man to death with your fists."

"I lost my temper," the Grigori admitted, followed by a sigh of exasperation. "He was just so damned stubborn. Wracked with guilt over what he believed he had done . . . you should have seen how excited he was when he thought that he'd found them."

Remy felt himself becoming sick as the fallen angel attempted to justify his twisted actions.

"He didn't see the danger no matter how hard I tried to explain it," the Grigori said, his words fervent. "He told me that he was going to beg God to let them live . . . that because they had survived the flood He should allow them to exist. That they had earned the right to life."

Sariel actually seemed to believe what he was saying, and that Remy found even more disturbing.

"Here was our chance, Remiel," the Grigori leader emphasized. "Something to bring us that much closer to going home . . . to be allowed back to Heaven."

"But you killed him," Remy reminded the Grigori leader with a shake.

"Yes, I did," Sariel admitted. "Not sure exactly how *that* will be received, but at least we're finishing what the flood began. That has to count for something. I wasn't about to allow anything to prevent me from completing what should have been finished ages ago."

Sariel glanced at the hand still holding his lapel.

"It's done, Remiel," Sariel said. "This is how it was supposed to be. For us to finish what had already been put in motion; it was a test for us, penance for one of our greatest . . . misjudgments."

"Misjudgments?" Remy asked, scorn in his words. "But the children . . ."

Sariel looked to the corpses, distaste upon his pale, perfect face.

"An error better left forgotten," he snarled, removing Remy's hand from his suit coat. "They were twisted things, Remiel, neither of Heaven nor Earth."

"They were yours."

He searched the fallen angel's eyes, looking for even a small sign of mercy or compassion. It was like staring into a deep, dark hole. There was nothing there, and Remy knew that Sariel and his Grigori brothers were lost.

What they believed of the Chimerian was true of them—there was no place for the Grigori in Heaven, or on Earth.

Remy heard a sound, a howl of mourning from the throats of children born of Grigori and Chimerian women. He turned toward the song to see them, squatting at the edge of darkness, clinging to one another as they ached over the fate that had befallen their Mother.

The Chimerian lament filled the shadows, becoming louder, and their sadness became palpable. One by one, the Grigori dropped to their knees, supremely affected by the woeful song.

Perhaps I am wrong about them, Remy thought.

All were affected except for Sariel.

The Grigori leader looked upon his brothers with horror. "Get up!" he screamed, but either they did not hear him over the sad song or they chose to ignore his words, for they continued to kneel upon the ground soaked with the blood of innocents.

"Listen to it," Remy yelled over the forlorn sound. "Listen to the pain you've caused."

Blood started to seep from Sariel's ears. His body grew stiff, and began to tremble. Slowly his knees began to bend, bringing him closer and closer to the ground.

"I . . . ," Sariel grunted, stabbing the blade of his sword into the ground to halt his progress.

"Hear . . ." He fought the gravity of sorrow pushing down upon him, to struggle to his feet.

"Nothing!" And he sprang across the floor, murder in his gaze as he raised his tarnished blade to strike at those who would keep him from achieving that which he most desired.

That which would keep him from the gates of Heaven.

Remy sprang into Sariel's path, grappling with the fallen angel and driving him to the cold, hard ground. The Grigori flailed, lashing out with the pommel of his sword, striking Remy across the temple with a savage blow.

There was a searing flash of pain and color as Remy felt the Grigori squirm out from beneath him. He fought back the descending curtain of oblivion, flapping his powerful wings to rise to his feet.

The Chimerian babes had ceased their song as they watched the scene unfold with wide, frightened eyes. They hissed, baring razor-sharp teeth as Sariel loomed, sword raised above his head, ready to fall.

The Seraphim emerged with a roar, pushing aside the fragile shell of humanity Remy wore, burning it with the fire of Heaven. And Remy let it. He was tired of all the pain and death, tired of being manipulated in others' pursuits of Heaven.

With hands burning white with divine heat, he grabbed the Grigori leader, pulling him back away from his objectives.

Away from his children.

Sariel struggled in the grasp of the Seraphim, and his fine suit and the flesh beneath it burned with the supernatural fire. He spun on Remy, swinging his sword with a cry of fury and pain.

But the Seraphim was not impressed, capturing the blade in midswing, causing the weapon to warp and bend, and finally to melt.

Sariel's screams were entirely of pain now as his immortal flesh blackened and smoldered, but the Seraphim held him tight, refusing to set him free.

Allowing the power of God that seethed at his core to flow through him and into the fallen angel.

"You wanted to see Heaven again, brother?" the Seraphim spoke in the language of God's first creations. "See it now."

The Grigori leader still lived, but his body had begun to crumble, pieces of charred angel flesh breaking away to drift on the air like black snow.

"See it and burn."

And soon the angel Sariel was no more, as the last of him was consumed by the voraciousness of Heaven's fire.

The Seraphim flapped his powerful wings, dispersing his fallen enemy's ashen remains, and turned his attention to the others. They had risen to their feet, weapons in hand, staring at him with intense hatred.

And the Seraphim's mouth twisted in a cruel smile that told he was ready to share their master's fate with them. None moved.

Having no fear of them, the Seraphim Remiel turned his back on the Grigori to face the children of the deluge. They looked away from him with a hiss, the intensity of his light searing their sensitive eyes.

Diminishing his holy glow, he knelt upon the ground, opening his arms to them. Without hesitation they came to him, the three orphans crawling into the safety of the angel's embrace.

Its penchant for violence more than satisfied, Remy was able to usurp control from the Seraphim, putting the genie back into the bottle for another time.

He didn't know how much longer he could continue to do this, for the essence of the divine grew more powerful each time it was called upon. But that was a worry for another time.

He had the safety of the children to concern himself with now.

Walking through darkness in the bowels of the ark, he held the quivering offspring tight, consoling them with words that everything would be all right, having no idea if he was lying to them or not.

Stopping, he allowed the fire to burn from his hand again to see how far they'd come. To say that he was shocked by the sight of dead Grigori bodies strewn about the ground was an understatement.

Even more shocking was the sight of Francis, and Armaros.

"Hey," the former Guardian angel said. He clutched what looked to be a Bavarian Warhammer in one hand, while supporting Armaros with the other. "Sorry I'm late, didn't think they'd start the party without me."

Armaros pulled away from Francis and opened his arms to the Chimerian orphans.

"You saved them," he said as the three children leapt from Remy's arms to go to the Grigori.

"But they're the only ones," Remy said sadly.

Francis was staring at the Chimerian children, and by the look on his face, he clearly was not sure what to think.

"How does Sariel feel about that?" he asked.

"Sariel's dead," Remy said coldly.

Francis nodded, then reached out a tentative hand to pat one of the bald Chimerian heads. The child growled, swatting at the offending hand with its razor-sharp claws.

"Cute," Francis said as he quickly pulled his hand back. "He has his daddy's charming disposition."

"He was going to kill them," Remy said, speaking of Sariel. "Because they had the audacity to survive."

Francis nudged one of the Grigori corpses with the toe of his shoe.

"And he wasn't the only one with that bad attitude."

The wayward Guardian then sighed, and slung the medieval weapon over his shoulder. "So what now?" he asked. "Anything else that needs to be killed?"

Remy looked to Armaros for an answer.

"Sariel is dead, but the Grigori still live," he said, holding the Chimerian children. They were falling asleep, their large heads bobbing. "They won't give up that easily. We're going to need a safe place until some of this dies down."

"Troublemaker," Francis said from the side of his mouth, his comment directed at Remy.

"You know me," Remy responded with a shrug.

Francis nodded, rolling his eyes.

"Where will you go?" Remy asked Armaros, who had already started to turn away from them.

"Perhaps it is better that you don't know," the fallen angel said, carrying the sleeping orphans farther into the darkness. "Perhaps it's time for the Chimerian to again become lost to the world."

To be swallowed up by the gloom.

FOURTEEN

Remy returned to the cottage in Maine, not really sure why; it seemed as good a place as any at the moment. He wasn't ready to resume his life, to pick up where it had left off with Madeline's passing.

It was all too fresh. He didn't know if there would ever come a time when it wouldn't still be too fresh.

There had been a few inches more of snow, the winter's flailing last attempts to hold on before the inevitable.

He knew the feeling.

Sitting in the wicker chair on the front porch, Marlowe lying beside him, he tried to imagine life without her. She had been his hold on the world, the thing that kept him from becoming like the Grigori, and the others of his heavenly ilk.

She was his soul. And now, with her gone . . .

Remy tried to think of something else—anything else.

A few days past, as much as he was loath to admit it, the fallen angel Sariel had provided him with something he desperately needed. Something that took him away from his thoughts and pain.

Distraction.

If there was one thing for which he owed the Grigori

leader, it was that. He had temporarily taken Remy from his sadness, and he had liked how it felt.

He crossed his legs, pulling the cuff of his jeans down below his ankle, covering the top of his work boot. From the porch he stared out over the driveway, into the dark woods at the snow-covered trees, and beyond.

Staring into the future.

"What?" Marlowe asked, suddenly alerted, following Remy's gaze, probably hoping that his master had seen some food attempting to escape.

The dog scrambled to his feet with a bark, walking to the edge of the porch and sniffing the cool air, just in case.

"Do you see it?" Remy asked, feeling the darkness calling to him.

"No," Marlowe grumbled, turning back to him, his thick black tail starting to wag nervously.

Remy smiled, placing both feet on the floor and leaning forward in the chair, hands open to Marlowe.

Marlowe came to him happily, eating up the affection.

"It must've been nothing," he told the dog, allowing the animal to lick his face.

But Remy knew it was there, waiting to take him away.

A diversion from the heartache.

A distraction found in the affairs of angels.

ABOUT THE AUTHORS

A martial arts enthusiast whose résumé includes a long list of skills rendered obsolete at least two hundred years ago, **Jim Butcher** turned to writing as a career because anything else probably would have driven him insane. He lives in Independence, Missouri, with his wife, his son, and a ferocious guard dog. You can visit his Web site at www.Jim-Butcher.com.

Simon R. Green is a *New York Times* bestselling author. He lives in England.

Kat Richardson lives on a sailboat in Seattle with her husband and two ferrets. She rides a motorcycle, doesn't own a car or a TV, shoots target pistol, and has been known to swing dance, sing, and spend insufficient time at the gym. Visit her on the Web at www.katrichardson.com.

Thomas E. Sniegoski is a full-time writer of novels and comics. He was born and raised in Massachusetts, where he still lives with his wife, LeeAnne, and their Labrador retriever, Mulder.

THE DRESDEN FILES

The #1 *New York Times* bestselling series
by Jim Butcher

"Think *Buffy the Vampire Slayer* starring Philip Marlowe." —*Entertainment Weekly*

STORM FRONT

FOOL MOON

GRAVE PERIL

SUMMER KNIGHT

DEATH MASKS

BLOOD RITES

DEAD BEAT

PROVEN GUILTY

WHITE NIGHT

SMALL FAVOR

TURN COAT